The Legend of Sasquatch

William T. Prince

Copyright © 2008 by William T. Prince

ISBN 0-7414-4844-0

Registration Number TXu001573323

Published by:

INFINITY
PUBLISHING.COM

1094 New DeHaven Street, Suite 100
West Conshohocken, PA 19428-2713
Info@buybooksontheweb.com
www.buybooksontheweb.com
Toll-free (877) BUY BOOK
Local Phone (610) 941-9999
Fax (610) 941-9959

Printed in the United States of America

Printed on Recycled Paper

Published May 2009

For Sharon

Wife

Partner

Best Friend

With all my love

ACKNOWLEDGMENTS

A number of people helped me in various ways to complete this project, and although I cannot thank everyone, I must acknowledge those whose assistance was most crucial. Without their support, I might not have been able to see this through to fruition.

I would like to thank my nephew, Alex Eckler, for being my first reader. Alex, your initial words of encouragement were more powerful than you probably realized at the time, but the book in your hands is proof of their influence. I thank you, too, for a really good suggestion about one of my characters. You take care of my Girly-Goo & KJ!

My favorite Mensan, English teacher, and barroom singer, Jim Stanley, aka "jstan" to all you Brothers of the Leaf, deserves my gratitude for volunteering his services as a proofreader. Buddy, I will herf with you anytime, with or without your guitar!

My oldest brother, Glenn, made a vital contribution to my project. I love you, Big Brother! (Ooh, shades of Orwell there!)

Almost nine years ago, God blessed me with the singular honor of being a father to the sweetest, smartest, and most gorgeous fraternal twin girls He ever created, Lauren and Justine. My sweeties, your love kept me going, and I could not have done this without you. I love you more than I can say, but—no—you may not read this book anytime soon!

Most importantly, I must thank my wife and proof-reader, Sharon Housman Prince. Writing almost 100,000 words of fiction is much easier than coming up with just a few truthful words to describe my feelings for you. "So, what are you?" was a question of Providence. You are the smartest, funniest, and most beautiful person I know, and without you, this book most assuredly would not exist. Without you, I might not exist. I cannot imagine growing old with anyone else. I love you with all my heart.

I offer my love and heartfelt appreciation to all those named and unnamed who supported this effort.

Sincerely,
Will

No Small Matter

Clint pushed a finger against the small hole in his chest and realized that the bullet had barely entered his body. He could feel the small chunk of lead just below the surface. He briefly considered trying to squeeze it out as one might exude a blemish, but better judgement prevailed. It was a small caliber, probably .22 or .25, and although he was aware of some pain, there wasn't nearly as much as he would've expected. He didn't seem to be losing much blood, but he decided he'd better keep some pressure on the wound anyway, although it was a little more painful to do so.

Clint walked across the street to where the body lay across the curb, half in the street and half on the sidewalk. He squatted and touched the neck, but he already knew that there would be no pulse. The 240-grain semi-jacketed hollow point from Clint's .44 magnum Smith and Wesson revolver—yes, the very same as another Clint carried in the movies—had entered just off the bridge of the nose, pretty much the corner of one eye, and the guy had died at precisely the same instant. That eye was gone, of course, but the other remained open with that telltale empty stare.

The guy's expression was blank, and on the whole his face didn't look all that bad under the circumstances. Even so, Clint knew without turning him over that the void in the back of his head was considerable. There was significant blood and gray matter on the sidewalk, and let's face it—the chances of anyone surviving a .44 mag to the face are about the same as the odds of winning the lottery, perhaps less. The guy was dead, and there was no need to wait around for official confirmation.

Clint didn't see the guy's pistol and didn't feel compelled to look for it. It's not as if he would ever use it again. There was no sign of anyone around at the moment, and Clint didn't think that there would be anyone peeking right now. Virtually no one lived in this part of Dallas, and anyone who might have been lurking about probably hit the ground and covered up at the thunderous *ka-BOOM!* of the .44. Clint got in his truck, quickly stowed his sidearms and holsters, and drove himself toward the emergency room at Parkland Hospital.

On the way to Parkland, Clint continued applying pressure to the wound, and he tried to figure out why this had happened. A man was dead, and that is no small matter. Regardless of circumstances, no matter the justification, anyone who can cause the death of another human being and not feel some ambivalence about it is one sick bastard. Normal, compassionate people just can't feel good about killing and dying, even when killing and dying are necessary.

This was textbook self defense, excusable homicide. The dead guy drew first; in fact, he'd gotten off the first shot. Clint's only choice was between the snub-nose .38 on his ankle and the .44 mag in his shoulder holster, and that was only a choice in the most technical sense. Clint had been reaching for the big six-inch revolver when he felt the small slug hit him in the chest, and he'd gotten off his only shot after he realized that he'd already been shot. Could there be a clearer case of self defense?

Why had this guy come after Clint? Was it a simple robbery attempt, and had Clint merely been in the wrong place at the wrong time, a seemingly random victim chosen by virtue of convenience alone? Or was it something else, and had Clint himself set the wheels in motion? The more questions Clint asked, the more he realized that it was likely that this man had been sent to kill him. If so, it had to be Mike reaching out from behind bars to exact his revenge.

Clint's body count was now up to five—six including the vegetable. Killing was becoming a habit, and Clint realized that it was starting to bother him less each time. He feared that he was becoming desensitized to death, too accustomed to killing.

As Clint neared Parkland, he wondered if his buddies would be able to make this go away as they had before. Clint was certain that he would never be prosecuted, much less convicted, except for maybe a weapons charge. Even so, aside from the sheer hassle of having to defend oneself in a criminal investigation and perhaps prosecution, this was the type of problem that could derail his plans just at the time when he was beginning to get himself together. Besides, there are certain details of one's personal life that should remain private. Clint hoped that those details would never come to light, his skeletons locked away securely in a hidden closet somewhere. Otherwise his family would be heartsick.

Clint parked his truck in the designated area outside the Parkland emergency room and went inside. The ER was always pretty busy, and this night was no exception. It was a zoo. There were people all over the place, though no one seemed ready to die. It was cold out, and many of the patients and their obvious symptoms seemed consistent with the weather. Mostly folks were just hanging around waiting to be examined by one of the doctors or nurses, none of whom seemed to have any sense of urgency despite the backlog.

Clint worked his way through the obstacle course to a counter behind which a nurse sat writing in a chart and refusing to look up. After several minutes, the nurse—still writing and not looking up—finally spoke.

"May I help you?" she asked disinterestedly.

Clint answered matter-of-factly, "I seem to have a bullet in my chest."

The nurse abruptly stopped writing and looked up for the first time. An ER nurse at Parkland would never be surprised by a gunshot wound, but she did seem genuinely shocked that a gunshot victim could stand in front of her and calmly mention it as if talking about the weather with a buddy.

"I think it's a .22 or .25," Clint continued. "It's not very deep, but I figured I'd better keep some pressure on it. I don't think it will take much to fix. I'm sure one of the docs can pop it out of there and get me on my way in no time."

The nurse was excited but controlled as she shouted, "Doctor! Doctor! I have a gunshot over here! And someone find that cop. Where'd he go? Is he asleep again? Someone find that cop!"

"Ma'am, there's really no need to involve the police," Clint said. "This was just an accident, no big deal. Just take the bullet out, give me a tetanus shot, an antibiotic, and a Band-Aid, and I'll get out of your hair."

"Are you kidding me?" she said. "You've been shot! It may not be that simple, and I have to cover my ass anyway. Where's that cop?"

"I'm coming," said a middle-aged, overweight police officer, walking sleepily toward the counter while tucking in his shirttail, looking very much as if the nurse's conjecture had been correct. "You say he's been shot?"

The nurse replied, "That's what he says. I haven't looked at him yet."

Clint said, "Yes, sir, I've been shot—small caliber, no big deal. Could you call Detective Roy for me please?"

It seemed like an innocent enough request. Detective Roy (Roy being his last name) was an established star within the DPD, but apparently Officer Rip Van Winkle was more concerned with exerting a little of his authority. He was a full head shorter than Clint and visibly intimidated, and like a small dog confronted by a larger one, he used bravado in an attempt to mask his own fear. It wasn't working very well for him. Standing tall and puffing out his chest, he poked a finger toward Clint's.

The cop said, "You're telling *me* who to call? Listen here, punk. I'm in charge here, and I decide who needs to be called. Roy's a narc. He's got nothing to do with crimes against persons. Who shot you anyway?"

Clint insisted, "Please, just call Roy. He knows me. He'll take care of this."

The nurse interjected, "Excuse me, boys, but there's the small matter of a gunshot wound that we need to address. You reckon you can talk while a doctor and I take a look over here at triage?"

"No problem, ma'am," was Clint's reply to the nurse, and then to the officer he asked again, "Could you please? Just call Roy." Clint was thinking to himself, "Please be there!"

With an exasperated sigh, the officer relented and reached for the telephone on the nurse's desk. As he kept an eye on Clint and the nurse, and the doctor who finally came along to take a look for himself, the officer dialed the number for headquarters and asked to speak with Detective Roy. Luckily Roy happened to be at the station, which was very unusual.

After a brief exchange the officer yelled across the short distance to the triage station, "He wants to know who's asking for him!"

Clint responded with, "Tell him it's Clint Buchanan," pronouncing his last name "Buck Hannon" and not the more common "Bew Cannon."

Although he understood it, Clint still hated it when people mispronounced his family name, especially since there was a wildly popular soap opera character at the time whose name was Clint "Bew Cannon," a pretend Texan. The officer repeated the name into the phone, pronouncing it incorrectly.

Clint heard the officer say, "Yeah, the kid's *damn* big!"

Clint was indeed a big young man by the standards of his time. Almost 21 but still growing, he stood a little over six feet, six inches tall and weighed a solid 250 pounds, plus or minus a little from day to day. In both size and demeanor, he was similar to Jimmy Dean's "Big Bad John," and since his feet were size 16EEEE, it was easy to see how folks had come to call him Sasquatch.

Sasquatch hadn't been Clint's only nickname. At various times people had called him Bigfoot or Yeti or Lurch, after the butler on the "Addams Family" television show, but he tolerated Sasquatch. In fact, he rather liked it, and although Bigfoot is ostensibly synonymous, it seemed merely to poke fun at his big feet. On the other hand, Sasquatch seemed to refer to his whole person. Yes, Clint was willing to split that hair. If it had to be either, it had to be Sasquatch. He might have liked Yeti but thought it too arcane.

Many cops have nicknames. Clint's buddy Detective Roy, for instance, was called Hulk. He was a barrel-chested weightlifter, and he despised his first name, Carroll. Hulk hated that his parents had given him a "girl's name," and he had considered changing it to Carl. Most folks just called him by his last name or Hulk, and those who slipped up and called him Carroll generally regretted it.

Clint had pretty much embraced Sasquatch, thinking it lucky that he had come upon his nickname so young and so naturally. Clint, of course, wasn't a cop yet, and now he wasn't sure if he ever would be or even if he really wanted to be. Still, he liked thinking of himself as a legend, and the moniker also addressed his elusive loner quality as well as his size. Beast or human, though, this Sasquatch had a bullet in him that required attention.

After an examination and some x-rays, the doctor decided that the removal of the bullet would not require an operating room or a surgical team. Apparently the density of Clint's chest muscles had put a quick halt to the small, weak bullet. It had stopped just below the skin, and the doctor could take it out right there in the ER. Perhaps he had not used his best medical judgement, but Clint was not wont to argue with a guy who had "M.D." on his name tag. Besides, Clint wanted to get out of the hospital as soon as possible.

The Legend Begins

Clint had been forced to quit playing football only a few games into his sophomore season in high school due to a spinal disorder caused by rapid growth, and a conflict with the athletic director led to his getting kicked off the track team after his sophomore year. Coach Morris was the head football coach in addition to being the AD, and he was skeptical of Clint's back problem. He referred to it as a "piss injury," and after Clint quit the team, Coach Morris became fond of referring to Clint as a pussy, which hurt young Clint's feelings very badly, especially when the coach would say it in the presence of other students. The coach did that often and chuckled proudly at himself each time. The constant pounding that a football lineman's back has to endure made Clint's pain unbearable; it rendered him unable to walk at times. He had given football his best shot, but it just wasn't to be.

Track was another story. Clint did feel twinges in his back from time to time but nothing that hindered his ability to put the 12-pound shot close to 60 feet and to throw the 1.5-kilo discus around 180. As a mere 16-year-old he was good enough to place at the state meet that year, possibly to win, but Coach Morris' dictate that only juniors and seniors would be allowed on the varsity team prevented Clint from even having the chance to go to state—which, of course, was the precise reason for the policy. Moreover, Clint's throws in the junior varsity meet were good enough to be school records, but Coach Morris wouldn't let them count because Clint hadn't competed in a varsity meet. Coach Morris was just pissed off that he wouldn't have Clint to help his struggling football team, and he used his authority as AD to exact some measure of revenge.

Coach Morris was pretty young himself, only in his mid- to late-20s and clearly not fully mature yet, but this scenario was pretty doggone childish by anyone's standards. He set a really poor example for the students at the high school. During a heated exchange one day near the end of the school year, Coach Morris pushed Clint past his limit by calling him a pussy one time too many. When he laughed that time, Clint's blood boiled, and his visceral reaction was to punch the coach in the face. A short right hand knocked the coach out cold and broke his nose, and thus, Clint's days as a high school athlete were over before he even had a chance to peak.

This was devastating to Clint. He was a good athlete and loved sports, especially track, and he even had dreams of making the Olympic team. His hero was the great Al Oerter, the four-time Olympic gold medalist in the discus. If Clint could get to college and make the Olympic team by 1980, he might have a chance to challenge his hero's record. That dream was now out the window, and since Clint thought that a scholarship was his only hope of being able to afford college, even getting a college degree seemed doubtful.

Not being an athlete also caused Clint to lose standing among his classmates, so he spent his last two years in high school as one of the "uncool" kids, something of a nerd, which resulted in some rebellion that kept him from doing as well academically as he could have done. He went from being at or very near the top of his class to barely in the top quarter. All of this—no sports, lower grades, the uncoolness—caused him trouble at home and with his other relationships as well. It was a vicious cycle that would profoundly affect Clint for the rest of his life.

College right out of high school was not in the cards for Clint. By the time he graduated, he had a good job, at least according to the myopic perception of an 18-year-old, and didn't feel the need for higher education. That may have been a moot point, however, as he clearly had not earned any kind of scholarship. Clint had a job working as a security officer, and it seemed to fit his goal of becoming a police officer when he was old enough. Very quickly Clint made a name for himself, which wasn't a particularly difficult thing to do. In the security industry, duly noted for its warm body syndrome, the primary screening tool is to reach across the interview desk and to touch an applicant's neck. If there's a detectable pulse and the body seems reasonably warm, another recruit is ready to occupy a post, sometimes with a sidearm. It was patent on sight that Clint was more than a warm body, and when he had walked into the office of England Security and Investigations to complete an application, the personnel director had practically fallen prostrate at Clint's feet.

When Clint proved early on to be very dependable, never absent or late and always willing to work extra, he was earmarked an up-and-comer. Clint did great work, too. Although shy, he proved to have good human relations skills. He knew how to talk to people, knew precisely what to say and not to say depending on the person with whom he was dealing at the time, to elicit their cooperation before it became necessary to get tough. He always used good judgement, and his supervisors could see that he was destined to outstrip them. Some were okay with that; some weren't. Most importantly, the higher-ups saw his potential and shielded him from the supervisors who were obviously threatened by him and might be inclined to sabotage his career.

It's very unusual for security personnel ever to have to use force, and Clint always avoided it—not because he was scared of a fight, but because he genuinely believed that it was better to use his brains than his considerable brawn. He took great pains never to use his size to intimidate, except as a last resort. He was actually quite a nice guy, but God help anyone who threw the first punch!

Before long the powers that be began giving Clint the best assignments, higher profile posts where he could really show his wares. He quickly graduated from the industrial sites and shopping centers to cushy office buildings, and he ultimately found a semi-permanent home in the proverbial ivory tower—the Republic Bank high-rise in downtown Dallas. Executives with their fancy cars and huge salaries who would normally look down their noses at the building's guards would usually extend a hand and a warm greeting to Clint.

It was difficult for folks not to notice Clint—not just because of his size either. He clearly had a special quality that drew people to him. Clint became fast friends with one of the private investigators at his firm, Tom Whitely. Clint was having the time of his life! For the first time really, people treated him with respect, and despite being a contract guard, the lowest of the low in the security business, Clint was treated as a peer by Tom and others who might normally look down on entry-level personnel, if they even noticed them at all.

The company began taking Clint off post to assist them in their investigations, and that was very interesting work, even if a little seedy from time to time. It also brought Clint into frequent contact with police officers and detectives from various agencies in the area. Clint was having loads of fun, and at the same time, he was rubbing elbows with people who could one day help him get on with the Dallas Police Department or perhaps one of the suburban agencies. He had to do something between the ages of 18 and 21, and although college would have been nice, he thought that this was both more fun and more practical. At the time a college education was viewed as unnecessary to work in the police occupation, and this kind of real-life experience would benefit Clint greatly, both in getting hired and then later on the job. It seemed the perfect fit.

Clint's life at this time consisted primarily of two things: working and working out. He still tried to squeeze in a weekly visit to church, mostly to keep his mom happy, and he did manage to do a little dating—nothing serious, but he did like to get laid whenever possible. He was, after all, a big, strapping, handsome young man nearing his sexual peak, and in his uniform he was a babe magnet.

After a couple of years of not playing football, Clint found that his back had quit bothering him entirely. His doctor had said that everything would normalize as his growing slowed, and free from pain, Clint threw himself into a regular routine of health club, work, sleep, health club, work, sleep, and so on every day. In his workouts he focused on both cardiovascular training and weightlifting, and he began taking karate lessons again. The health club included a Tae Kwon Do school, and Clint took advantage of the one-stop shopping.

Years earlier while working at a gas station, Clint had taken some informal karate lessons from an unlicensed instructor who also worked at the station. The guy's name was Dennis, but everyone called him Japan. He had earned his black belt while serving in the Army in Korea, and upon his return home, everyone around town had taken to calling him Japan. Clint asked him about that one day.

"Where'd you say you got your black belt?"

"Korea."

"Then why does everyone call you Japan?"

"You ever heard a guy called Korea?"

"No."

"Well, there you go."

Apparently calling him *Korea* would have been too weird. Anyway, during the times at the station when they had nothing else to do, Japan would teach Clint some karate, Tae Kwon Do to be precise. Clint was pretty good, and before the station closed and they parted ways, Japan had told Clint that he was probably the equivalent of a brown belt, maybe close to black, except that his weapons training was very limited, just nunchuks or, as Japan had called them, chako sticks. Now Clint was taking lessons from a licensed instructor in a formal school and had earned his first-degree black belt, and combined with all his strength training and running, he was becoming quite the physical specimen.

While working an overtime shift for "Friday Night Fights" at Billy Bob's, a big honky-tonk in Fort Worth, a small-time promoter had spoken with Clint and piqued his interest in fighting professionally. There was an opening on the card for the following Friday night, and Clint signed a contract on the spot. The fight would be sanctioned by the Professional Karate Association, and Clint was to fight another young fellow who had won his first two fights, both by knockout. Assuming that Clint could pass the physical, which was a foregone conclusion, he would be a pro fighter in seven days. He would be paid 500 bucks, which at the time was more than twice his base salary for a whole week. It seemed like a great deal.

During the next week Clint continued his usual routine, except that he spent a little more time working on the punching bags at the gym and doing some extra sparring, which was always a big part of his karate workouts. His conditioning was not an issue. He was already in exceptional shape, and the fight would only be a maximum of four two-minute rounds. Clint figured that he could go toe-to-toe with anyone for eight minutes if necessary, but he also knew that his size advantage would make it difficult for his opponent to engage him in such a fashion. He didn't count on a great deal of action, but he was ready for it nonetheless.

Clint requested and received Thursday and Friday nights off, agreeing to work extra the following week in exchange. He told no one in his family about his upcoming fight, partly because he didn't think that they would approve and partly because he didn't want them to worry. He did, however, tell Tom Whitely and a couple of work friends, and they agreed to be there to show their support. Clint was very confident that he would perform well, and it made him happy to know that he would have some support in the audience.

Clint got a good night's sleep on Thursday, carbed-up at lunch on Friday, and reported to Billy Bob's two hours early. One of his karate instructors, Mark Green, had agreed to work his corner and met him there. Clint was feeling some butterflies in his stomach, but they were more from excitement than from nervousness. He was ready to get it on.

Clint's dad, Doug, had been a boxer in the Army after World War II. He had been pretty good, too, and probably could have had some success as a professional, but Doug knew that he didn't have the necessary killer instinct to survive for very long. He had a tendency to hurt his opponents and then back off, not wanting to injure them badly, and a person who feels that way has no business trying to make his living as a boxer. Still, when Clint was very young, Doug had begun working with him—not so much to turn him into a boxer as to make sure that he could defend himself if necessary.

Doug was not obsessed really, but he was insistent that Clint knew how and, more importantly, *when* to fight. He frequently told Clint, "It takes more of a man to walk away from a fight than it does to kick ass, but if he won't let you walk away, make him regret it." Clint took those lessons to heart. He walked away from fights whenever he could, and as a result, was sometimes labeled a coward—a pussy. Perhaps that's why he hated it so much when Coach Morris had called him one. Regardless, when it happened that the other guy wouldn't let Clint walk away, Clint's boxing skills proved more than adequate.

Clint believed that he could be very successful fighting in the PKA because of his superior boxing skills. He surmised that most kickboxers were predominately karate fighters who were more concerned with their kicks and that their skills in the Sweet Science were lacking. Clint thought that a real boxer could get inside and punish his opponents and that it would be difficult for a typical karate fighter, even a good one, to defend effectively against such an attack. In other words, Clint's hypothesis was that a kick*boxer* could beat a *kick*boxer, and he would now have the chance to put his theory to the test.

Clint's opponent was 22-year-old Keith Willis from Fort Worth, and he was significantly smaller than Clint at 6-2 and 210 pounds. Despite being much smaller, he had a chiseled body and was a skilled black belt who had won his first two fights with early knockouts. With that in Willis' mind, he had little fear of Clint. Clint was younger and fighting in his first fight, so Willis figured that Clint might be a little nervous. He was wrong. Clint was never intimidated by anyone at any time, and just because he had walked away from many fights in the past, more than he had fought, didn't mean that he was scared.

Perhaps because he had walked away from fights so many times, Clint might have felt that he had something to prove, so when that opening bell sounded, he wasted no time mixing it up with Willis in the center of the ring. Immediately it was obvious that Willis was surprised at Clint's ability to punch him squarely on the nose with an incredibly stiff left jab that almost knocked him off his feet. Willis stumbled around and tried to throw a couple of wild kicks, but Clint caught those on his arms and continued the onslaught with his fists.

When Clint did raise a foot for the first time, he faked a round kick to the chest, and when Willis lowered a fist to block it, Clint caught him with an overhand right to the forehead that immediately closed his eyes. Willis was out cold on his feet, but Clint didn't realize it because he was already executing a spinning heel kick. When Clint's foot connected with Willis' face, a hush went over the crowd, and when all of Willis' 210 pounds fell to the canvas in a heap, the sound seemed amplified, almost as if a bomb had exploded. The fight, if one could really call it that, was over in 38 seconds.

Mark in Clint's corner said, "Shit, he's dead."

Clint stood in the middle of the ring, barely sweating and looking lost, almost moronic, and could only manage to say, "Aw, fuck."

It turned out that Mark had been wrong, technically speaking. Keith Willis was not dead per se, but he would never walk, speak, or even think again. He would spend the rest of his life looking much as he had in the ring that night—just a lifeless mound of flesh. Clint had effectively ended this young man's life and felt truly awful about it, downright depressed.

Clint refused his paycheck, instructing the promoter to give it to Willis' family, not that a measly 500 bucks would do much good for them under the circumstances. Clint simply didn't want to have anything to do with the money, didn't even want to touch it. The promoter, of course, couldn't wait to get Clint back in the ring.

"Listen, kid, you're going to make a fortune! People come to fights to watch guys get hurt, and you maimed, almost killed a guy in your very first fight. Sure, that's going to scare the shit out of some guys, and we may have a little trouble lining up fights. But we can always dangle the carrot and find some dumb fucks that are desperate enough to make a few bucks. You and me, kid, we're going to make a pile of money!"

Clint's initial, heartfelt response was, "Forget it. I'm done."

"What? Are you crazy? You're going to retire at 1-0?" The promoter laughed hysterically for a moment before continuing, "Well, at least you'll be undefeated! Not many people can say that!" He laughed some more, wiped tears from his eyes, and added, "Seriously, kid, don't you want to be rich?"

Looking very much like a kicked dog, Clint said, "No, not like this. I don't want to get rich like this."

The promoter didn't want to listen at first. Even months later he would still call Clint periodically, and there were others, too. In fact, there were many offers to fight, both karate and regular boxing, but Clint never listened. All he could think about were the sickening thud of his foot making contact with Willis' head and the explosion of his body hitting the canvas.

Clint recalled Willis' body jiggling after it hit the canvas, similar to a dollop of Jell-O that has fallen to a plate from a spoon. It jiggled for a moment; then it quit jiggling. Willis had indeed looked dead, and on one level Clint was relieved that Willis was still breathing, albeit with the help of a machine. At the same time, Clint also knew that he wouldn't want to exist as Willis would from this point forward. Clint dwelled on the memory of his one and only professional fight, relived it regularly in his dreams, often with the roles reversed, and just sleepwalked through his life one day at a time.

Close Encounters of the First Kind

After the Willis fight, Clint became obsessed with his job and with working out. He had always been an industrious employee and devoted to the gym, but now he attacked it all like a young man possessed. Sleep remained part of his routine, of course, but it wasn't a viable option much of the time. He didn't sleep very well; the nightmares were frequent. Luckily his body didn't seem to require a great deal of sleep, and he seemed capable of functioning perfectly well on a mere two or three hours of sleep per day.

Both work and working out were taking up more time than before, and he had begun dating a little more frequently as well. Clint didn't date a whole lot of women and certainly wasn't wanton in his sexual habits, but he did maintain relationships with the same two or three women over an extended period. Barely 19 now, he wasn't ready to tie himself down to any one woman. He wasn't necessarily opposed to it; he just hadn't found the right one yet and wasn't in any particular hurry to do so. As long as he could have some companionship with intelligent conversation and a little poon, he was satisfied. Clint found the presence of a woman to be very soothing, a poultice for his wounds.

Tom Whitely and the other investigators at England began using Clint more frequently. A lot of it was "domestic" work—husbands spying on cheating wives or vice versa. That's a pretty sleazy way to make a living, but then again, cheating on one's spouse is about as sordid as it gets. Clint had always thought that infidelity was among the worst sins, though he had begun to realize that real-life issues are usually more complicated than they appear. He figured that if it takes two people to make a good marriage, it must also take two to make a bad one. That helped him maintain his objectivity. His job was to collect information and to pass it on to a paying client. If that made him a whore, so be it. The world is full of them. Clint was very conscientious about his work, and he did it without passing judgement on any of the parties involved.

It wasn't all domestic work. Clint helped with other types of investigations as well. He really liked the credit card fraud investigations, and he proved quickly to be very adept at handwriting analysis. He could look at any two signatures and quickly discern whether or not the same person was responsible for both. Most of the banks and credit card companies had their own in-house investigators to handle such cases, but they only had time for the big cases and frequently farmed out the ones that were too big to ignore but too small to warrant more costly attention.

Clint had always been interested in accounting and at one time had considered majoring in it, so this work was fascinating to him. He also liked it because it wasn't as seedy as the domestic work, and it gave him the opportunity to work with some high-class private sector investigators, mostly people who had been cops and had left for greener pastures. He was meeting more and more people, the types of people that were good to know—people who might be able to help him one day.

One day Clint accompanied Tom to a credit card company to discuss a case with one of the in-house investigators there. As they were leaving after the meeting, Clint made eye contact with a woman who was entering the building, and he practically stopped in his tracks. Attempting to be discreet, he turned to check her out and caught her checking him out. They both blushed, turned back around, and went about their business. It was about 4:15 p.m., and Clint figured that the woman was one of the data entry operators arriving for the evening shift that started at 4:30.

Tom and Clint had ridden over in Tom's truck, so as Tom drove back to the office, Clint gazed out the window and daydreamed about the woman he'd just seen. She looked to be older than he, probably in her late 20s, and Clint thought that she was absolutely the most beautiful woman he'd ever seen. Clint's tastes weren't always in sync with what most men liked, and he realized that many men wouldn't have found her so attractive. Even so, she had an intangible quality that seemed to reach deep inside him and grab hold of his very soul. He had always been partial to dark-skinned women, and this one was clearly a mixture of some sort. Clint guessed that she was half black and half white, though he detected something else in the mix as well, maybe Indian. Regardless, she was gorgeous—beautiful face, wonderful skin, and fantastic ass.

Clint found himself wondering what the woman was like. He hadn't seen a wedding ring, but he didn't actually remember looking for one either. It was a very brief encounter, and he hadn't exactly handled it with aplomb. He wondered if she was married and whether or not their paths would ever cross again. He certainly hoped that they might meet again, and it wasn't entirely out of the question. Clint knew where she worked, and he might have a reason to go there again. If not, he might invent one. By the time Tom pulled his truck into the parking lot at the office, Clint had such an erection that it was awkward for him to exit the truck. He waited for a few minutes for things to return to normal.

A few nights later Clint was on a stakeout. The firm had been hired by a woman who suspected that her husband was cheating on her, and Clint was maintaining surveillance on the husband. The husband apparently was cheating because Clint had observed the man enter a motel room near Valley View Mall in Dallas. Someone was already in the room and opened the door for the husband when he knocked, but Clint couldn't see who she was because she was hidden behind the door. Clint had snapped a few pictures with a 35mm camera—the guy in his car in the parking lot, the guy walking toward the room, the guy knocking on the door, and the guy entering the room.

Clint wasn't actually a licensed investigator, so he wasn't supposed to do anything but take a few pictures and maintain a constant visual until Tom or another investigator arrived. After a while no one had showed up yet, and Clint was getting bored. He couldn't resist the temptation to get out of his truck and try to get a closer look. He walked toward Room 17 of the small motel, and when he arrived at the room, he realized that there was a small crack in the curtain that allowed him to see part of the room inside. Being as careful and quiet as a fellow his size could be, Clint peeked through the crack and was able to see the husband. He was standing naked next to the bed receiving fellatio— from another man!

Clint thought, "Oh, man, I've got to get some pictures of this," but he realized that he'd left the camera in the truck. He ran back to the truck and grabbed the camera, but he wasn't as quiet as he should have been. Apparently the men inside the room had been spooked, and they looked out the window just as Clint was returning toward the room with the camera at the ready. As Clint tip-toed up to the window, assuming that the men were still engaged, suddenly the door flew open and both men—still buck naked—jumped Clint and caught him completely off guard.

The camera hit the ground immediately as the two naked men flailed viciously at Clint, and it took Clint a few seconds to regain his composure. The men were hitting him all about his head and upper body, but they were swinging widely and wildly. There was little force behind their blows, and Clint thought, "They hit like girls!" Once the element of surprise had worn off, Clint was able to make quick work of the two men. The image of Keith Willis still clearly in his mind, Clint consciously held back. As the men cowered near the door of their motel room, Clint picked up what was left of the camera.

Just then Clint heard, "Freeze, motherfucker! Police! Hands on the wall!"

The voice was loud and clear, and as Clint dropped the camera again and put his hands against the brick facade of the motel, he turned his head just enough to look over his shoulder and see a large, rather intimidating cop. He was wearing plain clothes and had his badge on a lanyard so that it hung around the middle of one of the biggest chests that Clint had ever seen, and the cop was aiming a Browning Hi-Power 9mm pistol at the center of Clint's back.

The cop asked, "What the fuck is going on here? Is this some kind of queer porno thing?"

"No, sir," Clint responded. "One of those guys is cheating on his wife. I've been following him. I expected his friend to be a woman."

"Private dick, huh? You got a license?"

"Well, uh, no sir, not exactly."

"You packing?"

"No, sir. Well, I do have guns in my truck over there, but I'm not carrying any on me."

As the cop frisked Clint for weapons, a small crowd began to gather on the sidewalk as other motel patrons began exiting their rooms to see what was happening. One slimy-looking character a few doors down saw the cop and took off running.

The cop pointed in the man's direction and boomed, "That's our guy; stop him!"

A couple of other cops whom Clint hadn't even seen took off running after the guy and caught up with him quickly, taking him down hard in the parking lot.

Finishing his pat down of Clint, the big cop yelled, "The rest of you, in your rooms. This is police business!" He then cuffed Clint behind his back, led him into Room 17, and forced him down into a chair.

To the two naked men, the big cop yelled, "Okay, you two, get in here and get your goddam clothes on!"

As the men scrambled to get dressed, the other two cops showed up with the slimy-looking fellow. He, too, was cuffed behind his back, and his face looked as if it had scraped the pavement badly during his take-down. Perhaps that was no accident.

One of the cops said, "Hulk, what do you want us to do with him?"

Hulk responded, "Hold him down in his room until I sort this shit out, and make sure you search that room."

As the other two cops led their suspect back down to his room, Clint heard a vehicle outside. It pulled up and stopped, and then a door opened and closed. Clint heard footsteps approaching.

"Roy, is that you?" It was Tom Whitely. "I see you've met Clint."

"Hey, Tom, long time no see. You know this guy? Which one?"

"The big kid you have cuffed there. Yeah, I know him. He works for me."

"He said he has no license. You know better than that."

"Yeah, and so does he," Tom replied.

Looking a little perturbed but halfway smiling, Tom turned toward Clint and said, "You really stepped in a big pile this time, huh? I told you to wait until someone else got here. You're lucky this guy didn't beat your ass or shoot you."

Turning back toward the cop, Tom asked, "Can we get the cuffs off, Roy?"

"I ought to leave them on for a while, maybe teach him a lesson." After a short bluff, he removed the cuffs and said, "Sorry, kid."

Clint said, "No problem," and then winking, he added, "but you owe me!"

"Well, since you two haven't been properly introduced, allow me," said Tom. "Clint Buchanan," stressing the correct pronunciation, "meet Detective Carroll Roy, also known as Hulk."

Hulk immediately snapped, "Goddammit, Tom!"

"Oh, sorry. Detective Roy, also known as Hulk. Just forget the . . . ."

"I get it," Clint interrupted. "He doesn't like his first name. Can't say that I blame him."

"Listen, kid," said Hulk, "we don't know each other well enough for you to crack wise. Just shut the fuck up." Hulk's tone was harsh, but he couldn't hide a slight grin. He already liked Clint.

No one said anything or made eye contact for a moment, and then the little light bulb switched on above Tom's head. He looked at the other two guys in the room, and his eyes went back and forth between them.

Looking a bit puzzled and pointing to the client's husband, Tom said, "That's the husband." It was almost a question.

"Yeah," Clint said wryly, "and that's the other woman."

"Ah, shit," said Tom, shaking his head and looking disgusted. "That's an image I could do without." Turning to the husband he said, "You better have a damn good lawyer because your wife's about to take you to the cleaners."

Hulk said to the husband and his friend, "Okay, you two can get back to whatever it is you were doing before Sasquatch interrupted you." Directing Tom and Clint toward the door, he said, "We can finish this outside."

Once outside, Clint said, "You nailed it, Hulk. People call me Sasquatch."

Hulk responded, "Well, that don't exactly make me a damn genius. I rarely run into men bigger than me, and once I saw those damn clod-hoppers, that sealed it. What are those anyway, 15s?"

Looking as if he were tired of answering that question, Clint sighed and said, "16, quadruple E."

Hulk's eyes widened as he exclaimed, "Jesus Christ, kid! And you had the nerve to make fun of my name!"

The three men walked across the parking lot and gathered briefly at Tom's truck. The detective explained that he and his team had come there to serve a warrant on the slimy-looking fellow, and they arrived just as Clint was picking up his camera. When they saw him with the camera and then the two naked men, both of whom looked scared and slightly beaten, they figured they had to intervene.

"Okay, now I've got to go finish my official police business over here, and you two wannabes can talk about your little domestic situation," Hulk said sarcastically.

Tom said, "Okay, okay. Seriously, Roy, the three of us need to get together for drinks sometime. I want you and Sasquatch to meet all proper like, get to know each other. He's still young and stupid and wants to be a cop, and I figure you could give him some pointers, maybe even talk him out of it. I'd love to have him keep working with us. The kid's got promise."

"Yeah, sure, I'd love to pick your brain sometime," Clint said, a little too awestruck.

As Hulk walked toward the slimy-looking fellow's motel room, he said over his shoulder, "Fine. Stop by choir practice sometime. You remember the place."

Clint was puzzled, and he asked, "Choir practice?"

Tom responded, "He just means a shift party—cops unwinding together after work, mostly getting drunk. Cops got a lot of steam to blow off. Sometimes they overdo it and blow chunks, too."

"Why do they call it choir practice?"

Tom shrugged and said, "Search me; no one really knows. Anyway, they don't usually ask civilians. You must've made a good impression." Then he added, "Now, let's talk about our dick-smoking husband. You got pictures, right?"

Tom wouldn't like the answer.

Choir Practice

Tom and Clint entered a small bar called Cassidy's that was wall-to-wall coppers. Even though they were all wearing their street clothes, it was obvious that everyone in the place was a police officer. Tom told Clint that Cassidy was a retired DPD sergeant and that he had opened the place as a haven for cops. Every now and then civilians wandered into the place by accident, and though they weren't thrown out, they weren't exactly welcomed either. Generally they didn't stay very long. Tom explained that cops don't like civilians as a rule. They protect them; they serve them. Sometimes they even die for them, but they rarely drink with them. Clint puzzled over the paradox.

As Tom and Clint walked through the bar, every eye was on them. Clint was used to that. He was almost always the biggest person in the room, and people practically got whiplash anytime they caught a glimpse of him. Clint often thought, "I guess your parents didn't teach you that it's not polite to stare." Folks always stared, and usually they didn't even bother trying to be discreet about it. Tom once said that Clint had an aura about him and that people couldn't help themselves. In this case, though, the cops were taking notice that two civilians had trespassed onto their turf, and they were waiting to see if the visitors would somehow desecrate the hallowed ground of Cassidy's.

An older gentleman behind the bar saw them and yelled out, "Whitely, is that you? Damn, it's been a long time!"

"Yeah, Sarge, it's me. Figured it was time to revisit the old stomping grounds," Tom replied, shaking hands with the old fellow. "Sarge, this here's Clint Buchanan. That's 'Buck Hannon.' Be sure to pronounce it right, or he gets really pissed. Clint, meet Robert Cassidy. He was my sergeant for a while before he retired."

"Pleased to meet you, sir," Clint said, extending his hand.

The old man sized up the kid, shook his hand, and said, "Kid, you must've eaten every vegetable your momma ever cooked!"

"Oh, yes, sir! I surely did. Didn't miss too much of the meat either, or the desserts for that matter. And just think how big I'd be if I hadn't drunk coffee every day since I was four!"

The three men shared a laugh, and then Tom and Cassidy reminisced for a while. Clint had known that Tom was a cop before becoming a private investigator, but Tom was tight-lipped about the particulars of his police experience. In only a few minutes of listening to the two men hark back to old times, Clint learned a lot about Tom that he hadn't known before. Clint thought it very odd that Tom had resigned before locking in his retirement, but the secret of that decision would have to wait.

"Sarge, we're here to meet Detective Roy. You seen him tonight?"

"No, Hulk ain't been around in a week or two."

"Well, I guess he's just running a little late. Probably got tied up at the station doing paperwork or something."

"Yeah, if he said he'll be here, he'll be here—unless he's dead. Even then he'd probably call first." They all laughed. "What'll y'all have while you're waiting? Damn, I should've asked already 'stead of yapping away like that."

Tom replied, "Don't worry about it, Sarge. Give me a Bud draft."

Cassidy looked at Clint and said, "You don't look like you're even shaving yet kid. You old enough to drink?"

Clint replied, "Oh, yes, sir. I'm 19. Want to see ID?"

Cassidy chuckled and said, "No, kid, I was just yanking your chain. What'll you have?"

"Give me a 101 on the rocks, sir." Clint did like his Wild Turkey, and he liked that the legal age in Texas was only 18.

Cassidy replied, "If you'll quit calling me sir, I'll give you one on the house. I ain't no sir."

"Yes, sir. Oh, shit!" They all laughed, and Clint said, "Don't worry. It won't happen again."

Tom and Clint sipped their beer and bourbon while Cassidy excused himself and resumed the business of running a bar. They chatted for a while, finished their drinks, and ordered another round. None of the cops paid them much mind anymore. Apparently Cassidy's warm welcome assured them that these outsiders were okay. Tom and Clint were just about to give up when Hulk came bursting through the door. He didn't burst through the door literally, but it always seemed that way with him.

Everyone turned to look, and most shouted in unison, "Hey, it's Hulk!"

After several minutes of handshakes and back slaps, Hulk finally made it over to the corner of the bar where Tom and Clint were waiting.

"Hey, Sasquatch! How's it hanging, kid?" Hulk shook hands with Clint and Tom and then continued, "Sorry to keep y'all waiting. You know, fucking scumbags don't have any respect for the fact that I had people waiting for me."

"That's okay, Roy," Tom said. "I remember what it was like. We weren't waiting long. Besides, it gave me a chance to catch up with Sarge. The old fart looks good—probably outlive us all."

"Damn right he will," Hulk said, and then turning to Clint, he asked, "Well, kid, what do you think of this place? Think you fit in with this bunch?"

"Oh, I don't know about that," Clint said. "Maybe some day. I hope."

Hulk said, "That table in the corner opened up. Let's grab it. Hey, Cassidy, send me over the usual."

Cassidy said, "That stuff's going to kill you one of these days, Hulk."

Hulk responded loudly, "Well, that's why they call it *ta-kill-ya!*"

Everyone in the place seemed to hear and gave the obligatory laugh at Hulk's joke. He, Tom, and Clint made their way over to the table in the corner, and Cassidy came over with a shot glass and a full bottle of Cuervo.

Cassidy set the bottle and glass on the table in front of Hulk and said, "Hulk, you don't have to drink the whole bottle just because it's there."

Hulk said nothing. He just looked at the old man, winked, poured a shot, slammed it down, poured another, slammed it down, and then poured a third. Cassidy sighed and walked away, shaking his head.

"Damn, it's been a rough day, guys," Hulk said with a sigh. "I'm sorry you had to wait, but I'm glad you did. Sasquatch, it's good to see you again. Sorry about the other night, by the way. We okay?"

Clint said, "Oh, sure, think nothing of it. It made an interesting night more interesting."

Hulk said, "Oh, yeah, what about your cheating husband? What's happening with that case?"

Tom answered, "It took the guy about a minute to lawyer-up and make the wife an offer she couldn't refuse, which was real good since our big-footed friend over here broke the damn camera and didn't have any pictures."

Clint responded defensively, "Now, Tom, you know that the pictures didn't matter. I saw him with his dick in another man's mouth, and he didn't even deny it. In fact, I got the distinct impression he was relieved to come out of the closet."

"You're right, Clint," Tom said. "It's okay. I'm just having a little fun with you. The lady paid the bill, and that's all that really matters anyway."

Hulk yelled to Cassidy, "Hey, another round over here for my friends!" He turned to Clint and asked, "So, kid, why you want to be a one of us?"

With a perfectly straight face, Clint said, "Because I want to wear a badge and a gun and go out and fuck with civilians."

Hulk was in the process of drinking that third shot of tequila, and he laughed so hard that it spewed all over Tom and Clint. He continued laughing heartily for a moment. When Hulk had regained his composure, he poured another shot, held it up to Clint, and said, "You're hired!" Hulk threw back the shot, and they all continued laughing for a minute and then resumed the conversation seriously after Cassidy had dropped off another round for Tom and Clint.

"To tell you the truth," Clint said, "I want to be a cop because I want to help people. I know that sounds corny, but it's true. I'm not saying that I want to get all touchy-feely with folks. I'm no bleeding heart. But I want to help fight drugs, and that's helping people. I want to put criminals in jail, and that's helping people. That's it in a nutshell. All joking aside, that's my answer."

Looking very serious, Hulk said, "Well, you know, kid, this whole drug war thing ain't all it's cracked up to be. We can sit here all night and drink whiskey, tequila, and beer until we puke, and tomorrow I'll put someone in jail for smoking weed. We can smoke cigarettes and chew tobacco until we get cancer, but we get our shorts in a wad over some poor schmuck taking uppers to stay awake so he can drive a truck to feed his family. Some asshole can pound his wife and kids all day and night, and we look the other way— unless we happen to spot a nickel bag on the coffee table. Does any of this make sense to you?"

"Well, no, not really. I guess I never really thought of it like that," Clint said, pondering the subject seriously.

"Hulk's a little jaded, Clint," Tom snuck in.

"Oh, shut your pie hole, Tom! I'm a realist. I been trying to make sense of this shit for almost 20 years, and I just don't see much logic behind it all. There's emotions, lots of strong feelings, but there's not much science to it all. Half the shit—no *more* than half the shit we tell kids about drugs ain't even true. We just make it up as we go along to try to scare them. We forget that scare tactics don't work. It just makes them want to do it more. When will we learn?"

Hulk paused for a moment, looking deep in thought, and then sighed and said, "Sorry, Tom. You're right. I *am* jaded." The three men sat in silence for a minute or two, each sipping his legal drug of choice.

Hulk finally turned toward Clint, scooted a little closer, and said, "Kid, this line between the drugs people can use and the ones we throw them in jail for is an accident. It's just a fucking accident! What narcs do doesn't always make sense. Most of the time it doesn't. Prohibition should've taught us a lesson or two, but we haven't studied our history. We just block a whole decade out of our memory. You know, there's a reason we repealed Prohibition. Because it don't work! It does more harm than good."

Lightening up a bit, Hulk slapped the table and said, "You know what, though? The City of Dallas don't pay me to brood over this shit. None of that matters. The law is what it is, and if the people don't like it, they need to elect some politicians who'll change it. Until then, I'm going to enforce the law. I don't have to like it. I don't have to understand it. But I get paid to enforce it, and that's what I'll do to the best of my ability until I pull the pin or die."

There was another pregnant pause while Hulk let it all sink into Clint's young mind. He could tell that the kid was taken aback.

When the silence started to become uncomfortable, Hulk added, "But let me tell you something else. These dealers are absolute scum. They're fucking vultures. They prey on the weak and the young, and they deserve anything and everything that the law can throw at them. And when it comes to throwing the law at these worthless pieces of shit, I'm an All-Pro quarterback. I'm Roger Fucking Staubach!"

Clint was both surprised and awed by the detective's revelations. He was very impressed that the man could hold two contradictory thoughts in his head at the same time without short-circuiting his brain, and Hulk's single-minded devotion to his job despite considerable underlying ambivalence was something that Clint hoped he could emulate.

Many people like to view things as dichotomous. They think that there are only two possible answers to any question: the right one and the wrong one. That view certainly makes life simpler; one needn't think. Clint, though, was starting to realize that things are rarely so simple. The real world is not black and white. It's gray, and the shading varies according to each person's perception. As Clint matured, he realized more and more that the truth generally lies somewhere near the middle of a continuum between the two extremes. Rarely is the simple, thoughtless, extreme answer the right one.

Hulk was the perfect example of this truth, and as of that moment, Clint had a new hero. He wanted to be just like Hulk, and he couldn't help but think, "Hulk and Sasquatch, what a team!" It was a dream, but it was one that conceivably might come true one day.

"Well, Hulk, you've certainly given me a lot to think about," Clint said. "I appreciate your time. I hope we get to talk again sometime."

"Boy, you're talking like you're about to leave," Hulk responded. "Hell, the night's young. I ain't got to work for a couple days, and I plan to get rip-roaring drunk!" Effecting a haughty accent, he held up his glass and added, "I have not yet begun to party!"

The three drank and talked, talked and drank, until the wee hours of the morning. Once he had several Wild Turkeys in his belly, Clint started thinking of Keith Willis again and became sullen. That always happened when he drank. Being a cop and a drinker, Hulk knew that guys just get like that sometimes, so he didn't press the issue. He and Tom were content to swap war stories, cops' favorite pastime—next to getting laid, of course.

One time when Clint got up to visit the head, Hulk asked Tom, "Does he always get like that when he drinks?"

Tom glanced toward the men's room and then said, "Roy, you remember that fight over at Billy Bob's a while back, the one where the guy almost got killed? You hear about that?"

Hulk answered, "Yeah, I think I remember hearing something about that, but I don't recall the particulars."

Tom said, "Well, it was Clint that did that to him. I was there, Roy, and you wouldn't believe this kid. He's scary awesome. You'd never believe that such quickness and strength and fight savvy could be combined in one package. First pro fight, and he fucks the guy up big-time. We're talking 'lights out'—nothing but a machine keeping the guy alive, if you want to call it that. Clint's taking it pretty hard."

Hulk took another drink, shook his head, and said, "Damn! That's some tough luck."

"Yeah, for both of them," Tom added.

That was all the discussion they had time for before Clint made it back to the table. He said nothing, just sat there nursing his drink, deep in thought. The three sat quietly for a while, and Hulk contemplated whether or not to say anything. He didn't really know the kid well enough yet to judge that. Finally Hulk decided to proceed cautiously.

"Kid, you okay?"

"Yeah, Hulk, I'm fine."

"You want to talk about it?"

"No, sir, I'd rather not."

Hulk reached into his shirt pocket, retrieved one of his DPD calling cards, wrote his personal phone number on the card, and handed it to Clint.

He said, "Well, kid, here's my card. It has my office number at HQ and my home number. I don't give that to just anyone. You ever decide you want to chat, you give me a call. A guy's a cop long enough, he learns a thing or two about what might be eating another guy up inside. We all get that way sometimes. You don't want to talk now, fine. But one of these days you will, and I'll listen."

"And I'm here for you, too, Clint. You know I am," added Tom. "We're not going to push you, but when you're ready to talk, we're ready to listen."

Clint said only, "Thanks, guys," but he made it a point to look up and make eye contact with each of them, adding a nod of acknowledgement.

At precisely 1:45, Cassidy yelled out, "Last call!" Most everyone in the place, including Tom, Clint, and Hulk, had another round.

At straight up 2:00, Cassidy yelled out, "All right, all you motherfuckers out of this place! It's 2:00 closing time, and I don't need the state on my ass again. Finish your drink, pay your tab, and go home and climb into bed with something warm and wet."

Cassidy made his way over to the table in the corner and told Tom, Clint, and Hulk, "You guys are okay. I won't serve you no more booze, but I got a pot of coffee brewing. I'll stay here with you as long as you want. As long as no one drinks any booze, everything's kosher. I'd like to talk to y'all, and none of you needs to be driving anyways."

Cassidy was right about that, and drunk driving is the most violent crime in America. After everyone else had paid their tabs and made their way out the door, Cassidy locked the door, went back to the kitchen, and made his way back to the corner table. He was carrying a tray with four coffee cups and a full pot of fresh coffee. That was about 2:20, and Cassidy's lone employee left around 3:00. No one else would leave the bar until after sunrise.

The four men sat there through the night, drinking black coffee and telling stories. Clint mostly just listened, hanging on every word. At one point he thought, "I'm learning stuff here that I could never learn in college," and as the night wore on and the whiskey wore off, he cheered up and became a little more like Clint again.

Scooter Tramps

Clint was something of an enigma. On the one hand, he seemed perfectly at ease in social situations. He rarely seemed hesitant or shy in any way, and people often commented on his savoir faire. People were actually drawn to him, and at first blush he never seemed to push them away. On the other hand, he had an intense need to be alone much of the time, and in order to ensure that, he rarely let people get close to him.

Clint had grown up in Allen, a small town near Dallas, and he had known many of the same people for as long as he could remember. Even so, Clint had only one close friend: Milton Vaughan. Like Clint, Milton had been something of an outcast in high school, so he had grown used to being alone. To say that each was the other's best friend was a bit redundant; each was the other's only real friend. Clint was beginning to make some new friends now, guys like Tom and Hulk, but they were still a long way from really being close to Clint. Milton, on the other hand, was like a brother.

Milton was a couple of years older than Clint, and after graduating from high school he had briefly dated a girl at Clint's school who happened also to go to Clint's church. Milton would go with the girl to church on Sundays and then usually accompany the youth group on their Sunday night pizza ritual. It just wasn't Sunday without a Pizza Casa Supreme—the one with everything but the kitchen sink on it, including jalapeños and anchovies. It was about the only time when Clint hung around other kids.

Milton's girlfriend was Ginny Rodgers, and Clint had a bit of a crush on her. That might normally have made two guys rivals, but in this case it would ultimately have the opposite effect. Because Clint tended to try to sit near Ginny, he naturally wound up sitting near Milton as well.

One night as Clint sat directly across the table from Milton, Milton asked Ginny, "Why do elephants paint their toenails pink?"

"Oh, no, Milton! Not more elephant jokes!"

Ginny clearly didn't want to listen, so Milton turned to Clint and asked, "Hey, Clint, why do elephants paint their toenails pink?"

"I don't know," Clint said, knowing that the answer would be a real groaner.

"So they can hide in cherry trees." There was a bit of pause before Milton asked, "Ever see an elephant in a cherry tree?"

Thinking that this was pretty silly, Clint said, "Uh, no."

Smiling widely and thinking nothing of the disapproving looks on the other faces, Milton said, "See how well it works!"

Yes, it was a groaner, pretty childish, but Clint was intrigued by the apparent fact that Milton knew this and didn't care. With only a slight pause, Milton launched right into his next elephant joke.

"Hey, Clint, what do you get when you cross an owl with an elephant?"

"I don't know," Clint said, hoping that this one would be better.

"A dead owl with one huge orifice!"

As Ginny groaned, Clint and Milton burst into laughter, and Clint said, "Okay that was much better!"

That's how it all started. That led to more jokes and conversation. Soon Clint and Milton discovered that they were similar and had common interests, and they began spending some time together. Ultimately Milton didn't date Ginny for very long, but after they broke up, he and Clint continued their friendship. Clint and Ginny never got together.

Clint and Milton had two main things in common: motorcycles and guns. Generally when they were together, they were either on their scooters or at the shooting range—or perhaps riding their scooters to the shooting range. They both liked to eat, too, and they both preferred bourbon to beer. Moreover, each had a keen intellect that often escaped others who only knew him from a distance. As individuals, people often said that each marched to his own beat, but luckily for them their respective beats were more-or-less in sync most of the time.

Truthfully, Clint and Milton probably weren't particularly different from most young men their age, but what was markedly different about them was their preference for solitude. Most guys run in packs; they didn't. They were perfectly happy with the one friend or alone. They bonded quickly and securely, and although each continued to spend a great deal of time alone, they also spent a lot of time together. Often they were riding their motorcycles, which seemed the perfect thing for these two. They enjoyed taking long rides together, but inside their helmets, each remained alone with his thoughts. It was the best of both worlds.

Despite their solitary nature, Clint and Milton did share a great deal with one another, and Clint in particular seemed to open up and share most everything with Milton. More than anyone else in the world, Clint could talk to Milton and be confident that Milton would listen, not pass judgement, and keep his secrets. Clint genuinely loved his friend as a brother and trusted him implicitly. Although they didn't spend as much time together now as they had in the past, if either needed to talk, he always made time to seek out the other.

Milton was the only person to whom Clint turned for any kind of support after the Willis fight. Neither said much about it. Clint could barely tell Milton what had happened, and Milton didn't really know what to say to make Clint feel better. Clint said what little he had to say for the sake of catharsis, and Milton just listened. He was always good about that. They were kind of like an old couple and took comfort in just being together. A lot of their communication didn't require speech.

Today they were planning to take a ride. They hadn't ridden together in a few weeks, and each had arranged time off for this outing.

"Where do you want to go today?" Clint asked. "Wichita Falls?"

Milton responded, "Nah, it's boring, and we went there last time anyway. Let's go somewhere else, maybe Austin. We haven't been down there in a while."

"That's kind of far. You planning to spend the night and come back in the morning? We could take a shorter ride and then go to the range in the morning, fire off a couple hundred rounds."

"I'm up for the overnight if you are. We could go to Li'l Abner's tonight and then catch some Zs in a cheap motel before the flip-flop."

"Ah, shit, Milton," Clint said, shaking his head. "You going to drag me to a titty bar again?"

Clint had no inherent opposition to watching women dance naked. In fact, Clint had introduced Milton to strip clubs. Milton had become a little obsessed, though, and Clint often thought, "I've created a monster!" Clint's problem was that he tended not to like the typical clientele of a strip joint, and as titty bars go, Li'l Abner's wasn't exactly high class. Clint was always a little nervous around drunk rednecks, and Li'l Abner's seemed to have more than its share. He'd had some trouble there before.

Milton said, "Yeah, sure. Why not? We'll just go for a couple of hours and have us some Turkey. Maybe Trixie will be working tonight."

"I still can't get over that name," Clint said. "Isn't that supposedly her real name?"

"I've never seen her birth certificate, but yeah, that's what she says."

"What were her parents thinking? Nothing like dooming your daughter from the outset to a life on the pole."

"Oh, come on, Clint. Don't be so judgemental. She's a nice girl. She's going to community college, too."

"I'm sure that's true. All dancers take their clothes off to pay tuition."

"Forget it. Are we going or not?"

"Well, okay, but you're buying."

Clint never argued a whole lot. He argued often but only half-heartedly. It was kind of a little game they played, but he wanted to go. He hadn't had anything to drink since his choir practice bender a week ago, and he hadn't been to a titty bar in several months. He figured it was about time to go again.

"No problem, Sasquatch. I just got paid. Besides, I think it's my turn anyway."

"Damn right it is. Okay then, let's go. I'll take the lead."

The two strapped on their helmets and made their way through Dallas to I-35 for the drive south. Both of them rode Japanese motorcycles—Clint a Kawasaki and Milton a Honda. They referred to them as "rice-burners." Each badly wanted a Harley-Davidson but couldn't really afford it, and it somehow made them feel better to deride their own bikes.

Truthfully, Clint and Milton both liked to ride fast, and the Japanese motorcycles were faster and handled better. Still, Clint always felt a little unpatriotic about it, and he hoped that one day he could save enough money to buy a Harley. Yes, those 45-degree V-twins do tend to vibrate and leak oil, but they're American and have a certain mystique that no foreign bike can match, not even those fancy Beemers.

It was a good day for riding—clear, just a slight breeze, and not too hot. They made good time on the interstate and stopped to eat at a Fina truck stop in the little town of Jarrell. They were most of the way to Austin, but they liked to stop here because the restaurant, even though it was a bit of a dive, served a hearty and surprisingly tasty Tex-Mex combo plate. It was also cheap, so Clint ate two, as was his custom. After they had eaten and visited the men's room, they decided to top off their gas tanks before starting the last 40 miles or so into Austin.

They had filled up and paid and were getting on their bikes to leave when they heard the characteristic rumble of Harleys. That was always like a magnet for Clint and Milton both, so they looked up and saw three bikers pulling into the station. These were *real* bikers. They were wearing the colors of the Bandido Nation, and Clint realized too late that he and Milton were staring at them.

"You eyeballin' me, boy?" the lead biker barked as the three pulled up on the other side of the island.

"No, sir, sorry. We were just leaving," Clint responded just before he turned the key to start his Kawasaki.

Milton had started his Honda, too, and they were getting ready to make a run for it when one of the bikers pulled around the island and stopped in front of them, blocking their exit.

"What's your hurry, boys?" the biker in front of them asked.

By that time Clint and Milton were more-or-less trapped. The biker in front had been joined by another behind, and getting around them would have taken some really fancy maneuvering. Clint decided to try to talk his way out of this jam. He was normally good at talking to people, but he wondered if that was really relevant here.

"Sorry, guys, we weren't staring at you. We were staring at your bikes. Harleys have that effect on us. We're stuck with these shitty rice-burners, and we'd love to get us some real bikes like those." Clint crossed his fingers in his mind.

"Oh, is that so?" the lead biker asked. "I guess y'all are just a couple of dirty, low-down, good-for-nothin', snatch-eatin' scooter tramps like us, huh?" All three bikers enjoyed a good laugh.

Clint responded, "Yes, sir! We take that as a compliment!"

"Now you're getting smart with me!" the lead biker snarled.

He had gotten off his Harley by now and was standing face-to-face with Clint. He was a pretty big dude, probably about 6-2 and 240, and Bandidos were noted for being vicious. Clint knew that this opponent would have absolutely no fear.

Clint glanced at Milton and could tell that he was very nervous. Milton was capable of being pretty tough under normal circumstances; however, this circumstance was not normal, and Clint could see that Milton was intimidated. He would have his hands full with the one biker nearest him, and Clint would have to try to take the other two. Normally three-on-two would have been a pretty even fight for Clint and Milton, but with these three being outlaw bikers, all bets were off. Weapons would almost certainly be involved, and Clint and Milton had none.

"No, sir, I don't mean to sound smart," was all that Clint got out before all five of the men noticed the Highway Patrol cruiser pull into the parking lot and head straight for them.

Two troopers got out of the car and one asked, "Is everything okay here?"

"Oh, yes sir, I was just telling these gentlemen how much I envy their rides, and they suggested that we trade our rice-burners for some good American machines," Clint said. "I figure that's good advice. Now my buddy and I need to be on our way."

Looking very much as if he understood the situation, the trooper looked at Clint and Milton and said, "Well, then y'all should just go ahead and hit the road. We need to talk to your three friends for a little while."

"Yes, sir," Clint said to the trooper, and then turning to the lead biker, he added, "Nice to meet y'all. We appreciate the advice."

With a cold stare, the biker responded flatly, "We'll be seeing you."

There was an underlying menace in the biker's voice. Clint and Milton pulled away toward the on ramp, entered the interstate, and rode quickly to Austin. They made the last 40 miles in about a half hour. Clint had misgivings about continuing their outing. He shuddered and thought, "Damn, we should have turned north and gone home!"

They made their way to the University of Texas campus for some sight-seeing. They rode around for a while but then decided to get off their bikes for a closer look. There was never a shortage of nubile women at UT, and Clint tended to draw more attention from them on foot than hunched over the handlebars of his rice-burner.

At one point they saw a voluptuous young woman wearing a tight T-shirt stretched across her large breasts. The front of the shirt said: "If God had not intended for man to eat pussy . . . ." That certainly got their attention, and as she walked past them chuckling, they saw that the back of her shirt said: "Then why did he make it look so much like a taco?" Clint and Milton were completely dumbfounded, and they could hear the young woman laughing at them as she walked away.

"Does it really look like a taco, Clint?" Milton asked with a huge laugh. "I've never been that close to one in the light!"

"You know, I never really thought of it, but yeah, I guess it kind of does! But I stay away from the crunchy kind! Only soft tacos for me!"

They laughed all the way to the LBJ library. Milton was interested in architecture, and he always liked to take an up-close look at the unique building. He admired the structure if not the man for whom it was named. After circling the building and making a quick run through the ground floor, they headed back toward their bikes.

It was a nice day, and Clint and Milton were enjoying the fresh air and scenery. It seemed that few of the young women on campus were shy, and most enjoyed showing off their bodies. They liked being ogled, and these two young men were all too happy to oblige.

"I'm hungry," Clint said. "You want to stop by Stubb's for some barbecue?" It had been less than three hours since they had eaten in Jarrell, but Milton hadn't been surprised by Clint's insatiable appetite in a very long time.

"Yeah, sure," Milton said. "I could handle a sandwich."

Stubb's Bar-B-Q was as famous for its music as it was for its food. Willie Nelson, Johnny Cash, Stevie Ray Vaughn, and other famous musicians often performed there, sometimes for their supper. As Clint and Milton were getting off their bikes to go inside, they were wondering who might be playing this evening, and they heard Harleys getting louder. Their hearts stopped as they turned toward the rumble, and they were relieved to see a couple of clean-cut weekend "bikers" ride past.

"Damn!" Clint said, shaking his head.

Milton tried to reassure him by saying, "Relax. They can't find a needle in a haystack."

"You're forgetting that I'm more like a baseball bat."

They went inside and were only slightly disappointed that no one famous (yet) was playing. A lot of the local talent was just as good as the big names, some arguably better. The guys playing tonight had an eclectic repertoire. Clint and Milton didn't stay long, but they heard a little country, rockabilly, and blues.

Milton ate a pulled pork sandwich and marveled as Clint finished a three-meat combo plate with brisket, sausage, ribs, potato salad, cole slaw, and beans, and then topped it off with blackberry cobbler—with the requisite scoop of Blue Bell Homemade Vanilla ice cream on top, of course. It dawned on Milton that tonight might not be the best time to share a small motel room with Clint. He hoped it would have a good fan and a window that opened.

Killing some extra time before heading over to Li'l Abner's wasn't a bad thing. The best dancers rarely work the early shift, so it's better to arrive after the late shift starts. By the time Clint and Milton walked into the place, it was already packed, and the smoke was thick. No tables were open, so they squeezed into a space at the bar and ordered their usual.

"We'll have 101 on the rocks—both of us," Clint said.

"Coming right up," the bartender replied.

Clint reached into his case and retrieved a cigar. Clint's tastes exceeded his means, but he really enjoyed a premium smoke, especially those from a certain island south of Miami when he could get them. This one was not a Cuban. It was a milder smoke—and a legal one—from the Dominican Republic.

Clint cut the head of the cigar, put it to his lips to test the draw, and then toasted the foot for a little while before lighting it all the way. Milton always found the ritual a bit comical, but he said nothing this time. Clint was in full herf mode by the time the bartender placed the two glasses of whiskey on the bar in front of them. Each reached for his drink and took the first sip simultaneously.

In unison, Clint and Milton said sharply, "Sour mash!"

"Bartender, if you don't mind," Clint said, "please replace this Jack Daniels with Wild Turkey 101. We're partial to bourbon."

"Aw, shit, sorry guys. My mistake," replied the bartender as he reached for their glasses. "Y'all starting a tab by the way?"

"Yes, sir," Clint replied and then blew a nearly perfect smoke ring. His practice was paying off. "Here's my card."

Milton looked at Clint questioningly, and Clint said, "Yeah, I know you're supposed to buy. You can pay me later. This is just for the tab." Clint was proud of his new Master Charge because very few people his age had their own credit card. He watched as the bartender checked the number against the warning bulletin.

"You won't find it in there," Clint said, impressed that the bartender even bothered to look because he knew that many merchants did not, a fact that made life much easier for the fraudsters.

"I still have to look," the bartender replied without looking up. "You'd be surprised how many I find, and I get

50 bucks every time I do." Closing the bulletin and putting it back under the bar, he said, "Nope, not in there. You're good. Just so you know, I'm going to ask you to close out your tab before you go over 50 bucks. It's a pain in the ass to call for an authorization, especially on a busy night. You can always start another tab if you want."

Clint nodded and said, "No problem. We're not planning to be here all night anyway."

The bartender made their drinks and set them on the bar. Clint and Milton picked up the glasses and turned around on their stools so that they could see what they had come to see. They sipped their whiskey, and Clint puffed his toro.

Milton looked around and then asked the bartender, "Hey, is Trixie working tonight?"

To Milton's eternal heartbreak, the bartender said, "No, she doesn't work here anymore—been gone a while."

"She must've graduated," Clint said to his buddy. He couldn't resist digging a little, so with a chuckle he added, "Probably a banker now, maybe a doctor."

"Quit being a prick, Clint," Milton said before settling into a long-term sulk.

That put a damper on the evening. Milton was seriously bummed, and even the sight of some other nice flesh couldn't lift his spirits. Clint was actually somewhat relieved because he knew it wouldn't be difficult to get Milton out of the place at a reasonable hour. Clint was tired, and he hoped he might get a little more sleep than usual. Perhaps another drink might help.

After a while Clint turned and said, "Bartender, another . . . ." Clint was about to order another round, but someone bumped into him.

"Hey, what the fuck is your problem, man?" seemed an odd question coming from the fellow who had bumped into Clint as he sat on his stool with his back turned.

Turning back around, Clint said, "I don't have a problem. I was just sitting here minding my own business, and you bumped into me. But no big deal. Don't worry about it."

"You big guys always act like you own the place. You think you can just push the rest of us around. Well, I'm tired of being pushed around by big assholes like you!"

Clint thought, "Oh, shit, a Napoleon complex!" He noted that the other fellow was all of 5-7 and maybe 140 pounds. That would be 140 soaking wet with a rock in his pocket. Clint couldn't help but chuckle.

"What the fuck is so funny, you ugly fucking gorilla? You think you can take me?"

Still not able to stifle his laughter, Clint said, "Man, I'd break you in half."

The man's response would be etched into Clint's brain forever: "Yeah, you're right, but I'll make sure you're one tired motherfucker before it's over!"

At that moment, Clint, Milton, the bartender, and everyone else within earshot broke into uncontrollable laughter. Even the little guy couldn't help himself. He doubled over in laughter with his hands on his knees.

When the little guy was finally able to take a breath, he looked up and said, "Man, I think I just pissed my pants!" Still more laughter ensued. This was a story that all would tell for years to come.

Clint finally said, "Let me buy you a drink, my friend. What'll you have?" There was a moment of relative quiet while the little guy composed himself to answer Clint's question, and Clint turned back toward the bar. He had been so preoccupied that he hadn't seen them come in.

Clint's blood ran cold when he heard a familiar voice from behind him say, "Well, what do you know? Here's a couple of dirty, low-down, good-for-nothin', snatch-eatin' scooter tramps!"

Clint turned just enough and just in time to catch a glimpse of the big biker's fist before it crashed into his head, and the blow turned Clint's body to the side. He slid off the stool and drove a back kick into the biker's groin. It was a good kick, and when the biker doubled over, Clint drove his elbow into the back of the biker's head, knocking him face first into the floor, only semi-conscious. Surprised that he'd been able to put the big man down so quickly but figuring that he'd be down for a little while, Clint turned his attention toward Milton.

One of the other bikers had knocked Milton to the ground and was about to pounce on him when the little guy who'd wanted to fight Clint shattered a longneck bottle over the biker's head. Unfazed, the biker turned and hit the little guy squarely in the face and then picked him up and threw him over the bar. The biker stopped just a moment to take a deep breath, and that gave Clint the chance to step in and throw a left-right-left combination that put the biker down—two down and one to go.

"You okay? Where's the other one?" Clint asked as he helped Milton to his feet.

"Yeah, I'm okay. I didn't see another one," Milton responded.

"Where's the other one?" Clint asked the bartender.

The bartender said, "I only saw two. Hey, I called the cops."

"Good, thanks," Clint responded.

Clint took a moment to look at the two bikers who were down. The first one, possibly a bit less of a man than he'd been when he entered the place, was struggling to his feet. He had one hand cupped over his package, and he reached awkwardly toward Clint with the other.

In a pained, shrill tone, the biker yelled at Clint, "You goddam motherfucker! It's busted! You ruptured one of my nuts, man! I'll kill you! I'll fucking kill you!"

The biker stumbled toward Clint and threw a wild punch with his free hand. Clint slipped the punch and drove his knee into the biker's solar plexus, and the biker dropped like a rock.

As the biker writhed on the floor in pain and gasped for air, Clint said firmly, "You'd better stay down this time." Clint looked at the second biker. He was starting to squirm a little now, but he didn't appear to be getting up. Keeping an eye on both of the bikers on the floor, Clint asked the bartender, "You sure there wasn't another one?"

"Yeah, I'm sure, man. There were only two. Y'all go ahead and book. I'll clear everything up with the cops when they get here. It's not like they're going to be all concerned about these two anyway. Here's your credit card." Tearing up their tab, he added, "On the house tonight. Consider it payment for entertainment and pest control."

Taking the card from the bartender and putting it away quickly, Clint said, "Thanks, man. Nah, I'm sticking around. I got nothing to run from," Clint said. Suddenly he thought, "The bikes!"

To Milton, Clint said, "You stay here and watch these two. If either tries to get up, kick the shit out of him. I'm going to check on the bikes."

"Okay, Sasquatch."

Clint trotted out into the parking lot and made his way to where they'd parked just in time to see the third biker slash the fourth tire. The man stood up and faced Clint, sneering, the big Buck knife in his right hand. Clint thought, "Damn, I hate blades!"

Calmly Clint said, "Alright now, I just made pretty quick work of your two buddies in there. The big one's going to be singing soprano from now on. The cops are on their way, and you need to put that knife down before I shove it up your ass."

The biker lunged at Clint with the knife. Clint was able to move to the side as the knife narrowly missed his belly. As the biker's momentum carried him forward, Clint grabbed the biker's right wrist with his own right hand and threw a short left to the biker's right ear. The biker dropped the knife and went down. Clint grabbed the knife quickly and threw it away, over some cars and into some bushes. In doing so, he had turned slightly away from the biker, and as he turned back around, the biker was getting back to his feet. Clint thought he saw something in the biker's hand and was confused. "I got his knife," he puzzled.

The biker made an odd motion with his right hand, almost as if cracking a whip, and then he swung something at Clint's head. Clint ducked instinctively, but he had no idea what he was dodging. As the biker continued to swing something, Clint heard a "swoosh, swoosh" over his head. He didn't have a clue what it was, but he didn't want to find out the hard way.

Clint bull-rushed the biker, driving his head hard into the biker's chest, wrapping his arms around him, and taking him down. Even Coach Morris would have been proud of Clint's tackling technique. Clint rarely went to the ground in a fight. In fact, he preferred to avoid it at all costs, so he didn't intend to stay there long. He gave the biker two quick, short rights to the face and jumped to his feet.

The biker was out cold, and lying a few inches from his right hand was the mystery weapon: a car antenna. Clint had never seen such a thing! The biker had broken it off a car when Clint turned briefly to throw the knife away, and it had apparently been in the down position. The biker's whip-like motion telescoped it to full length, providing the biker with a very formidable weapon. Had he been able to connect with it, it would have done some damage. Clint couldn't help but admire the biker's ingenuity.

Clint was just about to go back inside and check on Milton when he heard the sirens approaching. Clint thought, "Just in time!" He turned to face the oncoming cruisers, making sure that his hands were up where the officers could see them. There were three cars and four officers already there, and he could hear that more were coming. If the bartender had told the dispatcher that Bandidos were involved, half of the Austin PD would be there soon.

"Freeze! Keep your hands where I can see them!" one of the officers yelled.

All four officers were out of their cruisers now, and each had his sidearm drawn. Clint found that a little unsettling, although he understood the need. Two of the officers ran up and frisked Clint while the other two checked on the fallen biker. He was starting to move a little, but he wasn't saying anything or making an effort to get up.

"What's going on here? Where's the other biker? We heard there were two," a man with sergeant's stripes inquired.

"Well, sir, actually there are three of them—that one there and another two inside. My buddy's watching them, but you'd better get in there and check on him."

"Your buddy is watching them?" asked the sergeant. "What? Y'all got them tied up or something?"

"No, sir," Clint responded. "They're just out on the floor. They took a pretty good pounding."

Clint could tell that the sergeant was having a hard time wrapping his mind around the concept that three Bandidos were on the losing end of a bar fight. His eyes went back and forth between Clint and the biker on the ground. He eyeballed Clint from head to toe and then shook his head.

Pointing to one of the officers, the sergeant said, "You wait with that one. An ambulance is on the way." Pointing to another cop, he said, "You get a statement from this badass here." The sergeant smiled and winked at Clint.

There was one cop left, and the sergeant turned to him and said, "You can come inside with me. This should be interesting."

Clint began giving the officer a blow-by-blow account of what had happened, and an ambulance arrived. The EMTs got out and had just begun checking the biker on the ground when the sergeant stuck his head out the door.

The sergeant yelled toward the EMTs, "Hey, guys, you better radio for help. We got two more Bandidos in here, and they both probably need to go with that one."

The EMTs and the cops in the parking lot glanced around at each other, almost as if to say, "Did I hear him correctly?" No one could believe that three people needed to be transported, that all three of them were outlaw bikers, and that this baby-faced kid was still standing there talking to the cop, seemingly unscathed.

Clint heard someone say, "What the hell?"

Another said, "Well, this is certainly one for the record books."

Still another added, "Yeah, the stuff of legend."

The cop who was taking Clint's statement said, "You hear that, kid? You're going to be a legend."

Clint resisted the urge to gloat, realizing that this could have serious repercussions. "Every Bandido in Texas is going to be gunning for me now," Clint said in a resigned tone.

"Yeah, you're probably right, kid. Be a good time to make yourself scarce," said the officer. "Anyone in there know you, know your name, anything about you?"

"No, sir, not really. My buddy knows me, of course, and I guess the bartender may remember my name from my credit card. No one else, though. We're not from around here."

"Where you from?"

"Dallas. Well, near Dallas really."

"What do you do up there?"

"I'm a security officer, and sort of a private investigator-in-training."

"Know any cops?"

"Yeah, I know a few."

"You need them to put out feelers—keep an ear to the word on the street. Texas is a big state, though, and hopefully these bikers won't know where to look. You might've had an easy time of it tonight, but these are some bad dudes. They come after you again, they won't do it with two or three. They'll kill you, kid, and they'll make sure you hurt damn bad before they do. You just stepped in a big, steaming pile of shit."

"Yeah, that seems to be a habit of mine."

Clint was genuinely perplexed. He liked to think of himself as a nice guy, and he never looked for trouble. Somehow, though, trouble kept finding him; bad things kept happening. At least this was different than the Keith Willis situation. Clint certainly didn't feel much remorse about hurting these bikers. Clint didn't know yet how badly they were injured, but he was certain that they would all fully recover and go on to lead normal lives—well, "normal" for outlaw bikers anyway.

These bikers were mean guys. They sold drugs and were into all manner of illegal activities, and maybe they deserved to be roughed up a little. At least that would be Clint's rationalization. Regardless, he had tried to avoid trouble, to walk away as Doug had taught him, and he was certain that the bikers were presently wishing that they had let him. He thought, "Dad would be proud." Of course, his dad would also be very concerned.

Milton was okay. He'd taken a hard fist to the face and had a small laceration, but he could probably do without a stitch. His pride was hurt more than his face, and he was still bummed about Trixie being gone. The little guy who'd wanted to fight earlier was okay, too. He'd tried to do his part, but once he landed on the floor behind the bar, he'd decided that discretion was the better part of valor. He just played possum until the fracas was over, and once the dust had settled, he realized how fortunate he was that Clint had such a long fuse.

The little guy wondered if he would have been able to make good on his threat. If three Bandidos couldn't get Clint tired, he probably had little chance. Yes, he was glad that Clint hadn't pushed back, and he thought that perhaps the time had come to put his little man's complex to rest. There weren't a lot of guys as good-tempered as Clint around, especially not big ones who knew how to fight, and the next time he might not be so lucky.

The bikers would all be okay. The big one had been right; one of his testicles was indeed ruptured by Clint's initial kick. He also had a concussion from the elbow to the back of the head, as well as some broken ribs from the knee to the torso. The second biker whom Clint had taken down inside the bar with the three-punch combination had suffered multiple fractures—jaw, cheek, and nose—but would probably have no long-term problems, save for being a bit uglier than before. The biker from the parking lot who had used the car antenna as a whip had a lacerated ear, a fractured eye socket, and a pretty bad concussion, but he, too, would ultimately be okay.

The biggest blow suffered by these three was to their standing in the Bandido Nation. While the gang would rally behind them and seek revenge for their beating, they would never command the same level of respect, and that would serve only to make them even more determined to find the big kid who was responsible and to make him pay dearly. While lying on the floor of the bar in a cloud of smoke and pain, one of them had heard him called "Sasquatch."

Moving Out

"I'm getting an apartment," Clint told Doug matter-of-factly.

"Well, that's come about all of a sudden. Are you sure you're ready for that?"

"Yes, sir. I'm 19. I have a pretty good job, and I can afford it. Besides, I'm sure Mom is tired of feeding me."

"It's not a chore she minds."

"I know, Dad, but it's expensive. Y'all won't take room and board money from me."

"Would you rather pay us something and stay here?"

"No, sir, not really. My schedule and habits are pretty crazy, and I know I disturb you and Mom sometimes."

"Ah, that's nothing, Son. You don't bother us. We're concerned about you sometimes, but that's what parents are for. Don't let that be the reason."

"I just think the time has come. Besides . . . ." Clint caught himself before saying something he hadn't planned to mention, and he said, "Never mind."

"No, Son, go ahead. I'll be honest with you. You're the only kid we've still got in the nest, and we're in no hurry for you to leave. Whatever it is that may be bothering you, you need to level with me. You've come up with this idea all of a sudden, and I need to know the reason, the real reason. You're right. You're an adult. You have a decent job, and maybe it is time for you to try being on your own. I'm not going to stand in your way, but I can see something's bugging you. I'd like to think that you trust me enough to tell me what it is."

"I do trust you, Dad. I really do, but I'm not ready to talk about this. Just give me a little space right now, and I'll come clean when the time is right."

"Come clean? I don't like the sound of that. Have you done something wrong, Son? Do I need to be hiring us a lawyer or something?"

"No, no, Dad, nothing like that. Nothing illegal. Don't worry about that. It's just . . . ."

"Please, Son, I can tell you're hurting. You know I love you, and that love's unconditional. Whatever it is, Mom and I can help you deal with it."

"No, Dad! Not Mom! She can't know about this!"

"Son, your mom and I don't keep secrets from one another—never have and never will. You know that. That's how we taught you to be. We don't keep secrets in this family."

"All families keep secrets," Clint said, almost to himself.

"No, Son, not this one."

"Well, Dad, I'm asking you to make an exception. I can talk to you about this, but I can't handle Mom knowing. Please. I'll level with you right now, but you have to promise me that you won't tell Mom."

"Alright Son, I can't promise you that I won't ever tell her, but let's get this out on the table right now. Once I know what it is, you and I can discuss whether or not Mom needs to know. That's the best I can do. Fair enough?"

"I don't know, Dad. I guess it is, but it's hard . . . ."

Clint paused for a moment. He wanted to be honest with Doug. They had gone through several rough years as most parents and teenagers do, but they'd gotten past that. For the last couple of years they'd grown closer than ever before, and Clint's dad was his best friend—well, other than Milton, but that's a different kind of friend. Clint didn't like keeping a secret such as this, so he took a leap of faith.

"Dad, some people may be after me, some really bad dudes. They may even want to kill me, and I can't take the chance of them finding me here with you and Mom. I couldn't live with myself if anything happened to y'all because of something I've done."

Much to Clint's surprise, Doug said nothing. He just sat there in stunned silence, not believing—or not wanting to believe—what he had just heard from his baby boy.

After a minute Doug finally said, "Why in the world would anyone want to kill you? Does this have anything to do with your job?"

"No, sir, it doesn't. Milton and I had a run-in with some Bandidos down in Austin. That's a motorcycle gang. They got hurt pretty bad."

"The bikers got hurt bad?"

"Yes, sir."

"How many were there?"

"Three."

"You and Milton got into a fight with three members of a motorcycle gang? And y'all are okay, but the bikers aren't?" Much like the cops down in Austin, Doug was having a difficult time grasping the concept.

"Oh, they'll be okay," Clint said. "It's nothing too serious—just a few broken bones and a ruptured nut."

"A ruptured nut?"

"Yeah, I kicked one in the balls, and my foot won the battle." Clint really didn't take pleasure in hurting the guy, but he was trying to lighten the mood a bit.

"No, I expect not too many testicles could withstand a good kick from one of those big feet of yours. What happened, Son? How did you and Milton end up in a fight with these guys?"

"Well, sir, it's kind of a long story, but believe me when I say that we didn't start it. And we tried to walk away. We actually rode away from them, but they hunted us down. Somehow they found us. I don't know if they just happened to be going to the same place or if they looked around and got lucky, but somehow they found us. And the second time we couldn't get away. One of them sucker-punched me from behind, and we had to fight. Well, I did most of the fighting, but Milton tried."

"Whoa! So now you're telling me that you took down three of these biker guys pretty much by yourself?"

"Yes, sir. One of them had a knife, too, and a car antenna."

"A car antenna?"

"Yes, sir. He broke it off a car and used it like a whip."

"I never heard of such a thing! And you didn't get hurt at all?"

"No, sir. Not really. Just one little bump on the head where the first one hit me."

Doug couldn't help himself. He smiled widely and said, "Man, I wish I'd been there to see it!"

"Yeah, I used a little of my karate on one of them, but the other two I pretty much took out the way you taught me. I tagged one real good with a jab-cross-hook combination, and he wilted like a wet wash rag."

"That's my boy!" Then reality set in, and Doug asked, "But do you really think they'll come after you now?"

"The cops think so, and it makes sense. That's pretty much the biker code. You fuck with one of us; we *all* fuck with you."

"Not the 'f' word, Son. You know we don't use that kind of language in our house."

"Right. Sorry. Anyway, the cops said to watch out, that they'd probably be gunning for me."

"You say this happened in Austin?"

"Yes, sir."

"Where in Austin?"

"Uh, a place called Li'l Abner's."

"And just what type of place is this Little Abner's?" Doug was pretty perceptive, and he pretty much knew what Clint's answer was going to be.

"Well, uh, okay," Clint said, cringing. "It's a strip joint."

"Dangit, Clint! I've told you to stay away from places like that! Every guy in a place like that is just looking to be the one to take a big man down, get a notch in his belt."

"But, Dad, it didn't start there. We were gassing up our bikes at that truck stop in Jarrell where you and me and Mom stopped that time on the way to San Marcos to visit Jack. These guys rode in, and Milton and I kind of stared at them a little. That's all it took. They were ready to fight us there at the station, but some troopers came in just in time, gave us a chance to get back on the road. Somehow they tracked us down at Li'l Abner's. I don't know how."

"Still, if you hadn't gone to that sleazy little strip club, maybe they wouldn't have found you. That's just the type of place where those guys are bound to go. All the more reason to stay away."

"I know, Dad. You're probably right, but Milton wanted to go."

"Son, you're getting way too old to blame your bad choices on your friends. You're accountable for your own decisions. That's a requirement of growing up."

"I know, Dad. I know. You're right. You're always right."

"No, not always. But I am right about this."

Clint and his dad just sat there for a while at the kitchen table, sipping their iced tea. They always drank iced tea at the Buchanan house, the Texas way with sugar and lemon. Clint drifted off for a moment and recollected a few memories of their past in the little cracker box house in Allen where Doug and Lucy had struggled to raise their three kids on teachers' salaries.

The house had three bedrooms, a bath and a half, and was barely a thousand square feet. Clint and his brother Jack had shared a double bed until Jack left for college when Clint was in junior high. Sissy was the lucky one with a room to herself. The Buchanans had lived in the little pink brick house since Clint was in diapers. He'd been only six months old and 35 pounds when his parents bought the house, and he would forever remember it as "home." Unlike Jack and Sissy, Clint had known no other.

Clint's mind wandered back over holiday dinners right there at the table where he sat with his dad, and he had a flash of sitting in his maternal grandmother's lap as she taught him to mix peanut butter with Karo syrup to put on pancakes. She had died when Clint was only five years old, so he couldn't have been more than four at the time. It was one of his oldest clear memories.

The Buchanans never seemed to have more than just enough money to get by, but as corny as it may sound, they did have each other. They certainly weren't a perfect family, but they had no shortage of love for one another. So much of his life, of their life, took place in that little house, right there at the table in the tiny kitchen, and Clint got a little misty as he thought about leaving.

Finally Clint said, "Dad, you're right. I should've turned around and come home after the run-in at the truck stop, and I sure didn't need to be throwing my money away in a strip club. But now do you understand why I want to go? Why I *have* to go?"

"What's the name of that cop friend of yours? Roy something?"

"Actually Roy's his last name, but we call him Hulk."

"You talk to him about this yet?"

"Yes, sir."

"What's he think?"

"He thinks I probably don't have much to worry about. This is a long way from Austin, and they don't know my name or anything about me. They don't really have much way of tracking me down."

"But they found you in Austin, right?"

"Yeah, that's what I told him. It's like they had radar or something."

"Well, does he think you should move out, get your own place?"

"He said it wouldn't hurt. He actually offered to let me stay with him for a while."

"Maybe you should take him up on that."

Clint had given that some serious thought. He liked Hulk a lot, but he didn't know him well enough yet to impose.

"No, I don't think so," Clint said. "We barely know each other."

"How about Milton? Y'all could be roommates and watch each other's backs—split the rent, too."

Clint and Milton had, in fact, talked about getting an apartment together, but as much as Clint loved his friend, he wasn't confident that they'd be compatible roommates. Milton was still living with his folks, too. They lived way out in the boondocks, had a large family still at home, with plenty of guns and no one shy about using them if necessary. He probably didn't have much to worry about.

Clint's and Milton's jobs were far apart as well, so they probably wouldn't be able to find a location convenient for both of them. Everyone kind of figured that Clint would be the main target anyway, so it would probably be better if the two didn't live together.

"No, Dad, I want to be on my own. You know I'm a loner, and I like my privacy too much. Milton and I will still be able to spend time together."

"Well, okay, I knew this day would come sooner or later. It might as well be now. Is there anything I can do to help? You need a little cash boost to get you started?"

"No, sir, I'm okay. I'm pretty flush now, and I have my savings if I need it."

"Are you planning to dip into your college money? How much you got now anyway?"

"I've tucked away a couple thousand, but I'll probably never go to college anyway."

"Don't touch that. You're only 19, and you may change your mind about college later. You'll need that. How much will that pay for anyway?"

"Probably two or three semesters at a state school."

"Well, that's a start. Leave that alone, but add to it when you can. If you need any help with deposits or up-front rent, anything at all, you let me know. I don't mind helping you out."

"I know, Dad, and I appreciate it. But I don't think it'll be necessary."

"Okay, I'm just saying. Don't be afraid to ask."

"I understand. Now what about Mom?"

"She's not going to be too happy about this—her baby leaving home and all."

"No, I mean what about the other—about telling her?"

Doug sipped his tea and chewed on that question for a moment before saying, "Okay, Son, I guess the reason for this can be just between us for now, but there may come a day when I have to tell her. She finds out I've been keeping something from her, she'll kick my butt. You know that. Right?"

"Yeah, she's a tough one alright!"

Lucy was indeed a tough woman. She had grown up on a farm, the eldest of eight children, and she may as well have been a boy as far as her parents were concerned. They didn't exactly follow the traditional sexist division of labor. They had put her to work at a very young age, and she never seemed to mind. She had done her duty without question or complaint, and it had instilled in her a profound sense of responsibility and devotion to family.

Lucy was big, about six feet tall and 200 pounds, and she was stronger than a lot of men. Even so, she was a gentle soul and very much a nurturing mother and loving wife, in that order, but she could be pretty intimidating when circumstances called for it. Doug was right. If she found out that he'd kept a secret, she'd be plenty pissed, and that was a side of her that no one ever wanted to see. She had a long fuse but a powerful payload.

Doug sighed heavily and said, "Okay, I won't tell her, Son. Not for now."

"Thanks, Dad. That's fair enough. Thank you for everything."

"You're welcome, Son. I love you, and I do what dads are supposed to do."

On Clint's next day off, he set out early in the morning to start the job of finding an apartment. He'd never done this before, so he had no idea how long it might take. He had assumed that one day would be enough, but he wasn't sure. He'd worry about moving when the time came.

Finding a place near his job was tricky because he didn't always work at the same place. He was still more-or-less assigned to the Republic Bank contract in downtown Dallas, but he was working there less and less. He was helping Tom and the other investigators more often than not, and while England's headquarters was on the northwest side of Dallas, they worked all over the area.

Clint ultimately decided to try to find a place in Plano or Richardson. It would still be reasonably close to his parents, to Milton, and to the health club where he still worked out almost daily. The commute down Central Expressway would be a bear when he worked the day shift downtown, but he figured he could tolerate that. No matter where he lived, his job would require a good bit of driving anyway, and he didn't really mind it a whole lot, especially since he could ride his motorcycle a lot of the time.

Clint had one apartment complex in mind that he'd already decided to try first. It was close to a Jack in the Box in east Plano where he and Milton stopped sometimes for a burger when they were out riding. It wasn't new or fancy, but Clint couldn't afford new or fancy. It looked nice enough, a little old perhaps, but well kept. He pulled up in front of the leasing office at the Village Green Apartments just as the manager was opening the door for business at 8:30. By 9:00 he'd rented his very first apartment.

The manager had referred to the apartment as a one-bedroom unit, but it was really an efficiency. There was no door, nor even a wall, between the living area and the bedroom, but that didn't really matter to Clint. It was almost half the size of the house where he'd grown up, so he figured it was plenty big enough for one. The day was still young, so Clint took his motorcycle back home, loaded everything he owned into his truck, including the bike, and was moved into his new apartment by noon. Clint was quite impressed with himself. "Well, that was easy!" he thought.

Doug and Lucy had offered to let Clint take the bed and dresser from his room at their house, but he'd declined. It was old and a little boyish, and he figured it was best to leave it there so his parents wouldn't feel obligated to spend their own money to fill the void. The only stick of furniture he had was a rickety old stand for his cheap mail-order stereo.

The apartment manager had turned Clint onto a place where he could rent the little bit of furniture that he needed, so he hopped on his bike and headed over to check out the place. It took him about an hour to get there, pick out what he wanted, and get back to the apartment to await the delivery. By the end of the day, he was sitting on a rented sofa watching a rented television and getting ready to eat two TV dinners. Two revolvers and a shotgun were handy and loaded.

Sasquatch the Teacher

Clint enjoyed living in his little apartment. His parents had always given him a great deal of freedom, but having his own place did make him feel more mature. For a while he'd felt a bit embarrassed any time it came out that he was still living with his parents, and he was proud finally to be on his own. Moreover, although he knew that his parents missed him and were probably struggling a little with the empty nest syndrome, he also knew that they would enjoy their privacy. They'd started their family only a year into their marriage, and after 25 years of raising kids, they'd certainly earned their time alone. Clint was happy that they'd finally have the chance to be a couple again.

The job was going well. Clint was only working at the Republic Bank building a day or two a week now, and he missed that some. Even so, he was glad to be doing other things, and he was building a reputation for being good at whatever anyone threw his way. He was beginning to be viewed as Tom's sidekick, and neither had a problem with it. They worked well together and enjoyed each other's company, and Clint was learning a lot. They had made another visit to the credit card company, but Clint had not seen the woman of his dreams. At this point, she was quite literally the woman of his dreams—almost always.

Tom and Clint met Hulk for choir practice again, but no one had as much to drink off his mind this time. They remained sober, and as Cassidy herded them toward the door at closing time, they'd decided to get together again the following day. Technically it would be later the same day.

"Hey, I have to go out and requalify tomorrow," Hulk said. "Why don't you guys meet me at the range? You free?"

"Maybe we can be," replied Tom. "What time did you have in mind?"

"Well, since we don't have a drunk to sleep off, we could meet early, say around 9:00. That work for y'all?"

"Make it 10:00," Tom replied. "I need a little more sleep than I used to."

"Pussy," Hulk said with a grin. "Okay, I'll give you an extra hour of beauty sleep. How about you, Sasquatch?"

"I don't need beauty sleep," said Clint with a grin. "Unlike a couple of guys I know, I'm still young and good-looking." The other two men groaned, and Clint added, "Yeah, I know. I'm not that good-looking. Anyway, which range are we going to?"

Tom said, "Just meet me at my place around 9:30, and we'll drive over together. What are we shooting this time, Roy?"

"I have to requalify with both my nine-millimeter and .357. Y'all bring whatever you want. Let's just stick with the pistol range, though. I don't feel up to shooting a rifle, too."

"What's the matter, Roy? Afraid my boy over here will outshoot you with a long gun?"

"You know that's not my strong suit, Tom."

"I'm just yanking your chain, Roy, but in all serious-ness, this kid's no pushover with a handgun. He can give you a run for your money."

"That right, kid?" Hulk asked. "You shoot pretty straight, huh?"

"Yes, sir, I do."

"You up for a little wager?"

Tom jumped in, "Come on, Roy. I said he could give you a run for your money, but you've been a cop for a long time. Don't take advantage of the kid."

"I can speak for myself, thank you very much," Clint said. Although pretty reserved most of the time and not normally what one would call cocky, Clint was nevertheless confident in his abilities, especially when it came to riding a motorcycle or shooting any kind of gun. He asked, "What did you have in mind, Hulk?"

"Ah, nothing big-time, maybe lunch. Loser buys lunch. How about that?"

"You're on," Clint responded without hesitation.

Tom added, "Okay, let's make it a three-way. We all compete, and the loser buys lunch for everyone." Tom figured he was letting Clint off the hook. He knew that he wasn't as good with a gun as either of the other two, even on a good day, and he was a little rusty.

"Fair enough," Hulk said, "but let's decide now where we're going to eat. What do you think, Sasquatch? You feel like a hunk of beef?"

"Yes, sir, how about the Trail Dust? I could go for a Bull Shipper."

Hulk laughed loudly and slapped his thighs. "I should have known! A man after my own heart! Sound good to you, Tom?"

Tom sighed and said, "Yeah, sure. My kid needs braces, but I'll just go ahead and max out my Master Charge buying three-pound steaks for you two. The wife is going to kick my ass."

"Pussy," Hulk said again with a laugh. Clint chuckled a little but felt a bit guilty about it. Tom didn't laugh.

Clint rode his bike home and tried to sleep, but he didn't have much success. He was still thinking of Keith Willis from time to time, but he was starting to have those bad dreams a little less. He had begun having more pleasurable dreams instead, usually of the mulatto woman at the credit card company. In this case, though, his difficulty sleeping was more the result of his excitement about going to the range.

Clint was no stranger to a shooting range, of course, but he was going to be there with a cop and a former cop. This was going to be a chance to show his stuff to a couple of guys who would know good stuff when they saw it. Tom had seen him shoot once before when he qualified for his security officer commission, but this would be different. Clint wanted to make a good impression on both men.

Clint was ritualistic about taking care of his guns, as he was about a lot of things. He checked them, made sure they were clean, but then decided to go ahead and clean them again anyway. He decided that he would take three revolvers: his six-inch .44 and .357 magnums as well as his snub-nose .38 special, all made by Smith and Wesson. Clint's bias was strong, virtually inflexible when it came to revolvers.

Clint decided also to take his HK91, a .308-caliber semi-automatic rifle from Heckler and Koch, often referred to erroneously as an "assault rifle." By definition, a true assault rifle is fully automatic; thus, the notion of a semi-automatic assault rifle is an oxymoron. Regardless, Hulk had made it clear that he didn't want to shoot rifles, but Clint thought, "Just in case." If nothing else, he could show it off to Hulk and Tom and anyone else who might be interested. It was a pretty uncommon weapon at the time.

Before he set off on his adventure of doing guy stuff with a couple of grownup manly men, Clint made himself a hearty breakfast: a half dozen eggs over easy, a can of corned beef hash, hashbrowns, grits, four slices of toast, and a quart of orange juice. Clint loved cooking and eating breakfast, and he wasn't sure how much time there would be between breakfast and his free Bull Shipper. He didn't want hunger pangs to interfere with his performance, so he figured he needed to eat well.

After breakfast, Clint cleaned the kitchen, brushed his teeth, and then loaded his weapons into his truck and drove over to Tom's. Tom lived in a nice middle-class neighborhood in Carrollton, pretty near the office at England, in a comfortable four-bedroom house with his wife and two kids, a boy and a girl. Tom came out the front door just as Clint was stepping onto the porch.

"Morning, Clint. How's it going?"

"I'm okay. How about you? Something wrong?" Clint could see that there was.

"Oh, it's nothing—just a little trouble in paradise. "

"Darn, Tom, I wouldn't call that *nothing*. I'm sorry to hear it. Do you need to stay home today? Hulk and I can get by without you—let you stay here and take care of family stuff. It's okay. We understand a man's got to have his priorities straight. Just tell me how to get to the range, and I'll meet him over there."

"Thanks, Clint. I appreciate that, but I wouldn't want to welsh on our wager."

"Oh, come on! Don't you think about that for a second. That's just all in good fun. You need to stay here, stay here. Period. Hulk and I can make our own bet."

"You sure?"

"Of course I'm sure! If there's one thing I learned from my parents, it's the importance of family. Don't you let anything—*anything*—come between you and the three people behind that door."

"It seems kind of odd for me to be taking family advice from a single teenager."

"The only thing that matters is that it's good advice. I don't have a family yet, but I hope to some day. When I do, nothing is going to come between me and them, and frankly, that will include you and Hulk."

"Clint, that's a little easier said than done sometimes, but frankly, this isn't one of those times. I do need to skip our outing today, and that's exactly what I'm going to do. Please give my regrets to Roy. I appreciate your understanding."

Tom gave Clint directions to the shooting range where he would meet Hulk. It wasn't far, and Clint had no trouble finding it. He made the drive from Tom's house in about 20 minutes, and once he pulled up in front of the place, he realized that he'd driven past it before.

Clint didn't know what Hulk would be driving today. He usually drove something that a drug dealer had forfeited, so it changed frequently. They often joked about Hulk's "car of the week." Clint didn't even know if Hulk owned a vehicle of his own. He was about to go inside when he heard the faint rumble of a Harley and turned in that direction to take a look. He looked at Harleys now more than ever. He could see a big man on a bike coming his way, a good bit down the road but closing fast, and then the rider turned into the range parking lot. Hulk rode up and parked next to Clint's truck.

"You prick!" Clint shouted. "You have a Harley! You never told me you had a Harley! Wait a minute. Is that yours, or did you get it from a dealer, too?"

"Yeah, from a motorcycle dealer," Hulk said with a chuckle. "It's all mine."

As Clint watched Hulk getting off his bike, he noticed how similar Hulk was physically to the big Bandido in Austin. He hadn't realized that before. The difference was that Hulk was more solid, bigger in the chest and smaller in the waist—and cleaner.

"Sorry, Sasquatch. It just never came up. You jealous?"

"Damn right I am! I'd give my left nut for one of those!"

"Careful what you wish for. I heard about a guy who lost a nut recently," Hulk said with a wink. "Where's Tom?"

"Tom couldn't make it after all. He sends his regrets." Clint wasn't sure how much Hulk knew or needed to know.

"That's okay. We can get by without him. Bet still on? Loser buys Bull Shippers?"

"Oh, yes, sir! I never turn down a free meal!"

Hulk laughed and said, "You're pretty sure of yourself, kiddo. We'll see. We'll see. Well, get your stuff and follow me."

As Hulk retrieved a handgun case from the back of his Harley, Clint grabbed his cases, including the long one, from his truck.

"Whoa, man! I said no rifles today!"

"Sorry, Hulk. I couldn't resist. I have to show it to you even if we don't shoot it."

"What's in there? AR-15?"

"Nope."

"Mini 14?"

"Nope, even better. HK91."

"Damn, a .308?"

"Yeah, it's a much better round than the .223."

"That's a matter of opinion, but I'd never argue the point. That's a heckuva weapon. What did it set you back?"

"About 400 bucks."

"Damn! What are Tom and those guys paying you? Can we trade jobs?"

"Can we trade motorcycles?"

Hulk laughed and said, "No, no, I don't think so. I'm allergic to rice. Okay, let's go."

As they walked toward the building, Hulk said, "Okay, if you don't mind, let me get my qualifying out of the way first. It won't take long. There's a lieutenant waiting for me in there, and I have to qualify with my Hi-Power and my Model 66. Once I'm done with the department stuff, we'll have some fun. Okay?"

"Sure, no problem. Can I watch you qualify?"

"Yeah, it's not a closed range, not even a police range. You'll be able to get close enough to watch. Just be cool— act like you've been there before."

This was a nicer facility than the places where Clint and Milton did their shooting, and Clint browsed a little while still making it a point to watch what Hulk was doing. The lieutenant seemed like a nice enough fellow, though perhaps a bit stiff, and Hulk clearly treated him with the deference that his rank required.

Clint didn't watch the clock closely, but Hulk was finished in about 45 minutes. He qualified easily with each weapon—shooting 245 out of 250 with the pistol and 248 with the revolver. Clint tried to maintain his poker face, but he could already taste the beef.

As they settled in and got ready for their little competition, Hulk asked, "You need to warm up?"

"Oh, maybe a little. Give me two cylinders with each. That'll be ten rounds with the .38 and 12 with the other two."

Clint remembered a favorite of his dad's lessons. Doug had been a fair bowler in his younger days, and he'd discussed the fine art of sand-bagging with Clint. Shooting is not bowling, of course, but the same basic concept applies. This might be a little more overt, though, perhaps closer to what pool shooters call hustling. At any rate, although they'd already agreed to a wager, Clint wanted Hulk to be overconfident. It might give Clint a little more of an edge. At the very least, it might have an entertaining result.

With each of his three revolvers, starting with the little .38 and working up to the .44, Clint fired a full cylinder, reloaded, and then fired another at a silhouette that was ten yards away. He made sure to disperse his rounds in the nine, eight, and seven rings, and he threw in a couple of six-ring flyers to boot.

Making sure to look both surprised and disgusted when he and Hulk examined the targets up close, Clint offered the necessary, "Ah, shit!"

"You sure you want to do this, kid? It's not too late to back out," Hulk said.

"No, no, I'm not backing out. A deal's a deal. I'll do better when it counts."

They discussed for a moment that their choice of weapons didn't exactly allow for an apples-to-apples contest. They each had a .357 magnum, but Hulk's had only a four-inch barrel compared to Clint's six-inch barrel, which would seem to give Clint an advantage, especially as the distance increased. Hulk magnanimously offered that the longer barrel would serve as Clint's handicap, thus leveling the playing field. They agreed that both would fire the standard target round, a .38 special "+P" wadcutter, and that they would fire simultaneously, side-by-side.

The two men fired a standard qualifying scheme consisting of a total of 50 rounds of ammunition fired double-action only from distances ranging from ten feet to 25 yards, including some weak-handed shooting as well as some rounds fired from behind barrels. Each round inside either the ten or nine ring would be worth five points, so the maximum score was 250. Eight-ring shots were worth four points, and seven-ring shots were worth three. Any fliers outside the seven ring didn't score anything.

When the smoke had cleared and the points had been tallied, Hulk's score was the same as his official department qualifying round with that weapon: 248. Clint had shot a perfect 250.

Hulk's face was red as he asked the inevitable question, "Did you just fucking hustle me?"

"Yes, sir, I surely did!"

"I should've known." Hulk wanted to be pissed, but Clint's big grin was disarming. It was hard to be angry with Clint.

Laughing a bit, Clint said, "But in the true spirit of sportsmanship, I'll give you a second chance. This first round counts for squat. We start from scratch, and I'll shoot the .44. You can take your pick."

"So let me get this straight. You're saying that nothing was riding on that first round? We shoot another round, and you'll shoot your Dirty Harry special against my revolver or my pistol—my choice?"

"Yes, sir, that's exactly right. I assume you'll be shooting the revolver again?"

"Sure, of course. It's more accurate than the pistol."

"Okay, and just so you don't shit your pants, I should warn you that I'll be firing magnum ammunition."

"You're going to shoot .44 mags against my .38s?"

"Yes, sir, that's exactly what I'm saying, and by the way, I like my steak rare." Once someone got Clint out of his shell, he could be a nervy ass.

"Okay, boy, let's get it on!"

Hulk was certain that firing .38 wadcutters from his heavy, K-frame .357 would give him an advantage over Clint with his cannon. He was wrong. Hulk did manage to squeeze an extra round into the nine ring this time and finished with a 249, and he couldn't believe it when Clint managed another 250.

"Holy shit, kid! You just shot a perfect round with a .44 magnum! No one in the whole department has ever done that to my knowledge! We need to hire you just to shoot in combat matches! Damn, this is the stuff legends are made of!"

Clint got a bit of a chill and said, "I wish people would quit saying that."

Clint looked around and realized that quite a crowd had gathered. A .44 magnum tends to draw a lot of attention, and so does someone Clint's size. Combine the two, and you've got a real traffic-stopper. The whole place had effectively shut down so that everyone could watch the show. That meant, of course, that Hulk couldn't wallow privately in his defeat. Everyone knew about it, and several people there knew Hulk and wouldn't be shy about rubbing it in. Clint saw the lieutenant in the crowd.

The lieutenant said, "Roy, please tell me I didn't just see what I think I just saw! A snot-nosed kid with a .44 magnum just beat one of DPD's finest, twice?"

"Well, lieutenant, what can I say? The kid's good. He ate his Wheaties and apparently his carrots, too. I shot a good round, two good rounds, but he beat me fair and square. I'm man enough to admit it. There's no shame in that. Besides, I can still kick his big young ass."

Someone in the crowd shouted, "I wouldn't be so sure about that!"

Clint could see that Hulk was a little thrown by the challenge. Over the years Hulk had earned a reputation for invincibility, so this was an affront not only to his manhood but also to his standing in the department. Clint was concerned that Hulk might be compelled by some code—either as a man or as a cop—to prove that he could, in fact, beat Clint's young ass. Luckily Hulk was a bigger man than that.

"Well, it don't matter anyway," Hulk said. "Sasquatch here is my good buddy, and right now we have a date over at the Trail Dust with a couple of Bull Shippers. Looks like it's on me."

"Wait a minute," Clint said. "Let's shoot the rifle a few times before we go."

"Ah, I guess," Hulk replied. "I'm hungry, but I guess we got time." Then turning to the crowd he said, "Kid's got him an HK91. He's going to put on a little show."

As Clint and Hulk prepared to move over to the rifle range, one fellow stepped forward toward them.

Hulk said, "Hey, I know you. Sorry, don't recall your name."

The man reached out a hand to Hulk and said, "Detective Roy, I'm Patrolman Joe Long. I handled the preliminary for you on a drug shooting a year or so back over in South Dallas. Homicide let you take it because it was one of your snitches."

"Oh, yeah, I remember. Clint Buchanan, this is Joe Long of the DPD."

"Pleased to meet you, sir," Clint said as he shook the patrolman's hand.

"Same here," Long replied. "You know, I'd kind of like to see that HK91."

Clint removed the rifle from its case and handed it to the patrolman, sans magazine. After a cursory examination, Long handed it back to Clint.

Long said, "Nice, very nice. But I'm still partial to my AR-15. You might say it's been modified."

"Ah," Clint said with a knowing smile and nod, "you mean it's fully automatic. I guess that's pretty cool, but I'd just as soon use a semi-auto myself. Outside of a jungle, I don't see much sense in spraying rounds willy-nilly. I'd just as soon take aim and make sure I hit my target." Realizing too late the implications of his statement, Clint added, "But to each his own."

It wasn't enough. Clint had inadvertently thrown down the gauntlet, and Long couldn't resist.

"Well, why don't we just do a little side-by-side comparison?" Long asked. "I'll be right back."

As Long went to his car to retrieve his machine gun, Clint and Hulk started making their way over to the rifle range.

Along the way Clint said, "Hey, maybe I can get you off the hook for lunch."

"What do you got in mind?"

"I make a wager with Machine Gun Long. If he loses, he buys lunch for both of us. Is he a good sport?"

"Hell, I barely know him. I don't really know, but I'd be for finding out. I'd been counting on Tom to buy lunch. It wouldn't bother me to pawn it off on someone else."

"Okay, just hang on to your wallet. You won't need it this afternoon."

"You know, Sasquatch, sometimes you try too hard to come across as this shy little bumpkin, but you are one brash son of a bitch. I like that in a guy, especially in a cop. You want a little advice, though?"

"What's that?"

"Be careful, son. One of these days someone's going to take you down a notch."

"Okay, I'll consider myself duly warned."

Long met Clint and Hulk at the rifle range, and many of the people who had gathered to observe Clint and Hulk's handgun competition had followed them over to the range anticipating another show. Too, any mention of a fully automatic weapon around gun nuts is bound to give most of them wood. Long offered his rifle to Clint to take a look, and Clint gave the requisite compliments.

Handing the rifle back to Long, Clint said, "Well, show us what you can do with that thing. Everyone around here is dying to see a full auto in action."

Without even setting up any kind of target, Long put a 30-round clip in the rifle and wildly spewed out all 30 rounds in roughly five seconds.

As Long stood there all too proud of himself, Clint said, "That's impressive, but it's kind of like seeing how loud your stereo speakers will go without busting. You want to know, but it doesn't accomplish anything. Can you actually hit anything?"

"Yeah, sure. This thing was tried and true in Vietnam—well, essentially the same gun anyway. I can hit what I want with it," Long said defensively.

Clint asked, "Are you a sporting man?"

"You want to bet me something?"

"Sure. Nothing big, though. Just lunch."

"What are we betting on?"

Clint thought a moment and said, "Okay, here's the deal. First off, loser buys Bull Shippers at the Trail Dust for Hulk and the winner. Just to be clear, Hulk gets his free beef no matter who's buying. We're betting on who can put the most kill rounds in a paper target in five seconds at 25 yards."

"How we going to measure that?"

"We use handgun targets, silhouettes. We set five targets across five lanes at 25 yards. Whoever puts the most rounds inside the seven ring or better in five seconds wins."

"Separate targets?"

"Yeah, most rounds inside the seven ring on separate targets. We shoot separately. Someone times us, and we each get five seconds to shoot. Whoever kills the most silhouettes wins, and the loser buys Hulk and the winner steaks at the Trail Dust."

"Bull Shippers," Hulk interjected.

Clint chuckled, "Yeah, Hulk. We wouldn't want anyone to misunderstand that important fact. Fair enough, Long? We got a bet?"

"Fucking A, you got a bet!"

"Okay, you go first."

A couple of onlookers volunteered to set up the first five targets. As they were doing so, Clint glanced at Hulk, and Hulk's eyes seemed to ask, "You know what you're doing, kid?" Clint smiled at Hulk and nodded.

Another man volunteered to be the timekeeper, and when everything seemed set, he said, "First shooter, whenever you're ready."

Long put another 30-round clip in his rifle, stood still for a few seconds, jacked a round into the chamber, put the rifle to his shoulder, took a deep breath, and fired. Just as he had before, he fired on fully automatic and emptied the clip in about five seconds, but he only aimed slightly better than he had before. Clint had been counting on that—and on the fact that Long simply wasn't much of a shooter.

The timekeeper said, "I think he actually got a little more than five seconds, maybe five-point-five."

Hulk said, "You using your second hand over there?"

Sheepishly the guy said, "Uh, yeah."

Hulk rolled his eyes and said, "Maybe next time you don't volunteer to be timekeeper. I know there's bound to be a stopwatch around here somewhere." Hulk shook his head and thought "dumbass."

Clint said, "Doesn't matter. Close enough for government work. Let's count the kills."

They retrieved the targets and took a close look, but Long had already reached a high pucker factor before anyone started counting. Of the 30 rounds he fired wantonly, only eight had hit paper, and only two hit inside the seven ring on separate targets. His kill rate was only 6.7 percent. He'd let Clint sucker him into a losing game, and he knew it.

Long sighed and said, "Okay, I see how this is shaping up. You got me. I buy."

"Oh, no, we can't do that," Clint said. "We had a bet, and I have to shoot. Who knows? I could break my trigger finger loading my rifle."

Clint didn't even have a magazine loaded, so as he started to load precisely five rounds of .308 ammunition into a clip, the two guys from before trotted out to ready five new targets.

"Don't worry about that," Clint yelled at the men. "I can use the same ones."

The two men shrugged and trotted back behind the line.

Clint cycled a round into the chamber and asked, "Timekeeper ready?"

"Timekeeper ready!"

Without hesitation, Clint raised the rifle to his shoulder and switched off the safety in one quick motion and then fired one round at each target.

When Clint had fired the last round, he yelled, "Time!" The timekeeper said, "About four seconds," and Hulk rolled his eyes again.

No one needed to retrieve the targets to know the outcome, but when they took a close look, each of Clint's five rounds had hit the ten ring in the center of a different target. His kill rate was 100%, and he'd done it in less time. He'd also saved 25 rounds of ammo.

Clint looked at Long and said, "Your rate of fire means nothing if you don't aim and can't control the recoil. That's why I don't bother modifying this H&K. It's more useful to me when I know I have to aim. Someone wants to come after me with a machine gun, let them. I'll be fine with this—or my .44 mag."

"Point well taken," Long said and seemed to mean it.

"Well, I guess I owe you two steaks."

"Not just steaks. Trail Dust Bull Shippers!" said Hulk. He was hungry and didn't bother trying to contain his excitement.

Hulk said loudly, "Let's go! Show's over!"

The Trail Dust Steak House started back in the 60s on Highway 380 east of Denton, but now they had a location on Restaurant Row at Stemmons Freeway and Walnut Hill Lane on the west side of Dallas, not far from the range. They were famous for their "no neckties" policy. If you entered the building wearing a necktie, they'd cut it off and tack it to the wall with your business card or a note. Many a bad Christmas present wound up on those walls! Men like Clint and Hulk, though, didn't wear neckties. They were more interested in beef, and it didn't get any better than the 50-ounce mesquite-grilled porterhouse called the Bull Shipper.

Joe Long turned out to be a good sport after all. Oh, he seemed a little pissed at first, but he got over it quickly. The three men got over to the Trail Dust and sat down at one of the picnic tables. This wasn't the busy time of day, so they had it to themselves. Clint loved the Trail Dust, but he hated that he normally had to eat elbow-to-elbow with total strangers. Whenever he went there, he preferred to go during the slow times of day so that he could have his privacy, and today he was lucky.

As they waited for their steaks to be grilled, they munched on the roasted-in-the-shell peanuts, threw the shells on the floor (another Trail Dust tradition), and drank Lone Star beer. Clint wasn't crazy about the beer, but it was Texan and cheap. Besides, it was the meat that really mattered. The waitress brought their steaks, and they pretty much covered the plates. Clint and Hulk weren't surprised, of course, but it turned out that Long had never seen a Bull Shipper. His eyes were about as big around as the steaks.

"Jesus Christ, guys! Those are huge!"

It was a fairly typical reaction for the uninitiated. Luckily for Long, they were also very reasonably priced, as was everything at the Trail Dust. Although Long had not seen one before, he knew that he wasn't man enough to handle a 50-ounce steak, so he'd opted for the Cowboy, less than half the size.

The three men sat and had a really nice Texas-style meal together. They ate their steak and all the trimmings, drank their beer, told jokes, laughed, and just flat enjoyed themselves. Clint finished his steak first. In fact, he finished well before the other two.

Not being fully sated yet, Clint said, "Hey, guys, I'll bet you I can eat another."

Long about fell off the bench and said, "No, no way!"

Then Hulk said, "No, I don't think so."

Clint smiled. "No you don't think I can do it, or no you won't bet me?"

"No, I don't think we'll be fool enough to take that bet. You wouldn't make it if you weren't awfully damn sure of yourself."

Clint was disappointed but didn't make a big deal out of it. He ate apple cobbler with ice cream for dessert and figured that could last him until supper. Long had someplace he had to be, so he settled up with the waitress and excused himself.

"Detective, good to see you again," he said as he shook Hulk's hand. "I hope it's not the last time."

"Yeah, right," Hulk replied. "We'll have to do it again sometime. You get a chance, drop by choir practice at Cassidy's sometime. You know the place?"

"Oh, sure. Every cop in town knows the place. Look for me. I'll be there." Long turned to Clint, extended his hand, and said, "Son, you're a real badass on the shooting range. I suspect elsewhere, too. I look forward to seeing you again, maybe working with you someday. Thanks for the shooting lesson."

"Don't mention it, sir. I'll do just about anything for a good meal." They all chuckled, and Clint added, "Seriously, the pleasure is mine. Good luck to you."

Sasquatch the Student

Long may have been a good sport, but he was a lousy tipper. After he had excused himself, Clint and Hulk each left a couple more bucks on the table for the waitress and then headed over to the bar for another drink.

As they sat down, the bartender asked, "What'll it be?"

Hulk said, "Shot of Cuervo, please."

Clint said, "101 on the rocks, please."

"May I see some ID," the bartender said, not joking. Hulk shook his head and chuckled as Clint showed the bartender his driver's license.

"See, I'm 19," Clint said.

"Sorry," said the bartender. "You look young." He got their drinks and set them on the bar, and Clint started to reach for his wallet.

"No, this one's on me," Hulk said. He laid some cash on the bar and said, "Keep the change."

"Thank you, sir," said the bartender as he turned toward the register.

Not making eye contact with Clint, Hulk rolled the shot glass back and forth between his hands and said, "Boy, Sasquatch, that was one helluva show you put on today. I've got to tell you, kid. That was impressive—damn impressive."

"Thanks, Hulk. It means a lot coming from you."

"Is there anything you're not good at? What about singing? Can you sing?"

Chuckling, Clint said, "Well, actually yes. I can sing pretty well, and I play the piano, too."

"Motherfucker!" Hulk said and shook his head. "I'll ask you again: Is there anything you're not good at?"

"Sure, Hulk, there are lots of things that I'm not good at. For one, I can't dance. I mean, I can two-step a little, but other than that, I'm not worth a damn. Also, I'm a lousy multi-tasker, probably the most linear person you know. In case you didn't notice, I even eat one thing at a time. My right side is very dominant, too. I can't even jack off left-handed. It's all I can do to shoot a few rounds now and then with my left hand—takes a lot of concentration. To tell you the truth, that's the only thing I was worried about today."

Clint continued, "And to be perfectly honest, I'm not good at keeping my dick in my pants. My lack of self-control is probably going to get the best of me someday. I mean, I don't just run around fucking any woman who comes along, but if I find a woman who's attractive to me, I'll do her. Sometimes I don't use the best judgement."

"Well, kid, I don't know of many guys in this line of work who can't say the same thing. Why you think I live alone—why I've been divorced twice? Of course you know that's why Whitely ain't a cop anymore."

"What do you mean?" Clint asked. He had an idea now, but he hadn't considered it before.

"Ah, shit, man. I thought you knew. I shouldn't have said nothing." Hulk finally threw down his shot of tequila and said, "Well, cat's out of the bag now. You're a smart kid. You can put two and two together."

Clint had thought a lot of Tom, and the idea of him having cheated on his wife was a surprise. Hulk had as much as admitted it, too, but that didn't bother Clint quite so much for some reason—maybe because Hulk wasn't married now or because Clint had known Tom longer. Or maybe it was just the inherent differences in their personalities. Tom seemed like a nicer guy. Clint was sorely disappointed.

"You mean he screwed around?"

"Yeah, kid, that's the long and short of it. You know, they say the divorce rate for cops is 50 percent, but I think it's more, probably a lot more. It's because cops get more strange pussy than any other profession. We're just a bunch of dumb fucks, but chicks throw themselves at us. It's a helluva temptation, and a lot of us have trouble saying no. Yeah, Tom screwed around some, and his wife found out. He had to make a choice—her or the job. He chose her."

Clint felt a little bit better about that part, and he said, "Well, at least he made the right choice about that."

"Another round?" the bartender asked in passing. Clint had sucked down his whiskey without even realizing it.

"Yeah, sure," Clint said, figuring he might need it.

"Me, too," Hulk said.

The bartender got their drinks, and again Hulk picked up the tab. He was feeling a little guilty about divulging Tom's secret, and Clint certainly didn't mind letting him pay if it made him feel better.

"I'm not so sure," Hulk said, looking straight ahead.

"About what?"

"I'm not so sure that he made the right decision."

"Oh, come on, Hulk! How can you say that? The man's married, and he cheated on his wife. He's damn lucky she'd even give him a choice. A lot of women would have just kicked his ass out, and he'd deserve it, too." Clint was indignant. He was no saint clearly, but he drew the line at cheating. Hulk was very patient with him.

"Kid, you're young. I know you think you know everything, but you've still got a lot to learn. Don't try to judge a man without walking in his shoes. You get to be a cop, half the women in Dallas will want to fuck you. You think you can say no to them all?"

"I'll fuck them all until I get married, but once a gal puts a ring on this finger here, that's it. I'm hers and no one else's."

Hulk smiled and said, "Kid, I believe you really mean that right now, and for your sake, I hope you're that strong. Just don't be too hard on old Tom. He's paid a heavy price for his mistakes. He feels awful about cheating on his wife, and he feels awful about leaving the job. Now he's left the job before he could retire, got nothing to show for 15 years of putting his life on the line, and she's busting his chops every day about the cheating. And she's busting his chops every day about not being a cop anymore, too. He don't make as much money as he used to, and she don't like that."

Hulk continued, "You know, old Tom made a mistake, and he fessed up to it like a man. He's trying to make amends, but it's like she wants it both ways. That ain't fair. Cheating ain't right, and I won't try to tell you it is. But the way she's acting ain't right either. She didn't want to forgive him, she should've just kicked his ass out. Sometimes I think he should've called her bluff and stayed a cop. He wouldn't be any worse off."

"I don't know, Hulk," Clint said, sipping his drink. "I don't know. It's a tough call."

"Now kid, don't you be too tough on your buddy. I'd rather you not let on that you know, but I suspect that'll be hard for you. Try, though. For me, try. And trust me when I tell you that his penance has been harsh to say the least. The guy's in a lose-lose situation, and if anyone deserves to be forgiven, it's him. He's trying to do the right thing now, but she's making his life miserable pretty much every day. He needs our support."

"I guess that's why he begged off the outing today."

"Yeah, I suspect that had something to do with it. She don't like me anyway, and he's been spending too much time with us already. I know you work with him, but outside the job, we both probably need to give him some distance. Besides, me and you make a pretty good team. Right? We don't need no third wheel!"

"Yeah, I guess you're right about that, Hulk," Clint said.

Hulk paused for a moment and then said, "Okay now, I want to talk about something else for a minute. Tom told me about Billy Bob's, about that Willis kid. Anything you need to get off your chest now?"

Clint hadn't enjoyed their conversation about Tom Whitely. He was surprised at how hurt he was by the fact that Tom had been guilty of adultery, but he was going to try to assess that with an open mind. He was coming to realize that when dealing with human issues and faced with a choice between two opposing extremes, the truth always falls somewhere in between. If he could be objective on the job when he was investigating total strangers, he figured that he owed it to his friend to keep his emotions in check.

He would consider all that some more later, but for the time being Hulk had changed the subject and ventured into an area where Clint preferred not to go. Still, he felt like he owed it to Hulk not to shut him down. He decided that he might be ready to talk about it some, and for whatever reason he felt more comfortable discussing it with Hulk than with anyone else.

"What's to get off my chest? I fucked the guy up, but he knew the risks. No one made him fight me."

"That's right, kid, but I suspect your head and your heart aren't exactly on the same page. Am I right?"

"Yeah, I guess."

"Let me tell you something, Clint. This is as serious as I know how to be, so I want you to listen. You get to be a cop someday, you may have to hurt someone. You may have to kill someone. You think you could do that?"

"If I had to. If my life was in danger or maybe someone else's, yeah, I think I could do it."

"You think that's an easy choice to make?"

"No, probably not."

"Damn right it's not! It's never easy! That's what I'm getting at. You have to waste a dude, he could be the meanest, baddest dude on the planet, and you still feel like shit. That's a normal human reaction. I don't care who it is. I don't care how much he deserves it. Anyone who can kill another person and not think twice about it is evil. You want to be a cop, though, you've got to be able to do it. If push comes to shove and your life or your partner's life depends on it, you've got to be *able* to shoot, and you've got to be *willing* to kill."

"Okay, I understand that, Hulk, but I'm not sure what that has to do with Keith Willis."

"What I mean, kid, is that you fuck a guy up that bad, you're bound to have some guilt issues to deal with. That's okay. It's perfectly normal. Fact is, I'd worry about you if you didn't. You were just doing your job. You were paid to do a job, and you did it the best you could. What happened was an accident—nothing more, nothing less. It was just a damn awful accident, but there's no reason it should fuck up two lives. Police work is the same. You can't deal with this now, you won't be able to handle being a cop. You need to figure this shit out before it's too late."

"I can't just forget about it, act like it never happened."

"I'm not saying you should. You can't just forget something like that. You can't forget about ending someone's life," Hulk said, his voice trailing off a little at the end.

There was a question that Clint had wanted to ask Hulk before, but he knew it would be gauche. This seemed to be the right time, though. Clint waited just a moment, took a deep breath, and asked the unavoidable question, "Have you ever killed anyone, Hulk?"

Hulk just sat there on his stool looking at himself in the mirror behind the bar. It was almost as if the figure in the mirror were someone else and that the two were engaged in a stare-down contest. He didn't have to answer the question, but he did anyway.

"Yes, Clint, I have. This is the voice of experience talking to you, and that's why you should listen to me. It took me a long time to come to terms with it, and it cost me a marriage, maybe two. I like you, kid, and I don't want to see you torture yourself the way I did."

"So how do I deal with these feelings I'm having, the bad dreams and everything else? I go to work every day. I go work out. I hang out with my buddy Milton and with you and Tom. I have dates when I have time, enjoy my women, and I like to put up a good front, pretend like everything's okay. Most of the time I think I put on a pretty good show, but the truth is, this is killing me, Hulk. What do I do?"

The pain was obvious on Clint's face and in his voice, and though their glasses were empty and no one else was at the bar, the bartender conspicuously avoided them. Bartenders probably develop a sixth sense about such things.

"Son," Hulk said in his most fatherly tone, "we all have to exorcise our demons in our own way. You got to figure out what's going to work for you. But since you asked for my advice, you might think about going to see him."

"You mean what's left of him," Clint said harshly.

"Yeah, I mean what's left of him. You might just think about that."

Absolution

After a few days of thinking about Hulk's advice, Clint decided to give it a try. He knew that Keith Willis was in a nursing home in Denton, and he'd actually thought of going to see him many times before. Up to this point, though, he'd always managed to talk himself out of it, but now he was done with the rationalizations and excuses. It was his gut instinct to go see the guy, and since Hulk had suggested the very same thing, he took that as confirmation that it was definitely the right thing to do, almost as if God Himself had told Clint to do it.

It was a good day for a ride, so Clint took his bike. He rode north on Highway 75 to McKinney and turned west on Highway 380 toward Denton. He had ridden this road many times over the years and knew it like the back of his hand. Even so, he was slightly startled when he rode past the original Trail Dust location. When Clint saw the big red barn out in the middle of nowhere, it made him think of Hulk. He appreciated his new buddy's good advice, but he still couldn't help but wonder if he'd actually be able to follow it. Getting to the point of riding in the right direction was one thing; actually going into the nursing home and into Willis' room would be quite another. He said a quick prayer for strength.

Aloud inside his helmet, Clint prayed, "Lord, I know I don't talk to you nearly enough these days, but I'm asking you to forgive my many sins and to make me strong enough to do this. I know I can't do it on my own, so please help me. In Jesus' name I pray. Amen."

Clint had been raised in the Southern Baptist faith and had been "born again" at age eleven. At this point in his life, however, his visits to church were becoming less frequent, and even when he did go, it was mostly just to please Lucy. He remained a very spiritual person—just not a very religious one.

Clint had become very much turned off by organized religion. He tended to agree with Gandhi:

I like your Christ. I do not like your Christians. Your Christians are so unlike your Christ.

Clint knew that he shouldn't generalize, but knowing it didn't keep him from doing it. He didn't think of himself as better than other Christians; in fact, he thought that he was probably worse than a lot of them. He simply despised the overt hypocrisy.

Clint had begun to notice that people who professed to emulate Christ were often the most intolerant and uncompassionate, sometimes demonstrating overt hatred of individuals and groups merely for being different. He also despised the arrogance and closed-mindedness of people who thought that their particular beliefs were the only ticket to heaven. Clint's own views were more ecumenical, and he thought that people should focus on their similarities rather than dwelling on differences. Regardless, when times got tough, Clint did rely on the power of prayer, and this was certainly a tough time—and getting tougher with each mile. His brief entreaty to the Almighty had given him a boost.

Clint rode on into Denton and found his way to the Chasewood Manor Nursing Home near the campus of North Texas State University. One of Clint's old girlfriends attended NTSU and lived in the neighborhood, and he remembered seeing the place before. Some nursing homes are nice, but this didn't appear to be one of those. He guessed that it was all that Willis' family could afford, and that didn't exactly mitigate his guilt.

Clint had visited nursing homes before. Several of his relatives, including his grandparents, had been in nursing homes at one time or another, and he'd also visited with various church groups in the past. He remembered the way the old folks' faces used to light up when he would sing for them, and the thought made him smile for just an instant. He thought about how strange it would be to see such a young man in a place normally reserved for the elderly, the dying.

As Clint entered the front door, he was immediately struck by the stench. He looked around, and the place appeared to be reasonably clean. Even so, the smell was horrible, a sickening mixture of urine, feces, and death. He considered turning back but forced himself to press on.

Clint stopped at the nearest nurses' station and said simply, "Keith Willis, please."

An aide behind the desk looked up, smiled, pointed to the hallway to her left and said, "309."

"Thank you, ma'am," Clint said as he turned and began walking in that direction.

As Clint walked down the hallway, he tried not to look into any of the rooms, but he was nevertheless disturbed by the sounds emanating from them. From blaring TVs to screams of pain to the ravings of dementia, it was all very unsettling, but Clint kept going until he saw Room 309. He stopped a few steps away and leaned against the wall. The hallway seemed to be spinning a bit, and Clint had to hold onto the hand rail to steady himself. He took a few deep breaths and again spoke to God.

Silently in his mind, Clint prayed, "Lord, I can't do this. Please give me a little push. Amen."

Clint remained still for a few moments until the hallway quit spinning. Once he had regained full control of his faculties, he took a deep breath, stood up straight, and walked into Room 309. He regretted it instantly. The black, once Adonis-like body lay in the bed, already reduced to a soft lump of smelly flesh, and a middle-aged black woman sat beside his bed. Clint assumed she was Keith's mother, or maybe an aunt, and it was a complete shock to him. He foolishly hadn't even considered the possibility that relatives might be visiting.

The woman looked up, smiled, and said, "Hello, are you a friend of Keith's?"

"Uh, no ma'am, not really. I'm . . . ."

"Wait! You're that 'Bew Cannon' boy! Aren't you?"

"Yes, ma'am," Clint said. Now was not the time for corrections.

"It's about time you showed up. What took you so long?" The question surprised Clint.

"I don't know, ma'am. I'm sorry," Clint said as he lowered his head and looked at the floor, expecting the worst to follow.

Much to Clint's surprise, the woman stood up and stepped toward him, extending her hand. "I'm Ruth Willis," she said warmly, "Keith's mother. Pleased to meet you finally."

Clint looked up from the floor and made eye contact with Ruth as he shook her hand. She was smiling—*smiling!* How could this be? He was dumbstruck.

"Come on over here, son. Sit here with me." Clint sat down, and Ruth continued talking. "He's breathing on his own now. He'd been on the respirator for so long, and I finally told them to just go ahead and pull the plug. I guess the Good Lord wasn't ready to take my baby yet, though, because he just kept on breathing! Praise Jesus!"

Clint didn't have any idea what to say. He couldn't really understand how she could seem so happy, and he knew that if it were him, he'd want someone to put him out of his misery. "Forget pulling the plug," he thought, "Just shoot me!" There's no way he'd ever want to exist in such a state, and it pained him greatly to think that he had caused it, albeit unintentionally.

"I'm sorry, ma'am. I don't know what to say. I'm not even sure why I'm here."

"Son, I know why you're here," she said softly as she looked deeply into Clint's wet eyes. She reached out and took one of his hands. She held it between her own two hands and caressed it for a moment, and then she raised it to her lips and kissed Clint's fingers. She said again, even more softly, "I know why you're here."

They just sat there for a few minutes, though it seemed much longer. She continued to hold Clint's hand as he cried quietly. At one point, she reached up to the table next to Keith's bed and handed the box of Kleenex to Clint. He nodded his thanks and took the box, taking one of the tissues and dabbing his eyes. Then he wiped his nose and threw the tissue in the trash can.

They continued sitting silently, holding hands. Clint thought of his own mother, and realized that Lucy would probably behave similarly if the tables were turned. She was the most Christian person he'd ever known, and he thought that Ruth must have a similar faith. Clint wondered if he'd ever be able to tell Lucy and Doug about this.

"Ma'am," Clint started and then stopped.

Ruth was a very patient woman. She seemed perfectly content to let him move at his own pace. He decided to try again.

"Ma'am," he said, "I don't really know what to say. I'm just so sorry."

Clint's voice cracked at the end.

Ruth said, "I believe that, son. I really do."

"Ma'am, can you ever forgive me?"

"No, son, I won't forgive you." She paused for only a moment before continuing, "I won't forgive you because there's nothing to forgive. You got nothing to be sorry for— nothing to be forgiven for." Again, Clint was speechless.

Continuing to hold Clint's hand, Ruth reached with the other hand and touched his cheek, wiping away some tears with her thumb. "Son, you didn't mean to hurt my boy like this," Ruth said. "It was an accident. And it's not like you drove drunk and crashed into him and caused this. You young boys both wanted to do this, and both of you are too young to think about all the possibilities. You just tough boys doing what tough boys do, wanting to make some money and be famous. Keith wasn't no better or no worse than you. You boys is the same, probably more than you realize."

"But, ma'am, I didn't mean for this to happen. You've got to believe me!"

"I do believe you, son, and I don't need no more explanation. And no more apologies neither. I don't want to hear no more apologies. You got nothing to be sorry for. It was just a bad accident. The Lord had some purpose for it. Now you and me just got to figure out what that purpose is."

"Did you get the money? I mean my money from the fight."

"Yes, son, I did. And I appreciate that. It wasn't necessary, but I thank you for it."

"I could send you more. Maybe I could send you a little bit every time I get paid. I don't make a lot of money, but . . . ."

"No, no, no! I won't hear of it! Don't you even think about that."

"But, ma'am, I know this is expensive. It's got to cost a lot of money, and I want to help."

"No! I said no, and I mean no! Son, you're young. You're just getting started in your life. You didn't mean for this to happen, and there's no reason it should be a burden to you. And I don't just mean the money either." Ruth caressed Clint's hand with her hands again, raised it to her lips, and kissed it once more.

"Son, this is hard," Ruth said. "My whole life has been like the trials of Job, but I never imagined anything could ever be this hard. I won't try to kid you about that. Seeing my baby boy lie there like that, seeing his body waste away right in front of my eyes, knowing that he'll never hold his momma again and say, 'I love you.' That's the hardest part. And this place ain't cheap. I won't lie about that either, but I got me a little help—some family and government money. I'll get by. It's just another trial, and the Lord has some reason for it. I'll just be patient until I know what that is."

She continued, "But, son, there's no reason for you to put yourself through so much pain over this. Keith's life as we knew it is over, but you still got yours. Praise Jesus for that! This don't have to ruin you, too. Don't you let this horrible accident end another life. I don't want that, and my boy wouldn't want it either."

"Ma'am, I can't tell you how much what you're saying means to me. It's not what I expected, and I thank you for it. But it's a lot easier said than done. How do I do it? How do I let go?" The volume increased as Clint continued, "I can't forget what I did! I can't forget *that!*" Clint yelled as he pointed to Keith's body, wondering where his mind and soul had gone.

It was just too much to bear, and Clint fell to his knees and wept uncontrollably. Although it was almost unintelligible, Clint said over and over, "I'm so sorry! I'm so sorry!"

Ruth dropped to the floor as well, pulled Clint close to her, and held him in her arms. She stroked his hair and said softly, "It's okay, son. It's okay," almost as if speaking to the young man in the bed.

A nurse and an orderly trotted into the room to check on the commotion, and Ruth shooed them away. "Get on out of here!" Ruth shouted. "Everything's alright!"

As Clint's wailing continued, Ruth held his huge upper body in her lap, one arm around his chest and the other hand still stroking his hair. He could feel her face against his own, and now her tears mixed with his.

Again Ruth spoke softly, "It's okay, son. Everything's going to be okay. You just got to give it to the Lord. None of us is strong enough to make it through one day on our own. You got to give it to the Lord."

Then Ruth closed her eyes and began praying aloud, "Dear sweet Jesus, help this poor young man carry his burden. He's hurting, Lord. Please let him know Your peace. Please show him Your purpose. Help him find his way, Lord. No, help him find *Your* way. Help him know that I got no hard feelings, Lord. Let him see how much I want him to let go of this and get on living his life, Lord. I want him to *live*, Lord. Please give him the strength."

Ruth paused briefly and continued, "And please give me the strength, Lord, to go on living my life and taking care of my boy. We all need you, Lord. Help us feel Your presence. Show us Your way, and give us Your strength. We owe everything to You, Lord, and we praise Your holy name. And if it be Your will, Lord, please heal my baby. Let me see his sweet smile again. In the name of Your Son, our Lord and Savior Jesus Christ, I pray. Amen."

At that very moment Clint's sobbing ceased, and he felt as if the world had been lifted from his shoulders. He sat up and then stood up. He helped Ruth to her feet, directed her back to the chair, and sat down next to her. He took both her hands in his, and they just sat there smiling at each other for several minutes, their faces still wet with tears. This time Clint reached for the tissues and offered her one, and then he took one for himself. Clint looked at Ruth with an admiration that he reserved for very few.

Clint said, "Ma'am, along with my mom, you're the finest example I know of what a Christian should be."

"Oh, no son, I'm just a normal sinner like everyone else. I just try to live according to the New Testament. I do my best, but that's usually not good enough—not near good enough most days. But I thank you for saying that. It makes me feel real good to hear it."

"Ma'am, you say that I have nothing to be sorry about, but I am sorry—so very, very sorry. I've asked the Lord to forgive me for what I did to your son, and I know that according to the Bible, He's already done it. I have no right to be asking you for any favors, but I have to ask you for one, just this one. Please, Mrs. Willis, please say that you forgive me. I think it will help me put this behind me."

"Okay, I forgive you, son. I forgive you. Now you go out and live your life and don't you think about me and my boy no more, except maybe to say a prayer for us now and then."

"Ma'am, I've been praying for Keith and your whole family every single day since this happened, and I promise you—as God is my witness—I'll keep praying for you every day. I can see that you're good people, and good people deserve good things. I've got to believe that God has great blessings in store for you."

"I hope you're right, son."

Clint stood up with the intent of excusing himself, but something stopped him from turning for the door. He stood there for a moment looking at Keith's seemingly lifeless body and then stepped nearer the bed. He looked down at Keith and took his hand.

Ruth stepped up just behind and beside Clint. She placed one hand on Clint's arm and the other on his shoulder, as if to give him a bit of her own strength. Clint closed his eyes and bowed his head, and only he and God knew what he was thinking. Ruth did the same. After several minutes, Clint raised his head and opened his eyes, and he let go of Keith's hand.

Clint turned and embraced Ruth, squeezed her tightly in his arms, and said, "I love you, Momma." Clint wasn't sure why he'd felt the compulsion to say it. Ruth was startled by the words and pulled away slightly. She looked into Clint's eyes for a moment and then smiled.

Ruth buried her head in Clint's chest again, squeezing him as tightly as she could as she said, "Thank you, son. I needed to hear that."

Stumble & Fall

After his visit to the nursing home, Clint felt as though the cloud that had been hanging over him since the Willis fight was beginning to lift. He wasn't quite in the clear yet; however, he was feeling much better, and he was very glad that he'd made the visit. He was thankful that his friend Hulk had given him the nudge that he'd needed, but most of all he was thankful that God had given him the strength to follow through and had blessed Ruth Willis with such a kind and forgiving heart. Clint had lost a lot of faith in his fellow Christians in recent years, and Ruth had helped to restore some of it.

Clint had settled into life on his own, and his routine continued relatively unchanged. One difference was that he was sleeping better these days; the nightmares were both less frequent and less intense. With the additional rest he found that he had a lot more energy and a better overall attitude, and he began dating a little more. Clint had less money for dating since he moved out of his parents' house, but it wasn't much of a problem because he dated mostly older women who had more money and didn't mind spending it on a "boy toy." Still, he was careful not to tie himself down to any one of them.

One afternoon Clint was working the evening shift at the lobby desk in the Republic Bank tower. It was nearing the end of the work day for most of the people in the building, but he had only been on duty for a few minutes. The women's restroom was right around a corner from the lobby desk, and suddenly three women walked around the corner and stopped directly in front of the desk. They were obviously angry, and each was staring her own hole through Clint.

Clint looked at the three women and immediately knew that he was in some trouble. Over the past months he had been dating all three of them. Apparently they had been comparing notes in the restroom and eventually figured out that they were all talking about the same guy. Once again Clint had stepped in a big pile. He was going to have to learn how to break that habit.

There was virtually no dialogue between Clint and his three ladies that afternoon. Perhaps they were too angry to speak, or maybe they were thinking of other ways to get even with him—perchance both. The real conversation would come the following day when Clint was summoned to the headquarters of his employer.

Perhaps because they had grown close, Tom was the one who came out to the lobby and greeted Clint and then led him into the office of the personnel director, Greg Patton. Greg and the Republic account manager, Lester Mings, were waiting inside. No one looked happy, and Clint assumed that he was about to be fired. Once Clint was seated, Greg was the first to speak.

"Clint, does the term 'don't shit where you eat' mean anything to you?" Greg asked.

Clint responded, "No, sir, I'm afraid I'm not familiar with that turn of phrase."

"What he means, Clint," said Tom with a surprising harshness, "is that you shouldn't fuck around with women where you work, and if you do, you definitely don't fuck around with three of them at the same time."

Clint thought, "What are the odds of all three of them winding up in the restroom at the same time and talking about their extracurricular activities?"

Luckily Clint's better judgement prevailed, and he said instead, "I'm sorry I let y'all down. I should've known better, and I hope that my faux pas doesn't reflect poorly on the company or on any of you."

Lester said, "Well, it does. Your little 'faux pas,' as you call it, does reflect poorly on the company and on all of us. We have some egg on our face here. What do you suppose we should do about it?"

"Well, I assume you're probably going to fire me," Clint answered. "I hope not. I hope I get a chance to redeem myself, but I'm a big boy. I'll take my medicine—whatever it is."

The silence was deafening. The four men sat there without a spoken word for a couple of minutes, which seemed like a couple of hours under the circumstances. Up to this point, Clint could do no wrong, and he was genuinely sorry for the trouble he had caused. Finally Lester spoke again.

"Clint, you've done exceptional work up to this point. We've thrown a lot at you, and you've handled it all very well. No matter the task, you've done it without question or complaint, and generally you've done it better than anyone else could have. We've all expected great things from you, but this lapse of judgement gives us pause. I have to be honest with you. We did discuss firing you."

Again there was silence, and Clint thought it a little sadistic. Implicit in Lester's last sentence was the message that Clint would not be fired, but they nevertheless paused to make him wonder. Perhaps that was part of the lesson.

"Well?" Clint finally asked. "What did you decide?"

Lester answered, "We decided that you have too much potential for us to dump you for your first mistake. We're going to have to write you up, and this will be part of your personnel file, which is permanent. And it goes without saying that we can't send you back to Republic." With a nod in Tom's direction, Lester continued, "Tom went to bat for you, and he wants you to work full time with his group."

Tom immediately jumped in. "Don't you make any mistake about it," he said. "We're not rewarding your bad behavior, and don't you expect for a minute that you're going to be doing interesting work. You can expect a lot of dull grunt work, and if you can't handle that, then maybe

Lester or one of the other account managers can find you a nice warehouse to sit in all night on graveyards. Understand?"

"Yes, sir," Clint said. "Again, I'm sorry for my mistake, and I thank you for giving me a second chance," he added sincerely.

Greg had already completed a memorandum of reprimand, and he said, "Then all we need to do is complete the paperwork. This is a memorandum outlining everything we discussed here today. You need to sign it, and then we'll all sign it as witnesses. Then I'll put it in your file, and it will be part of your permanent record. Do you have any objection?"

"No, sir, I don't. I'm grateful that I still have a job." Clint signed the form without even reading it, and the other three signed it as well.

Greg added, "Okay, now you need to go home and think about things. We're suspending you for the rest of this week without pay, and when you come back to work on Monday, you'll be reporting to Tom."

"Yes, sir," Clint responded.

Clint stood up, and the others followed suit. Clint shook hands and said "thank you" to each of them before leaving. As Clint was sitting on his bike in the parking lot and putting on his helmet, Tom came out and walked over to him.

"Well, you certainly have an unorthodox way of getting what you want," Tom said, managing a weak smile.

"Tom, listen. I'm really sorry. I know I put you in a bad position, and that's the last thing I'd want to do. Please accept my apology."

"Ah, you're young. You're entitled to screw up now and then. Can we talk about it some more at happy hour?"

Clint smiled and said, "Sure, it seems I'll have plenty of time on my hands for a while."

"Okay then, I have some loose ends to tie up. Can you meet me at the Bennigan's on Beltline around 5:30? That's on my way home. I can't stay long, but we can have a drink or two and talk."

"Okay, see you then," Clint said as he started his bike.

The two men shook hands, and Clint rode away. He had a little time to kill, so he rode over to Addison Airport to watch the planes take off and land. Addison was the busiest single-slab general aviation airport in the world, and Clint loved hanging out there. He dreamed of one day being able to afford flying lessons. After an hour or so of watching the planes and dreaming of flying, Clint decided to head on over to Bennigan's, which wasn't far. He was thirsty, and he figured he could have a drink while waiting for Tom to get there.

On his way down Beltline toward Bennigan's, Clint decided to stop at a 7-Eleven for some Certs and Doublemint. He was afraid that he had dragon breath and didn't want to offend Tom or the wait staff at the tavern. He went inside, bought his breath mints and chewing gum, and came back out and stood by his bike. He crunched a couple of mints right away and began chewing a stick of gum. Clint walked over to the trash can to discard his wrappers, and as he walked back to his bike, he saw her.

She was getting out of a 1979 Ford Thunderbird, and she saw him, too. It was the beautiful mulatto woman from the credit card company. Clint realized that it was just down the road on the other side of the airport. For two obvious reasons, he was very happy that he'd stopped for breath mints and gum. They smiled at one another as Clint walked toward her. Clint thought he saw her blush a little, and he was certain that he had.

"Good afternoon, ma'am," Clint said somewhat hesitantly. "Haven't we met before?"

"Is that your best line?" she said with a chuckle. Oh, her smile was beautiful!

"Well, no, I have some others, but that one seemed most appropriate. We have met before, but actually I guess it would be more accurate to say that we've seen each other before. I'm sure you remember, but it's not like we were formally introduced." Extending his hand, Clint said, "I'm

Clinton (Clint) Buchanan. That's 'Buck Hannon'—not 'Bew Cannon.' That's the way my family pronounces it."

"Hi, Clint. I'm Dani Bailey. My family says it Bailey, and yes, I do remember seeing you before. It's nice to meet you, and I'd love to talk some more. But I'm running a little late for work, and I need to get in here first real quick."

"Can we continue our conversation another time? What time do you take your lunch break?"

"At 9:00, but I don't leave the building. I bring my lunch and eat it in the lunch room."

"I'm sure you brought a good lunch for tonight, but I hope it keeps until tomorrow. I'll be bringing your supper tonight. See you at 9:00. Okay?"

"Uh, yeah, okay I guess. Do you need me to come to the door to get you?"

"No, that's okay. I know security there. I'll just meet you in the lunch room."

"Okay, I'll see you then. Now I really have to go. Sorry!"

"That's okay, Dani. I'll see you soon."

As Dani walked toward the store, Clint couldn't resist the temptation to watch her walk away, but he didn't gawk. By the time she got back out to her T-Bird, Clint was cruising east down Beltline toward Bennigan's. When he arrived, Clint went on inside, grabbed a seat at the bar, and ordered a whiskey sour. Since it was happy hour, the bartender made two. Clint was determined to make them last, and he'd just finished the first one when Tom showed up, actually a little early.

"Hi, Clint, how you holding up? Bartender, I'll have a Bud draft, please."

"Well, to be perfectly honest with you, I'm fan-fucking-tastic!"

"Well, that's interesting. After our meeting this afternoon, I figured you'd be really down in the dumps. I was hoping to cheer you up a bit."

"I appreciate that, Tom, but someone else has already taken care of that job."

"What do you mean?"

"You remember that time we went down the road here to talk to that credit card investigator about a case?"

"Yeah, we've been there a couple of times."

"That's right. Well, the first time I saw someone on the way out. You remember me telling you about her?"

"How could I forget? After we got back to the office, you had to sit in my truck for ten minutes waiting to lose your boner."

"Yeah, well, if you'd noticed her you'd understand. Anyway, guess what? I *did* see her this afternoon! I bumped into her down the road at the 7-Eleven, and we had us a little chat. Her name is Dani, and I'm taking supper to her tonight at work."

The bartender returned with Tom's beer and set it on the bar in front of him.

Tom didn't look happy. He sighed and shook his head. "I'm sorry," he said. "I'm having a little disconnect. Think about this for a minute. We just had to discipline you for screwing around with women at work. That happened this very day—just a few hours ago. Now here you are all excited about getting involved with a woman who's connected to your job. You don't see a problem with that?"

That dulled Clint's excitement only slightly. "No, Tom, actually I don't. Any connection she has to my job is tenuous at best, and I don't see how this could come back on the company. Give me a break here, Tom. You're my friend. Right?"

"Yes, Clint, I am your friend, and you're probably right about this one. I just want you to be careful. I know a little something about screwing around—how it can get a guy in trouble. I just want you to be more careful than I was."

Suddenly the atmosphere had become awkward for both men. They sat there sipping their drinks without talking for several minutes. It was Tom who finally broke the silence.

"Clint, I've never told you this before, but I used to have a hard time keeping my hooter in my pants. When I was a cop, I couldn't hardly say no to a woman. I'm sorry to say that I didn't stop after I got married either. My screwing around cost me my career, the job I was born to do, and it almost cost me my marriage, too. Check that. You could say that it did cost me my marriage. We're still together, but it will never be the same. I'm ashamed to admit that, but I want you to understand how chasing poon-tang can come back and bite you on the ass. And I don't mean in a good way."

Not wanting to give Tom any reason to be mad at Hulk, Clint just said, "I'm kind of surprised, Tom. I figured you for the kind who'd be faithful to his wife."

"Yeah, I did, too. I did, too," Tom said pensively. They sipped their drinks for a moment, and Tom added, "By the way, you don't have to pretend that Roy didn't tell you about it. He fessed up already."

"Oh, okay."

"So you should understand. You should understand why I feel the way I do—why I want you to be careful. Clint, you've become almost like a son to me, or at least a little brother, and I'd hate to see you make a bad mistake like I did. Please be careful."

"Don't take this the wrong way, Tom, but I'm not married yet. A single man chasing pussy isn't the same as a married guy doing it. I'm not being judgemental. I'm just stating a simple fact. It's not the same thing, so try to lighten up a bit. I'm sorry about what happened at Republic, and I'll take my punishment like a man. But this isn't the same. It won't affect work."

"Yeah, I guess you're right. Maybe I'm just project-ing." After a brief pause, Tom said, "So, what's this about supper?"

"Yeah, Dani takes her lunch break at 9:00, so I figured I'd go get some burgers or something and take them over there."

"That sounds good, but don't get Whataburger or Dairy Queen. Stop by Chili's or J. T. McCord's. Get some good burgers—not fast food. You can't hardly go wrong with that."

"I've got to tell you, Tom. My heart's going pitter-patter over this one. This one could be special."

"Well, I'm happy for you, Clint, but don't go getting your hopes up. There ain't no such thing as love at first sight."

"I'm not so sure about that, but that's not what I'm saying—well, not really. There's just something about her. I don't know what it is yet, but I'm going to find out."

"Okay, well, good luck. I'll see you at work on Monday morning—bright and early at 0800. Oh, and by the way, you really should spend some time between now and then thinking about your mistake at Republic. You can certainly work your way past it, and I expect you will. But it was a serious matter, and you came *this* close to being fired. That's as serious as it gets, and you do need to ponder that some."

"Okay, friend, I will. I will."

Tom left some cash on the bar for their drinks, shook Clint's hand, and left. Clint looked at his watch and thought, "Shit! I need to get a shower." He had just enough time, so he didn't even bother finishing his drink. He practically ran out, hopped on his bike, and rode home as quickly as he could in evening traffic. Clint had showered before his big meeting earlier, but after being on his bike for a while, he needed to freshen up a bit before his date, even as informal as it would be.

Clint took a quick shower, got dressed, and put on some Aramis cologne. He went outside, hopped into his truck, and retraced his route back to the same neighborhood where he'd been that afternoon. He decided to stop at J. T. McCord's, and he ordered burgers and fries to go. When he had the bag in hand, he hopped back into his truck and pulled into the parking lot at Dani's work just before 9:00. Whew! He'd barely made it.

Clint trotted up to the employee's entrance and spoke to the security guard behind the bullet-proof glass. "Hi, Bob. Remember me? I'm Clint Buchanan. I work with Tom Whitely at England Security. We've been around here a couple times."

"Yeah, I remember you, kid. You're kind of distinct."

"Good. I'm here to meet someone for lunch at 9:00." Looking at his watch, he said, "That's right now. Mind if I have a visitor's pass?"

"Well, it ain't exactly kosher, but I reckon you're okay." He slid the pass under the window and said, "Don't forget to drop it on your way out."

"Oh, I won't. Thank you, Bob. I owe you one. Wait! I just remembered that I need an escort. There's a secured door between here and the lunch room."

Bob said, "Yeah, I was just about to remind you of that." It was a lie. He'd forgotten just as Clint had.

"Your escort's here, sir." Clint recognized Dani's voice and turned to see her smiling. "I can see you're punctual."

As they began walking through the corridors toward the lunch room, Clint said, "I'm sorry to be last-minute like that. I'm normally early."

"It's no problem, but I only have 30 minutes. I hope that's enough time."

Clint said with a smile, "Oh, I'm sure it won't be enough time, but there's always the next time."

Dani smiled and blushed. As they entered the lunch room, there was a small group of people, mostly women, at a table at the other end of the room.

One of the women shouted, "Woo-hoo, Dani! Good catch!"

An obviously gay man agreed with her assessment, yelling, "Dani, if you don't want him, I do!"

Everyone laughed, and Dani just waved in their direction. Hoping for at least a bit of privacy, Clint and Dani grabbed a table on the near side of the lunch room.

"What kind of coke do you want?" Clint asked as he walked toward one of the machines.

"I'll take a Dr. Pepper, please," Dani replied.

"How to know you're in Texas," Clint said as he dropped some change into the machine.

Dani chuckled. She had already sat down at the table and begun emptying the bag, separating their burgers and fries. Clint returned with her Dr. Pepper and his Pepsi and sat across the table from her.

"I wasn't sure what to get," Clint said. "I figured burgers would be safe, and I stuck to the basics—nothing fancy, medium-well, and no onions. I started to get cheese, but I was afraid you might be lactose intolerant or something. Is that okay?"

Dani smiled and said, "Sure, that's perfect. Cheese would have been okay, but I like them either way."

"Okay," Clint started right in, "since we don't have much time, let me just repeat, in case you've forgotten, my name is Clinton Buchanan, but I go by Clint. Make sure you get that last name right. It's 'Buck Hannon.' I'm 19 years old. I grew up about 20 miles from here in Allen, but now I have my own apartment in Plano. My parents are both schoolteachers in Allen, and I have two siblings, one of each. Right now I'm technically a security officer, but I'm doing mostly investigations, except I'm still too young for a license, so that's not really official. Once I turn 21, I plan to apply to be a police officer, hopefully in Dallas. And, by the way, I think you're one of the three most beautiful women I've ever seen in my life."

Dani swallowed a bit of burger and laughed.

"One of the three?" she asked, chuckling.

"Yes, absolutely. You're definitely one of the three most beautiful women I've ever seen, and if you're not married, engaged, or celibate, I'd really like to take you out on a real date sometime."

Dani laughed harder this time. "Celibate, huh? You really get right to it. Don't you?"

"Yes, ma'am, I do. Now tell me about yourself. How do you spell your name?"

"It's D-A-N-I, short for Danielle. I'm 29 years old, and no, I'm not married, engaged, or celibate. I'm divorced, and I have two kids, a boy and a girl. Oh, and in case you haven't noticed, I'm kind of black."

"Well, yes, as a matter of fact, I did notice that."

"And that doesn't matter to you?"

"No. Why would it?"

"It does matter to some people, probably most. I figured it didn't matter to you, or you wouldn't be here. But what about your parents? What would they say if you told them your girlfriend was black?"

"First of all, you're not my girlfriend—yet. I'm kind of hoping that we're headed that way, but we're not there quite yet. Secondly, just because I'm a white boy from a small town in Texas doesn't mean that I'm an ignorant racist cracker. I'm not. My parents didn't raise me that way."

"I'm glad to hear that, but when push comes to shove, sometimes people find out that they're not as open-minded as they thought they were. You bring me home for Sunday dinner, and you'll find out what your parents really think. With all due respect."

"Okay, so you're my girlfriend, and you want to meet my parents at Sunday dinner. Should I just go ahead and pop the question now?"

They both laughed. There was an obvious chemistry that neither could deny, and they were both thinking that there might be some potential for a relationship.

"No, no. Let's don't go getting ahead of ourselves," Dani said.

They sat there smiling, munching their burgers and fries, and chatting for a little while, and time started running short.

Dani checked the clock on the wall and said, "Listen, Clint. You're a gorgeous young white boy, but I'm a divorced woman with two kids—ten years older than you, too. Then there's the racial difference. Even if you say it don't matter to you, it matters to a lot of folks, and that could make things tough. This ain't exactly a match made in heaven."

"That remains to be seen," Clint responded. "Listen, right now I want kiss you so bad it hurts, but let me just say this: You're beautiful; I like you, and none of that other stuff matters. I'm not asking you to marry me. I'm just asking you to go out with me. You said it yourself—let's not go getting ahead of ourselves. I just want a chance. Will you go out with me?"

Dani checked the clock again and stood up. She said, "I've got to get back to work. Thanks for supper. Do you have a pen?"

"No, I don't," Clint said, but he knew why she had asked the question.

Looking across the room, Clint saw that the group at the opposite end was heading back to work as well. He yelled, "Excuse me! Does anyone have a pen?"

The gay man responded, "Sure, I have one."

Clint trotted across the room, and the gay man ogled him and said, "Mmmm, mmmm, mmmm! You look absolutely scrumptious!" He held out the pen to Clint.

Clint reached for the pen and answered, "Thanks. She must think so, too, because she's about to give me her number. I'll bring this right back."

"Don't worry about it. I've got to run to the little girls' room real quick. Just give it to Dani. And by the way, if she dumps you, you know where to find me," he said, winking at Clint.

Clint said, "I'll keep that in mind. Thanks again."

Clint turned to trot back across the room, and unbeknownst to him, Dani had walked up behind him. He bumped into her moderately and had to grab her to keep them both from falling. "Oh, shit, I'm sorry. I didn't realize you were there. Are you okay?"

Pretending to be a little woozy, Dani said, "Yeah, but did you get the license number of that truck?"

They both smiled. Clint held her for just a moment and handed her the pen. She had ripped off part of the burger bag, and she wrote her phone number on it.

Dani said, "Here's my number, but on second thought, let me ask you something. Are you doing anything tonight?"

As Clint tucked the number into his pocket, he said, "No, I'm not doing anything at all tonight, and I don't have to work tomorrow either. What did you have in mind?"

Dani asked, "You know that Bennigan's down the street?"

Clint grinned and said, "Yeah, I'm familiar with it."

Dani reached for Clint's hand and squeezed it. "I get off at 12:30," she said. "Meet me there."

Dani turned and trotted off to work. She was going to be slightly late getting back, but she didn't care.

Half & Half

Clint had a really difficult time waiting for the next several hours to pass. He drove back to the airport to pass some more time watching the planes take off and land, but he just couldn't sit still for it. After a few minutes, he just took to driving up and down Beltline Road and checking the clock on the dashboard every couple of minutes. Finally, when he was down to the final hour, he went on back to Bennigan's, figuring that he could nurse a drink until Dani arrived.

The place was actually pretty busy, so Clint just took a seat at the bar. He paid cash for a Guinness Stout and started perusing the tables. When he had identified the one he believed to be the coziest, he paid the hostess five bucks to make sure that he got that table when the couple who was there left. They did so at around 12:15, and as soon as the table was bused, Clint took possession of it as if he were one of his ancestors in the Oklahoma land rush of 1889. At precisely 12:38, Dani walked through the door, and Clint rose and met her halfway.

Clint took Dani's hand, kissed her cheek, and asked, "What took you so long?"

Dani just smiled as Clint led her back to the table. The waitress had seen her arrive and stopped by just as Clint and Dani were sitting down.

The waitress said, "Good evening, ma'am. What can I get for you?"

Dani said, "I'll have a Singapore Sling."

"And you?" the waitress asked Clint.

"I'll have another Guinness," Clint responded. "No, check that. Make it a Half-and-Half."

"Okay, I'll be right back."

"What's a Half-and-Half?" Dani asked.

"A beer for the indecisive," Clint said, smiling. "It's half Guinness and half Harp's."

Dani nodded and said, "Oh, I thought that was called a Black-and-Tan."

"No, actually a Black-and-Tan is Guinness and Bass, but it just doesn't seem right to me to mix the Irish and the British. Anyway, you can remember the difference with the 'b' and the 'h.' Black is Bass. Half is Harp's. I know that's not exactly correct, but it's a good mnemonic. But enough trivia. How are you doing? Have a good evening at work?"

"Yeah, it was okay. We didn't have too many authorization calls, so I was able to get a lot of keypunching done. I can make more incentive pay that way. They try to tell us that the authorization calls don't hurt our incentive pay, but that's not really true. They break the rhythm, and that slows you down."

The waitress returned with their drinks and discreetly placed them on the table without disturbing their conversation. She just made sure to make eye contact with Clint, and he nodded his thanks.

Clint said to Dani, "Oh, so you do work in data entry. That's kind of what I figured."

"Yeah, I've been doing it for a couple of years. It's not too bad. It's a pretty good job for someone with a GED. I do okay."

"Good. I'm glad to hear it. I got the impression it was a decent place to work."

"That day—that day when we first saw each other. What were you doing there?"

"Well, I heard you were there, of course, so I came to check you out!"

Dani laughed and said, "Yeah, I saw you checking me out!"

"If you ask me, the 'checking out' seemed pretty mutual," Clint said, "but seriously, I was there with an investigator from my job. We were working on a little case for your investigators, and we had to discuss some stuff with one of them. I'm just really, really glad that I went along that day—and that we timed it just right."

"Yeah, me too," Dani replied.

They were holding hands across the table now, and Dani looked at Clint and flashed a big smile, showing off a marvelous set of perfect white teeth.

Clint smiled back and said, "Damn, you're beautiful!"

"Who are the other two?" Dani asked.

Puzzled, Clint asked, "The other two?"

"You said that I was one of the three most beautiful women you'd ever seen. I demand to know who the other two are!"

"Oh, yeah," Clint said, chuckling. "Yes, I did say that. Didn't I? Well, my mother and sister, of course. Other than the two of them, you're *the* most beautiful woman I've ever seen. I just didn't think you'd believe me if I said that right up front."

"Yeah, right. Like I'm going to believe it now."

They just sat there and smiled at each other for a few moments and sipped their drinks. Dani's left hand was in Clint's right, and he was holding it firmly and stroking the back of it with his thumb.

"Seriously, you are very beautiful," Clint said, "and I'm amazed that you're here with me right now. I just want to get to know you—to see if you're as beautiful on the inside as you are on the outside. I know that sounds pretty hokey, but I really mean it. And the initial indications are very promising."

Dani responded, "Yeah, I'd have to say the same thing."

"Good. I'm glad you feel that way," Clint said. "So, tell me about yourself—where you're from, your family, your kids, whatever you can cram into the next hour before this place closes."

"Okay. Well, I'm not going to talk for an hour. I'll make it short. I'm from West Texas—Midland to be exact. I'm the baby of the family—fourth of four girls. Dad really wanted a boy, and he planned to name me after himself, Daniel Robert. But when I turned out to be another girl, he just changed that to Danielle Rose. But he always called me Dani. Most folks do. I got married during senior year and moved over here with my husband for his job. We had two kids, a girl named Leesah (L-E-E-S-A-H) and a boy named Marcus. They're ten and eight now."

"Leesah's ten, and Marcus is eight?" Clint asked.

"Yeah, Leesah's the oldest."

"How long you been divorced?"

"Well," Dani started, obviously somewhat uncomfortable, "to tell you the truth, we're not exactly divorced."

Clint was a bit taken aback. "Uh, what exactly does 'not exactly' mean?"

"Clint, listen. I want to be honest with you about this. Then you can decide whether or not you still want to see me. Truth is, Antoine and I have been separated for about three years, but he won't give me a divorce. And I can't afford a lawyer to keep hounding him for it. So, I've just decided not to push it. If I have to some day, I will, but for now I don't have to."

"Wow," Clint said, shaking his head, "that's a bit of a bomb you just dropped on me. I have a pet peeve about cheating, and even though you're separated, you're still married. I'm not sure how I feel about that."

"Clint, listen. There's more. I've been going with someone else for a long time, too, and we just broke up. He's kind of possessive, and he doesn't want to admit that it's over. He'd go crazy if he knew I was here with you now."

Clint was speechless. He let go of Dani's hand and sat there silently. He was really stung by Dani's revelations, and also quite conflicted. He didn't know what to think or to say.

"Clint, I hate that you're upset, but I'm not going to apologize for being honest with you. We just met, and I like you. I like you a lot, and that's why I have to be honest with you. Would you rather I lied about it?"

"No, Dani, I'm glad you were honest. I just don't know what to think about it. I'm disappointed—not disappointed in you, just disappointed about the situation. That's all. Please don't take it personally. I'm not being judgemental."

Just then the waitress returned and said, "Folks, we're going to be closing before too long. Are you going to want anything else?"

Without even thinking about it, Clint said, "Yeah, bring us another round with the check." He thought for a moment as the waitress walked away, and he reached and took Dani's hand again and said, "Look, Dani, I'm glad you were honest with me, and I'm going to be honest with you. I can't say that I'm completely okay with the situation. Truth is, I still don't know what to think. But what I do know is that I like you enough to want to get to know you better. I know I'm jumping the gun here, but I think we might have something more than 'like' in our future."

"Good. I agree," Dani responded with a smile, looking relieved.

"Okay, so when do I meet the kiddos?" Clint asked, not to earn brownie points but because he genuinely wanted to meet them.

"Wow! You do move right along. Don't you?"

"Yeah, I do," Clint answered. "When I have something in my sights that I want, I tend to go right for it. That's not necessarily a good thing all the time, but I think it is here. I like kids, and I've always been good with them. I used to work in my church nursery, and that was always loads of fun. Ten and eight are good ages, and I'd love to meet Leesah and Marcus. But if you think it would be rushing things, I can wait—for a day or two maybe." They both laughed before Clint said, "I'm just kidding. We can take it at your pace—whatever you think is best."

The waitress returned with their drinks and check. Clint took a quick glance at the check and handed the waitress his Master Charge.

The waitress said, "Thanks. I'll be right back."

"Seriously, Clint, I'm happy that you want to meet my kids, but I think it's too soon. A few minutes ago you weren't even sure you wanted to keep seeing me."

Clint interrupted, "No, I knew I wanted to keep seeing you. I was just trying to wrap my mind around what you told me about still being married—technically. And that's my rationalization—that you're only technically married."

Dani continued, "I'm not even quite sure what you mean by that, but anyway, I think it's too soon for you to meet the kids. I'm not sure how they'd react to me bringing home a big white boy. The race thing, the age thing . . . . I need to think on those for a while. Let's you and me get to know each other a little better, and then we'll see."

"Okay," Clint said, "I guess that's fair enough. Do you work the weekends? Can we go out on Saturday night maybe?"

"I'm off weekends unless they have us on overtime." Then Dani smiled and said, "As luck would have it, I'm off this weekend, and Leesah and Marcus are going to be with their dad. If you want, we can do this again on Friday night after work, and then we can have Saturday and part of Sunday, too. I won't have to be back to work until 4:30 Monday afternoon, but Antoine will be bringing the kids back home Sunday afternoon around supper time."

Clint was thinking, "Wow, what a great time to be suspended!" He almost said it, too, but then he realized that it would have been pretty stupid. Dani might have been okay with the suspension, but Clint didn't exactly want to broach the subject of *why* he'd been suspended. Clint was pretty ashamed of being suspended, and he wasn't exactly proud of the reason. It was definitely not something to interject into the discussion—not now, and not with this woman.

The waitress came back, gave Clint his credit card, along with the charge slip, and said, "Thanks, y'all. I hope you've had a nice time. Come back and see us."

Clint looked up and smiled at the waitress and said, "Thanks. You've been great. We'll see you again soon."

Without thinking, Clint winked at the waitress. It was a habit of his, and like a lot of habits, he often did it without thinking.

"Good night," the waitress said with a smile. She glanced at Dani, nodded, and walked away.

"I saw that, young man!" Dani said playfully. "I saw you wink at that pretty young white girl. Do you always flirt like that?"

Clint was embarrassed and felt himself blush. "I don't know—maybe. Sorry about that. I just wasn't thinking. I guess I should break that habit, huh?"

"Damn, right! You might get away with that with a white girlfriend, but us black women are jealous. We don't put up with that shit. You'd better watch out. You don't want me going left on you!"

Dani was still yanking Clint's chain, and he was still blushing. He enjoyed it, though. He liked that she was the playful sort.

"Yeah, yeah, yeah. I hear you. You won't have to tell me twice." Clint glanced at his watch and said, "Well, I guess we should finish our drinks and get out of here. They're going to close up and run us out pretty soon."

Suddenly Dani stood up, came over to Clint's side of the table and sat next to him, and she kissed him squarely on the lips. It was a great first kiss—no tongue, not all passionate and wet, just a nice, soft kiss that lingered for a moment. Clint was a little surprised that Dani had kissed him first, but he wasn't really disappointed. He didn't mind her taking the initiative; in fact, he rather liked it. It actually made him feel a little more secure that she genuinely liked him.

Dani looked at Clint with her big brown, puppy dog eyes and said, "Then I'm going to sit right here until they make us leave."

Clint smiled and reciprocated the kiss, giving much as he had gotten. "Good," he said. "I don't want to leave either."

Clint looked at his Half-and-Half and realized that in the middle where the Guinness and Harp's blended together, the color was about the same as Dani's skin.

At precisely that moment, Dani said, "You know, Clint, it's funny that you would be drinking a Half-and-Half while you're sitting here with one."

Clint was clearly shocked. "Do you read minds?" he asked. "I was just thinking about that!"

"Wow, that's pretty cool. So you know I'm a half-breed?"

"Well, yeah. I hope this doesn't sound bad, but it's fairly obvious."

"I guess so, but sometimes I wonder."

"So, since you brought it up, what are you exactly—I mean, besides human?"

"Sometimes you might not be so sure about that, especially when I first wake up," Dani said with a chuckle. "Seriously, my dad is black, and my mom was half white and half Indian."

"Was?"

"Yeah, she passed a few years back."

"I'm sorry to hear that."

"Thanks."

"You mean American Indian. Right? Not the other kind."

"Right—feathers, not turbans."

"I guess that explains the hair and the cheek bones."

"Yeah, and I can kind of go on the warpath sometimes, too," Dani said with a grin, and they both chuckled.

Clint replied, "Yeah, I'll bet that's true, but you know, technically you're not a half-and-half. You're a half-quarter-quarter." Clint winked, and they both laughed again.

Clint asked, "By the way, which tribe?"

"Apache. I'm a distant relative of Geronimo, or so Mom's people used to say. I think a lot of Apaches probably say that."

"Really? That's interesting. I have a wee tiny bit of Apache blood in me, too. You reckon we're related?" Clint asked with a wink.

"Oh, God, I hope not! That could really throw a wrench into things."

"Indeed it would complicate matters. You know, my mom comes from New Mexico, and my family has always spent a lot of time there. I remember one vacation, probably about ten years ago. We stopped to eat at a restaurant near Ruidoso. I think it was on the Mescalero Apache Indian Reservation, and there was an old Indian in there who claimed to be Geronimo's grandson. You got any kin on the reservation?"

"Maybe, but I don't really know. I think my mom's family was from New Mexico, so it's possible. Anyway, like I said, I think a lot of Apaches claim to be related to Geronimo. Mom was proud of her Indian blood, but she wasn't part of the tribe. I don't know that much about it to tell you the truth. I'm more black than anything, so I just consider myself black. That's how folks see people like me anyway."

"Well, it doesn't really matter. It's just a subject that interests me. A lot of subjects interest me, come to think of it. But no matter what you are or where you're from, you're here with me now, and that makes me very happy."

"Yeah, me too." Dani's smile melted Clint's heart.

All the lights came on, and Clint said, "We're going to have to get out of here pretty soon. They're getting ready to close."

"Yeah, I guess you're right," Dani said with obvious disappointment on her face and in her voice.

They finished their drinks quickly, and then Clint double-checked the Master Charge slip to make sure he'd given the waitress a sufficient tip. He was a little obsessive-compulsive, and he often double-checked himself.

"Well," Clint said, "as much fun as this is, I guess we need to get out of here."

They slid out of the booth and walked toward the door. Clint saw their waitress on the way out and waved another "good-bye" to her, and then he said the same to the hostess who opened the door for them on the way out. He saw Dani's T-Bird, and they walked in that direction, holding hands.

When they arrived at Dani's car, Clint pulled her close and kissed her passionately. This was no little peck—no first kiss. This was a long, lustful, whole-mouth kiss—the "I wish we were naked and sweaty" kind of kiss. They both thought of being naked and sweaty. They embraced tightly and held the kiss for a long minute, neither one caring that they were in a public place.

When they finally pulled their lips away slightly, Dani said, "My God! I can't wait until Friday night. You'll meet me here—12:30 again, just like tonight?"

"Okay, you talked me into it. Now you'll have a little more to think about between now and then."

"No, not a little," Dani said as she got into her car. She started the car and then rolled the window down and said, "You will be here on Friday. Right?"

Clint leaned in the window and gave her another hard kiss, though not as long as the one before.

"Yes, Dani, I'll be here. I promise."

It wouldn't be a hard promise to keep.

Backup

After leaving Bennigan's, Clint drove east on Beltline Road toward Central Expressway. He turned north on Central and headed toward Plano, and he was so elated after his date with Dani that he almost didn't notice them—a group of four Bandidos. They were riding northbound on Central in the standard staggered formation, and they passed him in the fast lane. Clint was driving slightly over the 55-mph speed limit, and they passed him quickly, probably going around 70-75. They were well past him before he realized who they were, so he didn't get a chance to see if he recognized any of them from Austin.

The Bandidos were a fast-growing gang, and though their range did include the DFW Metroplex, they tended to spend most of their time in other parts of Texas. Seeing them in North Dallas was somewhat rare, so Clint was obviously concerned. New clubs were springing up in Oklahoma, though, so maybe they were just on their way up there—maybe. Clint hoped that there was an innocent explanation for their presence in the area, but he decided to speed up and follow them at a discreet distance for a while. He thought of the .44 magnum and the 12-gauge in his saddle blanket, but they gave him little comfort. He decided that he would stay with them as far as the Red River, and if they crossed into Oklahoma, he would turn around and go home. It would only be a couple of hours out of his way, and he probably wasn't going to sleep much tonight anyway.

Clint was vexed when they took the 15th Street exit in Plano. At this point, they were very near his apartment. Was it a coincidence? At least Clint was in his truck and thankful for it. He would have been a lot more conspicuous on his bike, and he was better armed in his truck. After exiting the expressway, the bikers turned into the Pit Grill, and Clint cruised right on past them as they entered the small café. He turned into a dark parking lot about a block away and thought for a moment. He should probably call Hulk, or maybe Tom, but he didn't want to expose himself at a pay phone. He decided to drive back by the Pit Grill, and as he did he saw that the four bikers were seated at the counter. Since they were apparently ordering something to eat, Clint decided to drive to the Sak-n-Pak about two blocks west and use the pay phone.

Hulk answered after the fourth ring. "What!" he answered loudly, not at all like a question.

"Oh, good, I caught you home. You off tonight?"

"Yeah, Sasquatch, I'm off tonight. It would be kind of hard to answer the phone otherwise."

"Don't be a smartass, man. I need your help."

"Sorry, kid, but I was just about to get laid. You're lucky I answered at all."

"Ah, shit. Sorry. Should I call Tom?"

"No, no, kid. It's okay. What's up? You sound a little out of sorts."

"I'm in Plano, and four Bandidos just stopped at the Pit Grill for a late-night snack. Have you heard anything lately?"

"No, there's been no word about them at all. Listen, Sasquatch, I understand your concern, but I wouldn't worry about it. It's probably just a coincidence. Did you notice which way they were going before they got there?"

"Yeah, they blew past me northbound on Central. Thank God I'm in my truck tonight."

"You packing?"

"Yeah, I've got my .44 and my shotgun."

"Where you at?"

"I'm at the Sak-n-Pak on 15th Street, a couple of blocks west of Central."

"Okay, kid, sit tight. I'll be there ASAP, and don't you even think about leaving until you see my ugly mug."

"Hulk, you don't have to do this—really. This is probably nothing. I'll just head on home."

"Quit talking, kid. I'm hanging up the phone now, and I'm on my way."

The phone went "click" before Clint could say anything else. He knew that it would be a good half hour at least before Hulk showed up. He didn't like the idea of leaving his truck, but his nerves had made him thirsty. He decided to run into the store and buy a coke for the wait.

Clint entered the store, went back to cooler, and grabbed his customary Pepsi, and on the way back to the register he grabbed a pack of Peanut M&Ms. Glancing out the front door toward the street, he put his drink and snack on the counter, reached into his wallet, and handed the cashier two dollars.

"How's it hanging, dude?" the kid behind the counter asked.

"It's okay. Listen, man, could you do me a small favor?"

"Depends what it is."

As he took his change from the clerk and grabbed his stuff from the counter, Clint said, "It's no big deal, but I'm going to be waiting for someone in my truck out there. If you see four bikers ride up and stop, call the cops. Okay?"

"Yeah, sure, no sweat. You have some trouble with them?"

"You could say that. Just so you know, an off-duty cop is already on the way. He may be on a Harley, too, but he'll be by himself and won't be wearing colors. But if four Bandidos ride up, call the cops immediately. Okay?"

"Yeah, sure, sounds like some excitement."

"I hope not. Thanks," Clint said on his way out.

Clint got back into his truck and waited. He opened the M&Ms and ate them quickly, and he started on the Pepsi. He felt a little silly for being so paranoid, but then again, they had found him in Austin. It wasn't out of the question that they might find him again. He finished the Pepsi and immediately wished that he'd bought two, but he didn't want to chance leaving the truck again. He reached down with one hand and patted the guns in his saddle blanket, but they offered little reassurance.

After a wait that seemed like hours, he heard the rumble of a Harley—just one. Clint checked his watch and noted that it had been 34 minutes since Hulk had hung up on him. Hulk rode up on the left side of the truck, and Clint had already rolled his window down.

"Hey, Sasquatch. How's your nerves?"

"Well, to tell you the truth, they're a little frazzled. Thanks for coming."

"Yeah, kid, I'd rather be coming at home, but I figured this was important. I already rode by the Pit Grill, and they're still there. I figure you should just go on home and let me tail them for a little while. I'll stop by your place later when I'm done."

"Are you kidding me, man? I can't let you do this alone!"

"That's exactly what you're going to do," Hulk said in a tone with which Clint didn't dare argue. "I'm a cop. I have my guns, and unlike some people I know, I also have a badge. Now you just go home and sit tight. I'll drop by your place as soon as I can."

"Four on one just doesn't sound very good to me. If they see a guy riding alone, they may just decide to have a little fun."

Hulk grinned and said, "Kid, don't forget: You ain't the only badass around these parts. Those four motherfuckers ain't all that. I deal with worse every day. Anyways, we need to shut up now. You just get on home and wait for me. I'll see you soon."

"Okay, Hulk. You're the boss. Thanks again, man. I feel guilty about dragging you away from pussy."

"Yeah, well, payback's a bitch," Hulk said as he rode away.

As he watched Hulk head eastward on 15th Street, Clint turned and headed westbound on 15th and then cut across Custer to 14th Street and headed back to his apartment in East Plano. He felt a little ashamed to be taking the long way around while his buddy was checking out the four bikers alone, but he thought it prudent nonetheless.

When Clint got back to the complex, he checked to make sure that the cover was on his bike; then he parked, went inside, and locked the door. He left the two weapons in his truck but made sure that he had a couple more handy. He loaded his 12-gauge bird gun with magnum #4 buckshot and his .38 with "+P" rounds, 125-grain semi-jacketed hollow points.

Clint was tempted to turn on the TV, but there wasn't much on in the middle of the night; so he turned his stereo to the local classical station but kept the volume low. The DJ had just spun Beethoven's Piano Sonata No. 14 in C-sharp minor, the "Moonlight Sonata." Clint leaned back on the couch, closed his eyes, and listened closely to one of the most beautiful piano masterpieces ever composed.

Clint tried to put the Bandidos out of his mind and focused instead on his time with Dani. He couldn't help but smile, and then he remembered that Beethoven had dedicated this particular sonata to a beautiful young countess with whom he was in love. Clint was particularly fond of the opening adagio, which Hector Berlioz had said "is one of those poems that human language does not know how to qualify." Clint had learned to play it pretty well years before, and he wondered if he could still do it justice. He thought that he might like to play it for Dani one day. Although he had wanted to stay awake until Hulk got there, he couldn't fight sleep now. He drifted off and dreamed of Dani.

The hard knock on the door shocked him awake. In his dream he and Dani were naked and wrapped in each other's arms, and he awoke in a disoriented funk. He sat there for a brief moment and then grabbed his .38. Then he felt silly, realizing that the Bandidos wouldn't have knocked. Just then he heard another knock, a little louder than the first.

"Sasquatch! You in there? Open up; it's Roy!"

Clint opened the door with his .38 in hand and said, "Come on in, Hulk," and Hulk saw the snub-nose revolver and smiled.

"You think those bikers would knock first?" Hulk asked with a smile.

"No, I reckon not. How'd it go?"

"Oh, fine. You got any beer?"

Clint said, "No, but I have a bottle of 101."

"Any tequila?"

"No, just the Turkey. That'll have to do."

"Okay, then Wild Turkey it is."

As Clint retrieved the bottle of whiskey from the freezer and grabbed a couple of glasses, he asked again, "Well, how'd it go?"

"I almost missed them. When I got back to the Pit Grill, they'd already saddled up and left. Since you said they'd been headed north, I decided to light a shuck in that direction. I caught up to them just the other side of McKinney and followed from about a half mile back. I turned around in Denison when it looked like they were going to keep going into Oklahoma. Then I headed back here. I would have been here sooner, but I got pulled over by a county mounty near Van Alstyne. He was willing to show me a little professional courtesy, but I had to humor him with some cop talk for a few minutes."

"So it was probably nothing. Right?" Clint asked, needing Hulk's reassurance.

"Yeah, kid, you're okay. They weren't on any scouting mission or nothing like that. They were just out for a ride, maybe heading up to Durant. I hear they may be starting up a chapter in southeastern Oklahoma. Anyways, the bottom line is that I don't think you have anything to worry about."

"Shit, Hulk, I feel awful. I feel like such a pussy for freaking out like that, and I feel even worse about dragging you away from a piece of ass."

"Ah, don't sweat it, kid. She was a bit of a skank anyway—probably give me clap, or worse." Hulk was smiling, but Clint wasn't sure that he was really telling the truth. He still felt guilty about Hulk's sacrifice.

"Well, I'm sorry anyway," Clint said. "I'll try to be more of a man next time. Here," he said, handing Hulk a shot of bourbon, "maybe this'll make you feel better."

"No, booze never makes me feel better, but it don't stop me from trying," Hulk said, just before slamming down his shot. "No, not better. Give me another."

Clint poured Hulk a bigger shot this time and said, "Here, this one's bigger. Maybe that will help."

Hulk slammed it down and said, "No, still not better. Give me another."

The third shot was even bigger, and Hulk slammed it down and said, "Yeah, that's starting to make me feel a little better. You know, the stuff's pretty good neat and cold. I'll have to remember that. Say, what's that shit you're listening to?"

Clint listened for a few seconds and said, "Oh, that's Antonín Dvořák's Ninth Symphony, 'From the New World,' second movement. You may have heard that largo melody as a funeral hymn called 'Going Home.' It's really quite a remarkable composition, probably my favorite symphony."

Hulk stood open-mouthed, staring at Clint for a while before shaking his head as if to banish an unwanted image from his mind.

He said, "Jesus Christ, Sasquatch! I can't listen to that shit when I'm sober. I sure don't want to listen to it while I'm drinking."

"Well, I guess I could break out my Barry Manilow and John Denver eight-tracks," Clint said with a smirk.

"Ah, shit, kid. That was beyond the limits of good taste. You trying to make me puke for sure?"

"Seriously, you like Marty Robbins? My dad's a huge Marty fan, and a little of it rubbed off on me."

"Yeah, sure. Put in old Marty. I love those old western songs of his."

Clint put in the eight-track tape, and Marty Robbins began singing, "Out in the West Texas town of El Paso, I fell in love with a Mexican girl . . . ." Clint and Hulk sat down on the couch with their drinks. It was morning now but still felt like night.

"Hulk, are you leveling with me about those Bandidos?"

"Yeah, Sasquatch, you know I am. I'd never lie to you about something like that. If these guys really come after you, I don't want you to be blind-sided, and for the record, I hope I'm right there beside you. Yes, I'm telling you like it is. I always will."

Clint just looked at his drink and nodded, so Hulk added, "And listen here, kid. Don't feel bad about calling me tonight. You got good reason to be a little jumpy when it comes to those guys. You'd be a damn fool not to worry some. Don't give it a second thought. It's like a cop calling for backup—no need for what we call 'tombstone courage.' Trying to be too brave can get a guy dead in a hurry. Better safe than sorry."

"Okay, thanks, Hulk. You're a good friend."

They sat there listening to some of Marty's best western songs; the stereo played the eight-track album over and over. Though they continued to drink whiskey, they kept a moderate pace and didn't get too drunk. Eventually they both dozed off. After a while, Clint woke up and made his way to his bed, fell across it, and went back to sleep immediately.

Clint awoke to the smell of coffee and bacon. He looked at the clock and saw that it was almost 2:00 in the afternoon. As he got off the bed, Hulk saw him and said, "Kid, you eat pretty good for a single guy. I got nothing but beer and moldy Chinese leftovers in my fridge, but yours looks like your mom does your grocery shopping."

"What can I say? I'm a hungry guy. I like to eat well, breakfast especially."

Hulk said, "Well, we got bacon, eggs, hashbrowns and biscuits this morning—uh, I mean afternoon—plus orange juice and coffee. Got to get that whiskey out of our heads before we go to work."

"Go to work? What do you mean?"

"You're going to work with me today. Time for you to see what being a cop is all about."

"Is that kosher?"

"Sure, you can do what we call a ride-along anytime. We just got to get my boss's okay, and you got to sign a release form. You got to promise you won't sue us if you get killed."

They both chuckled, and then Clint said, "It sounds like fun, but I should probably take a rain check. I have a couple of errands that I need to run, and I haven't seen my folks in a while. Can we plan to do it another time, maybe in a week or two?"

"Yeah, sure, there's no rush. We can do it anytime."

Clint watched as Hulk put the finishing touches on their breakfast. He was a little surprised that Hulk knew his way around a kitchen, but then again, Clint knew his way around a kitchen, too. Lots of men do. Hulk loaded up their plates as Clint set up the TV trays by the couch. Clint turned on the radio and turned the dial until he heard country music coming through clearly, and once everything was ready, they sat at the couch and began eating. Clint hadn't bothered to get a kitchen set yet because he didn't really have enough room for it anyway.

As they ate, Clint said, "You know, Hulk. I had a date last night. I think this woman may be special."

"The mulatto chick Whitely told me about?"

"Damn! News travels fast, but yeah, that's the one. Just don't call her a chick, though. I've never liked that term, and I especially don't think of Dani that way."

"You're not in love. Are you kid? Please tell me you got more sense than that."

"No, I can't really say that I'm in love—not yet anyway. But I am feeling something that I've never felt before."

"You're just wanting to taste a little lump of brown sugar; that's all. But trust me—pussy's all pink on the inside."

"Come on, Hulk. That's pretty fucking crude," Clint said, obviously offended. "I'm not thinking like that at all. I really like this woman. Show a little support for a friend."

"Hey, the fact that I'm here right now shows my support, my friend. I'm sorry if I touched a nerve. I just don't want to see you get mixed up in something that could turn out badly, and interracial relationships in Texas have a way of doing that."

"You're right, Hulk. You're here because I needed a favor, and you jumped out of bed and came running without a second thought. That proves you're a good friend, and I don't take that for granted. I appreciate your concern, but you don't have to be so crude. Just don't talk about Dani like that—please. I'm not just in this for sex. I really like her, man. Okay?"

"Yeah, sure, kid. I'm sorry. So, when are y'all getting together again?"

"Tomorrow night, and hopefully the whole weekend. In case Tom didn't tell you, I'm suspended until Monday morning, and Dani's kids are with their dad this weekend."

"Yeah, I talked to Whitely, which is partly why I'm so concerned. What's this about kids?"

"Dani has a couple of kids, a ten-year-old girl and an eight-year-old boy."

"A ready-made family. How long she been divorced?"

Clint pushed his eggs around on his plate for a moment. "Well, uh, she's not exactly divorced yet."

"Holy shit! You mean you're looking to fuck a married woman?"

"There you go again. No, I'm not just looking to fuck this woman at all. I'm hoping for a relationship. Regardless, she's been separated for a while, but her old man won't give her a divorce. She's just not pushing it yet—can't afford to. I'm trying not to worry about that right now."

"Listen here, kid. You'd better worry about that. I'll tell you that much right now. You'd better think long and hard about getting involved in all this. Black, married, kids," Hulk said, his voice trailing off as he shook his head. "For Christ sakes, Clint, you're just a fucking teenager! I'm sorry, son, but you're getting in way over your head."

Before he had time to think twice about it, Clint heard himself saying, "I haven't even told you the worst part yet."

"Oh, shit, this just keeps getting better and better!" Hulk said, obviously quite perturbed. "Okay, so what's the worst part?"

"Forget it. I'm sorry I mentioned it."

"No, kid, I'm not letting you off that easy. You did mention it, and if it's any worse that what you already told me, then I *really* need to know what it is."

Wishing that he'd kept his mouth shut, Clint said, "She just broke up with someone who's crazy jealous."

"Oh, that's sweet!" Hulk said in his most sarcastic tone. "Black, kids, husband, *and* a jealous boyfriend! What, the Bandidos don't scare you enough?"

Clint would never admit that his buddy had made a good point. Clint had enough to worry about right now without getting mixed up in potentially more drama. This situation had "Warning: Stay Away!" written all over it, and Clint's head had no trouble grasping that truth.

Unfortunately Clint's heart would overrule his brain. He'd already crossed a threshold of sorts with Dani, perhaps even fallen halfway, and he was just stubborn enough to see it through. Besides, despite his objections to Hulk's crudeness, Clint's dick was probably doing some of his thinking.

They had both finished their food now, and Clint gathered up their dishes and took them to the kitchen. "You want more coffee or orange juice?" he asked Hulk from the kitchen.

"Yeah, if you have a mug I can take with me, I would like another cup of coffee."

"Okay, no problem. What time do you have to be at work?"

"I don't punch a time clock, but I need to be there around 1600 hours." Hulk paused for a moment and then added, "You never answered my question."

135

Clint played dumb, asking "Which one was that?"

"Don't the Bandidos scare you bad enough?"

"I'm sorry. I thought that was a rhetorical question. Yeah, the Bandidos scare me badly enough. I don't worry about one or two, maybe even three of them, but if it comes to a showdown, I doubt if my odds will be that good."

"That's right, kid. You really want to add more shit to the pile you're standing in? Knee deep ain't enough for you—you like it up to your waist?

They just looked at each other for a minute. It was a bit of a stare-down, and Clint blinked first. He had poured coffee into an insulated mug, and he averted his gaze as he handed it to Hulk.

Clint said grudgingly, "I reckon you're probably right."

"Think about it. Now I've got to go. Thanks for the coffee. I'll get the mug back to you later," Hulk said as he opened the door.

"Hulk, stop," Clint said as he stepped toward the door and held out his hand. As they shook, he said, "Don't worry about the mug. Listen, I'm sorry to get you out of bed in the middle of the night for a false alarm, but I want you to know that I really appreciate it. I owe you one, and I won't forget it."

Hulk smiled and said, "You're welcome, Sasquatch, and you can quit thanking me now." Hulk winked, turned around, and walked toward the parking lot. As he turned at the end of the sidewalk, he yelled back over his shoulder, "You think about what I said!"

Clint said nothing as he shut the door and locked all three locks. He heard Hulk start his Harley and rumble away.

Clint felt guilty for lying to Hulk. He didn't have any errands that couldn't wait, and he'd just seen his folks at Sunday dinner. The truth was that he needed some time to himself. He was suffering a little social overload and needed simply to be alone for a while. Clint doubted that Hulk would understand, and he definitely didn't want Hulk to think that he didn't want to go to work with him. Clint did want to ride along with Hulk—just not today.

Backup

Clint changed the radio station back to classical and started cleaning the kitchen. At first the station was playing Gershwin's "An American in Paris," which Clint could barely tolerate, but luckily it was near the end. The next piece was Tartini's famous violin sonata, the "Devil's Trill." Clint loved that one, and he wondered if it had anything to do with Charlie Daniels' current hit, "The Devil Went Down to Georgia." By the time the violin quit trilling, Clint had finished his chore.

As the classical music continued on the radio, Clint picked up John Irving's *The World According to Garp* and sat on the couch. He found his place and began reading Garp's short story, "The Pension Grillparzer." What was left of today was going to be real vacation—nothing but rest, relaxation, and peaceful solitude. He propped his feet on a chair and, completely comfortable now, drifted off into his own little world of music and literature. This was heaven to Clint in a way that few could understand.

Six Feet Six & Bulletproof

For the rest of Thursday and most of Friday, Clint was alone and thankful for it. He caught up on some reading, and he listened to a lot of good music, all classical. Clint enjoyed many different types of music, but nothing could calm or stir his soul the way that classical music did. No matter what he was feeling or needed to feel, classical music seemed the right choice more often than not, and it always created the perfect frame of mind for reading. Clint figured that if he ever had enough money that he didn't have to work, he could be perfectly content with a good stereo and a nice collection of classical records and books—well, and maybe a Harley.

Clint's range of reading material was as broad as his tastes in music. He really didn't read a lot, not nearly as much as he would have liked, but truth be told, he would read just about anything. Although he was partial to fiction, especially a good character study, his tastes were quite varied. He had memorized huge chunks of the 1977 *Shooter's Bible* and had a genuinely encyclopedic knowledge of firearms and ammunition. At the same time, he was so moved by Irwin Shaw's *Rich Man, Poor Man*, and by the character of Tom Jordache in particular, that he had read the novel three times—the first two consecutively.

Of course, Clint had also spent countless hours reading the Holy Bible and could impress most ministers with his command of Scripture, but even he would confess that he was allowing himself to get rusty in that department. Although he occasionally felt guilty about it, most times he didn't particularly care. His heart was Christian—his mind agnostic.

It would be a considerable understatement to say that Clint was conflicted. He loved spiritual issues—matters of God—and prayed frequently, but he hated religion. He rationalized that God had not created religion—that it was a man-made adulteration of what God had in mind. It was a constant struggle. At any rate, his Bible was gathering dust, and today had been a day of mostly *Garp*. He had read "The Pension Grillparzer" twice and marveled at Irving's skill.

As his date with Dani drew nearer, Clint grew more and more excited. As much as he enjoyed being sequestered in his little apartment, he was ready for her company. The fluttering of the butterflies in his stomach made him feel a bit silly. After all, he was no stranger to a woman's company; he had been on many dates. Even so, this one felt different—special. It was almost as if it were his first, and he felt like a schoolboy. He decided to go buy a single red rose to give to Dani that night.

Being a Friday, Clint knew that he would need to arrive a good bit early to scope out a table. He arrived a full two hours before Dani could be there, but he still had to wait for a spot at the bar. He felt jittery being crammed onto a stool between strangers, but at least it gave him plenty of time to make sure that he had a table by the time Dani arrived. He ordered a 101 straight up with a Guinness back and started a tab.

Two pretty young women sat across the bar from Clint. They were friends, obviously together and without dates. They kept trying to make eye contact with Clint, but he conspicuously avoided it. He hoped they'd get the message, but they didn't. As one of them watched and smiled, the other made her way around the bar to where Clint sat.

With a slight giggle, the young woman said, "My friend over there would like to meet you." Her friend blushed, and Clint winked at her.

"Oh, is that so?" Clint responded. "I think you probably want to meet me, too. Am I right?"

"Well, yeah, I guess so. Why don't you come over and talk to us?"

"You see, there are a couple of problems with that. First, there's no room over there, and there's not a table in the place to be had right now. More importantly, I'm actually here to meet someone else, which is why I have the rose," Clint said, holding up the rose. "She won't be here for a while, but I imagine she'd take a pretty dim view of me chatting it up with you and your friend when she gets here. So, as tempting as your offer is, I'll have to pass this time. Please don't take it personally."

"Uh, okay, sure, no problem. Sorry to bother you."

"Oh, it's no bother—just bad timing," Clint said as she walked away.

Clint watched as the young woman relayed what he'd said to her friend. The friend looked at him, smiled, and shrugged her shoulders. Clint got the bartender's attention and told him to put their next round on his tab.

Although crowds often made Clint uneasy, he was fond of watching people. He enjoyed looking at individuals, couples, and groups and trying to figure out what people were talking about and thinking. It had been a pastime of his for several years, and he was actually getting pretty good at reading lips.

Clint thought that he could understand a third or maybe even half of what people were saying at times, and that was often enough to catch the gist of a conversation. Even so, Clint found great sport in trying to fill in the blanks via non-verbal communication and other subtle factors. He enjoyed trying to read minds, and it seemed clear to him that people often didn't say what they were thinking. He figured that all this would make him a better cop one day, so he worked to hone his skills.

Clint was able to catch the hostess as she walked through the bar area. It was the same one who'd been working on Wednesday night when he and Dani were there, and she remembered him. He slipped her a ten this time to make sure that he and Dani had the same table. As soon as it was available, he settled up with the bartender and moved over to the table to wait for Dani. Clint checked his watch, and it was almost midnight. He figured that the next 40 minutes or so would pass very slowly.

Suddenly Dani appeared. Clint hadn't seen her come in, and it was as if she had beamed to that spot Star Trek style.

"You're early!" he said quite loudly.

"You're not disappointed. Are you?"

"Oh, God no!" Clint stood up and kissed Dani. They sat on opposite sides of the table so they could see each other better. Clint handed the rose to her.

"I hope you're not allergic."

Dani flashed that beautiful smile of hers, and her whole face lit up. She said, "No, I'm not. Gee, I can't remember the last time anyone gave me a flower. It's beautiful. Thanks."

"Well, I thought of reciting one of Shakespeare's sonnets, but I figured that might be a little over the top at this stage. Maybe some day, but for now the rose will have to take the place of flowery speech."

"The rose does just fine," she said, beaming.

They gazed happily into each other's eyes for a moment, and then Clint asked, "How'd you manage to get off early tonight?"

"I just talked my boss into letting me leave a little early—said it was real important. It wasn't the easiest thing to do with all the authorizations on a Friday night, but I just couldn't wait. Lucky for me she never comes here, and if any of my friends show up, they won't rat me out."

"Well, I'm glad I didn't have to wait any longer. I'm very happy to see you; plus now I won't have to fight off all the women in the place who keep coming on to me," Clint said with a chuckle and a wink.

"Are you kidding me? Ladies been hitting on you? I'm not surprised. Place like this. Friday night crowd. Figures. But it ends now!"

Just then the waiter arrived, looked at Dani, and asked, "What'll it be tonight?"

"I'll have a Singapore Sling," she answered, smiling at Clint.

When the waiter turned his way, Clint smiled back at Dani and said, "And I'll have a Half-and-Half."

"Be right back," the waiter said and then turned and walked away.

"We may as well wax nostalgic for our first date," Clint said. "It was a whole two days ago."

Clint and Dani both smiled. They spent the better part of the next two hours much as they had on Wednesday night. They held hands, talked, laughed, and got to know each other a little better. Dani was impressed with what she perceived to be remarkable maturity for a kid so young, but more than that, she just really, really liked him. He was smart and funny, very sweet and gentlemanly, and despite his baby face, he was quite handsome. He also had an amazing rock-solid body that she couldn't wait to see naked, but she hoped that he wouldn't be disappointed with what two kids and a hard life had done to hers.

Clint was just as impressed with Dani. Although she hadn't been to college and probably wasn't as "book smart" as he, she was a sharp cookie. He also liked her sense of humor and how easy it seemed to be to talk to her, and of course, she was also gorgeous. Yes, there was that, and he ached to hold her, skin to skin. He had seen and touched her face, kissed it. It was the most beautiful shade of brown and oh, so soft. He wanted to see, to touch, to kiss, all the soft spots of her body. He wasn't certain that it would happen tonight. He wasn't the kind to push such things, but he knew it would happen—and probably soon.

Clint asked the waiter for the check a little early, and by the time he'd settled up, he and Dani were practically running toward the door. Unlike the last time, they were both in a hurry to leave tonight. When they got outside, it dawned on them that they were in separate vehicles, so they stopped to discuss what would happen next. They stood on the sidewalk, facing each other and holding hands. Dani raised the rose to her face, sniffed it, and smiled.

"You want to come to my place?" she asked coyly.

"Sure, or we could go to mine. I may be a single guy, but I keep the place pretty neat. It's not too far—just over in Plano."

"I'm much farther, but we might be more comfortable there."

"Where do you live?"

"South Oak Cliff," Dani replied, curious how Clint would respond.

"Sure, you're probably right. We'd probably be more comfortable there. It really doesn't matter to me either way, just so we have more time together."

"You don't mind driving all the way over there? Oh, and just so you know, there aren't a lot of white folks over that way."

"It doesn't matter to me," Clint said honestly. "That's my truck over there. I'll just follow you."

"You sure you don't mind?"

"No, of course not, but let's get going before the sun comes up." As Dani giggled, he added "Here, I'll walk you to your car."

They walked hand-in-hand, and about halfway to Dani's T-Bird, Clint heard someone say, "Nigger."

Dani wanted to keep going, but Clint stopped in his tracks. He turned to face two young men, probably in their early 20s. They were well-dressed but obviously ill-mannered. They didn't appear to be sloppy drunk, but Clint assumed that booze was talking to some degree. They had stopped about ten feet behind Clint and Dani, and they just stood there simpering. They were both average size, around six feet and 160 pounds or so. Clint thought, "Yeah, it must be liquid courage."

Clint released Dani's hand and discreetly assumed a defensive T-stance. He thought he knew which one had made the remark, so he looked that one straight in the eye.

"Excuse me?" Clint asked.

"You heard me, Big Tex. I called her a nigger, and that makes you a nigger lover." The other one laughed so stupidly that Clint wondered if his family tree branched.

"Come on, Clint. Let's just leave," Dani said, tugging on his arm. Clint could feel his blood starting to boil, but at the same time, he heard Doug's voice telling him just to walk away, or at least to try.

Making intense eye contact with the guy doing all the talking, Clint said, "Listen. It's late, and you're drunk. So I'm just going to walk away, and in the morning you'll wake up and realize what a big mistake you almost made." Against his better judgement, Clint turned his back to the two men, took Dani's hand in his, and started walking toward her car again.

Dani whispered in Clint's direction, "See what I mean?"

Clint could hear the men following behind, so he turned to look over his shoulder. Just then a third man came trotting down the sidewalk toward the first two guys. As the third guy approached his two buddies, he said, "Sorry guys. Had to piss. What's up? Our car's the other way."

"We're just following this nigger lover and his nigger WHORE! That's all."

Clint stopped again and turned around to face the three men, and again Dani tugged at his arm. This time she pleaded with him to leave, but he stood his ground.

"Dani, I want you to go to your car and wait for me. I'll be there in a minute. We're just going to have a quiet discussion about etiquette. It won't take long."

Looking very afraid, Dani did as Clint said. Clint couldn't help but notice that the third guy was much larger than the first two. In fact, he was about Clint's size, if not slightly bigger, but he looked a little soft.

As calmly as he could, Clint looked at the big guy and said, "Listen, I don't want any trouble here tonight, so you need to take control of your buddies. My lady friend is not a nigger, nor is she a whore. I'd appreciate it if you guys would just be quiet and let me walk away. How about it?"

The big guy was in a jam. Clint could tell that he didn't want to fight, but he didn't want his friends to see him back down either.

As the big guy considered his options, Clint told him, "And just so you know, if anything happens here, you'll be the first to hit the concrete." Clint meant it, and the big guy knew that Clint meant it.

"Come on, guys. Let's just leave," the big guy said to his friends. "We don't need any trouble."

"What do you mean, Trace? You're as big as him, and there's three of us. We can take him. You know I hate niggers, and I don't cotton to nigger lovers. Whites and niggers don't mix. Let's teach this boy a lesson." He had the mouth, but he was clearly expecting Trace to do his fighting.

"Trace," Clint said, seething. "Are you really going to let your friend get your ass kicked tonight? Because that's exactly what's going to happen if you don't get this ignorant, in-bred cracker out of my face right now."

Apparently that flipped a switch in the guy with the mouth because he suddenly lunged forward and threw a wild punch in the general direction of Clint's head. Clint slipped the punch, spun, and kicked Trace in the chest. The big guy didn't go down, but he stumbled backward, looking both shocked and scared.

"We don't have to do this, Trace," Clint said as he took a step forward, but apparently Trace felt locked into it now.

Trace came at Clint swinging wildly with both fists. Obviously no one had ever taught him how to fight. A boy or a teenager can get by on his size alone most of the time. He can talk a good fight and intimidate folks into backing down, and sometimes brute strength—and luck—can win a fight against an unskilled opponent. At about 18 or 20, though, a guy reaches a point when that's not enough anymore. There are people out there who will flat-out kick your ass if you don't know what you're doing, and they'll take extra pleasure in the fact that they took a big guy down. Trace was about to learn a lesson the hard way.

As Trace waved his big fists awkwardly around Clint's upper body, Clint stole a glance at his buddies and realized that they had no intention of fighting. Maybe they had watched Trace get lucky before, and they expected it to happen again. They had started this, but now they were mere spectators. Clint stepped inside Trace's wild swings and popped him squarely in the mouth with a good jab.

Trace stumbled backward and Clint said, "You can still quit," but Trace regained his footing and stepped forward again, not saying anything but continuing to throw wide, harmless punches, if one could really call them that. Again Clint stepped up close, but this time he popped him twice—two stiff jabs right on the kisser.

"I'm telling you, Trace. You need to end this right now. Just stop," Clint pleaded. Trace just shook his head and plodded forward. Clint glanced again at Trace's buddies, and they were still just watching. Clint shook his head and sighed. "Okay, Trace, if this is the way it has to be."

Clint wanted to end it quickly. This wasn't fun, and he had better things to do. When Trace came forward again, Clint faked an overhand right, and Trace threw both hands up to block it. When he did, Clint gave him a solid round kick to the chest, spun, and followed it with a back kick to the same spot. Trace went down and didn't get up. Clint stepped up to take a look. He was relieved when he saw that Trace's eyes were open.

When Trace turned his eyes to meet Clint's, Clint said, "I tried to warn you. Now stay there. Even if you can get up, don't." Trace made no attempt to get up, so Clint turned toward Trace's buddies. They had the proverbial deer-in-the-headlights look.

Clint said, "It doesn't seem fair for Trace to be lying there in pain, probably with some broken ribs, maybe some busted teeth, when you two are the ones who started this. Now you have two choices: Go over there and apologize to my lady, or do your own fighting. And as much as you deserve to be beaten—and as much as I'd enjoy kicking the shit out of you right now—I hope you choose the apology.

She deserves that much. I'll give you three seconds to decide. One, two . . . ."

The two were running toward Dani's car, and Clint ran after them to make sure that they had no nefarious intent. Rather than getting in the car, Dani had waited at the driver's door and had watched the whole thing. The two crackers stopped a little short with Clint literally breathing down their necks. The Mouth turned and looked at Clint and then turned back toward Dani and grudgingly said, "Sorry."

"Sorry, what?" Clint asked.

The Mouth turned back toward Clint and asked, "What do you mean?"

"If you were apologizing to your mother, what would you say?"

"Sorry, Mom?"

Exasperated, Clint said, "You really are a dumb bastard. Aren't you? Sorry, *ma'am*. Call her *ma'am*."

The Mouth paused for a moment. He didn't want to say it. Finally he said, "Sorry, ma'am." He wasn't very convincing, but Clint let him slide.

Clint turned and looked toward Trace. Someone had helped him up, and he was leaning, kind of half-sitting, on a car bumper. A small crowd had gathered, exiting patrons and some of the staff. Clint turned back toward The Mouth's buddy and said, "Now you, and say it like you mean it."

"I'm sorry, ma'am," he offered a little more convincingly than his buddy had said it.

Clint said, "Now you two come here."

They followed Clint to the rear of the car. Clint stepped between them and Dani, and they turned to face him. Clint reached and grabbed each man around the neck. Holding one man in each hand, and without as much effort as one might expect, he lifted the two men high off the ground and held them there. Clint was not choking them, but it was still quite uncomfortable for them. Their faces were white with terror. Each wrapped his hands around Clint's and tried to break free, but it was no use. They looked to Dani in desperation, but she said nothing.

Clint finally said, "I hope you assholes know that I could kill you right now, but I'm not going to. I only hope you learned your lesson, but something tells me no. Now you just get over there and help your buddy, and I hope he kicks your asses when he's feeling better. I get the impression he's a decent guy, but he needs to find new friends."

Clint placed the men gently on the ground and let go of their necks. They turned and ran quickly toward Trace. The crowd had grown much larger, and Clint was surprised that he hadn't yet heard an approaching siren. Bar fights tend to get a quick response from any cop who's free. Perhaps no one had called the police.

Clint returned to Dani, hugged her, and asked, "Are you okay?"

"Yeah, sure, I'm fine. You see what I mean when I say that whites and blacks together can lead to trouble?" Dani looked very serious, and it worried Clint.

"Come on, Dani. Time's are changing. Don't let a couple of racist pricks ruin things for us. Let's just get out of here. We can talk about it if you want at your place, but I'd just as soon drop the subject."

Dani happened to look over Clint's shoulder. She gasped, and her eyes widened. Clint turned quickly, and one of the crackers—The Mouth—was walking quickly toward Clint. In his right hand he held a revolver, and he was pointing it toward Clint's face.

"Get down, Dani," Clint said calmly as he stepped toward the guy with the gun. Dani took cover in front of her car and watched as Clint and the other guy met in the middle of the parking lot.

One of the onlookers screamed, "He's got a gun!"

Another yelled, "Someone call the cops!"

Clint and the other guy had stopped and were standing at arm's length in the middle of the parking lot. Clint said, "You don't want to do this . . ." and then quickly threw out his left hand toward the gun.

Clint had hoped to wrap his hand around the cylinder to keep it from turning, which would prevent it from firing, but he was just a fraction of a second too late. Clint was deafened by the report of the gun, and he felt a powerful stinging sensation above his right eye. He could smell the gunpowder. Several people screamed, but Clint couldn't hear them.

At this point Clint had wrapped his powerful hand around the revolver, and he easily wrested it from the other fellow's grip. The guy dropped to his knees and cried, "Momma!" Clint smelled shit and realized that the guy had soiled himself.

As blood ran down the right side of Clint's face, he calmly unloaded the revolver, five live rounds and one spent casing, and made note that it was a .357 magnum Smith and Wesson. Clint thought, "At least he has good taste in guns." Clint stuck the ammo in his pocket, and then he looked up and saw a man wearing a Bennigan's shirt who had the look of a manager. Clint walked over toward the man and held out the gun with the cylinder open.

Clint said, "Here, do you mind holding this for the police, please? It's not loaded."

The man replied, "Yeah, sure. Are you okay? You're bleeding a lot."

Dani had run up to Clint, and when she saw his face, she screamed, "Oh, my God! You're shot!"

Clint realized that his shirt was soaked, and the blood had made its way down to his jeans. He reached up and felt the wound. The bullet had just clipped him. Part of his right eyebrow was missing, including a chunk of flesh beneath it. He didn't think it was a particularly bad wound, but any head wound is likely to bleed a great deal. It would probably leave a decent scar, too. Clint's ears were still ringing, but his hearing was coming back.

Clint said, "I'm okay, Dani." Then turning to the crowd, he asked, "Anybody got a hanky?" Clint could hear the sirens now. A middle-aged fellow in a three-piece suit stepped forward and handed Clint a handkerchief.

The man said, "Here, it's clean."

Clint nodded and replied, "Thank you, sir. I appreciate it."

Clint folded the handkerchief and pressed it against his eyebrow to staunch the bleeding. Dani was sobbing now, so he turned to her and placed his free arm around her. "It's okay, honey," Clint said. "I'm alright."

Trace had regained some of his strength now and looked thoroughly disgusted. Conspicuously avoiding Clint, he limped over to his stinky friend, who had curled into a fetal position and was still bawling for his mother. Trace said, "You stupid motherfucker," and gave his former friend a good kick in the gut.

As Stinky sucked for air, Trace pointed an accusing finger at him and said, "This is on you, asshole. It's all on you. That's your gun. I didn't even know you had it. I ain't taking no rap for you on top of the whooping I just got. FUCK YOU!" Trace looked around for his other buddy, but the guy was gone. He had lit a shuck about the time Trace's foot made contact with Stinky's belly. Maybe he wasn't so dumb after all.

A couple of Addison police cruisers arrived on the scene, followed shortly by a Dallas unit. The Dallas officers were slightly out of their jurisdiction but had apparently been summoned as backup. Suburban agencies sometimes did that. Even after it became clear that the Dallas cops weren't needed, they stuck around and observed while the Addison officers sorted things out. It must have been a slow night in Big D.

The police interviewed all of the participants and several of the witnesses, and it quickly became clear to them what had happened. They arrested Trace and The Mouth and placed them, cuffs behind, in separate cruisers so they couldn't speak to one another. The other cracker was nowhere to be found.

Clint and Dani were leaning against her car. He still had one arm around her while the other hand held the handkerchief against his wound. She had stopped crying but was still shaken by the ordeal. Despite Clint's objections, one of the Addison officers had called for an ambulance, and when it arrived, two EMTs checked Clint's wound.

One of them said, "It looks a little nasty and probably needs some stitches, and the doctor will want to give you an antibiotic, maybe a tetanus, too. It's not too bad, though. You want us to take you somewhere, or can you drive yourself?"

Clint waved them off. "I don't need a ride, thank you," Clint said. "I can drive myself."

"Okay, suit yourself. Just be sure to get that taken care of tonight. Don't wait."

"Okay," Clint said, disappointed that he still couldn't go to Dani's.

One of the Dallas officers approached Clint and said, "Excuse me. You okay?"

"Yeah, I'm fine."

"One of our detectives heard some of the radio transmissions, and he asked me to find out if your name is Clint."

"Yeah, I'm Clint, and you can tell Hulk that I'm okay. And tell him thanks for asking. How'd he know it was me?"

The officer laughed and said, "Well, one of the radio calls said something about 'a cross between Randy White and Bruce Lee,' and he put two-and-two together."

Clint smiled and said, "Well, now we know how he made detective." Clint and the officer both laughed.

"Truth is, Roy's a helluva narc, maybe the best we have. How do you know him?"

"A retired cop I work with introduced us," Clint said. "He's become a good friend, and I'm damn lucky to have him looking out for me. Listen, officer, I don't mean to be rude, but it's been a really bad night. I've had a fight. I've been shot. My lady is scared to death, and I still have to stop by the ER before I can take her home. I'd really love to chat, but this isn't the best time. Maybe I'll bump into you at choir practice sometime. I go to Cassidy's with Hulk from time to time."

"Sure, kid," the officer said. "Sounds good. I'll let Roy know you're okay, and you take care now. Good luck to you." The officer shook Clint's hand, nodded at Dani, and returned to his patrol car. He said something to his partner as they were getting back in their cruiser, and then he made a radio call.

"Officer!" Clint yelled in the direction of the primary Addison cop. "May I go now?"

The officer walked back over to Clint and said, "Yeah, kid, we have everything we need at this point. A detective will be calling you soon to get a formal statement. You'll need to come to the station for that. And at some point I'm sure you'll have to testify—unless these yahoos get smart and cop a plea. We have all your information, and we'll be in touch. You be sure to get that head taken care of right now. Okay?"

"Yes, sir, I will," Clint said as he shook the officer's hand, and the officer walked back to where he and the other cops were still interviewing witnesses.

Clint let out a huge sigh and said, "Damn! What a night. Are you okay, Dani?"

"Yeah, Clint, I'm okay. I'm just really shook up and exhausted."

"Maybe you should just go on home and get some sleep, and I'll go get my head checked out."

"Not on your life, young man! You just got shot sticking up for me. I think I'll see this through."

"You sure?"

"Yes, I'm sure. Now where do you want to go?"

Clint thought for a moment and said, "Let's just scoot over to Campbell and go to Owen Memorial. Hopefully it won't be too crowded, and then when they're done with me, we can go to my apartment. Is that okay? We both need some rest, and that's a lot closer than going all the way to South Oak Cliff."

"Yeah, sure, that's fine with me. Do you think I should leave my car here?"

"No, I wouldn't. Just follow me." Clint put both of his big arms around Dani and hugged her tightly. Then he pulled back, cupped her face in his hands, and kissed her gently.

"I'm sorry about all of this," he said, "but I promise to make it up to you."

"Okay," she said with a tired smile.

Clint made his way to his truck, and Dani followed him to the hospital on Campbell Road in Richardson. They were lucky. The ER wasn't crowded, and the medical staff got to Clint quickly. He exhibited no symptoms of concussion, and an x-ray confirmed no skull damage. Clint talked the doctor out of stitches, opting for the butterfly tape instead.

A nurse gave Clint a couple of shots, presumably an antibiotic and a tetanus booster, though Clint was too tired to ask. Clint left with a prescription for an oral antibiotic. The doctor had offered him something for pain, but Clint declined. He and Dani walked out of the hospital hand-in-hand, stepped into the morning sunlight, and drove to Plano. Clint and Dani parked next to one another at the complex and walked, holding hands, toward his apartment.

"That's my bike under there," Clint said, pointing toward the gray cover. "Maybe I can take you for a ride later."

"Sure, I'd like that," Dani said, sniffing the rose again.

They made their way to Clint's apartment, and Clint opened the door. "Just a minute," he said. Clint stepped into the apartment first, flipped a light switch, and took a quick look around. Stepping back to the door, he took Dani's hand. He said, "Okay, you can come in."

Dani stepped in and immediately said, "Wow! You're right. This place is pretty neat, neater than mine."

"Well, I don't have kids."

They stepped over to the couch. Clint held out his hand toward the couch, and Dani sat down.

"Listen," Clint said, "I really need to get out of these clothes and get a shower. Is that okay? Will you be okay out here by yourself?"

Dani yawned and said, "Yeah, I'll be fine. Maybe I'll just lie down and snooze until you're done." She stretched out on the couch and fell asleep immediately. Clint bent over and kissed her cheek softly and then headed for the shower.

Clint got undressed and stood in front of the mirror to survey the damage. He had a lot of dried blood from head to toe, except where they'd cleaned him up at the hospital, but other than the crudely trimmed eyebrow, he had only a few minor contusions where Trace's ineffective punches had landed.

He turned on the water and stepped into the shower. Clint had never really cared for hot showers, preferring tepid water instead, but he did run it a little warmer this time. He lathered up and scrubbed himself thoroughly. Being as careful as he could not to get his wound wet, he shampooed his hair, rinsed completely, and stepped out of the shower for another look in the mirror. Then he ran a tub of cold water and put his bloody clothes in it to soak. With a towel wrapped around his waist, he stepped out to check on Dani.

She was sound asleep on the couch, so he went over to the bedroom and put on clean underwear and a pair of workout shorts. He then folded back the covers on the bed and returned to the couch. In one smooth movement he bent over and picked up Dani, and he carried her back to the bed and laid her down gently without waking her up. He removed her shoes, admired her beautiful feet for a moment, and pulled up the sheet to cover her. Clint lay down next to Dani but outside the sheet, kissed her cheek, draped one arm over her body, and joined her in peaceful slumber.

Getting Lucky

Dani awoke disoriented, and it took a moment before she was able to shake loose the cobwebs. She looked at Clint and smiled; then she looked around for a clock. It was almost noon. She lay there for a little while but needed to go to the bathroom, so she slipped out of bed. She was glad to see that she hadn't awakened Clint.

After using the bathroom, Dani nosed around the cabinet and happened to find a new toothbrush, still in the package, so she brushed her teeth. She noticed that the toothpaste tube was squeezed neatly from the bottom, and it made her giggle. This young fellow of hers was anal-retentive, and she was not. She hoped it wouldn't be a problem for them.

Dani drained the pink water from the tub and wrung Clint's clothes as much as she could. She looked at them, shook her head, and thought, "That blood's there to stay." She left them in a pile on the floor, undressed, and took a shower. When she was done, Dani stepped out of the shower, dried off, and hung Clint's clothes on the shower curtain rod. She started to put her clothes back on but stopped herself. Deep in thought, she stood looking at the beautiful, brown, naked woman in the mirror. Eventually she smiled and opened the door.

Dani walked back over to the bed and lay down beside Clint. He was lying on his back, and she studied the full and considerable length of his body and was amazed by its firm beauty. He had both bulk and definition, but not like those freakish body builders, and she had witnessed his almost superhuman strength. She admired his washboard stomach and then softly touched one of the bruises on his chest and thought about the night before.

Dani remembered being utterly scared to death—but also sexually aroused. She stood at her car door and watched as he calmly faced the big guy named Trace and was astonished that such a large man could move so quickly and smoothly. Oh, those moves! Watching him spin and kick and punch had made her wet. Even now the realization embarrassed her.

Clint had tried to walk away. He was bound and determined not to fight, and had it worked out that way, she would have thought no less of him. He only fought when it became clear that there was no alternative. Moreover, although it was patent that Clint could have pummeled Trace to death, he used only the amount of force necessary and not an ounce more. She had never known anyone—certainly not a man—with that much self-control.

Dani remembered watching as Clint effortlessly lifted the two men completely off the ground as if they were a child's rag dolls. She recalled their terrified expressions as they looked to her for intervention, and as she made eye contact with them, for a moment she wanted them to die. She had a flash of Clint ripping their throats open, and for an instant it would have pleased her. She was ashamed of herself for imagining it, for wishing it, but luckily Clint had a cooler head than that.

Perhaps more than anything else, Dani was in awe of Clint's courage. Throughout the whole battle, Clint was completely fearless and in control. Even when facing a man with a gun—even after being shot—Clint was calm and deliberate. She had never seen anything like it, and had she not witnessed it firsthand, she would never believe the story.

How could a young man, this *boy*, learn to be so brave? He couldn't possibly have had enough experience to have learned it. He must have been born that way. It came from his family regardless, and she was looking forward to meeting them. She hoped that Clint had made an accurate assessment of their racial tolerance.

Clint stirred a little but didn't wake up, and Dani began stroking his massive chest and marveled at the difference in size between it and his waist. When Dani's fingers touched a nipple, she lingered to caress it for a moment, and Clint's body shifted. She leaned over and kissed the nipple, massaged it with her tongue, and let a hand wander slowly southward. She slid her hand beneath the waistbands of his shorts and underwear, and her fingers found his penis. Clint stirred still more and whispered her name. She raised her eyes to see his face, but even now he slept. Dani smiled.

Dani began kissing all over Clint's chest. She started gently, but her kisses became progressively harder. She was manipulating his penis now, and it, too, became progressively harder. She felt his hand touch her back, and she looked up. He was awake. He smiled at her and whispered her name sweetly, and she kissed him hard. He pulled her on top of him, wrapped his long arms around her, pulled her very tightly against his body, and kissed her with more passion than she had ever experienced. After a while she sat up and moved her bottom downward to his penis. Though there were two layers of cloth in the way, it had found the spot and was trying its best to break through.

Suddenly Clint turned her over on her back. As she lay there expecting—and wanting—him to mount her, he began merely to look at her body. He started at her face and smiled, and he began moving his gaze slowly, slowly, down her body as if trying to memorize it. When he finally reached her feet, he turned her over on her stomach and went through the same ritual, except that he started at the feet and worked slowly upward.

When Clint had seen everything and committed it to memory, he touched the back of Dani's neck gently and then ran his hand slowly over her back to her buttocks. Pausing for a moment at the butt, Clint dropped to his knees on the floor at the foot of the bed and began moving both hands, gently and slowly, down the back of Dani's legs to her feet.

He caressed one foot, raised it to his lips, and kissed it all over, and then he kissed each toe and stroked it gently with his tongue. He repeated the ritual with the other foot, and Dani felt a chill run down her back—a good one.

When Clint was finished with Dani's feet, he returned his hands to her buttocks. As he squeezed her butt, Dani could hear his breath quickening. Then he bent over and began kissing her buttocks. He slipped off his shorts and underwear and got back up on the bed and began simultaneously kissing and massaging her butt, and after several minutes he scooted upward and began massaging her back, starting just above her butt and moving slowly upward. As Clint's hands moved farther up Dani's back, he adjusted his body upward as well, and by the time his hands reached her shoulders and neck, she could feel the rock between his legs against her butt. It was fiery hot and pulsing. Her juices were absolutely gushing now, and she wanted him inside her.

Clint slid off Dani's back and gently turned her over. He leaned over and kissed her passionately for a long time as one hand kneaded her breasts, first one, then the other, and then both at the same time. Oh, what hands! Then Clint lowered his head and kissed her breasts, again making sure that he neglected neither. She just knew that he would finally mount her at any second, but then he surprised her.

Clint's kisses moved from Dani's breasts to her belly— then farther downward. Clint repositioned himself so that Dani's legs were draped over his shoulders, and he buried his face between her legs. Dani experienced cunnilingus for the very first time. Clint was as good with his tongue as he was with everything else, and Dani had the most explosive orgasm of her life—then another. She had never felt anything like it.

Dani was running her hands through Clint's hair and squeezing his head against her body as she came several more times. She wondered how he could breathe. This went on for quite a long time, and then Dani forced Clint's head up so that they could make eye contact. He smiled, and she mouthed the single word "now." Clint lowered his head and tongue one more time, and he began running his tongue slowly upward. He lingered again momentarily at her breasts and then ran his tongue up to her neck, then along one jaw to her ear. He stopped there and nibbled the ear gently, then pulled away slightly and looked into her eyes with a depth of feeling that made her eyes well up instantly.

Clint did the unthinkable: He whispered, "I love you."

Then Dani did the unthinkable: She whispered back, "I love you, too."

They kissed each other gently, then harder, then passionately. Dani spread her legs, and without releasing the kiss, Clint moved over between her legs. Dani stretched her arms to reach his butt, grabbed it, and pulled him inside of her. She gasped at the penetration. His penis felt like a branding iron, and for a moment she feared that she was really on fire. It was the most surreal sensation—concurrently painful and intensely pleasurable. Almost instantly she started to have orgasms again, powerful orgasms that shook her from head to toe. She wasn't sure how many more she could have without losing consciousness, and she knew that Clint had more stamina than she.

With her hands on Clint's butt cheeks, Dani began to increase the tempo, moving her own body in unison with his powerful strokes. With each orgasm that she had, she increased the pace a little more, and she could tell that Clint was getting more and more excited. He was drawing pleasure directly from her own; the more he pleased her, the more he was pleased by her. Eventually they were moving very quickly. Clint's breathing became very rapid, and Dani could tell that he was starting to lose control a little. His penis grew harder and she thought, if possible, hotter. Finally, as Dani reached one final, incredible climax, she felt his wet warmth inside her and knew that he had come, too.

Although the pace slowed dramatically, Clint did not stop stroking. He continued to move in and out slowly. His penis lost some of its size and heat, but it didn't go completely flaccid. He just kept going, and she was amazed.

He looked at her and smiled. She smiled back, and they gazed deeply into each other's eyes, into each other's souls.

"Dani, I mean it. I love you."

"I know, Clint. I meant it, too."

"I know it's a little crazy. After all, we've only known each other a couple of days."

"I know what you mean, but it just feels right. Doesn't it?"

"Yes, it does. You know, after last night, I was afraid this might never happen."

"I know. Me, too."

"Thank you, Dani. Thank you for giving me a chance."

They were both misty-eyed. Clint wrapped his arms around Dani, squeezed her tightly, and kissed her. She gave him a nudge, and he knew that she wanted him to turn over. Very deftly, without removing his penis, Clint turned over and pulled her over with him. He was still inside her. With her hands against his chest, she pushed herself up into a sitting position and began moving her body back and forth, slowly but firmly.

After a while Dani could feel Clint's penis getting bigger again, and as it got harder, she ramped up the speed. Pretty soon they were back at a moderate speed, and once again a wave of orgasms took over her body. When Dani was no longer able to maintain the rhythm, she dismounted and assumed an all-fours position, and Clint got up on his knees and penetrated her from behind.

Clint grabbed Dani's buttocks, one in each hand, and massaged them firmly as he drove his penis in and out, in and out. Dani dropped to her elbows to improve the angle, and Clint could feel her tighten. She pushed her butt firmly against him, and he became more aroused and increased the speed, with each stroke driving himself as deeply into her body as he could.

Dani's orgasms started again. She began to push harder against him, moving her butt back and forth, round and round, all the while pushing, pushing. Clint got more and more excited. The speed of his drives and his breathing increased. Eventually Clint and Dani were a blur of movement and sound, the sweat covering both bodies and dripping, soaking the bed.

Clint leaned over Dani and wrapped one arm around her belly, pulled her against him, and maintained balance with the other arm. She pushed her head back against his, and he twisted to nibble her neck. Dani was still coming—loudly—and then Clint started to groan, louder and then louder still. All at once there was a massive explosion of physical and psychic release, and they dropped to the bed together. Clint quickly rolled over and pulled Dani against him. Her head on his chest and his arms wrapped around her, they lay there and caught their breath. It took a while. For several minutes they said nothing. Dani shifted a little and raised her head.

"Clint, you did things to me no one's ever done. The feet, and that thing with your tongue. Wow!"

"You've got to be kidding me!" Clint exclaimed with genuine shock.

"No, I'm not. That was the very first time that anyone has ever done that to me."

"Well, now you know what you've been missing!"

Dani laughed, "Yeah, you're right about that, and I can tell you one thing for sure: I like it!"

Looking very serious, Clint said, "Dani, I love you. It's my job to please you—any way I can, as much as I can. If I can't, then I don't get much out of it either. I don't see much point in being with a woman if I can't bring her to climax a whole bunch of times. Both of us might as well masturbate. Truth is, it takes two to have bad sex, and it takes two to have good sex. You've got as much to do with it as I do."

Clint paused for a moment before adding, "Dani, this is the first time I've ever made love to a woman I was in love with, so I just had to make it good. I never wanted so badly to please a woman."

Dani shook her head and asked, "How old are you again? Because I can't believe you're only 19. Most boys your age are just wham-bam-thank-you-ma'am. All they care about is getting their rocks off."

"Oh, yeah? And just how many 19-year-old boys have you been with?" Clint asked playfully.

"Just one up until now actually, and that was my husband. You knew what I meant," Dani said with a teasing punch to Clint's shoulder.

Clint said, "Well, I haven't always cared so much about pleasing my women. To be perfectly honest, I used to be pretty much like you said. It took me a while to figure out what it's all about—and just how much pleasure I could get from a satisfied partner." With a chuckle, Clint added, "I guess Dad's talks paid off."

"You talked to your dad about sex? About how to please a woman in bed?"

"Oh, yeah, we talked about it, and he always stressed that it's important to find out what pleases your woman—and then to do it often and to do it well."

"Your mom is one lucky woman. And me, too!"

"Yeah, Mom and Dad are lucky, and so are we—both of us." They smiled at each other and kissed.

Dani asked, "Did your dad teach you how to fight, too?"

"Yeah, Dad taught me the boxing part, and he taught me to walk away whenever I can. He always said, 'It takes more of a man to walk away from a fight than it does to kick ass,' and I took that to heart. I always walk away if I can. I have nothing to prove. I only fight when there's truly no other option. Of course, Dad also said to make them sorry when they won't let you walk away."

"Something tells me that those guys from last night are sorry."

"Yeah, I think so, too. I hope so. I hope they learned their lesson."

"Have you ever thought about going pro? You could probably make a lot of money."

Clint's face went white, and he said, "No, Dani, I could never fight for a living." His expression and tone told her to drop the subject.

"Clint, I just have to say something. That's the best sex I've ever had in my life. I never dreamed it could be so good."

"Me, too, Dani," he said, shaking his head. "It's mind-boggling. We're really lucky we found each other. It's about time something went my way."

There was a loud knock on the door, and it startled Clint and Dani. They looked at each other, and Clint got out of bed and grabbed a revolver from under the mattress. It surprised Dani. There was another loud knock.

"Clint, you in there? Wake up! Roy and I come to check on you."

"Just a minute, Tom!" Clint yelled toward the door as he put the gun back under the mattress. To Dani, he said, "Sorry. They're friends of mine. Do you want me to let them in?"

Dani said, "Sure, I'll just go get dressed."

As Dani headed for the bathroom, Clint found his underwear and shorts and put them on. He walked over and opened the door and greeted Tom and Hulk.

"Howdy, guys. I appreciate you dropping by, but this is kind of a bad time."

Hulk sniffed loudly and said, "Uh, yeah, we can smell that." Both men smirked.

Clint said, "Well, come on in. Dani's in the bathroom." Hulk and Tom stepped in, and Clint closed and locked the door.

"Well, let's take a look at you," Tom said. Tom and Hulk eyeballed Clint from head to toe, and then they focused on the eyebrow.

"That doesn't look too awfully bad, but why didn't they stitch it?" Tom asked.

Clint answered, "I told them not to. I figured the butterfly would be enough."

Hulk offered, "I'm not so sure about that. That .357 had to leave a pretty wide groove."

Clint shrugged and said, "You may be right, but it doesn't matter. It's no big deal."

"How you feel?" asked Tom.

"Apparently he feels good enough for a hard fuck," Hulk said.

"Come on, Hulk. You know I don't like you being that crude."

"Oh, right. Sorry. Looks like you feel okay, though."

Clint nodded and said, "Yeah, I'm okay."

Dani came out of the bathroom and walked over to the three men. She looked a little embarrassed, but she was trying not to show it. She had done a pretty fair job of sprucing herself up, except for her hair—not much she could have done with that in a couple of minutes. It was pretty obvious what she and Clint had been doing, especially to a couple of old coppers like Hulk and Tom. Still, she was putting up a brave front.

"Hi," she said. "I'm Dani."

Putting a hand to Hulk's shoulder, Clint said, "Dani, this is Detective Roy of the Dallas Police Department. We call him Hulk; you can see why. He's the one who asked about me last night." Clint nodded toward Tom and said, "That's Tom Whitely. We work together. Starting Monday, he's going to be my new boss."

Both men shook hands with Dani, and Hulk said, "We just stopped by to make sure old Sasquatch here is okay."

"Sasquatch?" Dani asked.

Clint said, "It's a nickname."

Dani smiled and replied, "Well, it fits."

"Let's all get off our feet," Clint said.

Dani walked over and sat on the foot of the bed so that no one else would have to. That would have been awkward. Hulk and Tom sat on the couch.

Clint asked, "Anyone want anything to drink?"

Dani said, "I'll take a Dr. Pepper, or whatever kind of coke you have."

Hulk asked, "You still got some of that ice cold whiskey?"

Clint said, "Yeah, we didn't drink it all last time." Turning to Tom, he asked, "And you, Boss?"

"I'll take a coke, too. Any flavor is fine."

As Clint walked over to the kitchen to get the drinks, Hulk asked Dani, "So, you saw all of what happened last night?"

"Yes, sir, I did. I was scared to death, but Clint was amazing."

"Yeah, all the cops were pretty impressed with what they heard. They said they wish they'd actually seen it." Hulk turned toward the kitchen and raised his voice a little, saying, "Hey, Sasquatch, one of those Addison cops was really pissed at you, though."

From the kitchen Clint asked, "Yeah? Why's that?"

Hulk chortled and said, "You scared that shooter so bad he filled his britches. I don't know what he'd been eating yesterday, but the cop didn't even make it to the station before he had to pull over and barf on the side of the road. And the station's only a half mile!" Hulk let out another belly laugh, and everyone else enjoyed a good laugh as well.

Dani said, "You wouldn't believe how this young man of ours kept his cool. He didn't act scared at all. To tell you the truth, I was surprised to see all the blood when he got shot. I expected ice water."

"Well, it may have looked like that, Dani," Clint said, "but looks can be deceiving. I feel fear. I just try not to show it to my opponent."

Tom offered, "Doesn't surprise me a bit. When the kid gets down to business, he's scary serious. Y'all should have seen that Willis fight at Billy Bob's." In the instant after the words passed his lips, Tom thought, "Whitely, you dumbass!"

Clint looked at Tom for a moment, the most pained look on his face that one could imagine, and then looked down. Hulk nudged Tom with an elbow and looked at his feet. Tom let out a deep sigh and allowed his gaze to move toward the floor as well, and Dani glanced around at all three men. There was a pregnant pause in the conversation. Clint had leaned over with his hands on the kitchen counter, almost as if he was having trouble standing. Finally he looked toward Dani.

"Dani," Clint said. "It's pretty obvious that Tom just slipped and said something that I really wasn't ready for you to know." Turning toward Tom, he added, "It's okay, though. Tom, buddy, don't beat yourself up about it. I was going to tell her anyway."

Looking sufficiently contrite, Tom said, "Sorry, Clint."

Clint answered, "It's okay, Tom, really. Don't sweat it." Then looking toward Dani, he said, "Dani, is it okay with you if we talk about this later?"

"Sure, Clint, no problem."

Clint finished gathering up everyone's drinks, distributed them, and then sat on the bed and put his arm around Dani. He pulled her to him and kissed her forehead. Looking into Dani's eyes and smiling widely, Clint said, "Tom, luckiest day of my life was the day we bumped into this beautiful gal."

In a very serious tone, Hulk said, "Sasquatch, with all due respect to your lady friend, I'd say that today is the luckiest day of your life. You're damn lucky to still be here among the breathing."

Revelations

Tom and Hulk didn't stay long. Once they'd satisfied themselves that Clint was okay, they left him and his new lady friend to do—well, whatever. Dani retrieved a bag from her car that contained some clean clothes, makeup, and such. Clint didn't ask her why she carried something like that in her car. They took a shower together—only a little mild hanky-panky—brushed their teeth, and got dressed. They were discussing what to do with the rest of the day.

Clint asked, "Are you ready to find out what Tom referred to earlier, about my first and last pro fight?"

"Sure, if you're ready to talk about it."

"I'd rather show you. Do you want to take a ride on my bike?"

"Absolutely! Sounds like fun!"

Serious in expression and tone, Clint said, "Fair warning: The ride may be fun, but what I'm going to show you won't be."

"Uh, okay," Dani said, wondering why Clint was being so cryptic.

Clint grabbed his spare motorcycle helmet from the closet, handed it to Dani, and said, "Here, try this on. I don't even want to think about that pretty face of yours hitting the pavement."

"Well, hopefully you're a better rider than that!" she said as she tried on the helmet.

"Oh, I'm a good rider, but unfortunately a bunch of folks out there aren't good drivers. Truth is, I never ride without a helmet. As far as I'm concerned, anyone who straddles a bike without one is a complete moron. Riding without a helmet is sheer idiocy. I've seen a head cracked like a melon, and it ain't pretty."

The helmet fit, and they went outside. Clint took the cover off his bike and quickly checked the gas, oil, the air in his tires, and his chain. They would need gas later, but they had enough to get to their destination. Clint put the motorcycle cover in his truck, came back, and removed the Kryptonite wheel lock from the rear wheel and stowed it in a case on the rear of his bike.

Clint got on the bike and pushed it backward out of the parking space. He delicately put on his own helmet and told Dani to get on. She strapped on her helmet and got on behind Clint, and he started the bike. It was a big four-cylinder bike, what some folks refer to as a "crotch rocket." It sounded awfully powerful to Dani, and she was more than a little anxious when she looked over Clint's shoulder and saw that the speedometer went to 160. Dani almost had to yell for Clint to hear her over the motor.

She asked, "Have you ever gone that fast?"

"What?"

"Your speedometer says 160. Have you ever gone that fast?"

"Not quite," Clint answered, not exactly making her feel better.

Clint took off and made his way westward to Central Expressway, Highway 75, and turned north. Clint drove near the speed limit, and they arrived at the Chasewood Manor Nursing Home in Denton in about an hour. Clint felt a twinge on his eyebrow as he removed his helmet. He retrieved the Kryptonite lock and secured the rear wheel, and Dani fussed with her hair for a moment in one of the bike's mirrors.

Clint said, "Oh, you look beautiful. Don't worry about it."

Clint took Dani's hand and led her toward the entry. They carried their helmets. Dani wondered what they were doing there, whom they might be going to see, but she didn't ask any questions. Clint knew the way now, and he led Dani directly to Room 309. Ever the faithful mother, Ruth was at Keith's bedside. When she saw Clint walk in, her face lit up, and she leapt out of the chair to bear hug him. "Praise Jesus! It's so good to see you! How you doing, son?" Ruth hugged Clint as if she were catching up on all of Keith's hugs that she'd missed. When she pulled back again, she noticed the eye. "What's wrong with your eye? You know, it's bleeding a little."

Clint stepped over and looked in the mirror. Apparently his motorcycle helmet had irritated his wound. One edge had opened up a little, and it had just started to trickle. He grabbed a couple of Kleenex and pressed them against the wound.

"Oh, it's nothing. Don't worry about it. I need to introduce y'all. Dani Bailey, this is Ruth Willis. Ruth, this is my girlfriend, Dani. I brought her over to meet you and Keith. I hope you don't mind another unannounced visit."

"Oh, heavens no!" Ruth said with a wide smile. Expecting a handshake, Dani held out her hand, but Ruth wrapped her in a big hug and said, "Oh, I'm so happy to meet you!" Ruth turned toward Clint, slapped him on the arm, and said, "Son, you didn't tell me you had a girlfriend—and such a pretty young black girl, too!" Ruth's expression grew dim as she turned toward the bed. "Dani, this is my boy, Keith."

Clint felt a lump in his throat when he noticed how much further Keith's body had deteriorated. He stepped over to Keith's bed and took his hand. The two women stepped over to Clint, one on each side, and each put a hand on one of his shoulders. As Clint held one hand to his wound and held Keith's hand with the other, he bowed his head and closed his eyes for a minute. The women said nothing, but Ruth, too, bowed her head and closed her eyes. Dani watched as the two prayed silently over Keith's virtually lifeless body. She noticed a tear streak one of Clint's cheeks.

When he was finished, Clint said, "Dani, Keith is the reason why I can never be a professional fighter again. I'm the reason he's like this." That's all it took; she understood completely. At this moment Clint seemed strangely vulnerable, a far cry from last night, and she loved him just a little bit more. He was human after all.

Clint and Dani had a wonderful visit with Ruth. The two women really hit it off, and Ruth made Clint promise to bring Dani back for another visit. He said that he would.

Before they left the room, Clint returned to Keith's side, placed a hand on his forehead, and said, "I'll keep praying for you, brother." Clint patted Keith's hand, turned, and gave Ruth another big good-bye hug. Just as he had at the end of his first visit, he said, "I love you, Momma." This time it didn't startle her. She had expected it, and she smiled.

"Thank you for speaking for my boy," Ruth said.

"Actually I was speaking for both of us," Clint said with a wink, and Ruth's smile widened.

Ruth and Dani hugged, and Ruth told her, "I hope to see you again real soon."

Dani replied, "I expect you will, ma'am."

Clint said, "Bye, now," took Dani's hand, and led her back to the parking lot. When they got to the bike, Clint said, "So now you understand? That's what happened in my first and only professional fight, and I can't take a chance of it ever happening again—never, not to anyone."

"Yes, lover, I understand completely."

Clint smiled and said, "Lover? Ooh, I like the sound of that!" They hugged and kissed before they went through Clint's pre-ride ritual again, after which they strapped on their helmets and mounted the bike. Just before pulling away, Clint turned and said, "Dani, do you realize that we haven't had anything whatsoever to eat today?"

"Well, you did actually," Dani said with a laugh, and Clint blushed and laughed as well.

"Yeah, yeah, I reckon you're right about that, but you know what I mean—sustenance. We haven't eaten any *food* today. You up for a good steak?"

"Sure, that sounds great. You know a place around here?"

"It just so happens I do. We passed it on the way over," Clint answered before starting the bike and riding away.

Clint refueled at a Texaco station on Highway 380 before heading east to the Trail Dust. Although it was pretty late, the place was still crowded. On weekends they had live music and dancing, and many two-steppers closed the joint. Dani didn't like the country and western music, but they enjoyed their supper nonetheless.

Surprisingly Clint cajoled Dani into a couple of dances. The two-step was the extent of Clint's dancing repertoire, and he wasn't very good. Even so, they had fun before leaving around midnight and heading back to Clint's place in Plano. Clint secured and covered his bike, and they went to his apartment.

Clint asked Dani, "I assume you're staying here tonight?"

"Well, I hadn't really planned to, but it is awfully late to be driving back to South Oak Cliff. I can stay tonight, but I'll have to go back home in the morning."

"Okay, at least we have the night. You want something to drink?"

"You got any alcohol?"

"Just a bottle of Wild Turkey 101, or what's left of it."

"You got any Coke to mix it with?"

"Just Pepsi."

"That'll do."

Dani sat on the couch as Clint went to the kitchen and retrieved the whiskey from the freezer. There wasn't a whole lot left, but there was enough for a couple of 101s and Pepsi. Clint had never mixed his Turkey with anything, but he wanted to have what Dani was having. He made their drinks and returned to the couch.

"Thanks," she said as he handed her the drink.

"You're welcome."

"You got any music we can listen to?" Dani stood up and stepped over to the stereo to check out the eight-tracks and records. As Dani perused Clint's collection, she said, "Oh, my God! Oh, shit!" She put a hand to her face and cried, "I'm in love with a man who listens to John Denver and Barely Man Enough! And what's this? Oh, no, country and western, and no. Could it be? Yes, it's classical!"

They both laughed, and Clint said, "What can I say? I like all kinds of music, especially saccharine love songs. But the classical—that's my favorite. It soothes my mind, body, and soul. It's better than sex—well, not really *better*, but it's damn good."

"Well, don't ever crank that shit up when I'm around. I'll have to slap you silly. Okay, well at least there's the radio." She tuned it to Dallas FM station K104. "Ah, now that's good music," she said as she returned to the couch and cuddled up to Clint. Teddy Pendergrass was singing "Close the Door," a song about bringing the day to a pleasant end.

"Damn," Clint said. "It's like they played that just for us."

"They did," Dani said as she cuddled Clint more tightly. "It's perfect."

They listened to the rest of the song, and Clint had to admit, "Yeah, that's very good. It's a great song, my kind of song, and I love his voice."

Clint and Dani cuddled on the couch and nursed their drinks for about an hour, all the while listening to a type of music that Clint had heretofore ignored. He was surprised at how well he liked it and realized that he needed to listen to it more frequently. Eventually it was clear that they both were tired and needed sleep, so Clint took their glasses to the kitchen and put them in the sink. He stepped over to the stereo and changed over to the classical station.

"As much as I've enjoyed that, this is a little better for sleeping."

"Oh, God," Dani said. "Must you?"

"Yes, ma'am, I must. This is one habit you won't break."

"Well, at least I won't hear it while I'm asleep."

"Oh, yes, you will. It will register in your brain even if you don't realize it. Anyway, it's time to turn in."

They went to the bathroom and brushed their teeth together and then took turns going potty. They weren't quite ready to share that yet. After a quick shower together, they returned to the bed. Clint sat on the foot of the bed, and Dani stood in front of him. Her hands were on his shoulders, and his hands were on her waist. They smiled and kissed. As she stood naked in front of him, he looked her up and down again, admiring her beauty.

Clint shook his head and said, "Damn, you're beautiful! I hope you never get tired of hearing me say that."

"I hope you never quit thinking it's true," Dani said before leaning over to kiss Clint again.

"Trust me, Dani. When we're sitting on the porch in our rockers with grandkids on our laps, I'll think you're just as beautiful as you are right now."

Dani flinched slightly and said, "It's probably too soon for talk like that."

"Maybe," Clint had to admit. After all, they'd only known each other a few days, and most folks would think it too soon even for talk of love.

"Let's trade," Dani said, and she pulled him to his feet and sat on the bed. She shook her head as Clint had and said, "Wow, you look awfully good yourself. Hi, Little General," she said as she reached up and patted the head of Clint's erect penis. "I see you're already at attention." Dani moved forward and gave Clint fellatio.

An oddity in many ways, Clint had never been crazy about head before, but this was something special. He pulled away just before his climax. "Damn, that's good, but I don't want to waste it. We'll call that a 68. You did me; now I owe you one."

Dani chuckled and said, "Ah, but you're forgetting that I already owed you one from this morning."

"Indeed. Well, I guess that means we're even, but that's going to change soon. You're about to owe me again," Clint said, and they both laughed.

"I don't mind owing you, but let me ask you something. How was that?"

"How was it? It was great! To be honest, that's never really done much for me before, but that was good—very, very good. I could definitely get used to it."

"It was my first time."

"I can't believe that—no way!"

"Yep, my very first time."

"Wow, unbelievable! You're just full of surprises." He kissed her and said, "Now, let's get back to business."

Clint dropped to his knees, pushed Dani back on the bed, and returned the favor. After she had come several times, he mounted her, and they made love—another remarkable outing, though neither as varied nor as productive as the first. Afterward they chatted only briefly before drifting off to sleep in each other's arms. They slept soundly and dreamed of each other.

The First Death

Clint's first several months on his new job were quite enjoyable. Tom had never really followed through on giving Clint only grunt work, and although their cases were often seedy, Clint had to admit that it beat a regular guard post. Clint was working directly for Tom, if not always physically with him, and Clint enjoyed that.

Tom was a good boss, and if truth be told, he actually let Clint do far more investigative work than he should have. If the Texas Board of Private Investigators and Private Security Agencies ever found out, they might yank the company's license, or at least give them a big fine, but then again, the Board had a reputation of profound ineptitude. The fear of potential repercussions didn't seem to bother anyone in the least.

One Thursday afternoon when Clint happened to be in the office working at Tom's desk, the receptionist called. "Clint," said the receptionist, "I have a call for you. Lady says her name is Ruth Willis. Do you want me to put her through?" Clint and Dani had visited Ruth and Keith several more times, and Clint had given Ruth his phone numbers at home and at work. She had never called him, though, so it surprised him.

"Uh, sure, put her through." The receptionist transferred the call, and Clint said, "Hi, Ruth. It's good to hear from you."

Ruth paused before speaking. Clint could hear her take a deep breath. Her voice quivering slightly, Ruth said, "My boy's at peace now. He's gone home to the Lord."

Clint dropped the phone. He fumbled with it for a moment, and once he had it under control again, he still couldn't speak. His throat was knotted, and he feared that untying it to try to speak would open the floodgates. Clint's eyes welled up with tears, and he glanced around the office to see if anyone was watching. He didn't want to make a fool of himself at work. He just sat there holding the phone for what seemed like an awfully long time. Finally he realized that he was going to have to say something to Ruth.

"Ruth, are you still there?"

"Yes, son, I am. You know I'm a patient woman."

"Yes, you are. When, Ruth? When did it happen?"

"Just a little while ago. I was holding Keith's hand and talking to the Lord, and I just told Him, 'Lord, Your will be done,' and my boy quit breathing. I was holding his hand, and he passed. Just like that. The funeral home is on the way."

His voice breaking, Clint said, "Ruth." He paused to compose himself before continuing, "Ruth, I'm so sorry. I'm sorry I . . . . I'm sorry I killed your son." Clint could hold back the tears no longer. They began to flow freely.

"Now don't you go talking like that, Clint! We done talked about that. You didn't kill Keith. It was an accident. I don't want to hear nothing about no killing."

Clint realized that someone was approaching the desk, and he looked up through a haze of tears and saw that it was Tom. Clint quickly looked away. Tom frowned and sat in the chair next to his desk. He looked at Clint and saw the tears pooling on the desk. He reached into a drawer for a box of Kleenex and gave it to Clint. Clint took one and covered his face with it, refusing to look at Tom and not able to continue his conversation with Ruth.

"What's wrong, Clint?" Tom asked quietly. He reached out and placed his hand gently on Clint's shoulder and asked again, "What is it?"

Clint just shook his head. He couldn't look at Tom, and he couldn't say anything.

"Take your time, son. It's okay. I'm here for you," Tom said, his own voice cracking a little. It pained Tom to see Clint so distraught.

Finally Clint put down the tissue, grabbed a pen from the desk, and on a notepad wrote the words: "He's <u>DEAD</u>!"

"Oh, my God," Tom said, "Who's dead?"

Clint wrote: "Keith Willis." He shook his head and handed the phone to Tom before standing up and trotting off to the restroom.

"Uh, hello," Tom said into the phone. "This is Tom Whitely. I'm Clint's boss. I'm also his friend. Who's this?"

"This is Ruth Willis. Where's Clint?"

"Ma'am, Clint's kind of upset right now. I don't think he can talk. He wrote me a note and told me about your son. I'm sorry, ma'am. I'm so sorry for your loss."

"Thank you, sir. Can you give Clint a message for me?"

"Yes, ma'am, certainly."

"The funeral home is going to be here any minute to pick up my boy. Please tell Clint that I'll call him later. I'll let him know when the services are so he can come. I want him and Dani to be there."

"Yes, ma'am. I understand. I'll let Clint know."

"Thank you, sir."

"Again, I'm sorry about your son."

"Thank you."

Ruth hung up, and Tom put the phone down and ran to the restroom. Clint was at the sink splashing cold water on his face. In the mirror he initially looked shocked when he realized that someone had walked in behind him, but he looked relieved when he saw that it was Tom. Tom walked over and put his hands on Clint's shoulders.

"Are you okay?" Tom asked.

"I don't know. I really don't know."

"Is there anything I can do for you?"

Clint shook his head. He splashed a little more water on his face and grabbed several paper towels and dried his face and hands. After discarding the towels, he looked at Tom and managed a weak smile. "Thanks, Tom. I need some coffee."

Tom followed Clint to the break room and watched him pour a cup of coffee. "You know, Clint, that looks like it's been there a while. It's probably boot polish by now."

"I don't care," Clint replied. He took a sip and grimaced. "Damn, maybe I should've listened." He flipped the switch on the coffee maker.

They sat down, and Clint sipped the scorched coffee. They said nothing for a long time. A couple of people started to enter the break room, but they could see that Tom and Clint didn't need an interruption. They tiptoed back out and didn't return.

Finally Clint said, "You know, Tom. I guess I knew this day would come eventually. I will never forget his face that night. Truth is, he died that night. Whatever happens to a person's soul when he dies, it happened to Keith Willis the night of our fight. He's been dead all along. I've just been pretending he wasn't dead. Just like his poor momma, I've been praying for a miracle. But I guess there haven't been any of those in a couple thousand years."

Clint paused for a moment, and Tom said nothing. He was a good listener, and he wanted to give Clint plenty of room on this one. Clint eventually continued, "I killed him, Tom. His momma—God bless her soul—keeps telling me it was just an accident. *Just* an accident! Dammit, Tom, that's just a fucking euphemism. I killed him. I killed him, and that's all there is to it.

"Yes, Clint," Tom said, "you killed him. There—I said it. I didn't try to soften it for you. I just said it. And you know what? The world didn't end. We're both still here."

"And Keith Willis is still dead."

"That's right. But you know what? You didn't murder him, Clint. You had no criminal intent, and you didn't kill him through recklessness or negligence. Bottom line: You're not culpable—period. Truth is, you're both right—you and Keith's mother. You killed him, but it was an accident. It's not a euphemism, Clint. It's a fact."

"It's just not fair."

"Life's not always fair."

"No offense, Tom, but it makes me want to puke every time someone says that. Dammit, life should be fair; it's supposed to be fair. People are supposed to get what they deserve. Good, bad, or in-between, people are supposed to get what they deserve. Whatever happened to just deserts?"

"I'm not sure I agree with that. I'm not saying it wouldn't be a good thing. It's just not reality. The real world isn't always fair—never has been, never will be. We don't live in a fairy tale world, Clint."

"You ever kill anyone?"

"No. Came close a couple of times, but no."

"Hulk has."

"I know."

"He told me a man is bound to feel bad after killing someone—even if the guy deserved it."

"He's right. Unless you're a psychopath, it's bound to affect you."

"Well, Keith Willis didn't deserve it, so how much harder is that going to make it for me? If a guy feels conflicted about killing someone who deserves it, how am I supposed to handle killing someone who didn't?"

"I don't know, Clint. I don't know, but I do know that you're the finest young man I've ever been around. Your whole life is in front of you, and your future is so bright—so very bright. Somehow you've got to get past this."

"Thanks, Tom. I want to."

"Good. Then you will, and I'm here to help you any way I can. Dani and Hulk, too. And don't forget about your family, and that buddy Milton of yours. You've got a lot of support. Don't be too proud to lean on us."

"Thanks. What did she say?"

"Who? Oh, Mrs. Willis. She said she'd call you later. She wants you and Dani to go to the funeral. Are you up to that?"

"No, but I owe it to her, so I'll be there. I'll probably make a damn fool of myself, but I'll be there."

"You should call Dani. Take the rest of the day off—tomorrow, too. I'll see you on Monday morning if you feel up to it. If not, just give me a heads-up. I'll cover for you as long as necessary."

"Okay," Clint said as he stood up. "Thanks, Tom."

Tom stood, too, and said, "You're welcome."

They stood there for a moment looking at each other. It was as if there was some unfinished business, something else that needed to be said or done. Suddenly they reached out for each other simultaneously, and they hugged.

Tom patted Clint on the back and said, "You're like a son to me. I hate to see you hurting. Whatever you need, just say the word."

"Thanks, Tom," Clint said. "I love you, too." As they pulled away from each other, Tom saw that Clint was smiling.

Tom said, "Smartass!" Tom was happy to know that Clint felt good enough to make a joke, though not really a joke. He just hoped that Clint would be able to survive the weekend. He knew how strong Clint was in so many ways, but he also feared that this might be his Achilles' heel—well, this or Dani. Tom knew that things hadn't been going well with her.

Clint started to call Dani before he left the office, but he looked at his watch and realized that she was probably on her way to work. He decided to go on home, wait for Ruth's call, and call Dani when he had all the details.

For the past several months, Clint and Dani had continued seeing each other as often as they could, but unfortunately it wasn't nearly enough, at least not for Clint. Clint was assigned to the day shift now, but his job sometimes required after-hours work as well. Dani worked evenings, and she still wasn't ready for Clint to meet her children, which meant even fewer opportunities to spend time together. That was a significant bone of contention between them, and Clint was growing frustrated.

Dani continued to profess her love for Clint at every opportunity, and he just couldn't understand why his race or age should still matter. Nevertheless, whenever they were able to be together, they made the most of it. They enjoyed each other's company, and of course, the sex was outstanding. They really seemed perfect for one another, and Clint just couldn't understand what was keeping them from taking their relationship to the next level.

There were other problems as well. Dani rarely let Clint come over to her apartment in South Oak Cliff, even when the kids were with their dad or their grandparents. In fact, there were some occasions when she simply forbade him to come over despite being alone, and Clint had grown suspicious. This bothered him sometimes, but he preferred not to think about it. Denial can be a powerful defense mechanism.

Clint went home and walked straight to the kitchen. He grabbed a glass from the cabinet and the bottle of 101 from the freezer. It was almost full. Clint was smart enough to know that a depressed person shouldn't consume a depressant drug, but he couldn't stop himself. He gulped about six ounces of whiskey standing in the kitchen and then poured some more and headed for the couch.

On his way to the couch, Clint took a little detour toward the stereo, looked through his record collection, and put one on the turntable. It was Gustav Mahler's "Kindertotenlieder" ("Songs on the Death of Children"). Clint really wanted to wallow. By the time Ruth Willis called, he was good and drunk, but he did a halfway decent job of masking it.

"Hello," he answered just before the sixth ring.

Ruth asked, "Clint, you okay now, son?"

"I'm okay, Ruth, but I'm a little embarrassed that you seem to be taking it better than I am. I'm sorry for being so selfish. I know this isn't about me. I'm so sorry for your loss."

"Thank you." In a disapproving motherly tone, Ruth asked, "You been drinking, son?"

"Yes, ma'am, a little." He felt like shit for lying, and he started sobering up quickly.

"The Devil's juice ain't going to do you no good."

"I know, ma'am. I'm sorry."

"Well, I called to let you know about the arrangements. I sure would like for you and Dani to come to the service."

"We'll be there, Ruth. Just tell me when and where."

"We're going to have a wake tomorrow night, but I kind of figured that you wouldn't want to come to that. It's going to be mainly just relatives, and I thought it might make you uncomfortable."

"The whole thing makes me uncomfortable, Ruth, but you're probably right. I've never even been to a wake. I wouldn't know how to act, and I wouldn't want to intrude on the family. Some of them might not be as forgiving as you are."

"That's okay, son. I don't expect you to go to that, but I would appreciate it if you could come to the funeral on Saturday afternoon. It's going to be at the chapel at Bluebonnet Hills in Colleyville. Service starts at 2:00. Can you make it?"

"Yes, Ruth, I'll be there, and I'll see if Dani can come, too."

"Clint, there's something else."

"What is it, Ruth?"

Ruth hesitated. "Clint, you remember that song you sang for me and Keith the last time you visited?"

"No, Ruth! No! I couldn't!"

"Please, Clint, it would mean so much to me."

"Ruth, there is no way, just no way on Earth that I could sing at Keith's funeral. I'm sorry. It's just not possible. If you recall, it was pretty tough before. I still don't know what possessed me that day."

"The Holy Ghost possessed you, that's what. Clint, I know you leading a sinful life now, rebelling against the Lord, but He's got special plans for you. Someday you'll realize that, and then you can get down to doing the Lord's business. I think He wants you to use that voice of yours."

"Maybe you're right, Ruth, but there's still no way I could possibly sing at Keith's funeral. I'd be lucky to get three words out. You're asking me to make a fool of myself."

"I'm asking you to help me—to help you and me both—say good-bye to my boy. I think it would do us both some good."

Clint had abandoned the glass a while back and had begun drinking straight from the bottle. He raised it to his lips to take another swig but thought better of it. He sniffed the whiskey and thought for a moment.

"Ruth," Clint started. He paused for a moment longer before saying, "I'll try. If it means that much to you, I'll try. I know what's going to happen, and don't say I didn't warn you. But I'll give it a shot. I owe you that much." He paused again before adding, "I owe Keith." Clint suddenly realized that he had never even had a conversation with Keith and thought it extremely odd that he would now be singing—or, rather, trying to sing—at Keith's funeral. How often does a killer sing at his victim's funeral service?

"Oh, thank you, son! Thank you!"

"I just said I'll try. Now where did you say the service is going to be?"

"Bluebonnet Hills in Colleyville at 2:00 Saturday afternoon."

"I'd better write that down." Clint had a very good memory, almost photographic, but that wasn't necessarily true when booze was interfering with the encoding of data. "Hold on a minute," he said. Clint fumbled around the apartment until he found a pen and paper and then returned to the phone. "Okay, Bluebonnet Hills, 2:00 Saturday afternoon. Got it."

"Thanks, son. I'll see you then. Dani's coming with you. Right?"

"Yes, ma'am. I hope so," Clint said, but he was far from certain.

"Well, okay, bye."

"Bye-bye now." Clint hung up the phone and said aloud, "Buchanan, you damn fool!"

Clint closed the whiskey bottle and returned it to the freezer. He needed some supper but didn't feel like cooking anything, so he put a TV dinner in the oven and set the timer. He picked up the phone and dialed the number to Dani's job. The evening guard answered the phone, and Clint asked for the data entry department.

Dani's supervisor answered the phone, "Data entry."

"Good evening, ma'am. I'm sorry to bother you, but I need to leave a fairly urgent message for Dani Bailey."

"Is this Mike?"

Clint was puzzled. "Uh, no, ma'am. My name is Clint. I need to speak with her, but it can wait until her break. Could you just ask her to call me on her break? She has the number."

"Yeah, sure, no problem."

"Thank you, ma'am," Clint said before hanging up. He wondered aloud, "Who the fuck is Mike?"

That question was at the forefront of Clint's mind while he waited for Dani to return the call. When the bell on the oven dinged, he went to the kitchen and ate his TV dinner standing at the sink. When he was finished, he threw his trash away and got a Pepsi from the fridge and returned to the couch. The question, "Who is Mike?" festered until the phone rang.

"Hello," Clint answered.

"Hi, lover, is everything okay?"

"No, it's not, Dani. Keith Willis died this afternoon. I thought you should know."

"Oh, God. Poor Ruth. Is she okay?"

"Yeah, Ruth is fine. That's one helluva strong woman. She's taking it better than I am. I made a damn fool of myself at the office this afternoon when she called to tell me."

"I'm sorry, Clint. Are you going to be okay?"

"What choice do I have?"

"You know what I mean, Clint. Are you going to be alright?"

"Yes, Dani, I took the news pretty rough at first, but I think I'm okay now. The funeral is Saturday afternoon, and Ruth really wants us both to be there. It's very important to her. Do you think you can make it?"

There was a noticeable pause before Dani answered. "Uh, I'm not really sure. I can maybe get Antoine or his mother to take the kids, but . . . ." She paused for a moment before continuing, "Yes, Clint, I can make it. I'll come up with something. Where is it—and when?"

"Bluebonnet Hills in Colleyville, 2:00 Saturday afternoon. I can pick you up."

"No, that's okay. Let's just meet there."

"I don't mind picking you up. It's not that far out of the way, and it makes sense for us to ride over together. Besides, we could use the extra time together. I'm going to need you to help me get through this."

"I know, Clint. I understand, but I'm not sure what I'm going to be able to work out with the kids. So it's better that I just plan on meeting you there. I can call over there and get directions, and then I'll meet you there on Saturday."

Again Clint thought, "Who's Mike?" He almost asked Dani but choked back the words before it was too late. Now wasn't the time. "Okay, Dani. We'll meet there. You're sure you can make it?"

"Yes, lover, I'll be there. I promise. Are you going to be okay until then?"

"Yes, I will. Tom gave me tomorrow off, and I have some things to do to keep occupied. I'll be fine."

"Okay, then. I'll see you Saturday afternoon. I love you."

Even with Mike on his mind, Clint did like hearing those words, and she sounded as if she really meant them. She always did. "I know, Dani. I love you, too. See you Saturday."

"Okay, bye."

"Bye-bye."

Clint put the phone down and stared at the wall for a while. He tried to put Mike out of his mind but couldn't.

Could he be the jealous ex-boyfriend? What if he's not really "ex"? All sorts of questions and scenarios were running through Clint's mind, and he didn't like any of them. Clint's thoughts were interrupted when the phone rang again.

"Hello," Clint answered, hoping it was Dani again.

"Hey, Sasquatch! How's it going?" Milton asked.

"Oh, hi, Milton. It's been a while—too long. We need to get together."

"Yeah, that's why I called. Dad's gone up to Amarillo to see about a job up that way, and the weather is supposed to suck around here tomorrow. We won't be able to work. Think you can get off?"

"Actually, I'm already supposed to be off. What did you have in mind?"

"Nothing in particular. The weather will probably be too bad for a ride or a trip to the range, so maybe we can just hang out, maybe shoot some pool or go to a movie, maybe both. What do you think?"

"Yeah, sure," Clint said. Clint had kind of hoped to have the day alone, but he missed Milton. He didn't want to let pass a rare chance for the two of them to spend some time together. "Milton, I need to tell you something."

"Sure, Clint. What's up?"

"Keith Willis died today."

"He's the guy you fought at Billy Bob's?"

"Yeah."

"Oh, shit, that's too bad. You okay?"

"Dani and I are going to his funeral on Saturday afternoon."

"Are you up to that?"

"No, not really, but what choice do I have? His mother asked me, and I owe it to her. If I'm going to kill her son, the least I can do is go to his funeral."

"I guess. So, Dani's going with you? How's that going—you and her?"

"Oh, God, Milton. I'm crazy in love with her, but I've got to be honest. It's not going well. She's acting pretty strange a lot of the time, acting like she's hiding

188

something—or someone. Tonight I called her at work to tell her about Keith, and her boss asked if my name is Mike. So who the fuck is Mike? I'm really out of sorts."

"That sounds goofy, my friend. I tried to warn you."

"Yes, you did, Milton. You tried to warn me that dating a black woman might be trouble, but this has nothing to do with her being black. Let's just not go there. Okay? I know you're a little racist, and I prefer not to think about it."

"You're right, Clint. It's probably best we don't talk about that. Let's just plan on getting together tomorrow. Hey! Let's just go ahead and get together now. Your couch open tonight?"

"Yeah, sure. You want to come on over now?"

"Yeah. That okay?"

"Sure. Can you make a detour on the way?"

"I guess so. Why?"

"Well, I'm low on whiskey, and I've been drinking out of the bottle some. I thought maybe you could go get another bottle of Turkey."

"Ooh, cooties!" Milton said with a chuckle. "Yeah, it's out of the way, but it would be nice to have a few shots of 101. I'll go get a bottle."

"Thanks, Milton. I'll see you in a little while."

"Okay, see you."

Clint hung up the phone and waited for Milton to arrive. Collin was a dry county, so Milton's detour would be significant. He'd have to go all the way to Dallas, and he'd be cutting it pretty near to closing time. Then he'd have to come all the way back to Plano. Even the way Milton tended to drive, it would probably take a solid hour or more before he got to Clint's apartment.

Clint decided on more wallowing—this time to Mahler's "Das Lied von Der Erde" ("The Song of the Earth"). Mahler was the king of self-pity. No one with a pulse could hear the final movement, "Der Abschied" ("The Farewell"), without being moved. When it ended, Clint played it again, and it was about a third of the way through when Milton knocked on the door.

"Hi, Milton. Good to see you," Clint said as he opened the door and stepped aside for Milton to enter.

"Hi, Sasquatch." Milton listened for a moment and shook his head. "Ah, shit," he said. "Mahler—just what you need. Why don't you just shoot yourself while you're at it?" Instantly Milton regretted his words. "You know I don't mean that literally."

"Yes, I do," Clint replied, "but don't think the thought has never occurred to me."

"You can't be serious." Milton was really worried. He knew how much it bothered Clint for Keith Willis to be in a persistent vegetative state. Now that he had finally succumbed, it would only be worse.

"No, not really. Relax. I'm not going to off myself." Looking at the bag in Milton's hand, he added, "I see you got the Turkey."

"Yeah, I did. You got some ice?"

Clint said, "Oh, yeah, I got plenty. I always keep a bag or two on hand in case I need to ice a joint or something. I normally keep my whiskey in the freezer and drink it neat, but on the rocks is okay."

Milton handed the sack to Clint, and Clint removed the bottle as he stepped to the kitchen. He threw the bag in the trash, got a couple of glasses, and filled them with ice. He poured each of them a tall glass of whiskey, stepped to the couch where Milton was now seated, and handed him a glass.

"To Keith Willis," Clint said as he clinked his glass against Milton's.

"Yeah, to Keith," Milton said. They sipped their whiskey, and Milton asked, "Why don't you put something else on? Mahler is really fucking depressing. You really shouldn't mix him with booze, and you definitely shouldn't mix Mahler, booze, and depression. Damn, that's one dangerous combo!"

"Yeah, I guess you're right," Clint admitted. He put the record away and tuned the radio to a country station. Looking toward Milton and smiling, Clint said, "I know how much you like John and Barry, so we'll just stick with this." Clint thought that he must be the only man his age who would admit to liking John Denver and Barry Manilow, or Barely Man Enough as Dani had referred to him.

Milton laughed and said, "Ugh, put that shit on, and I'll be the one committing suicide." Again he regretted his droll comment. "No, that station will be fine," he said before taking another sip. "So, what do you want to do tomorrow?"

"I don't know. I'm not much in the mood to have a good time—as ridiculous as that sounds. I guess we could shoot pool or something." Clint gulped some more whiskey and then played with his glass a little.

"Thanks, Milton. Thanks for coming over."

"Don't mention it, Clint. I'm here for you. You know I'll always be here for you. Let me ask you something, though. Have you talked to your parents yet?"

"No, they still don't know, and as far as I'm concerned, they'll never know. I can't tell them, and I can't imagine that'll ever change."

"Clint, you have great parents. They love you. They're understanding. They're supportive. You should tell them. That's what they're there for."

"Milton, knowing you're right and being able to do it are two different things. I can't. I just can't. No one in my family knows about this, and I'd just as soon keep it that way."

"Okay, that's your choice."

Just then there was a firm knock on the door, and Hulk's voice boomed, "Sasquatch, you in there?"

Clint got up and let him in.

"I just heard," Hulk said as he stepped into the apartment. "You okay?" Hulk eyeballed Milton. They knew of each other but had never met.

"Yeah, Hulk, I'm okay. Detective Roy, this is Milton Vaughan."

Milton stood and said, "Pleasure to meet you, sir," as the two shook hands.

"Likewise" Hulk said. Eyeing the whiskey bottle, he said, "Hey, I'll take some of that!"

"Sure," Clint replied, "but you'll have to settle for on-the-rocks. It's a fresh bottle." He'd already begun making Hulk a glass. He finished and handed it to him.

"Thanks. So, you holding up okay? I'm glad to see your buddy's here."

"Yeah, I'm fine, Hulk. I'm just fine now—two of my three best buddies are here to lend their support."

"Well, Whitely . . . ." Hulk was interrupted by another knock on the door.

Clint opened the door and told Tom, "Come on in and join the party!"

After introducing Tom and Milton, the four men got down to drinking. Clint thought a great deal of the other three men, loved each in his own way, and it was good to have them there. Even Clint had to admit that it was fun, and he felt a lot better. The impromptu get-together had accomplished its purpose: It had gotten Clint's mind off of Keith Willis, if only for a few hours.

Milton probably had more fun than anyone. He enjoyed hearing the old coppers swap their war stories, and he particularly enjoyed Hulk's telling of Clint's exploits at the firing range the day he won the two of them free Bull Shippers from Joe Long. Clint had told the story before; however, Milton had been a little dubious, and Hulk told the story better anyway. Hulk had loads of charisma and was a singular story-teller, and he enjoyed being the center of attention.

The four drank whiskey and swapped stories until the wee hours. They finished the bottle that Milton had brought with him, and they went ahead finished what little was left of the original bottle from which Clint had been drinking directly. Cooties be damned! When they were out of whiskey, Clint brewed some coffee, and they all drank some—even Milton, which was quite unusual. He was more of a tea drinker. Finally sober enough to drive, Hulk and Tom left just before sunrise, and Milton and Clint were asleep before the other two were out of the parking lot.

More Killing

Clint and Milton were only mildly hungover when they awoke early Friday afternoon. Clint made a hearty breakfast for the two of them, and they decided to go shoot some pool. The weather prognosticators had been correct, so motorcycle riding and the shooting range were out.

The two young men hopped in Clint's truck and drove down Greenville Avenue to a place called Shooter's. It was actually very near Hulk's apartment. Clint thought about calling Hulk but remembered that he would be working that day. The pool was cheap, and since they weren't drinking booze on this particular day, having had quite enough overnight, it would not be an expensive visit.

Clint and Milton were an even match on a pool table. Milton was probably the better shooter, but he took too many chances and sometimes got himself into trouble. Clint was more conservative and rarely beat himself. They normally played for drinks, but since they were only having cokes today, there wasn't much point. The sheer fun of the game and of spending time together was sufficient. Unfortunately the fun was about to end.

Clint had won the last game, so he was in the process of breaking to start the next one. He had his back to the door, but he heard it open. Milton, standing at the opposite end of the table, flinched in such a way that Clint looked up to see what was wrong. Milton's face had gone a ghostly pale, and he was staring over Clint's shoulder toward the door. Clint's first thought was "Bandidos." He slowly turned around and thought, "Damn, I hate being right!" Just as in Austin, there were three of them—and one a familiar face. The three bikers stepped into Shooter's as if they owned the place, and they surveyed their surroundings. One of them did a double take in Clint's direction. They had apparently stopped to get out of the weather, and they moved toward an open table at the other end of the large room. After the initial shock of seeing the three bikers wore off, everyone went back to their business—even Clint. He finally broke to start the new game, sank a couple of balls on the break, and moved to Milton's side of the table to take his next shot.

Without looking at Milton, Clint quietly said, "He recognized us, but we have to play it cool." Clint pretended to be considering his options for his next shot.

Milton replied, "I don't get it. What are they waiting for?"

Clint shook his head and said, "I don't know. Reinforcements?"

"Ah, shit," Milton said. He was scared stiff.

If truth be told, Clint was afraid as well, but he was better at hiding it. He went ahead and took his next shot, missing on purpose. He reached for his wallet and took out some cash along with something else and handed it to Milton.

"Here," Clint said. "Go buy us another round of cokes and then sneak back to the head. There's a pay phone back there. Hulk's business card is under that ten. Call him, and pray that he's there. I'll keep an eye out here."

Milton said nothing, but he did as Clint had told him. They were both sweating bullets. Clint stepped to one side of the table, chalked his cue, and studied the pool balls. His peripheral vision allowed him to keep an eye toward the bikers, and they seemed to be keeping an eye on him, too. He leaned the cue against the table and took a sip of the fresh Pepsi that Milton had given him before excusing himself. Clint discreetly kept an eye on the bikers while waiting for Milton to return.

After several minutes, Milton walked out of the restroom. His face was still white as a sheet, and he was shaking his head "no." He walked over to the table looking a bit lost.

Clint reminded him, "Your shot."

Milton retrieved his cue and tried to take a shot, but he missed it badly. He moved next to Clint and whispered, "He wasn't at either place, but I left a message on his machine at the house. We should make a run for it."

"That's exactly what I plan to do," Clint said, "but we can't be too obvious about it. I'd rather they didn't see my truck." Clint leaned over and sank one ball and then another. Everything seemed to line up for him perfectly, and despite his nerves, he ran the table. When he had sunk the eight ball, Clint said, "Okay, that's seven. Looks like you're paying today."

Clint and Milton put away their cues and retrieved all the balls from the pockets of the table, put them on the tray, and headed for the register. As Milton paid the young lady behind the register, Clint kept an eye on the bikers. They had stopped what they were doing, and all three were staring toward Clint and Milton.

Clint leaned toward the young lady and whispered, "You'd better call the cops. Tell them to send everyone— and a couple of ambulances, too. There's about to be one helluva fight in here."

"Hey, Sasquatch!" one of the bikers yelled across the room. "You think we're just going to let you waltz out of here?" It was the car antenna guy from Li'l Abner's parking lot. Clint didn't recognize the other two. All three were heading toward Clint and Milton now, pool cues still in hand.

Clint stole a quick glance toward the cashier and said loudly, "Make that call now!"

Clint stepped around Milton, putting himself first in harm's way. Luckily the pool tables created an obstacle course that kept the bikers from swarming Clint immediately, and they were essentially heading toward him in single file as the other patrons scrambled toward the perimeter.

The first biker, Car Antenna Guy, took a swing at Clint with his pool stick. He had turned it around so that he was holding the narrow end in both hands, and he swung it like a baseball bat. Clint threw up a forearm to absorb the blow from the heavy end of the stick and was able to grab the stick with one hand and punch the biker in the face with the other.

As the biker stumbled backward into his two buddies, Clint grabbed the stick with both hands, spun, and kicked him in the chest. As Clint gained control of the stick, all three bikers stumbled to the ground briefly, and Clint broke the stick in half. He now had the fat end of the stick in one hand and the skinny end in the other.

The three bikers got back to their feet quickly, but the pool tables frustrated them. One of them tried to run around a table and come up behind Clint, but Milton took care of him. It might not have been the best choice, but Milton instinctively grabbed a pool ball and threw it at the biker, striking him solidly on the temple and putting him on the ground. It was a lucky shot, but it worked. Milton ran around to make sure that he stayed on the ground.

Part of a pool stick in each hand, Clint assumed a defensive posture and waited for the bikers to make their next move. Car Antenna Guy was still in the lead, and he reached for something in his boot. When he did, Clint stepped forward and took a backhanded swipe at him with one half of the stick, stepped past him, and clocked the other guy with the other half of the stick. The second biker stumbled, and Clint drove a kick into his side that knocked him into a wall. Clint spun, kicked him in the head, and then caught him simultaneously on each side of his neck with the two halves of the pool stick. The biker fell like a sack of potatoes.

As Clint spun back toward Car Antenna Guy, he felt a sharp pain in the lower right portion of his abdomen. He thought, "What an odd time for my appendix to rupture!" He caught a glimpse of the knife and realized that the blood on its blade was his own. Car Antenna Guy was sneering like William Smith's character, Falconetti, in the TV miniseries "Rich Man, Poor Man," and there was something oddly appropriate about that.

Clint tried to step away, but Car Antenna Guy kept coming. Clint was able to hit him a couple of times with the sticks, but they weren't clean shots and had minimal effect. The guy that Milton had hit with the pool ball was apparently down for the count, and Milton had been able to sneak around behind Car Antenna Guy. Milton was able to get his hands on someone else's cue, and he swung it with full force at the back of Car Antenna Guy's head. Milton had held the stick by the fat end, though, and when the skinny end struck the guy's head, it barely distracted him.

Car Antenna Guy turned and lunged toward Milton with the knife. Milton was quick enough to step aside, and the biker's momentum carried him forward past Milton. Clint nudged his way around Milton and got between them.

"Just watch my back," Clint said to Milton as he stepped forward to engage the biker. As Milton watched the two unconscious bikers, Clint and Car Antenna Guy sized up each other. The biker held the knife in one hand and then moved it to the other. Clint stayed loose in a T-stance, still holding the two halves of the pool cue. He could tell that he was bleeding pretty badly, but he didn't feel as though the injury was severe.

"I see you got a new knife," Clint said to the biker, "but you know this is going to end the same way it did in Austin, maybe worse. I may just be mad enough to kill you this time."

The biker didn't exhibit his best poker face. Clint's last statement—and, more importantly, Clint's demeanor—worried him. He paused just a little too long while considering his options. Suddenly Clint was a blur. He was able to execute a scissors maneuver with the two halves of the pool stick, and the biker's knife went flying. Someone across the room dodged it, and it banged loudly against a wall. The biker had no realization of that, however, because

Clint had performed a beautiful spinning heel kick—the very same that put Keith Willis in his coffin. Perhaps the kick didn't land as cleanly as it did on Keith Willis, or maybe the biker simply had a harder head. Either way, the biker didn't go down, but he was clearly floundering. Clint dropped the sticks, stepped forward, and threw a vicious three-punch combination, all three landing flush against the biker's head. The third was a hook that would have made Joe Frazier proud, and the biker's lights went out. He wilted into a heap on the floor, and much to Milton's surprise, Clint dropped to the floor as well.

"You motherfucker! I'm not through with you yet!" Clint yelled madly. Clint grabbed the biker by the hair with his left hand, pulled him up almost to a sitting position, and punched him again with his right. There was a collective gasp in the room as Clint did it again—and again. The biker's face was mush, and Milton stepped toward Clint, though he was afraid to approach him too closely in his current state.

Milton yelled, "Clint, no! You're going to kill him!"

Clint paused just long enough to say, "That's the idea!"

When Clint hit the biker a fourth time, Milton had no choice. He stepped forward and grabbed Clint around the shoulders. "It's me, buddy. It's me," he said directly into Clint's ear as he grabbed him. Milton turned toward the cashier and asked, "Has anyone called the police? We need the police and an ambulance!"

"Yes, they're on the way," the cashier replied. She looked horribly frightened, as did all the rest of the spectators.

Milton pulled Clint backward a little. Clint leaned forward and took several deep breaths, and the crowd, sensing it was safe now, stepped a little closer to take a look.

To Milton, Clint said, "It's the second time that dirty bastard's pulled a knife on me. He stuck me this time, too. As long as he's breathing, I've got something to worry about."

Milton sighed and said, "You'll have something to worry about whether or not he's breathing."

Everyone heard sirens approaching now, and someone said, "Good—finally."

The next sound that everyone heard was a blood-curdling scream from one of the patrons, and the next was a stomach-turning thud as the heavy end of a pool cue struck the side of Milton's head. The first biker to go down—the one whom Milton had knocked out cold with the pool ball—had regained consciousness and exacted his revenge on the man who'd put him down. Milton fell face first to the floor.

Everything seemed to slow as Clint looked at his fallen buddy. Clint wasn't sure how badly Milton was hurt, but he considered the possibility that he might be dead. He jumped to his feet and faced the biker, who was still holding what was left of the pool stick, just a worthless piece of the small end. He barely had time to drop it before Clint let out a spine-chilling, Apache-esque war cry and attacked him in a blur of fists and feet. All present knew that the biker was about to die.

Although the spectators were aware of the sounds of blows landing, it was difficult for anyone to follow what was happening. The biker was clearly trying for a few moments to defend himself. Perhaps he even landed a blow or two; no one really knew. All they could see clearly was that Clint was moving forward and that the biker was moving backward, but no one had a clue as to what was keeping the biker's body upright. Eventually the biker did fall—at the feet of the first police officer to step through the door. The officer's sidearm was drawn.

The officer took a quick glance at the biker on the floor and then pointed his revolver at Clint's chest and yelled, "Freeze!" Clint didn't; he was out of control and took another step.

"No!" boomed another officer who jumped through the door and pushed the first officer's hand upward just as the gun went off, sending a .41 magnum bullet into the ceiling.

"No, he's okay," Hulk said, quickly noting that Clint had the appearance of a wild animal.

Clint was crazed. His eyes were wide; he was dripping sweat and blood, and he was breathing loudly. His autonomic nervous system had kicked the fight-or-flight syndrome into high gear, and he was on autopilot.

"Clint! It's me! It's Hulk!"

Clint stopped and looked at Hulk. It was almost as if Clint didn't recognize Hulk, but he apparently did. Hulk reached up and grabbed Clint firmly by his shoulders, and the two big men just stood there looking at each other for a moment as other officers filed into Shooter's. A couple of DFD paramedics rushed in and began examining the biker who fell near the door.

Someone yelled, "There's more over here!"

One of the paramedics got up to take a look and quickly yelled back to his partner, "Three more down! We need backup!"

"Hulk?" Clint asked, almost childishly.

"Yeah, Sasquatch? You back with us now?"

"Hulk?" Clint repeated.

"Yeah, kid, it's me. It's your buddy. You're okay now."

"How'd they find me, Hulk?"

"I don't know. I'm not worried about that right now."

"One of them had a knife. And that one hurt Milton."

Just then one of the paramedics said, "This one's dead."

"No!" Clint screamed as he turned and ran back to where Milton had fallen. Hulk had tried to hold him but couldn't. "No!" Clint yelled again as he dropped to his knees at Milton's side. Clint scooped Milton up in his arms and held him close to his chest, screaming yet again, "No!"

"You're not going queer on me. Are you?" Milton asked weakly.

"I thought. I thought," Clint stammered.

"I was talking about this one," the paramedic said, referring to Car Antenna Guy. "Jesus, his face is hamburger." The paramedic's expression betrayed his revulsion.

"You're okay! Thank God!" Clint exclaimed, pulling Milton close again.

"Careful," said the paramedic. "I need to examine him. That's a damn big knot on his head. Don't be jostling him around like that."

Hulk squatted next to Clint and Milton and asked Milton, "How are you, buddy? You're not going to check out on us. Are you?"

"Nah, I'll be okay. Clint can tell you I've got a hard head."

Tears were streaming down Clint's cheeks now. The adrenaline was getting back to a normal level, and he was regaining control of his faculties. He realized the gravity of the situation and was overcome by emotion. He wept for a few moments as Hulk held a hand on his shoulder. The paramedic had moved over to examine Milton.

"Now let's take a look at you," the paramedic said. "Damn, that's one helluva knot!" As the paramedic adjusted his position, he looked over and saw that Clint was covered in blood, so he asked, "Is any of that yours?"

"Yeah, that one stuck me with a knife," Clint said as he looked toward Car Antenna Guy.

Suddenly Clint retched, turned to one side, and emptied the entire contents of his stomach in one mighty explosion. Milton was sitting up now, so Clint moved away from him. Clint went to all-fours and retched some more—just dry heaves. His stomach was already empty, but still he retched and retched. As he did so, he got a look at his hands and realized that they didn't look much better than Car Antenna Guy's face. Each hand seemed likely broken, and the flesh was severely mangled. It appeared that a tooth was lodged in one of his knuckles, or was it a piece of bone?

When his body's attempts to vomit had ceased, Clint sat back and looked around. He reviewed the damage that had been done, and he thought about how different things looked than they always did on TV and in the movies. In Hollywood guys can pound on each other all day and come away with nary a scratch. Clint had always known that things are different in real life, but until now he'd never fully comprehended just how different they are. There is a limit to how much punishment a body can absorb before it breaks, and the threshold is much lower than people realize if John Wayne is the extent of their knowledge.

"You okay now?" Hulk asked. "Feel better?"

"Yeah, I'm okay," Clint replied. "I'm just very tired."

"You be okay without me? I need to go to work now. I'll be here for a while, and then I'll meet you over at the hospital."

"Sure, I'll be fine. Say, what are you doing here anyway?"

"Oh, shit, we couldn't have been luckier." Hulk took a deep breath and continued, "You see, I was on the way out the door, heading for work, when Milton called. I heard the phone ring and started to ignore it. I got all the way to my car, but something told me to go back. Call it divine intervention. Obviously I missed the call, but I got the message. So I called HQ and got over here as quick as I could. Thank God I live practically next door, and I got here at the same time as the uniforms."

Hulk paused for a moment before saying, "Clint, we almost had another funeral on our hands. If I'd gotten here a half second later . . . ." His voice trailed off. He looked down and shook his head, and then he walked away. This would be his investigation. He wouldn't normally handle this sort of case, but since he was the first detective on the scene and was so well thought of in the department, they would let him have it.

Shooter's became an absolute zoo. Other paramedics arrived, and there were cops everywhere. Although there was an appearance of chaos, Clint realized that everyone knew exactly what his or her job was and did it professionally. Clint was impressed. Seeing it as a good learning opportunity, he just sat back and tried to take it all in for a little while—until he remembered that there was a dead guy in the room. That has a way of putting a damper on things.

Ultimately Clint and Milton rode to the hospital in separate ambulances. Car Antenna Guy was dead already, so there was no rush to get him out of there. The biker whom Clint had put down last was mortally wounded and died en route to the hospital. One biker would survive with only moderate injuries, and one just had to wonder: Had Clint seen the last of this gang?

A Call for Help

"Hello."

"Mr. Buchanan?"

"Yes," Doug replied into the phone.

"Sir, this is Detective Roy with the Dallas Police Department. I'm calling about your son, Clint."

"I've heard my son speak of you. Is he okay?"

"Yes, sir, he's been injured, but he's going to be just fine. I'm here at the hospital with him. I'm afraid he got stabbed, but it's not bad at all. Don't you worry none. He'll be out of here in no time."

"Stabbed? What happened, Detective?" Doug sat down at the kitchen table and was thankful that Lucy wasn't home.

"Sir, Clint and that buddy of his, Milton Vaughan, were shooting pool in a place called Shooter's on Greenville. It's not a bad place, but some bikers came in . . . ."

"Bandidos?" Doug interrupted.

"Yes, sir."

"The same ones he had the fight with in Austin?"

"Oh, you know about that." Hulk hadn't been sure. Clint tended to be tight-lipped about certain things. "Yeah, one of them was the same. The other two weren't there in Austin. Anyway, Clint and Milton tried to leave the place, but these bikers jumped them on the way out. It got pretty ugly."

"Did these guys go there because they knew Clint was there?"

"We don't really know. I'm not sure how they could have known that. Right now I'm thinking that it was just a coincidence that they happened to be in the same place at the same time—just a really, really incredible coincidence. Clint seems to have some bad luck sometimes."

"Is Milton okay?"

"Yes, sir, he's got a bump on his head like I've never seen before. It looks like something out of a cartoon, but it's not anything serious. He's ready to go already. He'll be leaving when they're done with Clint."

"You sure my boy's okay? I have to be able to tell his momma that her baby is okay."

Hulk couldn't help but smile at the notion of anyone thinking of Clint as a baby. He replied, "Yes, sir. He'll be out of here as soon as they're done stitching him up. I'll have him home in an hour or two."

"Thank God!" Doug said with a big sigh of relief. "Thank you, Detective."

"No problem, sir. You've got a real fine boy, but . . . ." Hulk had to gather himself before continuing, "Sir, I think Clint needs some help."

"Help? He's at the hospital. What kind of help are you talking about?"

"Sir, I don't quite know how to tell you this, but I think Clint may need some kind of head-shrinker or something. Two of those Bandidos are dead, and . . . ."

"Dead?" Doug asked in disbelief, taking a moment to gather himself. "You mean my Clint . . . ."

"Yes, sir, Clint killed two of them. The third is going to be okay, but the other two . . . . Well, one of them was dead by the time we got there, and the other one died in the ambulance before they could get him to the emergency room."

"My boy killed two of these outlaw bikers?" It was the most surreal moment of Doug's life.

"Yes, sir, he essentially beat them to death."

"My God! I'm responsible! I taught him how to fight."

Hulk wanted to make Doug feel better. He said, "Now Mr. Buchanan, you're not responsible for this. Neither is Clint. These bikers just picked on the wrong guy. If Clint and

Milton hadn't defended themselves, they might be the ones dead, and this would be an entirely different conversation."

"I guess you're right, Detective, but you're telling me that my baby boy just killed two tough guys who fight for pleasure. Forgive me if I'm having a little trouble with the concept."

"I understand," Hulk said, "but trust me. I've been doing police work for a long time, and this case is pretty clear cut. That's how my report will read anyway. If anyone deserved to die, it was those bikers, but sir . . . . Sir, I think Clint needs to talk to someone. You see . . . ." This was tough for Hulk. He was about to betray a friend's confidence, something that he would never take lightly.

"Yes, what is it detective?"

"Sir, Clint didn't want you to know this, but it's not the first time—not the first time he's killed someone."

"Oh, God!" Doug said, completely beside himself. He was shaking uncontrollably, and it was all he could do to hold onto the phone and speak. "I don't know how much of this I can take!"

Hulk continued, "Sir, last year Clint had a fight—no, not a fight, not like this one. It was a professional karate match, kickboxing if you will. Some promoter offered Clint 500 bucks to fight a guy over at Billy Bob's in Fort Worth. It was a sanctioned bout—completely legit. Anyways, Clint knocked the guy out in the first round, not even a minute, hurt him real bad. He was in a coma for a long time, but then . . . . Well, he died . . . uh, yesterday. He just died yesterday, and the funeral is tomorrow."

"Do you mean to tell me that not two, but *three* men have died in the last two days and that my son killed them? He didn't shoot them. He didn't stab them. He didn't run them down with his truck. He killed them with his bare hands—and feet I guess. Is that what you're telling me?" This was a bona fide nightmare. Doug considered pinching himself to make sure that he was awake.

"Yes, sir, I reckon that's pretty much it. Now you see why I think Clint may need some help. That karate match hit him pretty tough, and with the guy dying yesterday and all—and his mom wanting Clint to go to the funeral . . . ."

"Wait! His mom wants Clint to go to the funeral? What's up with that? Did he even know the guy?"

"No, sir, not really. But Clint did go visit him some when he was in a coma, and he got real friendly with the kid's mom. She wants Clint and Dani . . . ." Hulk didn't know if Doug knew about Dani.

"It's okay, Detective," Doug said. "I know about his little half-breed. Wait!" Doug shook his head vigorously, an expression of disgust on his face. He was ashamed of himself. "I'm sorry, Detective. I don't mean to talk like that. I don't even think like that, not normally. I'm just not myself right now. I'm sure you understand. I just meant to say that I know about Dani. I even met her once. She's a nice girl—uh, woman."

"Anyway, Clint and Dani got to know this lady at the nursing home, got real friendly with her, and she wants them to be at her son's funeral. That's tomorrow."

"Why didn't Clint tell me about this before?" Doug was nonplussed. He hadn't realized that there were so many secrets in their family.

"Sir, he just couldn't. I think he knew that he should, but he just couldn't bring himself to for some reason. I think . . . . Well, I think he was ashamed, and I think he was afraid that you'd be ashamed, too."

"Detective, I don't even know you, and it hurts to be having this conversation with a complete stranger. Truth is, I thought Clint and I had a better relationship than that. I thought he knew that he could tell me anything. It's not like he raped or murdered someone—did some kind of horrible crime. I could never be ashamed of him for . . . for an accident."

"I believe you, sir," Hulk said, "but Clint had a really tough time dealing with what happened. I think he just didn't want to take any chances that it would affect your opinion of him. Now that I think of it, I think maybe it was a little bit of what the shrinks call denial or something. It was easier for him to deny it if he didn't have to talk to you about it. Right or wrong, it was just his way of dealing with it."

Hulk continued, "Anyways, I think his head may be a little messed up. I should've seen it before. I been a cop for a long time, and I've picked up a thing or two along the way. I should've recognized that Clint needed help. Maybe I'm not real objective when it comes to him."

"I'm his father, and I didn't recognize it."

"Mr. Buchanan, Clint's been carrying this baggage around with him for a long time, and I think it's been eating away at him. Then this Willis kid dies yesterday. Then his mom asks Clint to go to the funeral. I think he had a lot of pressure built up, and it just exploded all over these bikers. When I got to Shooter's . . . . Sir, Clint was crazy. I think he just snapped, went a little crazy, and took out all his frustrations on these guys. I'm not saying that they didn't have a good beating coming, but . . . . Well, I think Clint took things a little too far."

Doug didn't like the sound of that, and he was even more concerned now. "Is he going to be in any trouble over this? I mean, with the law?"

"I don't think so."

"You don't *think* so?"

"Well, sir, it's really up to the DA, but I've got a good reputation over there. I think they'll listen to me. There's certain things . . . . I'm just saying that the DA will go off of my report, what I say. I say it was self defense. I say he didn't mean to kill them. He's a big strong kid, and he's young. He just don't know his own strength. I don't think there'll be any charges filed."

"Detective?"

"Yes, sir?"

"Do you think Clint meant to kill them?"

Hulk took a moment to consider the question. "Well," he said, "just between you and me . . . . Yes, sir, I think he wanted to kill them. But remember what I said. When I got there he was like a wounded grizzly bear or something. He'd already been stabbed, and he wasn't thinking like folks normally do. It was what we call 'fight or flight,' and Clint ain't one for running. He may have wanted to kill them, but I don't know how conscious that was. He wasn't really thinking too clear. It's not like it was premeditated murder— not any kind of murder at all. Manslaughter maybe, but even that's a stretch."

"What? Manslaughter?"

"Sir," Hulk started. He stopped to think for a moment and took a quick look around. He'd stepped into one of the offices at the hospital to use the phone, so he had plenty of privacy. He just instinctively looked around to see who might have been within earshot. He continued, "Sir, I'm about to tell you something that's just between you and me. Okay?"

"I understand, Detective. Now be honest with me."

"Mr. Buchanan, Clint said some things during the fight. Milton said that Clint was completely out of control and said that he wanted to kill one of the bikers—the one who stabbed him. Some of the witnesses heard him say it, too. Like I said, though, his thinking wasn't too clear, and I don't think he was really responsible for his actions. So, well, I'm going to leave a few details out of my report. You have nothing to worry about. I'll make sure your boy doesn't get into any trouble over this."

"Thank you, Detective. Thank you for caring so much about Clint."

"I do, sir. That boy of yours is special. He don't deserve for something like this to ruin his whole life. But, sir . . . ."

"Yes, Detective?"

"Sir, Clint has his heart set on being a cop, maybe even working with me here in Dallas, and I don't think that's ever going to happen. People are going to know about this, and they're going to think that Clint's a hothead who can't be trusted with a badge and a gun. Either that, or maybe he's a risk for putting his gun in his mouth. I'm not sure that's right, but like I said, I'm not the most objective person when it comes to Clint. I can make sure he comes away with no criminal record, but I can't erase all these reports I'm going to have to write. And I can't do nothing about what people say. I mean, people are going to be talking about this fight for a long, long time. This is legendary stuff."

"Well, Detective, I appreciate your call—and everything you've done for my boy. We can talk about all of this stuff later. Right now I just want to be sure he's okay."

"Yes, sir, you're exactly right. We can talk about all this later, except the part about him needing some counseling or therapy or whatever they're calling it now. Clint will probably balk at that, and we need to present a united front. His boss, Tom Whitely, is a buddy of mine, and there's Milton, too, and your wife. And I guess maybe Dani, too. We all need to make sure he does this whether he wants to or not. I wish I'd done it when I needed to, but I had to learn my lessons the hard way. I don't want Clint to make the same mistake."

"Right. I understand, Detective. I've been taking care of Clint this long. I'm not about to stop now. I'll make sure he gets the help he needs. You just get my boy home to me. Forget his apartment. Bring him here. His mother and I will take care of him."

"Yes, sir, I will. I'll have him home ASAP. Now I need to make another call. I need to let the Vaughans know about Milton."

"You sure they're both okay?"

"Yes, Mr. Buchanan, I promise. Clint and Milton are okay—physically at least. You'll be seeing your boy real soon. Good-bye now."

"Good-bye, Detective. Thanks."

Doug held the phone to his ear until he heard it click. How was he going to tell Lucy about this? She'd been out at some kind of church thing. Luckily it had apparently run long, but she was going to be walking in the door any minute. This would probably be the toughest conversation of their marriage.

Going Home

"Mom, Dad, I'm okay! I'm okay!" Clint tried to reassure his parents, but they were overcome by emotion. They just hugged him and wept. "Ow! Watch the tummy, please."

Doug and Lucy stepped back, and Clint showed them the bandage on his waist. Doug felt a little light-headed, and Clint and Hulk helped him sit on the couch before he hit the floor.

"It's okay, Dad—just a little nick. Nothing's really damaged. I just needed a few sutures. Really, it's no big deal."

"Thank God, Son! Thank God you're okay," Lucy said. "And you, Milton, you're okay, too?"

"Yes, ma'am. It's not as bad as it looks. I want to get a picture of it before it goes down too much. No one's going to believe this if they don't see it."

"Mr. and Mrs. Buchanan," Hulk interjected, "they're both fine. Luckily that guy didn't stick Clint too bad, and this guy . . . ." Hulk turned toward Milton and smiled. He couldn't help chuckling. "This guy's head is like the Rock of Gibraltar or something. He took a full force blow from the heavy end of a pool stick, and it didn't even crack anything—besides the stick. He just has a mild concussion."

"I'm sorry to wimp out on you guys," Doug said from the couch, feeling better now. "This is all just a little too much. You can see who the strong ones are in this family."

"Well, sit down, y'all," Lucy said. "Anybody want anything to drink—coffee, tea, hot or cold?"

"No thanks, ma'am," Hulk answered. "I really need to be getting Milton home. His parents are as worried as you were."

"Yeah, my dad'll probably pass out, too," Milton said, and everyone laughed, including Doug.

Doug stood up and hugged Milton with tears in his eyes. He said, "Milton, thanks for being such a good friend to my boy. You're like a part of this family, and we love you."

"That's right," Lucy added with a hug of her own. "You're like our third son."

Milton wasn't one to be maudlin, but he did go a little misty and choked up. "Thanks," he said, obviously emotional and uncomfortable with it.

Doug reached out, shook Hulk's hand, and said, "Detective, I can't thank you enough. After hearing so much about you, it's a pleasure to finally meet you. You're my boy's hero, and I can see why."

"Don't mention it, sir. He means a lot to me, too." Was that a tear in Hulk's eye? He'd never admit it regardless.

Lucy stepped over and gave Hulk a big motherly hug. "Yes, thank you," she said. "Thank you for taking care of our boys here."

"You're welcome, ma'am. Normally I tell people, 'It's my job,' but it's more than just my job in this case. I have a vested interest." Hulk reached into his pocket and retrieved one of his business cards. He quickly jotted his home telephone number on it. Handing the card to Doug, he said, "Sir, call me anytime." Making intense eye contact, he added, "And don't forget what we talked about."

Doug took the card from Hulk and answered, "I won't."

"Sasquatch," Hulk said as he turned toward Clint, "you take care of yourself. I'll be seeing you again real soon. Don't you worry about none of this. I'll take care of it for you."

The two men started to shake hands but realized they couldn't, so Clint just threw his bandaged hands around Hulk's shoulders and gave him a big hug. Hulk was a little hesitant at first, but he did hug Clint back. Hulk didn't like sappy moments such as this, and he couldn't remember ever having hugged a man before. Even so, he couldn't deny the affection he felt for Clint.

After he had hugged Hulk, Clint turned and hugged Milton. The two young men couldn't have loved each other more if they'd shared blood, but they never articulated their feelings. They didn't need to; their love for one another was understood.

"Thanks for watching my back," Clint said quietly. "I wouldn't be here if it weren't for you."

"I'm not sure about that, but you're welcome. What are friends for?"

Hulk and Milton excused themselves, and that left Clint alone with his parents for the first time in a while. There was a minute or two of awkward silence before Clint finally said, "Mom, Dad, I'm sorry to put you through all this."

"Son, we're just glad you're okay," Lucy said. "There's a lot to talk about, but we don't have to do it now. It's late, and you need to get some rest."

"That's right, Son," Doug said. "I think we should hit the sack and do all our talking tomorrow."

"Dad?"

"Yes, Son?"

"Hulk told me he told you about Keith Willis, too."

"Is that his name? Yes, the detective did mention that."

"Well, Dad, his funeral is tomorrow afternoon, and I promised his mother I'd be there."

"Son, I'm sure she'd understand under the circumstances."

"Circumstances don't make any difference. I'm going to keep my word. If I'm breathing, I'm there."

"Just look at yourself, Son! You have a hole in your gut. Your hands are all bandaged up, and your face looks like it took a couple of punches, too. By the way, are your hands broken?"

"Yes, but they're all just fractures. No real breaks."

"They're *all*? Plural?" Lucy asked.

"Yes, ma'am. My hands and fingers are cracked up pretty bad, but nothing that's going to require surgery."

"Why didn't they put casts on them?" Doug asked.

"They're too swollen right now. Plus, the flesh got pretty chewed up, and that's going to take some time to heal. They don't really want to cover up any of the abrasions because of the risk of infection. They may put casts on them when the swelling goes down and the flesh has healed, but by then the bones should be well along to healing. I'm hoping I can avoid the casts. These bandages are bad enough."

"Oh, okay. Well anyway, I don't think you're in any kind of shape to go to that funeral. That lady will just have to understand."

"No, I'm going, Dad. I'm going, but I can't drive. I need a ride. Now will you take me, or do I have to call Tom?"

Doug sighed, thought for a moment, and said, "I'll take you, Son. I'll take you, but you need to get some rest now."

Lucy asked, "Do you need any help getting ready for bed?"

Embarrassed, Clint admitted, "Yeah, I probably do. I can't even get these bloody clothes off by myself."

Clint repined for his childhood when Lucy would help him get into his pajamas and then tuck him into bed with a hug and a kiss. She tucked him in every single night until he was 11 or 12, and she stopped only when he refused to let her do it anymore. He ached to go back in time and tell her, "It's okay, Mom. I'm not too big yet." Too, he longed to be a kid again so that his biggest problem would be getting ready for the next exam or sports contest—not death and funerals.

Lucy helped Clint get undressed and get a bath, which was tough to do without getting his wounds wet, which he wasn't supposed to do yet. He was embarrassed, as any young man would be, but he had no choice. It didn't seem to bother Lucy much. When Clint was all cleaned up, she gave him some of Doug's underwear. Clint was so thin around the waist that they actually wore almost the same size.

Clint lay down in his old bed and was soundly asleep in less than 30 seconds. Lucy went through his closet and found a suit that he had left there, along with a dress shirt and tie. They had been to the cleaners and were still wrapped in plastic. She checked the sizes and thought that he could probably still wear them. She found a belt, too, and it was about the right size. She dug around and found a pair of dress shoes and checked the size of those as well. They were 16EEEE, the same size he'd worn since he was 16 years old. She remembered how Clint's age and shoe size were pretty much in sync through age 16.

Lucy nosed around the closet some more. She had never gone through his room after he moved out. She just left everything as it had been, and she was surprised to see how much stuff he'd left there. It appeared that he'd taken most of his casual clothes and left all of his Sunday clothes. She thought about his declining church attendance and remembered that he hadn't worn a suit to church in quite a while. Had he left all his formal clothes here on purpose? She didn't like that he wore jeans to church, but that's what all the kids were doing now. She thought, "Well, I guess the Lord doesn't really care." She was just old-fashioned.

Doug and Lucy slept fitfully that night, what was left of it, and they didn't talk at all. They did hold each other, though—tightly. When morning came, Lucy got dressed and told Doug, "I'll be back in a little while. I need to go get a couple of things." She took Clint's keys and drove to his apartment. She had been there several times, but it still surprised her how neat it was. It wasn't spotless. There was some dirt and dust around, but everything was in its place.

Lucy went to the closet and found his underclothes folded neatly on shelves. She grabbed underwear, T-shirt, and socks, and then she went to the bathroom and picked up his razor and toothbrush. "I think that's it," she thought. She looked around just to satisfy her curiosity, and—sure enough—he didn't have any formal clothes whatsoever. He'd left them all at the house; it had to be on purpose.

By the time Lucy got back home, Clint was awake. He was sitting at the kitchen table while Doug made a big breakfast. "Where you been?" Clint asked.

"Oh, I just went to your apartment and picked up a few things you'll need today. We'll worry about everything else later. Right now we just need to get you through this funeral."

"Thanks, Mom. And thanks, Dad. Thank you both for everything."

They enjoyed a nice family breakfast together, and for a little while the world seemed right, except that Doug and Lucy had to take turns feeding Clint. They talked and laughed, reminisced about old times, and they didn't think about death. They didn't think about the circumstances that had brought Clint back home; they just enjoyed being together again.

Breakfast had been late and hearty, so they were able to skip dinner. In their family, the three meals of the day, in order, were breakfast, dinner, and supper. "Lunch" was something one carried in a sack, usually to eat for dinner at work or school. A little after noon, all dressed in their best Sunday clothes, they got in the car and headed to the funeral. Lucy decided that she and Doug should both go—not just to drive for Clint but to support him as well. She didn't know that she'd be meeting Clint's girlfriend for the first time. In fact, she hadn't even known that he'd settled down to a single girlfriend.

Doug took his time, and they still got to the funeral home a little early. Clint didn't see Dani's T-Bird, so they waited in the car for a little while. At about 1:45, they decided they had to go inside. "Wait!" Clint said. "We need to say a prayer. I don't think I can go in there without some intercession. Mom, will you?"

"Of course, Son. Let's bow our heads." They all bowed their heads and closed their eyes as Lucy prayed, "Our Dear Heavenly Father, thank You for this day and the many blessings You've given us. And thank You for being with my baby yesterday . . . ." Lucy's voice broke, and she took a moment to compose herself. Doug took her hand, and Clint put a bandaged hand on her shoulder. They all had tears in their eyes.

Lucy continued, "Thank You, Lord, for protecting Clint and Milton and for bringing Clint back home to us. And now, Lord, we pray that You'll be with us during this service for young Keith Willis. We didn't know Keith, Lord, but we pray that he's in Your care now. Please be with Clint, Lord. This is going to be tough for him, and he needs Your strength. And most especially, Lord, please be with Keith's mother, Ruth, and the rest of his family. Lord, they need You in a special way. Please give them Your peace and Your strength and, most of all, Your love that passes all understanding. In Jesus' name I pray. Amen."

"Amen," Doug and Clint said simultaneously.

They got out of the car, and Clint looked around. He still couldn't see Dani anywhere. He was sorely disappointed, though not completely surprised. When everything settled down, he'd have to get to the bottom of whatever was going on with her. They went inside the funeral home, and Ruth Willis had seen them and was running toward them.

"Oh, I'm so happy you made it!" Ruth started to hug Clint, but then she noticed the bandages on his hands. She looked at his face and saw some bruises. "Son, are you okay?" Ruth asked very seriously.

"Yes, ma'am," Clint answered. "I'm okay. Don't worry about me."

"Okay, son," Ruth said as she hugged Clint. Ruth squeezed Clint a little too tightly, and it hurt his belly wound. Clint couldn't help but flinch. Ruth pulled back and asked, "Are you sure you're okay?"

"Yes, ma'am," Clint said again. "I'm fine." Turning to his parents, he said, "Mom and Dad, I'd like to you meet Ruth Willis, Keith's mother. Ruth, this is my mom and dad, Lucy and Doug Buchanan."

"Oh, I'm so happy to meet you!" Ruth said as she hugged Lucy and then Doug. "This is one fine young man you've got here. I'm pleased to know him, and pleased to know the people responsible for raising such a fine boy."

Lucy and Doug were somewhat taken aback by Ruth's demeanor. How she and Clint had become friends was a notion that still puzzled them, as was her desire for him to be here at the funeral.

"We're pleased to meet you, too, ma'am," said Lucy. "We're sorry about the circumstances, though."

"Yes, ma'am, we're so sorry for your loss," Doug added.

"Well, I'm just so happy y'all could make it." Looking around, Ruth asked, "Where's Dani?"

Clint said, "I'm not sure, ma'am. She said she'd meet me here, but I guess she's running late."

"Ma'am, we're about to get started," said one of the men who worked for the funeral home.

"Okay," Ruth said. She shuddered and took Clint's hand.

They entered the chapel, and Clint walked with her all the way to the front row, hugged her, and kissed her cheek. She sat down, and Clint went back a few rows to the pew where Doug and Lucy had sat. Doug was on the end, and he scooted over to make room for Clint. Then Lucy insisted on switching places with Doug so she could sit between her two men. She turned slightly toward Clint and raised a hand to his shoulder. He patted her hand and smiled.

At this point Clint drifted off. He was vaguely aware of what was happening, but it was all like a dream. He was awakened from this state by a tap on his shoulder. He looked up and saw Dani smiling down at him. She noticed the bandages on his hands, and a look of shock took the place of her smile.

Clint stood, kissed Dani on the cheek, and whispered into her ear, "I'm okay. We'll talk later."

Doug had already scooted over to make room for Dani, but Lucy stood her ground for a moment. She looked at Dani with suspicion but did finally move over and let Dani sit between herself and Clint. Dani looked at Lucy and Doug, smiled, and gave each a quick "howdy" nod. This was the first time that Lucy had seen Dani, and she'd heard very little about her. Lucy hadn't known that Dani was black.

They all went back to listening to the preacher, and Clint was just about to drift back into his dream state when the preacher's words ensured that Clint remained fully alert. "Keith's mother, Ruth, has asked her friend Clint Buchanan to sing a special song for Keith today. Clint . . . ." The preacher yielded the pulpit and looked at Clint as if to ask, "Are you going to make it?"

Doug, Lucy, and Dani all looked toward Clint in shock. He hadn't told them he was going to sing, and they wondered if he had known in advance. Surely Ruth wouldn't just spring something like this on him without asking him first. Clint looked toward them and nodded. He smiled nervously, stood up, and very self-consciously made his way to the front. He made eye contact with no one, but he could see the glances toward his bandages and bruises. He sensed the eyes on his back.

When Clint got to Ruth, she stood up, hugged him, and whispered, "I'm praying for you, son. The Lord will make you strong."

Clint kissed her cheek and walked to the pulpit. He took his place and leaned forward, bracing himself against the sturdy platform. Doing so hurt his hands, but they'd just have to hurt. He wouldn't have been able to stand otherwise. He took a few moments to compose himself, and then he looked at Ruth.

Thankful for the microphone, Clint looked at Ruth and spoke quietly, "Ruth, you asked me here to sing today. I hope you don't mind if I say a few words, too." Ruth shook her head, and Clint continued, "Most of y'all are Keith's friends and family, and you don't know me. Those of you who do know who I am may feel as though I have no right to intrude on you at this difficult time, and if you feel that way, I'm sorry. My good friend Ruth asked me to be here today, so I'm doing this for her. To be honest, I didn't want to be here, but I couldn't say no to that fine woman on the front row." Clint smiled at Ruth.

Ruth smiled back and mouthed, "Thank you."

Several people around the chapel said, "Amen!"

Clint continued, "Keith and I weren't friends. Really we didn't even know each other, and for that I'm sorry. From what I can tell, he was a fine young man, and I would have been proud to count him as a friend. I guess that'll just have to wait until I join him in heaven."

"Amen!" and "Hallelujah!" rang out across the chapel.

"I know that Ruth loves the Lord, and I just have to say, along with my own mom back there, she's the finest Christian I've ever known."

More "amens" echoed through the chapel as Clint smiled at Ruth and Lucy, and they smiled back. Clint noticed Lucy look downward and dab an eye with a tissue.

"I visited Keith in the nursing home a few times, and Ruth was always there—always at his side. Ruth and I got to be good friends, but how could that be? A thousand times I've asked myself that question." Clint looked off into space and shook his head. He took a deep breath and continued, "How could this woman tolerate being in the same room with the man who killed her son?"

Everyone present gasped in unison. Most of them hadn't known, or hadn't made the connection.

Clint breathed deeply again and continued, "Yes, that's right. I'm the one who put Keith in that coffin." Looking upward and not at the closed coffin below, Clint said, "Keith, I'm sorry, but you know it was an accident. And I'll be sorry for it until I get up there and shake your hand, my brother."

There were a few "amens" and "hallelujahs" but not as many as before. There wasn't a dry eye in the chapel. Most people were looking downward and couldn't speak.

"The last time I visited Keith before he died," Clint continued, his voice breaking slightly, "I sang a song to him. I'm not sure why I did it. Something made me feel like I had to. I'd like to think it was the Lord who nudged me."

There were a few more "amens" and "hallelujahs" this time and a "praise Jesus" thrown in, and more people had looked back toward Clint.

"Anyway, I sang a song for Keith, and Ruth liked it so much she asked me to sing it again today." Clint bowed his head, closed his eyes, and prayed aloud, "Lord, I know this is Your will. Please give me strength. In Jesus' name I pray. Amen."

Everyone added his or her "amen" as well, and Clint steeled himself for the task at hand.

Without accompaniment, Clint's powerful baritone flooded the chapel. God answered his prayer, and his voice never wavered. To a melody from the second movement of Clint's favorite symphony, Dvořák's ninth, Clint sang William Arms Fisher's "Going Home." It was the very song he'd mentioned to Hulk once before.

Clint paused briefly after the first verse, and the chorus of "amens" and "hallelujahs" rang out again, virtually everyone this time. These folks were mostly charismatic— what some folks call "pew-pounders." They knew how to make noise, and they weren't afraid to celebrate at a funeral. After a moment, Clint sang the second verse.

Clint bowed his head when he was finished and received a standing ovation; tears streamed down each face. He stood there for a while, waiting for the "amens" and "hallelujahs" and "praise Jesuses" and all the clapping to die down. Everyone was stirred by the song—not Clint's singing necessarily, though it was an impressive performance, especially given the naked, a capella presentation.

Folks were moved by the message of the song and how it fit this particular occasion so perfectly. It wasn't an original song, of course. It had been around for decades, and some had heard it at funerals before. It just seemed to be particularly appropriate in this case, given the way that Keith lingered for so long before quietly slipping away to an afterlife free of suffering and grief.

Ruth believed that Keith had heard the song in the nursing home that day and that its message convinced him that going home to the Lord would be a good thing, a joyous occasion. It gave him peace, and she felt that the Lord had worked through Clint to convince her boy that it was indeed time to go home and that doing so was not the end of anything but, rather, the beginning. Ruth was hopeful that it would give Clint some peace as well. She also prayed that he would someday hear God's calling to use his voice for the glory of the Lord on a full-time basis.

When it was quiet enough to continue, Clint said, "Keith loved the Lord, and he's gone home now. He's with the Lord, and those of us who love the Lord will be there, too, one day." Looking upward again, Clint added, "Keith, I'll be seeing you soon."

Shocked, Doug and Lucy looked at each other, worried about that last sentence. Clint stepped around the pulpit and began walking back to his seat, stopping at the first row to give Ruth a big, long hug and another peck on the cheek. Ruth was crying freely, but she was smiling and looked very happy.

"Oh, thank you, son! Thank you! That was beautiful! God bless you!"

Clint made his way back to his seat and collapsed onto the pew. He leaned over, his head between his knees, and bawled like a baby. Dani put her arm around Clint while Doug and Lucy held each other and cried. Lucy handed Dani a tissue, and Dani gave it to Clint. He sobbed for a few moments, took a few deep breaths, and sat up again. He dabbed his eyes and nose with the tissue and put it in a pocket of his suit jacket.

The preacher had a few more words to say, but Clint didn't really hear them. He was happy to have survived the song. At the end of the service, everyone filed past Keith's casket to say their last good-byes. Ruth had opted to keep it closed. The sight of Keith's body would have been a shock to anyone, but to someone who had known him before that fateful night at Billy Bob's, it might have been too much. Instead of viewing Keith's actual remains, Ruth had pictures of Keith on and around the coffin so that people could remember him the way he was before. That's the Keith she wanted them to remember. There was even a picture of Keith in his karate gi, and Clint lingered on that one for a few moments. Dani squeezed his hand a little tighter then.

Clint shuddered to think of folks crying over his own dead body one day. It was a ritual that had always puzzled him. He just couldn't understand why people would make such a big deal out of a worthless pile of dead cells, and he had resolved that he would be cremated before his funeral. His parents were aware of his wishes, and though they didn't agree with him, they had promised to honor those wishes if—God forbid—he should precede them in death. Clint figured, and even Doug and Lucy had to agree, that if he needed his body at any point after death, the Lord Almighty would be up to the task.

After the funeral there was a short graveside service. Keith's grave was very near the chapel, so everyone walked over. When the service had ended, everybody made their way back to the main building. The family had another event planned, and many were leaving together. Ruth caught up to the Buchanans and Dani, though, and spoke to them one last time.

"I'm so glad you could make it," Ruth said to Dani.

"I'm sorry I was late. I meant no disrespect," Dani said.

"Oh, I know that. Think nothing of it. I'm just glad you're here." Turning to Clint, Ruth gave him a thorough look top to bottom, shook her head, and said, "Son, I'd love to talk to you about what happened, but I just can't right now. Are you sure you're okay?"

"Yes, ma'am. Don't you worry about me. I'm alright, and I'll be alright," Clint said as he leaned to hug Ruth. "Thank you for letting me be a part of this."

"Oh, son," Ruth said, pausing for a moment. "You sang beautiful, and it was the perfect song. Thank you. Thank you for singing it for Keith in the nursing home, and thank you for singing it again today. You gave Keith a real nice send-off. It wouldn't have been the same without you."

Ruth and Clint held each other for a long time. Finally Ruth pulled away, turned to Clint's parents, and said, "Mr. and Mrs. Buchanan . . . ." She smiled and said, "It took me a while to learn how to say that right."

"That's okay, ma'am," Lucy said. "It took me a while, too."

Everyone chuckled, and Ruth continued, "This boy of yours . . . . He's special. He's become like another son to me. Keith's daddy died when he was just a baby, and I never got married again. Keith was all I had, but your Clint . . . . Well, he's really helped me say good-bye to my boy. They say the apple don't fall too far from the tree, so I know you's good folks. Thank you for raising this boy up right so he could help me through all this." Ruth stepped between Doug and Lucy and hugged them both at the same time.

"We're so very sorry for your loss, ma'am, and thank you for your kind words," Lucy said.

"Yes, ma'am," Doug said. "Thank you for being so kind to our boy, and we'll be praying for you. We hope to see you again."

"Oh, I hope so, too!" Ruth beamed. She turned and hugged Clint and Dani one more time and said, "Good-bye now. Y'all don't be strangers."

"Don't worry," Dani said. "We won't."

"That's right," Clint said. With a wink, he added, "We love you, momma."

"Thank you, son. You know how I love to hear that."

With that Ruth turned and walked away. She got into a car with some relatives, and they drove away. The Buchanans and Dani watched them until the car went out of sight.

An Evening with Mom & Dad

Clint looked first at Dani and then at his mother and said, "Well, I guess I should introduce you two. Mom, this is Dani Bailey. Dani, this is my mother, Lucy Buchanan."

Lucy reached and shook Dani's hand and said, "Pleased to meet you, Dani."

Clint thought that Lucy was a tougher read than usual today. He perceived that Lucy wasn't really pleased to meet Dani, but he didn't really know why. Perhaps it was some kind of weird female competition thing, or maybe it was something else.

"Oh, the pleasure is mine, Mrs. Buchanan," Dani said, flashing those beautiful teeth of hers and shaking Lucy's hand vigorously. Then she threw her arms around Lucy, gave her a good, hard hug, and said, "I'm so happy to finally meet Clint's mother."

Lucy was definitely uncomfortable with the hug, and Clint thought, "Could it be the race thing?"

Dani released Lucy and hugged Doug, saying, "It's good to see you again, sir."

"Likewise," Doug said. Doug looked at Lucy. He'd noticed her discomfort, too.

Clint said, "Okay, why don't we all go out to eat? Mom, Dad, Dani, is that alright with you?"

"Uh, sure, I guess. I mean . . . . Sure, I can make it," Dani said awkwardly.

"Son, don't you think you need to get some more rest?" Lucy asked. "Dani, in case you didn't notice, our boy had a rough day yesterday."

"That's right! What happened to you?" Dani asked.

Clint exchanged glances with both his parents and said, "Well, uh, I'm not sure that this is the time or the place to discuss it. We should talk about it at supper, or after." Turning to Lucy, he said, "Mom, I'm okay. I can handle supper with the three most important people in my life. After yesterday . . . . After today, I could go for a good, relaxing meal with y'all."

"Sure, Son," Doug said. "You're right. Besides, it would give us a chance to get to know Dani a little better." Lucy still looked a little uncomfortable. She was trying to hide it but wasn't very successful.

"Okay," Clint said. "Why don't we meet up at that Cheddar's over by Six Flags? That sound okay to y'all?"

Clint and his parents often attended Texas Rangers baseball games at Arlington Stadium, and after the games, they always stopped at that Cheddar's to wait out the traffic. It was their favorite restaurant.

"Yeah, sure, Son," Doug said. "I assume you'll be riding with Dani?"

"Yes, we'll meet you there," Clint answered.

"Okay, Son, we'll see you," Doug said. "Dani, see you soon."

"Bye now," Dani said. "Bye, Mrs. Buchanan"

"Bye," Lucy said curtly.

Doug and Lucy got in their car as Clint and Dani got into hers. Doug drove out of the parking lot first, and Dani pulled onto the road behind him.

Dani told Clint, "Your mother doesn't like me."

"Honestly, Dani, as much as I'd like to disagree with you, I think you're right. It certainly seems that way. I'm just not sure why."

Dani chuckled and said, "I know why!"

"Oh, really?"

"Sure, I know why. It's exactly what I told you from the start. I'm black, and she don't like it. Simple."

"No, I don't think that's it," Clint said. "Well, I hope not anyway. That would be disappointing on more than one level."

While Clint and Dani were discussing the issue, so were Doug and Lucy.

"Honey, are you okay?" Doug asked. "You seemed a little uncomfortable with Dani."

"You could've warned me she was black."

"Does that make a difference? You know we raised our kids to think that everyone is equal. We're not racist people."

"No, that's not it," Lucy said. "Then again, maybe it is. I don't know. It was just a bit of a shock. We can talk about the races being equal and teach our kids to believe that, and that's all good when it's hypothetical. But when a black woman—a much older black woman—is standing there with my baby boy, it's just a little too real."

Doug didn't really know what to say. This was a bit of a shock, and he was having trouble digesting it. There was a pregnant pause in the conversation.

Finally Lucy said, "You know, Doug, she's probably a real nice woman, and I know I shouldn't feel the way I do. I'm a little ashamed of myself, but I'm not going to deny it to myself or to you." She thought for a moment and added, "And I just have trouble thinking of Clint having sex with a woman—any woman, no matter what color she is."

"Well," Doug said, "I guess that makes sense. But let's change the subject. What did you make of what Clint said up there? About going to see Keith *soon*? I mean . . . . He did a beautiful job with that song. I was impressed that he could do it at all, but to do such a great job . . . . That was something. But I've got to be honest with you. I'm worried about him, Lucy."

Doug continued, "Detective Roy told me some things. I don't want to get into it all right now, but he's concerned that Clint may need to see a psychologist—that his mind might be a little messed up. And that 'Keith, I'll see you soon' thing . . . ." Doug shuddered. "It gives me the heebie-jeebies. It sounds like he's thinking about killing himself!"

Lucy looked straight ahead and said, "Doug, our son has killed three men. One was an accident, and two were self defense. It's not like he's a criminal. But he's still killed three men. That's the simple truth, and it frightens me." Lucy started to cry, and Doug reached over and held her hand.

Her voice breaking, Lucy continued, "Normal people can't kill other human beings and just forget about it like it's no big deal, like they're animals. My heart is breaking for Clint right now. I just can't imagine . . . ."

She retrieved a tissue from her purse and dabbed at her eyes and nose. "I just can't imagine what he's going through, what he's thinking. And yes, what he said at the funeral bothered me, too. I'm very worried, and I'm sure Detective Roy is right. We have to get him some help."

Doug and Lucy drove the rest of the way to the restaurant in silence, and Clint and Dani continued their own conversation.

"Clint, it don't matter if your momma don't like me because I'm black. I'm used to that. Believe me, all black folks are used to that. As long as she's nice to me and treats me with respect, I don't care whether or not she really likes black folks. To tell you the truth, I don't like all white folks either."

"Fair enough," Clint said. "Besides, what Mom thinks doesn't really matter anyway. It's what I think that counts, and you know that your color doesn't matter to me. I wouldn't care if you were purple."

"I know, Clint. I love you, too. Say! What happened to you anyway? Good Lord! You look like you been through a wringer!"

Very matter-of-factly and without hesitation, Clint said, "Dani, I killed two men yesterday."

"You what?" She struggled to keep the car on the road. "Say again?"

Clint sighed and said, "Look, it's a long story, so I'll make it short. Milton and I got into a fight with some bikers in a pool hall. It was three of them and two of us, and things got really nasty—pool cues, knives, the whole works. One of them stuck me down here," he said, pointing toward the hidden wound. "It wasn't bad, but I took some stitches in the ER. My hands got all busted up, too."

"So two of the bikers died?"

"Yeah, I guess I got a little carried away. So much for your ice water theory."

"My God! I can't believe this! Are you going to be in any trouble?"

"No, Hulk says it was self defense. It's his investigation. He's writing the report and recommendation to the DA. He told me not to worry."

"Well, that's good. I guess . . . . Are you sure you're okay?"

"I'm fine, Dani. My gut will heal quickly, and I've had broken bones before. These aren't a big deal."

"That's good, but I don't just mean your body. How's your head? Still screwed on straight?"

"That remains to be seen," Clint said.

"Well, at least it's still screwed on."

They rode the rest of the way in silence.

The four managed to have a nice meal at Cheddar's. Lucy loosened up and seemed to have fun. She and Dani helped Clint with his meal and actually made a little game out of it. No one mentioned the funeral or the events of yesterday, preferring instead to put off the uncomfortable discussions until later. Doug and Clint argued briefly over who was going to pay, but Clint ultimately let his dad have the check. Before leaving the restaurant, the four discussed what they would do next.

"I still need to get my truck from Shooter's. Dad, can you and Mom help me with that?"

"Yeah, I guess so," Doug answered, "but can't you just leave it there a couple of days?"

"No, sir, I'd rather go ahead and get it now. I don't want anything to happen to it."

"Okay, y'all lead the way, and we'll follow. I can drive it back home for you."

Dani said, "Well, um, I'm not sure I can make it. I kind of have to get back home." Dani wouldn't make eye contact with Clint. He was very suspicious but didn't want to argue about it, especially not in front of his parents.

"Are you sure?" was all he asked.

Dani thought for a minute before saying, "Oh, forget it. Yeah, I can come."

"Good," Clint said. "I really want you to come over to the house with us." Dani looked a little uncomfortable but didn't say anything more.

"Okay, Son, you lead the way," Doug said.

"Bye now," Lucy said. "We'll see y'all in a little while."

With Clint giving her directions, Dani drove to Shooter's, and Doug and Lucy followed them. Something troubling occurred to Clint just as they were pulling into the parking lot: What if Bandidos were nosing around the place? Luckily he didn't see any Harleys parked there or nearby, so he figured the coast was clear. Even so, there was no point in lingering, and they didn't. It only took a minute before Doug was in Clint's truck and ready to go, and their little three-vchicle caravan drove to Allen.

The four had a nice visit at Doug and Lucy's that evening, and it really seemed that Lucy had gotten over whatever had been bothering her earlier. Perhaps Dani had won her over, or maybe Lucy was merely putting on a good show. Either way, they had a nice visit full of laughter, fun, and good conversation. Dani even let Doug play some Marty Robbins on the stereo, perhaps sensing that it was necessary to keep the laughter, fun, and good conversation going. No one dared disparage Marty Robbins in the presence of Doug Buchanan!

They were interrupted by phone calls from Tom and Hulk, and Clint called Milton to check on him, too. Clint assured all his buddies that he was okay, and he was happy to hear that Milton was doing fine, although Milton seemed to be a little bummed that his knot had already diminished substantially. At least he would have his pictures. Clint was a little concerned about how Milton's parents would react to what had happened, but Milton assured him that everything was copacetic.

As it got later, Dani seemed to grow a little restless, and eventually she excused herself. "I'm sorry, but I really need to go now. I have to get back home," she said. Again Clint had questions but elected not to ask them for the time being.

"Are you sure? We've had a lovely time," Lucy said with a smile that seemed genuine.

"Yes, ma'am, I'm sure. I've really had great time, too, but I need to go."

Everyone stood, and Lucy gave Dani a nice, warm hug and a kiss on the cheek. "I'm sorry I was a little out of sorts earlier," Lucy said. "I'm sure you understand it's been a rough couple of days."

"Yes, ma'am, I understand."

"It was so good meeting you and getting to know you a little," Lucy said. "I hope we can all get together again real soon."

"That's right," Doug added. "You're welcome in our house anytime." Doug hugged Dani as well.

"Thank you. Thank you both," Dani said. "It was good to spend some time with you, and I appreciate your hospitality. I'm sure I'll be around again before too long."

Clint walked Dani out to her car, and they paused there for a little while. They held each other tightly without speaking for several minutes. Finally Clint said, "Thank you for coming today—the funeral, the restaurant, here. It's been a good day with you. It wouldn't have been good without you."

Dani smiled and kissed him. She said, "I've enjoyed it, Clint. Well, actually the funeral wasn't much fun, but I've enjoyed the time with you and your parents. But I really have to go now. We'll get together again very soon, and we can talk some more about what happened yesterday. Are you sure you're okay?"

"Yes, I'm okay. I'm going to be just fine. You don't have to worry about me."

They kissed again and held each other for a few more moments, and then Dani got in her car and drove away. Clint watched her car until the taillights went around the curve near the end of the street. He lingered there a few moments longer, just staring into the distance, questions on his mind and butterflies in his stomach.

Meanwhile, inside the house Clint's parents were ending a brief exchange.

"Yes, honey, it was Oscar-worthy. Thanks," Doug said.

Lucy replied, "Our boy has enough on his mind without having to worry about whether or not I approve of his girlfriend."

Brother Collins

When Doug and Lucy awakened on Sunday morning, Clint was already awake and sitting at the kitchen table. He was just sitting there in his underwear, looking depressed and drinking a cup of coffee.

"Oh, my!" Lucy said. "Those hands look awful! Why are you out of your bandages?"

"You know, you do have to change them every now and then," Clint replied.

"There's no need for sarcasm, Son," Doug interjected.

"You're right, Dad. Mom, I'm sorry. I didn't mean to take that tone. Anyway, I just can't stand having my hands all bound up like that. I can't do anything for myself. I can't even hardly take a leak without making a mess. God forbid I should need to go Number Two."

"Okay, well after breakfast I'll dress them back up for you," Lucy said.

"No, Mom, I don't think so. I think I'll just drive my truck back to my apartment and try to get on with my life."

"I was hoping you'd at least go to church with us this morning. Brother Collins always asks about you," Lucy said.

"No, I don't think so, Mom. Brother Collins never did much for me anyway."

"Excuse me, young man? Brother Collins baptized you. He married your sister, and he'll probably preach my funeral when the time comes. He means a lot to this family." Lucy was indignant. Brother Collins was very high on her list and not only because he was her pastor.

"Your mom's right, Son," Doug added, almost half-heartedly. "You should show more respect." Doug didn't particularly care for Brother Collins either, but he didn't want to risk Lucy's wrath.

"Mom, Dad, you're right. I'm sorry. Please, just give me a little space right now. The last few days have been awfully rough on me. I feel like one of Grandpa's old horses that got rode hard and put up wet. My body hurts. My head's a little messed up, and to tell you the truth, I'm a little tired of being around people. I need to be alone. I need my 'me' time. You know how I am."

Lucy finally sat down at the table with Clint while Doug poured their coffee. She reached across the table and touched one of Clint's fingers gently as her eyes welled up with tears. "My poor boy," she said.

Doug put a mug of coffee in front of Lucy and then sat down and took a sip of his own. He took another sip, stalling. Finally he had the nerve. "Clint, it's that messed up head that we need to talk about."

"Dad, I wasn't speaking literally."

Doug looked Clint straight in the eye and said, "Son, three men are dead because of you. How do you feel about that?"

"Come on, Dad! Keith Willis was an accident, and those bikers had it coming. It's not like I'm a murderer."

"Yes, Son, I know that. You're not a murderer. You're not a criminal of any kind. You're just a young man who's killed three people recently, and I happen to think you're the kind of young man who can't just blow that off. They weren't animals."

"Well, I don't know about those Bandidos," Clint said with a smile.

Doug's expression didn't change. "Son, the death of a human being is nothing to joke about. I don't care if you're talking about a cold-blooded murderer being executed. He may have been a cruel killer and a sorry excuse for a human being, and he may have deserved to die. It's still nothing to celebrate or makes jokes about. You cried like a baby when you saw 'Old Yeller' and when we had to put your own Yeller down. Any person is worth more than a dog."

"Dad, I'm not so sure about that, but I get your point. I'm sorry. I shouldn't have cracked wise about it."

"Okay, Son, so answer my question. How do you feel about killing three people?"

Clint couldn't make eye contact. He tried to take a sip from his empty coffee mug; then he got up and refilled it. He sat back down, took a sip, and thought for a minute or two longer. Partly he was stalling, but he wasn't sure of the answer either. Lucy and Doug sat quietly, wanting to give him plenty of time to answer—and hopefully to do so honestly. Clint sat with his huge, mangled hands around his coffee mug and stared at the steam rising from the liquid.

Finally Clint said, "I feel pretty awful about Keith Willis. I just wanted to fight and make some money, maybe even make a name for myself. I wanted Coach Morris and everyone who ever called me a pussy—sorry, Mom—to know that I'm not. It never occurred to me that anyone might actually get hurt. Oh, sure, I know that's always possible, but what are the odds? I never thought it would actually happen—not to me. I mean . . . . You know what I mean. It hurts. It hurts real bad."

Clint's tears were starting now, and he took Lucy's hand. "Mom, Dad, you met Ruth Willis. She's one fine lady. Isn't she?"

"Yes, she is," Lucy said.

"That's right," added Doug.

"So the chances are good that Keith was a pretty decent guy. He graduated high school. He was going to community college, and they don't just give those black belts away. He had to have a lot of dedication, a good work ethic."

Doug nodded and said, "Yeah, son, that's probably right—a lot like you."

"Well, Dad, knowing all that just makes it tougher. I left a big part of myself in the ring that night, and I don't know if I can ever get it back."

"No, Son, I don't expect you can. I mean, the wound may heal if you treat it properly, but it's still going to scar."

Clint nodded and continued, "As for the Bandidos, well, I don't know how I feel about that. Dad, you always taught me to walk away if I could and to fight if I couldn't. These guys weren't going to let me walk away."

"We know that son," Doug said, "but do you think you may have gone a little too far? Couldn't you have stopped at some point before . . . ."

"Before I killed them? I don't know, Dad. I really don't remember a lot about the fight, and what I do remember is like a dream. There's holes, and I can't fill them. I do remember getting stabbed, and I remember the guy hitting Milton with the pool stick. That really set me off. I remember before and after, but I really don't remember a whole lot else. I don't remember . . . . I don't remember killing them."

"Son," Doug started, but then he looked away for a moment and gathered his strength for the next question. He turned back to Clint and asked, "Do you think they deserved to die?"

Clint didn't even take a moment to consider his answer. He immediately shook his head and said, "No, sir, I reckon not."

Clint's tears began to flow more freely, and Lucy got up and came around the table. As he sat in the chair and cried, Lucy stood behind him and wrapped her arms around him and laid her head against his. Doug reached across and took one of Clint's hands gingerly. They were all crying now. After a few minutes Lucy looked at the clock.

"There's no way we can make Sunday School," she said, "and we're going to miss worship unless we skip breakfast."

"Then let's skip breakfast," Clint said. He was smiling and wiping some tears away with a napkin from the table. "I'll go with you," he said. "I think my suit from yesterday is still presentable."

"Oh, good!" Clint had just made her day.

The Buchanans got ready for church, and before they left the house, Clint reluctantly let Lucy re-wrap his hands. Lucy really enjoyed the sermon, though Clint and Doug could barely remember it. Neither cared too much for fire and brimstone. They preferred teaching to preaching, so they tuned out and thought about other things—the same things in this case. As everyone filed out of the church afterward for the ritualistic handshake with the pastor, Clint was thankful that he wouldn't have to participate.

"Lucy!" Brother Collins said. "It's so good to see you. I always know you'll be here if these doors are open." Brother Collins gave Lucy a hug and looked over her shoulder at Doug and Clint.

"Doug," he said, shaking Doug's hand, "you could come a little more often, and Clint! How long has it been?" Noticing Clint's hands and face, he asked, "What happened to you, son?"

Doug jumped in, "Pastor, I'm not sure this is the time or place, but we'd love to have you and Julie over for dinner. Can you make it today?"

"Of course! No one can cook like your Lucy, but it will just be me. Julie's at her parents right now. Her mom's sick," the preacher responded.

"Oh, we're sorry to hear that," Lucy said. "We'll remember them in prayer. I'll make sure to feed you good today. See you in about an hour?"

"Absolutely! I wouldn't miss it," the preacher said. He noted that Clint still hadn't spoken, but he said nothing about it. Clint had always intimidated him.

As the Buchanans got in the car for the short drive home, Clint asked, "Okay, Dad, what's up with that?"

"Son, I'm sorry about that. I don't really like him much either, but I do respect what he knows about certain things. It might do you some good to talk to him."

"That's right, Son," Lucy said. "He might be able to help you."

Clint looked out the window as they passed his old elementary school playground. He had a flash of himself running with the football, dragging several of his classmates all the way across the playground to score another touchdown. Two or three kids could never tackle Clint; four or five had trouble. To no one in particular, he said quietly, "I'm not so sure the Good Lord Himself could help me now."

When they got home, Doug helped Clint get out of his coat and tie and then turned the stereo to an AM Gospel station. While Clint rested in Doug's recliner, Doug and Lucy changed into more comfortable clothes, and then Lucy went to work on dinner. By the time Brother Collins rang the bell, she had fried chicken, green beans, mashed potatoes, and gravy on the table. There hadn't been time to make a dessert, but they had some leftover chocolate cake that was still fresh.

Doug opened the door for the preacher, and the four shared a nice Sunday dinner. Much to Lucy's chagrin, Clint had unwrapped his hands again so he could feed himself, and though the preacher never said anything, he glanced frequently at Clint's hands and face. Sooner or later he would get around to asking the inevitable question. As was the Buchanan family custom, they ate their chocolate cake in bowls with milk over it, and the preacher marveled at how good it was.

"I still can't get over how good this is," he said. "Before I met y'all, I'd never heard of eating cake this way."

"Oh, it's just something my family's always done," Lucy said. "We wouldn't have it any other way."

After dinner, the three men moved to the living room to listen to the Gospel music on the radio, and Lucy came out a little later with coffee for everyone. Everyone had just begun to sip their coffee when Clint decided to have a little fun with the preacher.

Suddenly Clint said plainly, "I killed three people this week," and it was hard for him to hide his smile when the preacher spilled the hot coffee in his lap.

"Ow, that's hot!" Brother Collins said, jumping up and wiping at the wetness with a napkin.

Lucy ran to the kitchen and came back with a dish towel and gave it to the preacher. It was a little more effective than the napkin, but he would have some minor burns.

"I'm so sorry," Lucy said, looking embarrassed and hurt. Even so, Clint could only feel a little guilty. He really didn't like the man, and he definitely didn't appreciate the intrusion.

"Clint, you shouldn't have sprung it on him like that," Doug said, betraying just a little pleasure with the situation.

"Mea culpa," Clint offered unconvincingly. He was not contrite, and it showed.

"I'm okay, folks. Don't worry about it. I've had worse burns," the preacher said, casting a disdainful glance Clint's way. Sitting back down he asked, "Okay, Clint, now what's this all about?"

As Lucy went to get Brother Collins another cup of coffee, Clint just sat there and said nothing. Finally Doug decided to try to get the ball rolling.

"Pastor, last year Clint had a fight—not like a brawl. It was a professional fight, some kind of kickboxing match. Clint hurt the other boy real bad, and he died the other day. His funeral was yesterday."

"I'm sorry to hear that," the pastor said very sincerely. "Was he a Christian?"

Clint just nodded his answer.

"Good! At least we don't have to worry about that. Oh, but you said there were three." The pastor was puzzled, and finally Clint decided to speak for himself.

"The other two were bikers, members of the Bandidos motorcycle gang. They jumped me and Milton Vaughan in a pool hall down in Dallas," Clint said.

"Now, Clint, you know you shouldn't go to places like that. Were you drinking?" the pastor asked condescendingly.

"Yes, sir, I was drinking Pepsi, and Milton was drinking Dr. Pepper."

The preacher made a face but said nothing. Lucy was back now with another cup of coffee.

"Thank you, Lucy. I'll hold on to this one," he said with a smile.

As Lucy took her seat, she said, "Clint, I heard that. Please don't be disrespectful to our pastor."

"Sorry," Clint said. Again it was not a credible apology. "No, sir, we weren't drinking anything *sinful*. We were just drinking our cokes, shooting pool, and minding our own business when these three bikers came in. We'd had a run-in with one of them once before, down in Austin, and he remembered us, or at least me. We tried to leave, but they wanted to fight. We defended ourselves, and two of them wound up dead. That's the long and short of it."

"Did you use that karate of yours, Clint?" the preacher asked. He'd told Lucy long ago that he didn't approve of it, though he didn't state a reason. With Lucy he didn't have to. He was a Southern Baptist minister, after all, and only members of the Holy Trinity outranked a pastor in Lucy's book.

"Brother Collins, yes," Clint said crossly, "I used that karate of mine. I used the boxing that Dad taught me. I used the crude animal instincts that God gave me. When you're in a fight like that, when guys are hitting you with pool sticks and sticking you with knives and doing everything they can to kill you, you use whatever works to stay alive. You think the Good Lord has a problem with that? I kind of figure He wouldn't have given us a survival instinct if he didn't want us to use it. Would you rather I just lay down and let the guy cut me up like a Christmas turkey?"

"No, Clint, I didn't say that. The Lord doesn't have a problem with you defending yourself, but if you hadn't been hanging out in a place like that, it wouldn't have been necessary. Am I right?"

"Preacher, you could say the same thing about someone dying in a car wreck. How about that Wood boy who got killed last week? You tell his momma he shouldn't have been driving so fast with a couple beers in his belly? Would that make her feel better?"

"Now, Clint," Lucy said, "you know that's not the same thing."

"It's not that far off, Mom. I was doing nothing wrong. I'm not saying that Milton and I are little angels, but we did nothing wrong on Friday. He's trying to turn this thing around and make it like it was our fault, and I can't abide that."

"No, Clint, I'm sorry," the preacher said. "That's not my intent at all, but you're right. It's not fruitful to talk about that, so let's just move on. Clint, now I'm going to ask you a tough question. I want you to think about it, and I want you to give me an honest answer. Can you do that for me, Clint? For your mom and dad?"

"Yes, sir," Clint answered, "I'll give an honest answer for Mom and Dad."

Ignoring the slight, Brother Collins continued, "Okay then. Clint, did you mean to kill those men? Wait. I'm sorry; the numbers are confusing me. Were there two or three?"

"There were three of them, but only two died," Clint said, "And to answer your question . . . ." He looked downward and shook his head. "I don't know. I really don't know."

Doug jumped in at that point and offered, "Pastor Collins, I talked to the detective who investigated the, uh, the incident. He said that he didn't think that Clint was thinking clearly, that he wasn't himself. You have to remember that Clint was stabbed."

"Oh, really? Stabbed? I didn't realize that. Are you okay, son?" the preacher asked. He seemed genuinely concerned.

"I'm fine. It was just a nick," Clint said.

Doug continued, "It was a little more than a nick actually, but I'm not going to split that hair. The thing is, Clint was stabbed, and then he saw Milton get hurt. The detective said he just snapped and went a little crazy and got carried away."

"Is Milton okay?" the preacher asked. Milton had gone to the same church for a while, so Brother Collins was familiar with him.

"Yeah, just a bump on the noggin," Clint said.

"Were you arrested, Clint? Are you going to be in any trouble?" the preacher asked, and Clint just shook his head.

"No," Doug said, "the police said it was self defense."

The preacher thought for a moment and then asked, "Clint, what do you think?"

"Sir," Clint answered, "it's like I said. I don't know. I don't really remember much. I remember before the fight and after the fight, and I remember getting stabbed. And I remember Milton getting hurt. Other than that, it's just flashes, kind of dreamy. I really don't know."

Brother Collins leaned forward, looked at Clint, and said, "Son, it sounds to me like you bear no guilt here—not in the legal sense and not in the moral sense either. I'm okay with your explanation, and I think the Lord would be, too."

"Thank you," Clint said. It did actually make him feel a little better.

"But, son," the preacher continued, "that's not all there is to it. I know how you were raised, and I know you're a Christian. You may not be following God's path a hundred percent right now, but I think your heart's in the right place. I think you're a good person, just like your mom and dad, and your brother and sister, too. Are you okay with this? Can you put it aside, or is it something that's going to fester inside of you?"

Clint was actually starting to think that this talk was a good idea. "No, sir, I'm not okay with it, and I don't think I can put it aside." As Clint's tears started to flow again, he said, "I killed three people for Christ's sake! Sorry. I know I shouldn't take the Lord's name in vain. But I killed three people! *Three!* How many folks have to deal with something like that?"

"Not many. Not many," the pastor said with a sigh. He stepped over to Clint, put a hand on his shoulder, and said, "Clint, I remember baptizing you, and since then I've watched you grow toward the Lord and grow away from Him, too. But you know what? God is still your Heavenly Father, and nothing can pluck you from His grasp. He loves you, and He will never reject you—no matter what. Will you pray with me?"

"Yes, sir, please," Clint answered desperately.

"Join us," Brother Collins said to Doug and Lucy, and all four hit their knees on the living room floor. They formed a prayer ring, and Clint held Brother Collins' hand on one side and Lucy's on the other. The Buchanans were all crying, and even the preacher was a little misty. He seemed very sincere.

"Our dear Heavenly Father," Brother Collins prayed. "We come to You now with humble and heavy hearts. We ask that You hear our prayer and blanket us with Your love. Young Clint needs Your help, Lord. You know what's happened, Lord. You know the truth. You know how he's hurting. Lord, if Clint's done anything wrong in Your eyes, I know he's sorry for it. Please show him what it is so he can confess it and ask Your forgiveness. We know that if we confess our sins, You are faithful and just to forgive us our sins and to cleanse us of all unrighteousness. But Lord, sometimes it's hard for us to see what we did wrong."

Brother Collins shifted his position a little and continued, "Lord, please open Clint's eyes so he can see if he's displeased You and ask Your forgiveness. And, Lord, please lift this burden from his shoulders. He's young, Lord, and his whole life is in front of him. But he needs Your peace to go on. Please, Lord, take this burden from him and give him Your peace. Show him Your light, and lead him where You want him to go. Please help Clint to move forward and to learn from this and to do Your will in the future. Be with this good family, Lord. Help them all to deal with this tragedy. Manifest Your love to them, and bless them. In Jesus' name we pray. Amen."

Brother Collins stood up and took a seat again, and the Buchanans followed suit. After a short pause, Brother Collins asked, "Feel better, Clint?"

"Yes, sir, I do," Clint responded, "but is it really that simple?"

"Yes, sometimes it is, but not always. I know you've heard people say, 'God helps those who help themselves.' Sometimes a person needs a little more, and this seems like it might be one of those times. I'll be honest with you all. I took some counseling courses at the seminary. We all had to, but this might be over my head. You might need to see a real counselor, if you're open to that idea."

Clint looked at Doug and Lucy and asked, "Mom, Dad, what do y'all think?"

"I think you should, Son," Doug said. Doug thought it best not to invoke Hulk unless necessary. It might cause more problems.

"Me, too," Lucy said. "I think it would be a good idea."

"Okay then, I'll do it," Clint said. He was relieved, and it occurred to him that he had probably misjudged Brother Collins. Now that he thought about it, he couldn't even remember what had turned him against the man. He said, "Pastor, please forgive my behavior earlier. I haven't been myself lately. I know you understand. Truth is, I'm very grateful for your help."

"Oh, Clint," the pastor said, standing up to give him a big hug. "Of course I understand. You know, we've had our ups and downs over the years, but I know you're a good kid. I love you, and I'm proud of you, son. You're going to be alright."

Brother Collins also hugged Clint's parents, first Lucy and then Doug, and he told them, "Y'all need any help finding someone, you let me know."

"Yes, sir, we will," Doug said, giving the pastor another handshake as he made his way toward the front door.

"Thank you, Brother Collins," Lucy said. "I'll see you at church tonight."

"Oh, I know it, Lucy. I always know it," he said with big grin. "Oh, and thank you for dinner. As always, your cooking was something special."

"You're welcome, Pastor," Lucy replied, beaming. She loved making people happy, and her cooking worked every time.

After the pastor had made his way out to his car and driven away, Doug turned to Clint and said, "Son, I'm not sure we've been giving that man a fair shake."

"You're right, Dad. He's alright."

Smugly, Lucy said, "I've been telling you boys that all along."

Three's a Crowd

Later on Sunday afternoon, Clint called Tom and asked if he could take a week's vacation. Tom, of course, said it would be fine. Clint had the time saved, and he was entitled to use it. Tom told Clint to take all the time he needed to heal, physically and otherwise, and he promised to come see Clint in a day or two.

While Lucy was at church that evening, Doug and Clint drove to Clint's apartment and picked up a few more things. Doug floated the idea of Clint moving back home, but Clint didn't bite. He didn't mind staying with his folks for a few days, but he had no plans to give up his freedom and privacy.

Clint tried to call Dani, but she didn't answer. He thought it a little odd because she normally would have been home, but he wanted to think that she had just stepped out for a little while. He tried her again later, but she still didn't answer. Now he was concerned. Doug tried to reassure him, but Clint was still worried.

Except for not being able to speak with Dani, the next few days were nice. Lucy made breakfast each morning, and the three of them ate together before Doug and Lucy left for school. That left Clint home alone all day, and he spent the time reading and listening to music. Although his parents didn't approve of his smoking, he did manage to sneak a few cigars—always on the back porch, of course. He didn't even smoke inside his own apartment.

Clint's hands were doing much better. He was leaving the bandages off in the daytime now and wrapping them only at night. That allowed his wounds to breathe, and it gave him a lot more freedom. They still hurt a fair amount, but he was tough. He could take it. He'd already written off the notion of casts.

Lucy made some phone calls and found Clint a counselor in Plano. Ironically, his name was Keith. Clint's first instinct said "no way," but he decided to give the guy a chance. Mr. Blocher specialized in grief counseling. Clint didn't have insurance for this sort of thing, and Mr. Blocher was willing to charge on a sliding scale. Clint had his first visit on Thursday, and they agreed that he should probably come weekly for a while.

That first counseling session went reasonably well. Mr. Blocher was pretty informal about things, and Clint wasn't sure how much good he was going to do. Even so, Clint liked him and wanted to keep coming. Clint figured that he just needed someone to listen more than anything, and he found that he could talk easily with Mr. Blocher. Although Mr. Blocher preferred to be called by his first name, he understood when Clint said that he'd rather not just yet. He wouldn't have been worth his salt as a counselor if he hadn't understood that.

Clint was still having trouble with Dani. He had tried to call her several times, but she never answered. He really didn't like calling her at work and had only done that a couple of times, but he finally decided on Friday that he was desperate enough to do it. Much to his surprise, the data entry supervisor told him curtly, "Dani Bailey no longer works here."

Milton came over after work on Friday and ate supper with the Buchanans. He'd only taken a couple of days off before he went back to framing houses for his dad. After supper, he and Clint went for a drive. They just cruised Main as they'd done for years. The kids in Allen tended to congregate in the Dairy Queen parking lot, so Clint and Milton stopped in there a couple of times and chatted with some old friends.

One of the girls hanging out at the DQ was Laura Grimes, a high school girl from Clint's neighborhood who'd always had a huge crush on him. Laura was pretty, and Clint flirted with her for a little while before he and Milton took to the streets again.

"Why did you flirt with her like that, Clint?" Milton asked.

"Oh, I don't know. Was I leading her on?"

"Yeah, I think so. She's going to think you're sweet on her."

"Damn, Milton, she's pretty, but she's way too young."

"Pretty? Shit, Clint, she's more than pretty. I'd drink her bath water."

"What, you wouldn't eat a mile of her shit just to see where it came from? That's what you normally say," Clint said, chuckling.

"No," Milton said with a chuckle of his own, "she's not *that* good-looking!"

"Well, it's a moot point. She's jail bait anyway," Clint said.

After a couple more circuits of the main drag, they got bored and went back home. Doug was listening to Conway Twitty on the stereo, and Milton and Clint joined him.

"I think I'm going back to work on Monday," Clint said. "I'm going to call Tom tomorrow."

"You ready for that, Son?" Doug asked.

"Yeah, I'm feeling okay." That was that.

After Lucy and Doug went to bed, Milton stayed for another half hour or so. He had to work again the next day, and he didn't want to lose too much sleep.

"You sure you're okay?" Milton asked.

"Yeah, I'm fine. I just need to figure out what's going on with Dani. She's been acting all weird lately, and it just got weirder. I haven't been able to get her on the phone since last Saturday night, and apparently she's quit her job. This is really breaking my heart, man."

"Pardon my French, but you don't need that bitch's shit on top of everything else right now. Just write her off. She's trouble. I've been trying to tell you that all along."

"Milton, you know I can't do that, and don't talk about her like that either."

"Listen to me," Milton said as seriously as he'd ever spoken to Clint. "You're my best friend, and I can't imagine going through the rest of my life without knowing you're always going to be there." Milton stopped himself. He and Clint never spoke so frankly about their feelings, and he was self-conscious. They both blushed and broke eye contact for a moment.

Milton continued, "In case you haven't noticed, you've had some luck cheating death lately, but that luck's going to run out eventually. Even a cat only has nine lives. I have a very bad feeling about this chick. She's going to get you killed. You need to dump her. Forget about her. Please."

"I can't. I'm in love with her."

"Listen, Clint, I'll admit that I'm a bit of a racist. I'm not proud of it, but I'm not going to lie about it either. I know you're more open-minded, but we've always accepted each other at face value. In the beginning I didn't like you screwing Dani because she's black, and I hate the thought of race-mixing. But all this shit has nothing to do with her being black. It don't matter. Black, white, green, or whatever, this woman comes with baggage—the kind that winds up with people dying. I don't want you to be one of them."

"Milton, I love her, and I'm going to be with her—no matter what."

Milton just shook his head, and that's how their visit ended. Milton left, and Clint got a drink and went to bed.

The next day, a week after the funeral, Clint got up and had breakfast with his parents again. Afterward Doug helped him get his things in his truck.

"I don't feel real good about this, Son."

"I know, Dad, but I'm going back to work in a couple of days. I need to settle back in at my place."

After a family prayer and a long, teary good-bye, Clint left his parents' house and drove back to his apartment and unloaded his belongings. He went back outside, removed the cover from his bike, and started it. He had intended simply to let it run for a little while, but he decided to take a ride. He made sure that his hands could work all the controls, and they did, albeit painfully. He probably wasn't ready for this, but he did it anyway. He retrieved his helmet from his apartment, gingerly strapped it on, and took off.

Against his better judgement, Clint found himself driving toward South Oak Cliff. When he got to Dani's apartment complex, he parked a discreet distance away from her unit, took off his helmet, and waited. Dani's T-Bird was nowhere to be seen. There weren't a lot of white folks in that complex or, for that matter, the neighborhood, so Clint stood out even more than he usually did. A few people cast suspicious glances his way, but some recognized him from one of his few previous visits. If anyone saw Clint even once, they tended to remember.

After about 30 minutes Clint saw a young man walking toward him from across the lawn. Clint didn't know him but did recognize him. The guy often wandered the complex, sometimes smoking a joint openly. He seemed to enjoy annoying people, and Clint noticed that he was smiling smugly.

"Hey, dude, she's stepping out on you, man!" the guy said with a derisive laugh as he walked past Clint. "Yo lady done went back with huh suga-daddy. Long time ago." He just laughed and kept on walking.

"Motherfucker," Clint said under his breath. "Mike."

Clint sat there fuming. After another 30 minutes or so, he got tired of waiting and took off, angrily riding a wheelie down the street. The pain in his hands brought him back to earth, literally and figuratively, and he settled down a little. He drove around Dallas and the Mid-Cities area for a couple of hours and then went back to Dani's apartment complex. This time her T-Bird was there. He parked his bike, marched straight upstairs to her second-floor apartment, and knocked firmly on the door.

A pretty little girl—the spitting image of Dani—opened the door, took one look at Clint, and shut the door and locked it before he could say anything. Clint wasn't sure if she was frightened by his color or his size. It was probably both—not to mention the angry expression he couldn't hide. A moment later Dani came to the door and was just about as shocked as Leesah had been.

"Are you crazy?" she asked as she stepped outside and closed the door behind her. "You trying to get us both killed?"

"What are you talking about, Dani?" Clint noticed the bruises on her face. She had tried to cover them with makeup, but he could still see them. "What happened?" he asked. "Where did those bruises come from?"

Dani spoke to Clint in a weird combination of deliberateness and desperation. "Clint, you need to leave, and you need to leave *now*. Please. There's no time to explain. I'll call you later. If you love me, you have to trust me. Please, just go. I'll call you at home. I promise."

"Dani . . . ."

"No, Clint. Leave. Now. I'll call you." With that Dani went back inside and closed and locked the door.

Clint was angry, hurt, and worried, but he did as Dani had said. He lit a shuck back to Plano and assumed a position by the phone waiting for her to call. He didn't budge for several hours. Finally the phone rang, and he answered before the first ring finished.

"Dani!" he practically shouted.

"Yeah, Clint, it's me. Listen. I don't have much time, but I owe you an explanation. You remember me telling you about my ex-boyfriend, the crazy jealous one?"

"You mean Mike?"

"Yeah, Mike. Wait a minute. I never told you his name."

"Don't worry about it. I have my sources."

"Well, yeah, it's Mike. I can't get rid of him. I thought I could, but I can't. I'm sorry, but I just can't."

"Dani, I love you."

"I know. I love you, too."

"But you're with another man? I don't get it. Is he beating you? Is that where those bruises came from? And did you quit your job?"

Dani said nothing, but Clint could hear her crying. She cried for a few moments before continuing. Sighing heavily, she said, "Yes, he's hit me some, and yes, I quit my job."

"Oh, Dani," Clint said pitifully. "I can't believe this is happening. I can't believe you can stay with a man who hits you when you say you love me. You know I could never hurt you like that. Just leave, Dani. Just leave. Take Leesah and Marcus out of there and bring them over here now. I want you with me. I can protect you."

"Oh, Clint, you precious boy."

"I'm not a boy, dammit! Don't call me a boy. I'm a man, and I love you. I want to marry you." Clint hadn't intended to say that. It just popped out, but he meant it nonetheless. He waited for Dani to say something, but she didn't. She just continued to cry quietly.

Clint said, "I mean that. I want you to marry me."

"Oh, Clint . . . ." Dani paused to cry some more.

"Dani, please don't do this. We can fix this. We can get him out of your life somehow."

Finally Dani said, "No, Clint, we can't. We can't get him out of my life *nohow*. I'm sorry, lover, but I'm stuck. We're stuck. This can't be fixed."

"Dani, I've been through a lot lately, but I'll be alright as long as I have you. I can't take this on top of everything else."

"I know you've been through a lot, and I really hurt for you. But I can't see you anymore, and you're just going to have to deal with it—like I'm trying to deal with it. I'm sorry. I love you. Bye." The phone clicked, and Clint couldn't believe it. He sat there holding the phone for several minutes and then finally slammed it down.

Looking upward Clint said aloud, "God, when is it going to end? When are you going to quit throwing all this shit at me? I'm not Job. I'm not Ruth Willis. I can't take any more!"

The phone rang again, and Clint answered it quickly. "Dani?"

"Yes, it's me. I'm sorry. Listen, are you free on Monday? We could meet and talk about all this."

"I was going to go back to work, but Tom will let me beg off another day, or maybe change my shift. What did you have in mind?"

"Okay, I'll come see you—there, at your apartment— after I drop the kids off at school. Okay?"

"Of course it's okay. I'll be waiting."

"Okay, now I really do have to go. Bye. I'll see you Monday morning."

Clint said, "Dani, I love you," but the phone had already clicked.

Clint put the phone down but immediately picked it up again. He dialed Tom's number, and Tom's wife answered. "Good evening, ma'am. This is Clint Buchanan. I'm sorry to bother you at home on Saturday night, but is Tom available?"

"Just a moment," she said brusquely. She didn't know Clint well enough to dislike him, but she didn't like that he and Tom had gotten so close. She felt a strange sense of competition with Clint that reminded her of Tom's affairs, and that was something of which she'd rather not be reminded.

"Clint, is everything okay? I'm sorry I couldn't get by to see you like I promised. It's been, uh," Tom said and then paused briefly. "Well, it's been difficult."

"That's okay," Clint said. "I've missed you, but I'll be seeing you soon enough. Listen, I hate to put you on the spot. I know I said I'd be back on Monday, but can I make it Tuesday instead? If you'd rather, I could work Monday evening or night."

"Why? What's up?"

Clint was conflicted. He didn't really want to tell Tom the truth, but he didn't want to lie either. He thought for a moment and decided on the truth. "Tom, Dani's had some trouble with that ex-boyfriend of hers. We need to discuss some options."

"Oh, shit. This is trouble, kid—big trouble. It's not what you need, especially not right now."

"I know, but I need to look into this. Can we work something out on the schedule? I need to be here Monday morning for sure, maybe part of the afternoon."

"Sure, Clint, take Monday off. It's not a problem. I'll see you on Tuesday. Just be careful, son. Be very careful."

"Thanks, Tom. I owe you—more. And, yes, I'll be careful."

"Okay, I'll see you Tuesday. Bye."

Clint was beside himself. He went to the kitchen and drank a big shot of whiskey, then another. He browsed his music collection, but nothing jumped out at him. Finally he gave up and turned on the radio, tuning in a country station. He plopped down on the bed, fell back, and stared at the ceiling.

"I can't believe this is happening to me! After all I've been through!" he thought. "God, why are You doing this to me? Every time I start to try to turn back to You, You do something like this to push me away. What have I done to make You so angry? What's it going to take to get You off my back? I can't take any more, dammit! I just can't take it!"

For a moment Clint forgot about his fists. He jumped up from the bed and put the right one through a wall out of frustration. Immediately he crumbled to the floor in pain. He stumbled to the bathroom and washed fresh blood from his hand and wrapped a towel around it, and then he went to the kitchen for some ice. He emptied a bag of ice into the kitchen sink and buried both hands in it, removing one of them just long enough to grab the whiskey bottle and take a big swig.

Clint held his hands in the ice for as long as he could stand it and then examined the one that had punched through the sheetrock. It really didn't look much worse than it had before, except that the scabs had been scraped off of it. He wrapped the towel back around it, grabbed the whiskey bottle, and returned to the couch. He just sat there brooding and gulping whiskey for a while, and then the phone rang.

"Hello, Dani?"

"No, Son, it's Mom," Lucy said. "Are you coming to church with us in the morning?"

Very briefly Clint thought of his newfound respect for Brother Collins and said curtly, "No."

"Why not, Son? It would mean a lot to Dad and me, and to Brother Collins."

"I'm sorry, Mom. I have plans. I just can't make it."

"But I thought . . . ."

"Mom, drop it. Just drop it, please."

Clint did something that he couldn't remember ever having done before: He hung up the phone on his mother. A few moments later the phone rang again, and Clint just let it ring. He counted 12 rings before she gave up. Clint felt guilty about how he'd treated his mother, but he was too angry to care a whole lot. He went back to guzzling whiskey and feeling sorry for himself until he passed out. He slept on the couch and awoke to daylight.

Clint had a bad hangover; the combination of booze and anger had gotten the best of him. He got up, took a leak, washed his hands and face, and brushed his teeth. He remembered his conversation with Lucy and looked at the clock. He had just enough time to catch her before she left for church, so he hopped on his bike and rode quickly to his parents' house. He walked up on the porch just as Lucy and Doug were getting ready to walk out the door.

"Hi, Son," Doug said. "We're going to have talk about the way you treated your mother last night, but right now we're going to church."

Clint could see that Lucy was still very upset, and he said, "Mom, I'm so sorry. Dani and I are having some problems, and with everything else that's been happening to me lately, I just let my anger get the best of me. I'm sorry I took it out on you."

He hugged Lucy, and she hugged him back. She had a good nose and was very perceptive in general, so she immediately figured out that he had been drinking and was probably hungover.

With a frown she said, "Clint, I accept your apology. I'd ask you to come to church with us, but I don't think it's right to enter the Lord's house in your condition."

"I expect you're right about that, ma'am. I'm sorry," Clint said sheepishly.

"Will you stay here and have dinner with us after church?" Doug asked.

"Yeah, I guess so."

"Okay, we'll see you in a couple of hours," Lucy said. "You in the mood for liver and onions?"

"Oh, gosh yes! I'm always in the mood for that!" Clint did love Lucy's liver and onions and mashed potatoes. It was possibly his favorite meal, and no one could make it like his mom.

While Doug and Lucy were at Sunday School and church, Clint took the liberty of making himself some breakfast and a pot of coffee. It diminished his hangover, and he was almost a hundred percent by the time they returned. Lucy immediately went to work on lunch while Clint and Doug talked in the living room.

"Okay, Son, so what's this about Dani? What's bugging you so much?"

"Dad, I don't think this is really going to work out, and it's killing me. I just love her so much, and with everything that's been happening to me lately, I'm just not sure I can make it without her."

"I know it's tough to see right now, Son, but maybe this is for the best. Maybe y'all just aren't right for each other, or maybe it's just bad timing. Either way, you probably just need to walk away—let it sit for a while. If it's meant to be, it'll happen. If not, so be it. Live and learn."

"She's gone back to her ex-boyfriend, and he hits her."

Doug shook his head and said, "That's hard to figure, but we don't have all the facts."

"Well, I'm going to get some more facts tomorrow morning. After she drops her kids off at school, she's coming over to the apartment, and we're going to have us a talk and flesh everything out."

"Son, be careful. If this guy hits Dani, there's no telling what he'll do. He's obviously scum. Hitting a woman . . . ." Shaking his head, Doug paused briefly before he continued, "That's about as low as it gets."

"I know, Dad. I'd like to get my hands . . . ."

"No! No, Son. No, you steer clear of this mess." Shaking his head vigorously and looking very stern, Doug said, "Clint, first of all, your hands aren't in very good shape right now. You've already abused them a little too much lately." Doug looked and noticed the scab-less hand and said, "Hey! What happened?"

"Well, Dad, my anger got the best of me, and I kind of punched a wall."

Doug closed his eyes and shook his head. "You need to learn to control that temper of yours. They're going to make you pay for that wall, and your hands can't take much more punishment."

"I know, Dad. Sorry."

"How'd your session go the other day with that Mr. Blocher?"

"It went well. I'll be going every week for a while."

"Good. You be sure to talk to him about this, too. Maybe he can talk some sense into you. Anyway, what I was saying . . . . You don't need to be getting into any more fights—not now, not ever. You need to steer clear of that kind of trouble. Number two, this trouble with Dani and this guy . . . . It's a complicated thing, Clint. There's no simple solution to it. She's got to break free somehow—the sooner the better. But you can't force it to happen. Trying is just going to cause more trouble—for her and for you. Just give it some time, Son. Be patient."

"I can't, Dad. I love her, and, uh . . . . Well, I kind of asked her to marry me."

"Oh, God. Don't even think about that right now. You're too young, but aside from that, you're just not ready for it. Son, you've got some issues that you're just starting to deal with. This could wind up killing you. One way or other, you keep heading down this road, you're going to wind up dead. Your mom and me will be going through what poor Ruth Willis just went through. Please, Son, don't do that to your mom. Don't do that to us."

Just then Lucy called them to dinner. She was aware that they'd been having some type of serious conversation, but she hadn't been eavesdropping. She didn't know the topic or how serious it was. Doug and Clint looked at each other and then back at Lucy, and they both got up and went to the kitchen without saying anything else.

The three of them had a pleasant dinner, albeit a relatively quiet one. Clint ate his fill, thanked his mom, and excused himself. As he was hugging his mom at the front door, he looked over her shoulder to Doug. Clint wasn't sure that he'd ever seen his dad with such a distressed look on his face.

All Doug said was, "Be careful, Son." The phrase clearly had more than its usual meaning.

Clint was nervous for the rest of the day, but he kept his cool and stayed away from the booze. He rode out to Milton's place in the country, and they took a short ride. Afterward Clint returned to his apartment, listened to music, and read. At one point he thought, "I could be happy like this forever," but of course, human beings are social animals. They're not meant to be hermits.

Clint went to bed early and dozed off immediately, but he awoke early and couldn't get back to sleep. He shaved, showered, ate breakfast, and waited for Dani to arrive. He tried to read a little more; however, he was too anxious, and his mind kept wandering. Finally he heard a soft knock on his door at about 9:00, and he was up at the door in a second.

"Hi," Dani said when Clint opened the door.

She stepped inside, and they embraced. They held each other for a long time before making their way to the couch. They sat down and held each other some more. They kissed softly.

"I love you," Clint said. "I was serious about the proposal, too. I know it wasn't the best way to say it, but I did mean it. I want to get married."

Immediately Dani's tears began flowing freely. "Oh, Clint," she said, "I love you, too, and I'm not going to lie. I've thought about marriage, and I think we're perfect for each other in a lot of ways, most of the important ways. But, lover, it's just not meant to be. It's never going to happen. Mike would kill us first. At the very least he'd kill you, but he'd kill us both if he had to. We can't ever be together, and that's all there is to it."

"So when did you go back to him?"

"I never really left him for long," Dani admitted.

"What? What do you mean? You told me you broke up."

"Well, I tried. I really did try, but he wouldn't let go. We were apart for a little while, and then I fell in love with you. Clint, I loved you the first time I saw you."

"I know, Dani. Me, too."

It was the first time that Clint had admitted it to anyone, including himself. His mind knew that the concept of love at first sight was silly, but his first look at Dani had stirred a feeling in his heart that he'd never felt before or since. Obviously things between the two were not working out, but that didn't change the fact that they had, in fact, fallen in love at first sight.

"Me and Mike were still together when I first saw you, and then I tried to break up right before I met you again. I guess you might say I was on the rebound, but I never really loved him anyway. But I met you and fell in love with you and wanted to be with you. I'm starting to think I can be happy again and give my kids a real family like they deserve, and then this asshole steps back in the picture like he never left, thinks everything is going to be just like it was. But he don't remember it never was any good to start with."

"Is he living with you?"

"No, we never lived together really. We stay at his place mostly, but we still stay at mine a lot, too. He can't seem to make up his mind."

"And y'all have been together the whole time you've been seeing me?"

"Not the whole time really, but . . . . Yeah, I guess it's been pretty much the whole time actually. I can't lie about that anymore. Almost from the beginning, I've been seeing both of you."

"Have you been . . . sleeping with him?"

Dani's face turned beet red before she said, "Yes, Clint, when grown people stay together they sleep together. I've been sleeping with both of you. It makes me sick to my stomach, but I'm through lying about it."

"God!" Clint said, shaking his head in disgust. "I can't believe it!" He stood up and stomped around the little apartment and thought about putting another hole in the wall.

"Clint, listen. You've got to believe me when I say I love you. I love you more than I've ever loved anyone, except my kids. But I can't be with you, and I can't go on hurting you like this. We need to end it."

"How often does he hit you?"

"Not all the time."

"Not *all* the time? That's supposed to make me feel better?"

"Clint, he's never really hurt me much. He just slaps me around every now and then, mostly when he's been drinking. He doesn't use his fists very often."

"Does he do it in front of the kids?"

"No, not in front. But sometimes they're at home, and they're old enough and smart enough to know what's happening."

"Good God! How can you stay with someone like that?"

"Because, Clint," Dani said with a very severe look on her face, "he will *kill* me if I don't. There. That's it. I've laid it on the table. He will flat-out kill me if I try to break up again. He said he'll do it, and I believe he'll do it."

"Not if I kill him first."

"Yeah, right," Dani said with a chuckle.

"I'm not joking." Clint wasn't joking. He was deadly serious, and it showed.

"No, Clint! We're not having this conversation." Dani stood up and moved toward the door, but Clint grabbed her arm.

"Dani, please. Don't go. We need to talk about this."

"No, we're not talking about this no more. What you said . . . . It frightens me. We're not going to talk about it— not now, not ever. We're not ever going to talk again at all. Good-bye, Clint. I do love you."

Dani opened the door and walked out, and Clint wanted to go after her but didn't. He stood in the doorway until she walked out of sight, and he could hear her car door open and close in the parking lot. She started her engine and drove away.

Clint glimpsed two men in an old, beat-up Chevy Impala drive past in Dani's direction, but it didn't really register. They both turned and got a good look at Clint, but he was too distraught to notice. He stepped inside, closed the door, and locked it. It was time for more brooding.

Clint spent the rest of the day feeling sorry for himself and worrying about Dani. A man hitting a woman was despicable enough, but the notion that a woman could stay with such a man was equally mind-boggling. Clint couldn't understand it at all. Even so, the situation did give him pause, and he considered quite seriously whether or not he really wanted to pursue the relationship with Dani any further. Everyone kept saying that he should walk away, and he thought, "Maybe I should."

Clint did love Dani immensely, but he also had a certain innate human instinct that could not be denied: survival. Clint had enough going on in his life without complicating matters, psychologically and perhaps physically as well. He decided to give Dani some distance, at least for a while. All those close to him thought it wise. He threw himself back into his routine of work and working out, although the latter was reduced until his hands healed.

(Dead) Meat & Vegetable

Soon it was 1980, and Clint was excited about his first involvement in a presidential election. Although his parents were conservative Democrats, Clint openly embraced the Republican Party and supported George Bush in the primary. Clint liked Bush's open-minded, moderate stance on the issues, and he thought that Ronald Reagan was too extreme in his conservative views. Clint became disheartened as it became clearer that Reagan would win the party's nomination, but he perked up again when Reagan chose Bush as his running mate. So much for "voodoo economics"! Clint would happily and proudly vote for the Reagan-Bush team in November.

Before that election rolled around, though, 1980 would become famous for something else: the Texas Heat Wave. Even the old-timers had never experienced anything like it; it broke virtually every record in the book. Clint loathed hot weather; he preferred sub-freezing temperatures to anything above the mid-80s. The problem in 1980 was that the temperature rose to well above 100 each day, sometimes 110 or more, for most of the summer. Clint often ran at 4:00 or 5:00 in the morning when it was "only" 90 or so.

That summer rich people bought ice by the truckload to keep their pools cool enough for swimming. At one point Dallas had three straight days of 113, and with the humidity being what it tends to be in Big D, the heat index was off the charts. Clint was miserable and dreamed of Alaska, or at least Colorado, but despite the oppressive heat, he continued his intense workout regimen. He even added a bicycle and would sometimes take 50- or 100-mile rides on his days off. Milton tried to join him a couple of times but could never keep up.

That was also the summer when President Carter boycotted the Olympics, and Clint felt some ambivalence about it. He had some logical issues with the decision. It didn't really make sense, and Clint felt sorry for all the innocent athletes who would suffer for a futile political statement. Clint would also miss watching the events, especially track and field, and cheering on the Americans. At the same time, though, Clint was ashamed to admit that he felt a little relieved. For several years he had suffered a profound sense of regret for missing his chance to compete in the 1980 Olympics, and he needn't feel that anymore. In a strange way, he was off the hook.

Clint was still seeing Keith Blocher but only on a biweekly basis, and Clint had begun calling him by his first name. He had grown comfortable with having another Keith in his life, and he figured he'd better get used to it anyway. After all, it's a pretty common name.

Clint wasn't entirely ready to admit that the sessions were helping him, but he did have a more positive outlook and was sleeping better. It turned out that a bereavement counselor was pretty much what he needed, especially when he added the loss of Dani to the equation. The grief process is often the same for different types of losses—loss of life, loss of love, loss of innocence.

Despite his revised opinion of Brother Collins, Clint's church attendance was sporadic at best. Part of him wanted to go to church more, if only to make Lucy happy. Still another part of him didn't want to have anything whatsoever to do with God. Clint felt persecuted, and right or wrong, he blamed God. That part of his heart grew a little harder every day.

Clint and Milton were spending more time together now, but they resolved to stay away from strip joints, pool halls, or any other type of establishment where Bandidos might be inclined to pass time. They rode their scooters a lot and did a lot of shooting, and they weren't too old yet not to enjoy cruising Main in Allen from time to time. When they did, they seemed always to run into Laura Grimes, and she made it very clear that she wanted to go out with Clint. He liked her and was attracted to her; however, she was too young, and he loved someone else. Clint wondered if that would ever change.

Clint was still too hung-up on Dani to date anyone else, and he figured that celibacy had its benefits. For one thing, dating would have cut down on the amount of time that Clint had to spend alone. He now had more friends than he'd ever had in his life, and as much as he enjoyed spending time with Milton, Hulk, and Tom, he still needed his time alone. Dating would have crept into that. Not dating also meant fewer complications. Still, Clint continued to think of Dani often. He missed her, and he worried about her. Sometimes he felt guilty for not going after her, but he was able to rationalize that it was "for the best," as everyone seemed so quick to say.

August came, and Milton went with his parents on a family vacation to visit relatives in the Midwest. At the same time, Tom and his wife were having more trouble, which meant that it was difficult for him to get away, and Hulk was tied up with some kind of work that he couldn't discuss. That left Clint alone for a couple of weeks. He saw Tom at work, but he had no one to hang out with during his free time. For the most part Clint did enjoy his solitude, but he started to miss his buddies after a few days.

One evening after his workout Clint decided to go for a ride. Whether he was riding alone or with Milton, he often just took off without having any idea where he was headed. He just rode. That's how it was on this particular night, but before he knew it, he was in South Oak Cliff. He hadn't consciously intended to go there; it just happened. Once he was there, though, he couldn't resist the temptation of driving to Dani's apartment complex, and—sure enough— her T-Bird was there. She hadn't moved. Clint was careful not to linger. He just rode quickly through the complex and left.

The next day he did the same thing—and the next day after that as well. He was doing this after work and working out, so it kept him out quite late. He told himself that he had no particular purpose in mind. He just liked to ride, and Dani's apartment in South Oak Cliff was a good turning-around point, as good as any. He never stopped, though. He was careful always to ride through quickly and leave. It seemed harmless. It never occurred to him that anyone might see him and recognize him.

One night as Clint was pulling out of Dani's apartment complex, two guys in an old, beat-up Chevy Impala followed him. Clint didn't notice them at first. He stopped at a convenience store and bought a Pepsi and some Peanut M&Ms, and as he leaned against his bike consuming his snack, he saw them drive by. He probably wouldn't have taken note; however, they slowed and watched him very closely, and he thought that odd. "Haven't I seen them before?" he asked himself. Still, he shrugged it off until a few minutes later when he noticed them drive back by in the opposite direction, again watching him closely.

When Clint had finished his snack, he got back on his bike and headed north toward Plano. He checked his mirrors, but he didn't see the Impala. A little bit later, though, he checked his mirrors again, and there it was. Clint didn't panic, but he was concerned. He didn't think of himself as a prime target for robbery, but these guys were obviously following him for some reason. Clint exited the expressway, and they followed him. He turned on some side streets, and they were still there. He got back on the expressway, and they did, too. "Okay," he thought, "that cinches it."

Clint had had enough. He gave full throttle to his Kawasaki KZ-1000, the 1977 "King of the Superbikes," and left them far behind. At about 130, long before he topped out, Clint backed off and slowed to 80 and rode all the way to Allen. He drove east through Allen on McDermott and then Main, turned south on Highway 5, and rode back to his apartment in Plano. He immediately put the cover on his bike, went inside, and locked the door. Assuming that he'd easily lost the tail, Clint got ready and went to bed.

After a good night's sleep, Clint got up the next morning and got ready for work. As he was walking to his truck, he noticed something in the corner of his eye and turned his head. His gray motorcycle cover was cut to shreds; it was barely hanging on to his bike. He walked over to take a closer look, and he saw that his motorcycle seat had been cut and that both tires had been slashed as well. Frankly, Clint was surprised that the damage wasn't worse. Still, it was quite troubling.

"Motherfucker," he said aloud. "They know where I live."

The apartment office hadn't opened yet, so after Clint had been at work a while, he called the apartment manager to tell her what had happened. She immediately got defensive, but Clint assured her that he was merely letting her know— not trying to hold her responsible. He promised to take care of the unsightly problem forthwith.

Tom was out of the office that morning, but when he got back in the afternoon, Clint told him about his previous night's ride and this morning's discovery. Tom instantly came to the same conclusion that Clint had.

"It's the boyfriend, Clint. It's got to be," he said.

"Yeah, I know. I don't need my P.I. license to know that. It's a no-brainer."

"This is bad news, very bad," Tom said with a head shake. "You need to get out of that apartment."

"Well, I can't do it today, but I'll try soon."

"The sooner the better," Tom said. "In the meantime, you be careful, and let me tell you something else." Tom paused for a moment.

Clint asked, "What's that?"

"I don't know why I didn't do this already. I guess I thought this thing with Dani was over and done with."

"It is, Tom."

"No, Clint, it's not. I'm sorry, but how could you be such a dumbass? What are you doing hanging out over there?"

"I wasn't hanging out. I just drove through the complex."

"Damn, that's stupid, Clint. After all this time, why would you go and do something like that? They saw you! They probably think you and Dani have started up again, and that could be bad news for both of you."

"I'm sorry, Tom. You're right. It was dumb. But you were saying something. What's this thing you're going to do?"

"Oh, right," Tom said. "I'm going to look into this S.O.B.—try to find out exactly who he is and what kind of stuff he's into. We need to know who we're dealing with."

"You mean who *I'm* dealing with."

"No, Clint, I meant we."

Tom let Clint leave work early. On the way home, Clint stopped by the motorcycle dealer and bought new tubes and tires for his bike. They didn't have a seat in stock, so they put one on order for him, for which he had to pre-pay. The Vaughans were back from vacation now, and Clint was able to get in touch with Milton. Milton was more handy with these types of things, so he came over to the apartment to help Clint change the tires. Milton also had a compressor to air up the new tires when they were ready. It didn't take long before the bike was drivable.

Clint hopped on the bike and drove out of the parking lot, stopping at the dumpster to get rid of the shredded cover. He hadn't bought a new one because the tires and seat had taken about all the money he could afford, and at any rate, he wouldn't need a new cover right now. With Milton following behind him, he drove a circuitous route to his parents' house and put his bike in their garage. He told them what had happened, but he made it seem like just a random case of vandalism. He didn't want them to worry.

Doug and Lucy were like a lot of folks in this part of Texas. Because the high water table precludes building houses with basements, garages are generally used for storage. Doug and Lucy's cars had never seen the inside of their garage, and Clint did a good job of hiding his bike behind a lot of junk at the back of the garage. It wouldn't be visible from the street even with the door up, and he could leave it there indefinitely. He would just have to limit how often he rode it for a while.

Milton gave Clint a ride back to his apartment, and they discussed what Clint's next move would be.

"You need to get out of here," Milton said.

"Yeah, I know, but that's easier said than done. I've got myself a little overextended now, and I'm not sure I can afford it."

"I can help you out a little."

"No, I appreciate the offer, but I'll figure something out."

Milton said, "Well, you know .... You could come stay at our place for a little while."

"No, Milton, I don't think so. Again, I appreciate the offer, but your parents wouldn't really like that. Plus, God forbid any of my trouble should spill over onto you and your family. I wouldn't want to take the chance."

"Well, that's a good point," Milton had to admit. "Just be careful."

"I will."

"And stay the hell away from South Oak Cliff!" Milton was never shy about stating the obvious.

The next day Clint went back to work, and he told Tom what he'd done. Tom reiterated that Clint needed to move to a new apartment, and Clint assured him that he would as soon as possible. They both spent some time out of the office that morning. Tom had to meet with some clients, and Clint had to show a photo array to a salesman at a sporting goods store where someone had used a stolen credit card. When Clint got back to the office, there was a phone message for him, and he almost dropped the note. Dani had called.

Clint instantly felt his heart rate increase, and he wasn't sure if it was excitement or fear. He went to his desk and stared at the note for several minutes before picking up the phone and dialing the number.

"Hello," Dani answered.

"Hi, it's me," Clint said, trying to play it as cool as possible.

"I may not have much time. You been okay?"

"Yeah, Dani, I'm fine. You?"

Dani didn't answer the question. She said, "Why did you have to keep driving through here?"

"I don't know," Clint said, embarrassed. "I really can't explain it. I know it was pretty stupid."

"Yes, it was."

"Did it cause you any trouble?"

"Yes, Clint, it did. Please don't come around here no more. I miss you, but you just have to stay away. Don't make this any tougher than it has to be. You keep coming around here, it'll be bad for both of us."

"I'm sorry, Dani. I wasn't thinking. Did he hit you because of me?"

Again she ignored his question, but she did say, "I have to admit it's good to hear your voice."

Clint smiled to himself and said, "Yeah, it's good to talk. I've missed you."

Dani's tone changed dramatically, and she said, "Uh, I have to go now. Bye," and the phone clicked.

Clint thought, "Damn! Mike!"

All the old feelings rushed through Clint, and he ached to be with Dani again. Just like that—a single phone call—and he was completely hooked all over again. All the months of progress flew out the window. He accomplished very little for the rest of the day; he couldn't stop thinking of her.

Clint was able to stay away from South Oak Cliff for a few days, but he kept feeling the pull. He knew Dani was there, and he longed to be with her—to see her, touch her, hold her. Eventually he couldn't stand it anymore, and he tried calling her from his apartment one evening.

"Hello," Dani answered.

"Hi," Clint said with anticipation.

Dani abruptly replied, "Sorry, wrong number."

Clint festered on the couch for a little while until he couldn't stand it any longer. He got in his truck and drove to South Oak Cliff. He had no idea what he'd do when he got there, and he knew it was stupid to go. Even so, he couldn't help himself. He stayed away from Dani's apartment complex, but he drove around that part of town for about an hour. Eventually he found himself at the convenience store where he'd stopped before on his bike when he realized that the two guys in the Impala were tailing him.

Clint parked near the pay phone at the edge of the parking lot, and he sat there for a while. He looked at the phone for at least 15 minutes, and then he found himself getting out of his truck. He walked over to the phone, picked up the handset, and stood there thinking for another minute or two before dropping his quarter and dialing Dani's number. He knew it was stupid, idiotic, crazy. All those words ran through his mind has he heard the phone ringing. Something was driving him to do this, and whatever force it was, Clint was powerless to resist.

"Hello," Dani answered again.

"Hi, it's me. Can we talk?"

"No, dammit, quit calling here!"

"Dani . . . ." Clint said, and then everything went black.

Clint drifted off into some type of surreal state of semi-consciousness, and he wondered if he'd died. He felt as if he were floating above his body, but he couldn't really see his body below. He was vaguely aware of the presence of another man, and then a second. Clint sensed that something was happening, some type of activity, but he was unaware of his participation in it, or if he was part of it at all. He seemed to be a spectator, though one who was looking through dark, foggy glasses and couldn't really discern any of the action.

Clint had no idea how long this lasted; it may have been several minutes or only a few seconds. He caught a glimpse of what he thought might be two men lying in distorted positions on the ground. It lasted only an instant, and he had no idea who the men were or why they might have been lying there. Clint wasn't even sure whether or not he was one of them, or if they were really there. It was just a flash of two silhouettes he assumed to be male, and then it was gone.

Clint's next sentient moment occurred miles away. He was sitting in his truck in the parking lot of an office building at the corner of Central and Meadow. The truck's engine was running; the transmission was in "drive," and only Clint's foot on the brake kept the truck in place. Clint had no idea how he'd gotten there, but he was aware of an intense headache, the worst he'd ever had.

Clint put the truck in "park," felt the back of his head, and detected an abrasion and a huge knot. He switched on the interior light and twisted the mirror to take a look at himself, and he saw another significant bump on his forehead. His forehead was abraded as well at the site of the knot. Clint thought he was bleeding a little from both spots, or maybe the blood was already dry. He wasn't really sure.

Clint looked down and saw that he was spattered with blood, but because of the volume and patterns, he knew that it couldn't have all been his. He puzzled over what had happened, whose blood it might be, and why he couldn't remember anything, not to mention how he'd gotten to this location from another across town.

The pain in Clint's head was intense, and flashes of light dotted his field of vision. Still, he managed somehow to drive himself back to his apartment. He remained in such a dream-like state that he had no idea how dangerous it was for him to be behind the wheel of a two-ton missile fueled by 40 gallons of high explosive.

There was a firm knock on Clint's apartment door. He had washed his face before crashing on his couch and dozing off, but he was still wearing the same gory clothes. He didn't even think about that as he stumbled to the door and opened it. It was Hulk, and Hulk quickly pushed Clint back inside and locked the door.

"Okay, Sasquatch, it's time for you to level with me."

"Hulk? Is that you?" Clint said, still out of it.

"Yeah, Clint, it's me, Hulk. Detective Roy. Can you see me?"

"Sort of," Clint said drunkenly. "You're kind of fuzzy."

"You been drinking?"

"No," Clint said, and Hulk's nose concurred.

Hulk asked, "Where you been, and where'd all that blood come from?"

"What blood?" Clint looked down and said, "Oh, yeah, that."

"Whose is it?" Hulk asked.

"I think I got hit in the head."

"Who hit you?"

"I don't know."

Hulk didn't smell any booze on Clint, and he knew that Clint didn't use illegal drugs. He was very worried, so he led Clint back to the couch and made him sit down. Hulk moved a lamp closer, examined Clint's head, and quickly found both lumps, but he knew that there was way too much blood for all of it to have been Clint's own. Moreover, Clint's blood would have dripped downward onto his clothing; it wouldn't have splattered from in front of his body. Hulk also noticed that Clint's fists were damaged, though not as badly as they had been after the Shooter's incident.

Hulk said to Clint, "Listen, Sasquatch, I don't know what kind of state of mind you're in, but I need to ask you a very serious question. Do you know anything about where all this blood came from or how your fists got busted up?"

"Hulk, I'll give it to you square. All I know is I was trying to call Dani from a pay phone. Next thing I know, I'm waking up on the other side of town practically. Why? What's this all about?"

Hulk wasn't sure that he should say anything just yet, but he decided to go ahead. "Clint, we got two dead guys over in South Oak Cliff. Well, actually one ain't dead yet, but it's not looking too good for him. I guess it depends how lucky he is."

"You think I did it?"

"From where I sit, yeah, it sure looks like it. It's a convenience store near Dani's, and they were near a pay phone. And, uh, well, it kind of looks like your handiwork."

"Oh, shit, not again!"

"Now, Clint," Hulk said. "Listen to me. I'm going to clean you up a little, and then we're going to go to the hospital and get you checked out. Those bumps look pretty bad, and we need to make sure you're okay."

"Hulk, thanks. You're a good friend. I love you, you know."

"Oh, Jesus," Hulk said, embarrassed. "We don't need to talk about that."

Hulk took Clint to the bathroom, stripped off all his clothes, and put them in a trash bag from the kitchen. He cleaned Clint up and helped him get dressed. They went to the kitchen, and Hulk looked in the freezer.

"Good," he said. "Drink a little of this." Hulk gave the bottle of whiskey to Clint, and Clint took a swig. "Not too much," Hulk said.

Hulk took the bottle from Clint and then splashed a little whiskey on Clint's shirt. Hulk then took a mouthful himself and returned the bottle to the freezer, grabbed the bag of Clint's bloody clothes, and helped Clint outside.

Hulk put the bag in the trunk of his car and helped Clint get into the front seat, which was no small task because Clint didn't fit very well in the Firebird. It was actually Hulk's car-of-the-week, a recent forfeiture. Once Hulk had managed to cram Clint into the front passenger seat, he got in and drove Clint to the hospital.

Hulk drove Clint to Plano General, flashed his badge, and identified himself as a Dallas police detective. When the nurse asked him what had happened to Clint, he lied.

"You see, it was just a little accident," Hulk explained. "Kind of a freak thing really. My buddy and me were having a little drink at his apartment, and he stumbled. As you can see, he's a pretty big guy, so he fell a ways before conking himself on the counter top. And then he falls backwards and bangs his head on the other counter. I never saw anything like it. Boom-boom, and his lights went out. Now he's all fuzzy-like."

"What about his knuckles?" the nurse asked.

"Oh, he's into karate. They're always like that."

Hulk wasn't sanguine that she'd buy it, but she did. Maybe it was the fact that Hulk was a cop, or maybe that Clint seemed a little inebriated and smelled of booze. Either way, she didn't ask any more questions. She just went on about her normal business. While the nurse examined Clint, Hulk stepped out and called Tom, and Tom arrived about a half hour later while they had Clint in the x-ray room.

"You take it from here, buddy?" Hulk asked Tom. "I need to go look into this."

"Sure, I got it, Roy," Tom replied. "How are you going to deal with this?"

Hulk pulled Tom down the hall and into the chapel. It was empty, and when Hulk had looked around and satisfied himself that no one was within earshot, he answered the question.

"Tom, this is going to go away, and not like Shooter's either. Clint ain't got nothing to do with this. I'm going to make sure that no one connects the dots. He was drinking, and he fell in his kitchen. He hit his forehead on the way down, and then he fell backward after that and hit the back of his head on the counter on the other side. And his fists are always busted up because of his karate."

Tom made a funny look.

"Yeah, yeah," Hulk said. "I know it sounds a little fishy. But the nurse bought it, so that's the story. We stick with it. Okay?"

"Sure, Roy," Tom said. "Listen, you know you could be making a career decision here. Right?"

"Yeah, I know," Hulk replied without blinking.

"Are you okay with that? I mean, I know what it's like—making a career decision. And I know what it's like to regret making the wrong one. Are you going to be okay with this if the shit hits the fan? Are you sure Clint's worth it?"

"Yes, Clint's worth it, but I'm not sure how I'll feel if it costs me my job. We'll just have to make sure that don't happen. Honestly, it's impossible to answer that right now, but I know the risks. My eyes are wide open here, Tom."

"Okay, friend, I just need to make sure that we're clear on that."

"We are. Don't worry about me. I'm a big boy."

There was a brief pause while Hulk and Tom looked at each other and thought of the implications of this situation. If they got caught in a cover-up, it could indeed cost Hulk's job—and maybe Tom's, too. If he lost his P.I. license, he didn't know what he'd do.

Hulk said, "Okay, now you stay here with him. Unless there's a fracture, I don't think they're going to keep him. Well, overnight maybe. Probably I guess. Anyways, if they do release him, take him back home. If not, stay here with him. Either way, stick with him until I get back. Don't call his folks unless you've got to—unless it's something really serious. Even then, we stick to the story."

"Okay, Roy, you're the boss in these matters."

"Tom, you okay at home?"

"Ah, shit, things at home will never be okay again, but I can't do any more damage than I've already done. I'm not even going to worry about it anymore. My buddies need me, and you've got to know I've got your back."

As he shook Tom's hand good-bye, Hulk said, "Okay, I'm out of here."

Tom waited at the hospital with Clint. The x-rays came back negative; his skull was intact. He did, however, have a severe concussion, and they decided to keep him overnight for observation. Tom thought of trying to get a message to Hulk through DPD dispatch but then realized that was a bad idea. They didn't need anyone else knowing about this. While Clint slept soundly in a hospital bed that looked awfully small with him in it, Tom slept restlessly in a chair. He felt guilty about not calling Clint's parents.

The phone rang, and Tom answered, "Hello."

"It's me," Hulk said. "How's Sasquatch?"

"He's okay," Tom answered. "There wasn't any fracture. He's got a bad concussion, though, and they figured they'd better keep an eye on him for a while."

"You call his folks?"

"No, Roy, you said not to, so I didn't."

"Okay, good," Hulk continued. "Listen, Tom. This ain't going to be too tough after all. Truth is, we know these guys. They're buddies of one Mike Small."

"I knew it!" Tom practically shouted.

"Yep, the one and only," Hulk continued. "Bottom line is this just looks like a deal gone bad, or maybe they were out to collect from someone who got the best of them. Don't matter. Either way, no one's going to bust a nut looking into this. There is the connection with Dani, but no one's going to be looking at that angle. I'll make sure of it."

"That's good, Roy. Are they both . . . dead?" Tom asked with a shudder.

"No, one's still hanging on, looks 50-50 at best. Say, there was a baseball bat lying near these guys. We don't know which one swung it, but that's apparently what Clint got hit with. He said he was talking on the pay phone, trying to call Dani, and someone's head definitely hit the phone. So it looks like they hit him in the back of the head, and then his head bounced off the phone. It's a wonder it didn't kill him."

"Damn," Tom said. "I can't believe it didn't even fracture his skull."

"Damn straight! That boy never ceases to amaze me. Anyways, crime scene guys got some evidence, but I ain't too worried about anyone connecting it to Clint. Like I said, this one won't be high on anyone's priorities. This is my area. Anyone starts nosing around, I'll put the quietus to it in a hurry."

"Good," Tom said, relieved. "That's good news, Roy. Thanks."

"Now listen," Hulk said. "We got to talk about what we're going to do with our boy."

"What do you mean?"

"Well, he's got too many people wanting him dead. The Bandidos are bad enough, but Mike Small and these guys run with some pretty rough company, too. Clint needs to make hisself scarce around here. We need to convince him to move away somewhere."

"Damn, Roy, I hate to lose him. He's my best employee, and I can't even turn him loose a hundred percent yet. I can't imagine how good he's going to be eventually. And then there's . . . . Well, you know, the personal part."

"Yeah, I know. I don't want to lose him either, but we can't be selfish about this, Tom. We have to do what's right for him."

"I know. I know you're right. I just don't want to lose him, work or otherwise." Things had gotten so bad at home that Tom was closer now to Clint and Hulk than he was to his wife. He really couldn't bear the thought of losing a friend right now.

"I know, Tom. Me, too. I'll miss him as much as you." Hulk paused for a moment to think of how attached he'd gotten to Clint. In fact, both men thought of Clint as a son, and neither was ready to say good-bye to him.

"You heading over here?" Tom asked.

"Yeah, on my way," Hulk answered.

With that, their phone conversation ended, and Tom and Hulk individually pondered the potential of a life in which Clint was no longer a regular part. Each was thankful for the lack of witnesses.

Milton Plants a Seed

Tom and Hulk took turns keeping vigil at Clint's bedside until his release two days later. The doctors had expected to release him the day following the incident; however, his eyesight was coming and going, so more tests and observation were in order. Clint was half amused and half annoyed at the thought of being baby-sat, but Tom and Hulk weren't about to leave him alone, unguarded. All three did agree, however, that Doug and Lucy need not be worried and that Clint could wait until later to tell Milton what had happened.

When Clint was discharged from the hospital, Tom and Hulk were both there. Hulk drove Clint home, and Tom met them there to discuss what would happen next. It wasn't much of a discussion, though. Hulk pretty much dictated how things would be. He had already moved from his one-bedroom apartment to a two-bedroom unit at the same complex, and Clint would be staying there until they figured out a long-term solution.

Clint called Milton, and Milton came over after work that evening. As the four men huddled around a fresh bottle of Wild Turkey, Hulk explained what had happened on the night in question.

"Near as we can tell, it went down like this. Sasquatch is standing there talking on the pay phone. He's all distracted with trying to call Dani, so he's not paying attention to things. That's how these guys were able to sneak up on him. They park across the lot, tippy-toe over, and blind-side him. The guy with the bat swings for the seats and knocks old

Sasquatch's head against the phone. That's how he got knots on both sides like that."

"Jesus Christ!" Milton exclaimed. "How is it he's still alive? I mean, a pool cue is one thing, but a baseball bat?"

"I don't know," Hulk said. "It's a miracle that it didn't kill him—didn't even fracture his skull. It can't be explained. I guess the Good Lord, if you believe in Him, still likes Sasquatch for some reason. Anyways, all it does is knock him silly, but somehow he's still able to fight."

"You don't remember any of it, Clint?" Tom asked.

"No, I had some kind of out-of-body experience. It felt like I was floating above it all, but I couldn't see it. I had no idea what was happening until I woke up at the corner of Central and Meadow. I only knew where I was because I recognized the office building. I have no idea how I got there."

Hulk continued, "That's something else I can't figure, but somehow Sasquatch is able to defend hisself and then drive away. He does a number on these two guys just like he's awake. The dead guy's all busted up—ribs, organs, just about everything. Guy's all in pieces, and most of his pieces are in pieces. It's like he fell off a building or something. Apparently Sasquatch got the bat away from him and used it. His neck's broken, too, but that wasn't the bat. Looks like it was done manually."

Clint made a face, and Hulk added, "Uh, yeah, bare hands."

"Oh, God," Clint said, shaking his head and feeling nauseous.

Hulk asked him, "You okay?"

"No, not really," Clint answered, "but go ahead. We all need to hear this."

"The other guy," Hulk continued, "is still hanging on. They still don't know if he's going to make it or not, but if he does . . . ." Hulk paused a moment to take a good look at Clint.

"But if he does? Go ahead, Hulk. I can take it," Clint said.

"If he does," Hulk continued, "he's going to be a drooling vegetable like Keith Willis."

"I hope he does die," Clint said. "No one deserves to live like that—no one. And no reasonable person would call that living. Doctors keeping people alive like that," Clint said, stopping to give his head a good shake. "It's not natural. They're playing God."

"Some folks," Milton said, "think it's playing God to pull the plug."

"No, no way. I don't buy that. They've got it backwards. If they'd just let Keith Willis alone, he'd have died right away. That was God's will, and that's His will for this guy, too. A person like that's already dead. We just need to leave them alone and let them have their peace—let them drift off to whatever's next with a little dignity."

"I'm not saying I don't agree with you. I'm just playing devil's advocate."

Hulk interrupted, "Listen, you geniuses can save the philosophical discussion for later. I figure doctors are playing God no matter what they do. They all got God complexes. It's why they become doctors in the first place. Hell, it's what we pay them for. It don't really matter to me. Bottom line, this guy's either going to die now, or he's going to be a vegetable for a while and then die. I don't see as how it makes much difference."

Making eye contact with no one, Clint said, "That's four—five if you count the vegetable." Clint reached for the whiskey bottle, but Hulk grabbed it first.

"Uh-uh, Sasquatch. You need to lay off this stuff for a while. Doctor's orders." There was a long, uncomfortable pause as the four men sat quietly for a while. Finally Hulk poured shots for Tom, Milton, and himself. Hulk said, "Sorry, Sasquatch. I'm sure you want a little of this, too, but it's not good for your head right now." The three drank their shots while Clint stared a hole through the wall.

Hulk continued, "Now listen, Sasquatch, me and Tom been looking into this asshole Mike. Name's Mike Small, but he ain't no little guy. Fact is, he's somewhere between you and me, and he's a bit of a badass, too. He's kind of like the Leroy Brown of South Oak Cliff, except he likes to send his buddies to do his dirty work when he can. But push comes to shove, he'll mix it up. And he knows every dirty trick in the book—learned some of them in prison."

"What's Dani doing mixed up with someone like that?" Clint asked, not expecting an answer.

"No telling," Hulk offered. "Maybe she ain't the little angel you think, or maybe she don't know. Sometimes women ain't too careful about their men. I'm not sure it matters."

"You're right," Clint said. "It doesn't matter. It was a rhetorical question."

"Oh, yeah, you like those," Hulk said with a touch of sarcasm.

"Clint," Tom said, "like Hulk said, this guy's done some hard time, and he hangs with a rough crowd. They're basically small-time hoods, mostly drugs, gambling, a little prostitution. But you need to be afraid of them and stay the hell away from Dani."

"Does she know about any of this?" Clint asked, not rhetorically.

"There's no way to know for sure," Tom said, "but we don't think she's into any of his illegal activities."

"He takes decent care of her, though," Hulk interjected. "Money-wise anyway. She's bound to wonder where the money comes from, but she don't really want to know."

"Clint, it doesn't matter," Tom continued. "The bottom line is you need to get out of this apartment, and you're doing it tonight."

"That's right," Hulk added, "and that's that. Don't even think about arguing."

After a little more discussion, mostly Hulk giving more orders, the three healthy men loaded all of Clint's things, including his rented furniture, into his truck and Milton's and drove it over to Hulk's apartment and moved it in there. Hulk said that he would call Clint's apartment manager the next day and "smooth it all over." Things tended never to be quite as smooth as Hulk perceived, but with his shield and his mouth, not to mention his girth, folks tended not to ask a lot of questions. Clint went ahead and called Doug that night to let him know that he'd moved in with Hulk, but he didn't tell him why. Doug seemed happy with the decision and not at all surprised.

Oddly, the subject of Dani never came up again. No one mentioned her to Clint, and Clint didn't mention her either. Oh, he was still thinking of her, of course. He didn't think that would ever stop, but he'd reconciled himself to the fact that it was indeed finally over. He wondered if she knew what had happened—and if she had suffered any repercussions of her own.

After about a week of rest and recuperation, Clint went back to work with Tom and settled back into a normal routine. He worked; he worked out, and he spent time with his buddies. Clint became annoyed that they allowed him to spend so little time alone, but he knew that they were just looking out for him. At Hulk's insistence, Clint had begun carrying at least one sidearm virtually all the time. When practical, he carried two. It wasn't legal, of course, but Hulk could deal with the technicalities, at least in Dallas.

Despite the fact that it broke Lucy's heart, Clint had pretty much written off Brother Collins and church, but he did continue his biweekly visits with Keith Blocher, although he never mentioned the incident at the pay phone. Their sessions were completely confidential, but Clint never felt comfortable enough to broach the subject. Clint enjoyed the visits, and even though he always questioned whether or not they were doing him any good, he never felt the urge to stop going. That should've been a clue that they were doing some good.

Tom, Hulk, Milton, and Clint had discussed Clint's moving away somewhere, but it was ultimately Milton who had the bright idea. "Clint, how long has it been since your back bothered you?" he asked one evening while the four were drinking shots at Hulk and Clint's apartment.

"Oh shit, it's been so long I've forgotten. I haven't even thought of that in forever. Why?"

"Have you ever thought of playing college football? You're still young enough, and you could probably be pretty good. You certainly have the size and all the tools. Maybe you could get a scholarship."

"Ah, no way. I haven't played in so long. No one would give me a scholarship." Despite Clint's response, the notion did intrigue him. Milton was right. Clint was certainly big enough, and he was strong as an ox. He was a natural athlete, too, and he was in great shape. Maybe it wasn't completely out of the question.

"You could walk on somewhere," Hulk said. "Maybe you could earn a scholarship. Maybe not a major college, but probably one of the little ones. Hey, a free education is a free education, and it would get you away from here."

Tom asked Hulk, "Do you really think that's wise? Shouldn't Clint try to keep a lower profile?"

"You may be right," Hulk replied. "I'm not really sure about it to tell you the truth, but it's not like he's going to be getting his face in the papers every day, especially if it's a small school. A guy like him, he's going to be a lineman anyways. I'm guessing an offensive tackle. Those guys don't ever get mentioned."

"Unless they get called for holding," Milton said, and everyone chuckled.

"That's only in the pros," Clint said. "They don't humiliate the offenders in college."

"Anyways," Hulk said, "this might be a way for you to get away from here."

The four kicked the idea around for a while, but Clint didn't really expect it ever to happen. Even so, he had to confess that the discussion had piqued his interest considerably, and after that night he thought of it often, even had dreams about it from time to time.

Changing Seasons, Tough Choices

The November election was a happy event in Clint's life. Although he still liked Bush better than Reagan, the latter had grown on him some, and he was ecstatic when they won. The thought occurred to him that Reagan might serve two terms, and then Bush would have a chance to do the same. Clint convinced himself that things had worked out for the better.

November was a happy time for Clint for another reason as well: cooler weather. The summer had been so oppressive, and he was ready for some of "his" kind of weather—cold and hopefully some snow. Even ice would be better than the heat of the previous summer. Although Clint loved Texas and was proud of his heritage as a Native Texan, he thought often of moving to a cooler climate.

A couple of weeks before Christmas, it happened again. He got back to the office after being out for a while, and there was a message waiting for him—from Dani. This time, though, he wadded up the note and threw it in the trash, telling himself that he was done with her and would never call her again. His resolve lasted for about a minute, and once again all the old feelings flooded his mind and soul. Still, he didn't call her—for a couple of days. Finally he couldn't stand it any longer, and he dialed her number from home one evening.

"Hello," Dani answered the phone.

"Hi, it's me," Clint replied.

"Took you long enough!" she said as if nothing at all had happened. Clint could sense her smiling through the phone.

"To tell you the truth, I wasn't sure I wanted to do this."

"I understand, lover, but Mike's gone. I don't just mean right now. He's gone from my life."

Clint felt the room spin a bit, and he didn't really know whether this was good news or bad. He said, "So? What's that mean for us?"

"It means we can be together now if you still want me." Dani's voice told Clint that she still wanted him, but he wasn't sure how he felt.

"I don't know, Dani. The last time we talked on the phone, you weren't exactly polite, and then two guys tried to kill me. One of them wound up dead—both of them really, as far as I'm concerned. Truth is, I'm damn lucky to be alive."

"Clint, I had nothing to do with it. Surely you know that. I did hear about it, though. They were some of Mike's buddies, and I was happy how it turned out."

"You were *happy* about it?"

"No, not happy really. You know what I mean. I'm glad you're okay."

"I wasn't okay, Dani. I'm *not* okay."

"I'm sorry," Dani said with a dejected tone. "I just thought . . . ."

"You thought I'd just take you back with open arms? Just like nothing ever happened?"

"Yeah, I guess that was expecting too much."

"Maybe not," Clint said against his better judgement. "Maybe not, Dani. I don't know. Truth is, I do still love you, and I'd be lying if I tried to say that my heart's not going a mile a minute just hearing your voice again. But we're snake-bit. Fate hasn't exactly been smiling on us."

"I know it seems that way, but I really want to give this a try."

Clint asked, "So how is it that Mike is finally out of the picture?"

"Jail," Dani answered. "He finally screwed up and got caught."

"And what happens when he gets out of jail?"

"That's going to be a while, and by then we'll be somewhere else—somewhere he can't find us."

"I'm not sure that's possible. People seem to have a way of finding me no matter what."

"Can you meet me? Let's talk about this in person. How about that Bennigan's, our special place?"

"You mean the place where I got shot?"

"It doesn't have to be there. We can meet anywhere. You name it. I'm just dying to see you again. I don't care where it is." Dani sounded desperate, and it tested Clint's determination.

"Dani," Clint said very seriously, "I was dying to see you a while back, and I almost did die—for real."

"I know, lover. I'm sorry."

There was quiet for a long time while Clint argued with himself, and Dani anticipated his ultimate response. It was time to make a decision. After a wait that seemed much longer in silence, Clint finally spoke.

"Okay, I'll meet you." Even as Clint said it, he cringed.

They agreed to meet at Paddy's Irish Pub near downtown. It was essentially the halfway point between them, and it seemed like a good neutral location. Clint also figured that it wasn't the typical hangout for Bandidos.

Although Clint had to work the next day, he agreed to meet Dani that same night. Dani was able to get away because her next-door neighbor could sleep at her place with the kids. Clint told himself that he wouldn't be out late, and even if he did stay out later than expected, he had always been good at getting by on little or no sleep.

Clint took a quick shower, splashed on a little Royal Copenhagen, and left a note for Hulk. He drove his truck to Paddy's and hoped that the four-leaf clover on the sign would bring him good luck. Dani's T-Bird was already in the parking lot when he arrived.

Clint entered the pub, stopped just inside the doorway, and took a look around. He hadn't seen any Harleys outside, and he saw no bikers inside. This definitely wasn't their kind of place. For that matter, it didn't exactly look like Dani's kind of place either, but the fact that she stood out made her easier to find in the moderate crowd. He quickly found her sitting at a table in the corner, and he made his way over to her. He bent over to kiss her cheek, and she jumped up and hugged him tightly, as if holding on for dear life.

"Oh, thank God you came!" she said sincerely.

"I'm sorry I'm running late. I took a quick shower."

"That's okay, lover. I just got here."

"So, what's this all about, Dani? Why are we here?"

"Clint, we're here because I love you, and I'm free. I'm finally free! Mike's going away for a long stretch. His lawyer convinced him to plead guilty, and he's going to be gone for at least five years, maybe ten. We can be together now—finally!" Dani seemed very happy and sincere, and Clint felt his resolve fading. He didn't know what to say. He was thankful when the waitress interrupted their conversation.

"What'll you have, sir?" she asked.

"I guess I'll have a 101 on the rocks."

"That's Wild Turkey?"

"Yes, Wild Turkey 101—on the rocks."

"You okay, ma'am?"

"Yes, I'm fine," Dani replied. Her amaretto sour was almost full.

"Okay, be right back."

Clint fidgeted for a while, saying nothing and hoping to stay strong.

"Well?" Dani finally asked.

"Let's wait until she gets back with my drink. I don't want any more interruptions," Clint said somewhat brusquely. Dani frowned, and they waited.

The waitress came back and set Clint's whiskey on the table in front of him. She started to walk away, but Clint stopped her. "Wait! I don't need a tab. I'll only be having this one." He handed her a five and said, "Keep it." Clint sipped his drink and thought for a moment, and Dani's face grew more austere with each passing second. She feared the worst, and it came.

"Dani, I'm sorry. I can't do this. I love you. I can't tip-toe around that fact. I reckon I'll love you for a long time, but this isn't going to work. Even with Mike out of the picture, it just can't work."

With tears already streaming down her cheeks, Dani simply asked, "Why?"

Clint gave her the straight truth. "Because I don't want to die. That's why. People have accused me of having a death wish, and I've even wondered about it myself at times. But I don't. I don't want to die. I want to live. I want to go to college, get a degree, maybe even play some football. And after that, I want to have a career. For a long time I thought I wanted to be a cop, but now I'm not so sure about that. I just know that my whole life is in front of me, and I don't want it to end now."

"But Mike is going away. He can't hurt you. Please, Clint," Dani pleaded.

"Mike didn't hurt me before, Dani. I wouldn't even know him if he walked in the door right now and sat down next to me. To be honest, I don't even know if he's black or white—not that it matters one iota. Truth is, he sent someone else to hurt me before, and there's nothing to stop him from doing it again. Tell me, are all of his friends joining him in prison? Can you tell me that there'll be no one left to do his dirty work for him?"

Dani didn't make eye contact with Clint, and she said nothing. She simply shook her head.

"That's right. Hell, he could have someone waiting for me out in the parking lot right now! How do I know I'm even going to make it home after I leave here?"

"I don't know. I guess I didn't think this through all the way. I was just so excited. I want to be with you."

"I'm sorry. I don't like hurting you, but our timing is bad. Maybe someday things will be different, but I can't hope for that anymore. I have to get on with my life. We both do." Dani was weeping unreservedly now, and Clint felt awful. He hurt for Dani, and he hurt for himself. He was strong, though, and he stood his ground.

Clint continued, "Dani, I'm going to be going away soon. I don't know exactly when, and I don't know where. But I've got to get away from Dallas, and Dani," he said, trying somewhat successfully to stifle his own tears now, "you won't know where I am. Everyone who knows me will know not to tell you where I've gone." Clint swallowed and added, "I'm sorry."

Her voice cracking, Dani asked, "So this is it?"

"Yes, I'm afraid this is good-bye. If our paths cross again, it'll only be by accident. It's not because I don't love you. Truth is, this is killing me, but it's for the best—for both of us. It's time to move on. Just know this: I do love you so, and I'll never forget you."

With those final words, Clint stood up and stepped to the other side of the table. He bent over and hugged Dani briefly, and they shared one last, salty kiss. As Clint turned and walked toward the door, Dani looked up through her freely flowing tears and could barely make out his blurred figure. She knew it was Clint only because he filled the doorway.

As the huge young man walked out of her life and into the night, she whispered only to herself, "Bye, lover."

As Clint drove away from the pub, he couldn't believe that he'd actually been strong enough to do the right thing. It hurt every bit as much as he thought it would, but he'd stuck to his guns. He loved Dani, and part of him hoped that their situation might change at some point in the future. Even so, he knew that it was a foolish notion, a boy's dream. He was a man now, and he had to make tough choices like a man. The time had come to close the "Dani" chapter of his life. Clint was ready to move on and write the new stories of a young man's life, and college seemed the logical starting point.

Suddenly Clint heard a "Pow!" and cringed, and he felt the familiar "ka-thunk, ka-thunk" of a flat tire. He pulled over and took a look. The left front tire of his truck had apparently blown out. Clint took a look around and thought, "This isn't exactly where I'd like to be doing this," but he had no choice.

Clint was in a deteriorating industrial section of the city with virtually no traffic. It was dark, and there was no one around. Frankly, it was a scary place, and Clint thought, "Why did I come this way?" Apparently getting away from Paddy's was more difficult than getting to it, and with his mind on other things, Clint had taken a wrong turn.

Clint got his flashlight and set about the task of changing the tire. It wouldn't take long. When he had worked at the gas station, he had gotten very good at changing tires, and he knew he'd have this one changed and be on his way again in just a few minutes. Despite the dark and his weak flashlight, he had the spare on the ground in ten minutes. He threw the blown-out tire in the bed of his truck and stowed the jack and tire tool behind the seat. He was ready to roll.

As Clint stepped up with one foot to get back into his truck, he saw the guy across the street, and without registering a thought, Clint's right hand instinctively went for the .44 magnum under his coat. The guy was stepping off the curb into the street, and he had a small pistol pointed straight at Clint. He never said a word.

Clint thought of trying to make a run for it, but it was already too late for that. His second option was to use his truck door as cover. His fingers gripped his big revolver and began pulling it from its holster, and for the second time in less than 15 minutes, Clint heard a "Pow!" and cringed.

Using the door for cover had been a good idea, but the bullet missed the door by about half an inch and struck Clint near the center of his chest. In the next instant, Clint aimed at center body mass and squeezed off a round, but his aim was errant. This, after all, was not a friendly contest at a shooting range. This was a real-life gun battle, and it can be tough to shoot with a bullet in one's chest. When the .44 roared, the bad guy's body splayed backward and landed half in the street and half on the sidewalk. The bullet had freed his brain from his skull.

Epiphany at Parkland

By the time Hulk, in his usual manner, came bursting through the door into the emergency room, the doctor had already removed the bullet from Clint's chest, and he was sitting on a gurney chatting with Officer Rip Van Winkle, actually a career patrolman named Max Stratton. Once Stratton knew that Clint and Hulk were really buddies, he decided to be friendly, and he and Clint were swapping some stories. Of course, there were some that Clint would never tell.

"Hey, Stratton, how goes it? Can me and my buddy get some privacy?" Hulk asked.

"Yeah sure, Roy, no problem," he said as he ducked out.

"Can you walk?" Hulk asked Clint.

"Yeah, I can, but the doctor said not to yet. They want to keep an eye on me for a while. Plus, and he's not saying this, but he's not wanting to let me loose until you guys tell him it's okay."

"Okay, well we got to talk," Hulk said.

Hulk began wheeling Clint's gurney to a more private location. He didn't ask. He just did it, and no one questioned him. Hulk was the most naturally intimidating man Clint had ever seen—with or without a badge and gun. Clint's doctor watched as Hulk wheeled him into a room and closed the door. Hulk peered through the blinds to make sure that no one was eavesdropping, and then he turned to Clint.

"Your .44 got anything to do with a guy's brains getting spilled all over the street tonight?"

"Yes, I'm afraid I got another notch tonight, but he shot me first."

"Yeah, I can see that now, but it looks kind of fishy when you leave the guy in the street like that without so much as a phone call. This one might not be so easy to cover as the last one."

"Hulk, I'm not asking you to cover anything. Just do your job and let all the other cops do theirs. It was a righteous shoot. The worst you got on me is a weapons charge."

"Yeah, I know that, Sasquatch," Hulk said. Hulk sounded angry, but Clint assumed it to be nerves. "Remember: I'm the cop here, and I'm the one that told you to arm yourself. But let me tell you something else, my friend. Any hopes you ever had of being one of us just flew out the back of that guy's head. It was looking pretty iffy already, but you can forget it for sure now. You need to plan another career path."

"I'm sorry, Hulk. I don't mean to make light of this in any way. I'm just relieved to be alive. Thanks, man. Thanks for everything you've done for me. I owe you big-time, and I'll never forget it. And for the record, I was already having second thoughts about being a cop. No one would ever want to partner up with my bad karma. No one should have to."

"You got that right. Cops are superstitious. No one would want to be near you when your number's finally up. Hey, what were you doing over there anyway?"

"Okay, I know how this is going to sound," Clint started.

"Ah, shit. Dani, right? Fucking Dani. It's always fucking Dani! When are you going to learn? All this time I been thinking you're a smart kid, but you're not. You're a fucking idiot."

"I understand your frustration, but it's over. After tonight, it's finally over. Really. I met Dani to tell her that, and then I had a flat. I'd just finished changing it when this guy starts coming at me with that little pistol."

"It was a .25—just a little Saturday night special. They found it under his body, and not too far away they found the spent casing," Hulk said, his tone softening a little now.

"I figured it was a .25 or maybe a .22, but I didn't get a good look at it. The bullet didn't go in very far, and they took it out right here in the ER."

"Okay, so are you going to be okay, Sasquatch? It didn't hit anything important?"

"No, it barely scratched the surface. I'm fine. It's a good thing he didn't use a *real* gun."

"Whew! What a relief! I was worried sick, man. This shit is getting old, and sooner or later your luck's going to run out. We really do need to get you out of here—and fast. And I'm not just talking about the hospital. I mean Big D, just like we talked about."

"I know. That's what I told Dani tonight. You would have really been proud of me, man. I know I'm proud of myself. I told her that it's time for both of us to move on and that I'm going to be leaving Dallas soon, probably go to college and get a degree—maybe even play a little ball along the way."

"Yeah, well don't make the mistake of letting her know where you're at. I hear old Mike is going up the river for a while, but he's still got friends. That's why Tom and me didn't bother telling you yet. Matter of fact, our dead guy tonight's probably one of his buddies. If we're lucky, we can pin this on him, too, but that all remains to be seen."

"I know, Hulk. Don't worry. I won't let her find me. My head's finally screwed on straight. You and Tom had a lot to do with that, and I appreciate your patience. I know it wasn't easy waiting for me to grow up."

"You sure got that right, Sasquatch. Damn, I'm sure glad I never had kids!"

Clint continued, "You know, despite this hole in my chest, I feel like a million bucks. For the first time in a long time, I know what I want to do—not exactly, but close enough to head in the right direction. The past is behind me, and I'm moving forward. You know, Dani said something to me tonight about being free. Well, guess what? *I'm* the one that's free! Dammit, I'm really free! Finally I'm free of everyone and everything that's been holding me back—the ghost of Keith Willis, Dani and Mike, all the bodies falling around me, self-doubt, self-hate, all of it. I'm done wasting my time with all that worthless, self-defeating bullshit!"

"Oh, that's great, kid. I'm happy for you," Hulk said, smiling widely. He believed Clint, and he couldn't have been prouder of his own son if he'd had one.

There was a tap on the door, and Tom stepped into the room.

"That was quick," Hulk said.

"Are you okay, Clint?" Tom asked.

"Yeah, Tom, never better!"

Clint was beaming, and Tom was puzzled. He turned to Hulk, and Hulk had a big smile, too.

"Okay," Tom said, "will someone kindly fill me in on what's happening here? I've been sick to death. I just about killed myself getting over here, and this isn't exactly what I expected to find when I walked in the door."

Hulk answered, "Old Sasquatch here had hisself one of those . . . . What do they call it? An epiphany. Yeah, that's it. He had an epiphany. He was telling me that we finally got his head screwed on straight—that he's over Dani and ready to move on. Kid wants to go to college and get on with his life. He's even thinking of taking a shot at playing some ball like Milton said. That was a great idea, and I got a good feeling about it. One of these days we're going to be sitting on the 50-yard line watching him pancake people."

"Oh, that's great!" Tom exclaimed. "What finally did it, Clint? What made you see the light?"

Tom turned toward Clint, and at the same instant both he and Hulk noticed that Clint's face had blanched. His eyes were open, but he seemed to be drifting off. Something was gravely wrong.

Hulk stuck his head out the door and yelled at the top of his lungs, "We need a doctor in here now!" His voice seemed to shake the building, and everyone took notice. As medical personnel came running with a sense of urgency that they hadn't shown up to this point, Hulk and Tom rushed to Clint's side.

Clint looked up at his buddies and clumsily took each man by a hand. Looking at Hulk, he whispered in a frail voice, "We never did that ride-along."

Clint was quickly fading. He tried to say something to Tom, but he didn't have enough strength. Tom and Hulk felt his grip slipping, and he managed only a faint smile before his eyes closed.

Breinigsville, PA USA
07 July 2010
241360BV00001B/33/P